"Bound by Honor, Betrayed by Trust."

–Foreigner

Matthew and James Dale

Copyright© 2021

Matthew and James Dale

All rights reserved.

To request permission, contact the writer here:

eaton220@gmail.com or
rengadekrew@hotmail.com.

Paperback: ISBN 9798736670765

Author/Edited by Matthew and James Dale

Cover art by Dyshan and Ariiana Anderson

Poems by James Dale, Kimberly Waite, Rauwshan Ingram

Please check out our other published books:

Just another hope-full fool in love

Written in Vampire's Blood: The Stranger

Politricks: It's all Political

The Pen is Mightier than the Sword

Introduction

This story is about redemption and the atonement of past transgressions. Bound by Honor, betrayed by Trust, follows the story of Jean-Jacque, son of Haitian immigrants who came to the United States seeking a better quality of life. His parents discovered at a young age that he was a gifted musician. Through music, he made friends, and those friends became foes.

His father, Henri, experienced racism, and discrimination by his colleagues while working as a professor at MIT. They were wroth with anger and exhibited xenophobia against foreigners taking advantage of all the great opportunities here in the states that should only be available to Americans.

To avoid any further criticism or conflict with anyone else on campus, he accepted a new job as a professor at NYU. At the same time, the change in scenery was good for him and his wife. The vicious cycle of bigotry continued with his son Jean Jacque while attending NYC private school.

His son Jean Jacque, angry about how narrow-minded the world was towards foreigners, embarked on a journey where a system that swore to protect and serve–forced him to participate in a program designed for gifted foreign exchange students. After being charged with assault and battery in grade school for defending himself against being brutalized by a few privileged American students.

Jean Jacque uncovered the despicable truth behind *The Program* and through his resolve, he atoned for his involvement. With the help of a few good friends, he revitalized it to lend a helping hand to future foreign exchange students seeking a better education in the United States. Jean-Jacque vowed to change the narrative of being called foreigner in a place by the people where dreams become a reality.

Table of Contents

Acknowledgement

I would like to thank my grandparents (R.I.P) and my parents; without them I wouldn't be here. "Rest In Peace" Eilel "Calvin" Dale, my father, I know he's looking down on me and is proud of my accomplishments. I love and miss you dearly. My mother Lureen Jennifer Dale, the matriarch of the family. She's been the rock that held me down and the glue that held this family together.

To all three of my older brothers Valin, Devon and Matthew, I appreciate the tough love and guidance during my up brining. Without you all I wouldn't have survived growing up in the "Concrete Jungle."

To all my aunts and uncles back in Jamaica, I owe the level of perspective I poses to you all. Without a strong base to start, life is that much harder.

Uncle Donald, thank you for being that father figure throughout the years in the absence of my Father. Big up yourself!

To my wife Dionne and my kids Aaliana, Zavanaa and Naala; Daddy loves you. And to the most-high God, I give all the glory onto you!

Preface

"Bound by honor, betrayed by trust" is about a Haitian Mathematician named Henri Cadet and his wife a Botanist/Musician, named Flora. They didn't have much, but whatever they lacked in worldly possessions, they made up for it in love, pride, and ambition.

They started from modest beginnings; some people use this as an excuse to remain stationary, never trying to rise above their circumstances. Not them, they internalized their position in life, then used it as fuel for the fire that propelled them forward to realize their full potential. Impressing an indelible mark on the next force to be reckoned with.

Henri and Flora looked forward to living out their lives together. The promise of a bright future was all that Flora saw when she looked at her beloved husband, Henri. She believed in him with every fiber of her being. As for Henri, nothing brought him more joy than when he looked upon his beautiful wife, Flora.

Henri's love for Flora has grown since she became pregnant with their first child. There's nothing more important to them then to fill his or her world with love, shelter, and lessons that will prepare them for a bright future...

Chapter 1:

From Port O' Prince

Henri ran inside the house with a smile on his face. He was ecstatic and out of breath. Henri threw down his leather briefcase on the kitchen table and raised his hands in the air.

"Flora! Flora! Flora! Mwen jis te resevwa gwo nouvèl mwen te rekrite pa Inivèsite Ameriken an M.I.T. Disètasyon mwen nan Matematik te pibliye pa inivèsite a ak yo vle m 'ale nan bay prezantasyon nan travay mwen an. (Flora! Flora! Flora! I just got some good news. I was recruited by M.I.T, a University of America. My essay in Mathematics was published by the University and they want me to travel to Massachusetts in the United States, to give a presentation of my work.)

"Go… go ahead and pack your things. We're leaving Haiti, this is our chance," exclaimed Henri.

Flora sighed, frowned, and fixed her mouth to voice what was on her tentative mind…

Henri pointed his finger at Flora, shook his head and pounded his hand on the kitchen table. "Pa gen kesyon!" (No questions!)

"This is our opportunity. Our future will be solidified; think of the little one," Henri said.

Henri stepped over to Flora and rubbed her belly. She placed her hand on-top of his, as he massaged her very pregnant stomach.

Flora smiled at the notion of Henri fulfilling his lifelong passion. But was torn at what they would leave behind: Her vast garden, her instruments, and all of her students.

"Anri e lavi mwen isit la? Mwen pral sakrifye anpil. Kisa ki pral rive elèv mwen yo? (Henri what about my life here? I will be sacrificing a lot. What is going to happen to my students?) said Flora.

"We will start a new life in the United States. We've been

sacrificing all our lives, it's time, all of our hard work is finally paying off," Henri replied.

"Henri, don't get me wrong, I think this is wonderful news, but I am Efreye (Afraid) arèstasyon (apprehensive)... You hear so much about America."

"Efreye, (Afraid) of what, Flora?"

"Ou konnen Anri, Ameriken pa renmen etranje, ak nwa nan Amerik la." (You know Henri, Americans don't like foreigners, and blacks in America.) Look at us Henri, nou tou de se (we are both.) Even worst, they don't treat them well either."

"Listen! Flora, I know better, we're never going to be liked outside of Haiti. It doesn't matter where we go; blacks, and foreigners aren't liked anywhere in the world. We have to put our best foot forward. I'm confident that we will be able to handle anything that is put in front of us.

"As long as we are together, we can overcome any obstacle and win any battle. If we put our faith in God, and continue to move forward, any move in the right direction, is progress."

Flora didn't respond, but the flames of her uncertainty dwindled considerably. She heard the conviction in his voice and the confidence Henri had for their future together.

Henry looked into Flora's eyes, and she looked into his.

"We can go, but under one condition," Flora said.

"What is that my love?" replied Henri.

"When we get settled in the United States, I need a floral shop."

"Eh, eh! Okay Flora, we have to leave now the plane leaves in three hours. Go ahead and pack."

Flora walked away from Henri in haste, but he grabbed her by the wrist, pulled her back into his arms, kissed her on the lips. "Ti bebe, mwen renmen ou plis pase opòtinite sa a. Mwen kontan toutotan mwen pase lavi mwen avèk ou." (Baby, I love you more than this opportunity. I am happy as long as I spend my life with

9

you,) Henri said.

With such short notice, Flora didn't have enough time to pack everything that she wanted. She brought all her essentials and things that had sentimental value. As Flora packed, she thought about her garden, and she looked out of her window at all of the work, time, and effort that she put into her fruit trees like calabash, kowosol, abricot, herbs, her beautiful flowers like choeblock, and apocynaceae.

"I have to make sure I tell the neighbors to tend to the garden," she thought.

Flora was a Botanist by trade, but her passion was being a musician. In her spare time, she taught the local children how to play the piano and the violin. Exposing the neighborhood kids to music, who would not otherwise be privy to this type of exposure.

In the middle of folding her violin's bow into its case, Flora couldn't help feeling like she was abandoning not only her students, but also her community.

"Who else is going to teach my students," Flora exclaimed.

She has been vigilant in her community where Flora has grown so reliant upon. She owes her culture, her disciplines, and the way she approaches life in general to. Flora realized that her life outside of Haiti will be completely different.

Flora packed the last piece of clothing away and closed her suitcase. She itemized everything she had, and double checked it to make sure she didn't forget anything. Then Flora walked into the bathroom to wash up before their trip.

"Are you ready Flora?" asked Henri.

"Just about, I'll be out in a sec. Henri," Flora replied.

Henri carried Flora's suitcases outside, along with his, and they both stood there in front of their house for a moment.

"Mwen pral sonje kote sa a," (I'm going to miss this place,) Flora said.

They looked into each other's eyes, sighed, and entwined

their hands together. "Tout bagay soti Flora, osi lontan ke nou rete pozitif e nou gen youn ak lòt," (Everything will work out Flora, as long as we stay positive, and we have one another,) Henri replied.

The taxicab arrived and Henri helped his eight-month pregnant wife, into the back seat. Henri and the driver stuffed the luggage inside the truck, then he and the driver entered. The cab driver pulled away from the curb.

"Ah Oh Anri," Flora shouted.

"What is it Flora? Are you feeling pain?" asked Henri.

"No, I forgot to let Marie know that she should continue to tend to the garden!"

"No problem my wife, I made arrangements already."

He gently grabbed her hand and interlocked his fingers with hers.

When they got to 'Aerorport international Toussaint Louverture,' he paid the driver, they got out the taxicab, Henri took their luggage out of the trunk, and they walked straight to the departure gate. Henri took out his credentials to show the airport check-in-officer their boarding pass and the invitation from M.I.T. University.

The airport-check-in-officer looked over the paperwork and handed it back to Henri. "Konbyen sak wap tcheke? (How many bags are you checking in?) asked the airport-check-in-officer.

"Just these two bags," Henri replied.

"Ou jis fè li, ou se de dènye moun ki monte. (You just made it, you're the last two people to board.)

"Tout bagay tout nan lòd. Pase yon bon moman nan Amerik la," (Everything is all in order, have a good time in America,) The airport-check-in-officer said.

They both got to their seats, buckled their seatbelts and anxiously awaited the plane to take off.

Flora had never flown before, so she gripped her armrest as the plane took off from the tarmac. An hour and twenty minutes along in the flight, the plane hit a patch of turbulence. Flora looked down at her feet and saw a puddle of water. She felt in-between her thighs, and it was wet.

Flora tapped Henri on the shoulder and wrapped her hands around her belly. "Anmwe! Mwen panse ke mwen pral nan travay. Ti bebe a ap vini!" (Ahhh! I think I'm going into labor. The baby is coming.)

"Woy! Ou serye Flora!" (Yikes! Are you serious Flora!)

"Otès, tanpri ede madanm mwen, li pral travay," (Stewardess, please help my wife, she is going into labor,) Henri said.

"Wouy! Pilòt, pilòt nou gen nan peyi avyon an, yon pasaje ki pral nan travay," (Oh no! Pilot, pilot, we have to land the plane, a passenger is going into labor,) The stewardess replied.

The pilot grabbed the radio transceiver and pressed the sidebar.

"Pilot to air traffic control!" said the pilot.

"Este es el control del tráfico aéreo out of San Juan Puerto Rico; siga adelante con su mensaje." (This is air traffic control, out of San Juan, Puerto Rico; go ahead with your message,) air traffic control replied.

"We have an emergency situation here, where a pregnant woman is in labor on this flight, permission to land."

The pilot hovered over Puerto Rico, until air traffic control gave him permission to land the plane.

"Control de tráfico aéreo al piloto, aterrice el Aeropuerto Internacional de Isla Verde, personal médico de emergencia estará esperando su llegada, copia" (Air traffic control to Pilot, land the plane at Isla Verde International Airport, emergency medical personnel will be awaiting your arrival, copy.)

"Copia ese control de tráfico aéreo." (Copy that air traffic control.)

The plane landed in San Juan, Puerto Rico, and the medical

personnel rushed Flora to the hospital. "Anmwe! Anri, Anri, li fè m mal, mwen soufri anpil," (Ahhh! Henri, Henri, it hurts, I'm in so much pain,) Flora said.

The doctor saw that Flora was 10 centimeters dilated, placed her legs in the stirrups. "Push, I see the baby crowning," the doctor said.

"Wouch!" (Ouch!) said Flora.

Flora, huffed and puffed as the baby inched its way down the birth canal.

"I have the baby; nurse, give me the suction to clear the airway. Here it comes, you have a bouncing baby boy," the doctor said.

Flora laid there on the hospital bed, with sweat dripping from her as the nurses cleaned off the newborn baby. They checked his vital signs, put him on the scale. "He's 22 in. long and weighs 7 lbs-7oz," the nurse said.

The doctor walked out of the operating room and saw Henri pacing in the waiting room.

"Congratulations, you have a bouncing baby boy," the doctor said.

Henri jumped up and down in the waiting room. "Wololoy! Yon ti gason, yon ti gason, madanm mwen te gen pitit gason m ', (Whoaaa! A boy, a boy, my wife had my son,) said Henri.

"We understand here at the hospital that you, your wife, and your sons' circumstances surrounding the landing was unique. As a result, the airline made a courtesy adjustment for you and your family to fly out on the next available flight."

"Thank you, doctor, I'm at a loss for words. Words alone can't begin to express how grateful we are."

Henri was then fitted for a disposable isolation gown. He walked inside the delivery room and the nurse handed him the baby. He held his baby boy in his arms, smiled at his son, and looked at his wife, while the doctor safely removed the after birth.

Although Flora was tired from giving birth, she had a crooked smile on her face. Henri walked over to Flora and placed a kiss on her forehead.

"Flora what if we name him Henri Jr.," he asked.

"A Junior, no I want to name him, Jean-Jacque Dessaline, after the first leader of a free Haiti in 1804. The pride of our country, who led us to victory, and to our sovereignty from the French," she replied.

"No, no, no! He is going to have my name."

"How about we name him Henri Jean-Jacque Cadet, that way, he would be named after two great Haitian men," Flora said.

"Henri Jean-Jacque Cadet, I'll call him JJ," Henri said, smiled and shook his head in agreement.

Two days later, they were released from the hospital. A taxicab took them straight to the airport from the hospital. They boarded the plane without a hitch, and they made it to Massachusetts with enough time for them to settle in before Henri's presentation.

Henry woke up the next morning to Flora nursing Jean-Jacque, seated in a chair by the window in a hotel room.

"Good morning, Flora! Good morning, my son!"

Henri kissed his wife, put his finger in Jean-Jacque's palm, and he squeezed it.

"Flora, I must go and give my presentation."

Henri took a shower, then he put on his suit, and left the hotel room.

Hours went by, and Flora was startled out of her sleep by Henri opening the door to the hotel room.

"Henri, how did it go?"

"It went well, Flora, they offered me a permanent position as a mathematics professor there at M.I.T. That means a reasonable salary, enough to buy a house. You could start your garden."

"O! O! Wow Henri, that's great!"

Flora got out of bed, walked toward Henri, kissed him on the cheek, then scurried into the bathroom. "How soon can we move?"

"We can start looking at houses tomorrow."

The next day, Henri and Flora went house hunting. On their second viewing, Flora surveyed the house, then she walked towards the back yard and remained outside the entire time of the viewing.

"It seems like your wife made herself at home Mr. Cadet," the real estate agent said.

"It appears so, this house is beautiful; I'll check on her to see what she thinks," Henri replied.

Henry opened a window in the hallway and poked his head outside. "Cheri, ou renmen li?" (Honey, do you love it?) asked Henri.

Flora looked up with Jean-Jacque in her arms, smiled. "Anri, mwen renmen li; ou panse mwen ka jwenn grenn nan kay tounen, se konsa mwen te kapab plante yo nan jaden mwen an? Mwen pral bezwen yon ban enstale nan sant la, ak yon Gazebo tou." (Henri, I love it; do you think I can get seeds from back home, so I could plant them in my garden? I am going to need a bench installed in the center, and a gazebo too,) Flora replied.

Henri closed the window, turned to the real estate agent, shrugged his shoulders and put his hands out. "We'll take it!" said Henri.

Henri extended his right hand, and the real estate agent shook it.

"Great, allow me to retrieve the documents from my car, so we could get the process rolling. Congratulations Mr. Cadet, this is a beautiful home. You and your family will be very happy here," the real estate agent said.

A week later, Henri went off to work, and met with the chancellor out in front of M.I.T University. Henri smiled and shook his hand "Good morning, are you Mr. Benito?" said Henri.

"Yes, good morning, Mr. Cadet, I won't bore you with a tour of the campus right now. What I will do is escort you to your

15

classroom, so you can do what we brought you here for. I know you will do great; your students are already there in the classroom," Mr. Benito replied.

Henry stood in front of the heavy mahogany door with a glass in the center of it. He took a deep breath and opened the door. "Good morning, my name is…"

"We're so glad you came as soon as you did, Robert threw up all over his desk; where are all of your cleaning products?" said a disgusted college student.

At that moment, the janitor walked in behind Henri with a mop and bucket. All the students scowled at Henri, and one college student said, "Why did Mr. Benito send in a Haitian janitor's assistant, to teach us math? I want to learn arithmetic, not how to clean."

The classroom erupted in laughter, and Henry slammed his briefcase down on the desk, walked to the blackboard, picked up a piece of chalk, and wrote out: 'Good morning students, my name is Mr. Cadet, and I'm your mathematics professor. Simplify to lowest term:

$$\frac{x^6 + a^2 + X^3}{x^6 - a^4 + y^2}$$

Henry slammed the chalk down on the desk, and shards of chalk flew around the room. He picked up his briefcase, stormed out of the classroom, and slammed the door behind him. Mr. Benito was down the hallway talking with a student, and Henri marched up to him and wedged his way in-between them. "The students in there mistook me for a janitor. Didn't you inform them that I was black?" asked Henri.

"Mr. Cadet, please calm down, I assure you it was a misunderstanding. I will get to the bottom of this, take a deep breath, go into the teachers' lounge, and I'll sort things out," Mr. Benito said.

Over the next year, Henri experienced nothing short of blatant bigotry at M.I.T. Every morning Henri would pull into his parking spot, and he would have to remove a makeshift janitor banner above his name. Before every class, a mop and bucket would always be by the chalkboard. Henri would remove it and put the mop and bucket in the hallway outside the classroom, so every student had to walk past it before entering.

Henri reached his breaking point when a faculty member threw his car keys at him. "Hey garçon, park this for me, will you!"

He understood these events weren't at all coincidences, Henri grew weary of people on campus mistaking him for a janitor, security guard, or any position other than professor.

The atmosphere on campus was at times overtly racist. Henri befriended a colleague at the school who spoke French. "Monsieur Trudeau, je ne peux pas le supporter ici, j'ai envie de frapper quelqu'un au visage. Mais je vous garantis que si je le faisais, je serais immédiatement réprimandé. Les étudiants et les professeurs ont manifesté un comportement raciste à mon égard," (Mr. Trudeau, I can't stand it here, I feel like punching someone in the face. But I guarantee if I did, I would be reprimanded immediately. Both students and faculty has exhibited racist behavior towards me,) Henri said.

"Monsieur Cadet, je comprends votre frustration, mais deux ans de plus et vous aurez un mandat ici. Ne faites rien d'irréfléchi," (Mr. Cadet, I understand your frustration, but two more years and y'all have tenure here. Don't do anything rash,) Mr. Trudeau replied.

"Je dois partir au cas où les choses deviendraient hostiles; Je ne peux plus le porter. Je n'ai pas déménagé ma famille ici aux États-Unis pour cette merde Monsieur Trudeau." (I have to leave in case things get hostile; I can't bare it any longer. I didn't move my family here to the United States for this shit Mr. Trudeau.)

"Je comprends parfaitement mon ami. Je connais un poste de statisticien qui a été soulevé à NYU. Ce serait une excellente opportunité pour vous et votre famille. Je le prendrais moi-même, mais je suis si proche de la titularisation ici à M.I.T. Partir maintenant serait un suicide professionnel. (I completely understand my friend. I know of a statistician position that has come up at

17

NYU. This would be a great opportunity for you and your family. I would take it myself, but I'm this close to tenure here at M.I.T. To leave now would be career suicide.)

"Pour vous, cela pourrait être une issue sans aucune perte. Je ressens votre douleur M. Cadet. Croyez-le ou non, j'ai moi aussi vécu des fissures sages, elles confondent mon identité avec un peintre ou un plombier. J'ai vécu tout le poids de leurs remarques de condoléances. Cela étant dit, si je pouvais harponner quelqu'un ici, je le ferais," (For you this could be a way out without any loses. I feel your pain Mr. Cadet. Believe it or not, I too have experienced the wise cracks, them mistaking my identity for a painter or a plumber. I've experienced the full brunt of their condescending remarks. With that being said, if I could spear anyone here, I would,) said Mr. Trudeau.

Mr. Trudeau's words were calming, like your favorite dish that your mother makes. His time here has stirred up anger inside him. He developed a jagged edge. Henri wondered if he had made the right decision by emigrating to the United States. He knew Flora won't like having to move again, but her fears manifested itself in reality and became fully realized.

"Je le ferai, je prendrai le poste. Qu'est-ce que je dois faire? Je ne peux pas simplement déménager aveuglément à New York », a-t-il demandé," (I'll do it, I will take the job. What do I need to do? I can't just blindly move to New York,) Henri said.

"Rien, je vais tout régler pour vous. Après avoir fait savoir à ma contact que je ne prendrai pas position. Ils seront déçus, mais une fois que je leur ferai savoir que je vous recommanderai. Et que je vous tiens en haute estime. Je pense qu'ils seront bien si vous venez à ma place," (Nothing, I will sort out everything for you. After I let my contact know that I won't be taking the position. They'll be disappointed, but once I let them know that I'll be recommending you. And that I hold you in high regard. I think that they will be alright with you coming in my stead,) Mr. Trudeau replied.

Henri went home, and Flora prepared Joumou for him for dinner. He sat down at the dinner table and sighed. "Flora, I have good news, and bad news," Henri said.

"Henri, give me the good news first," Flora replied.

"The good news is that I was offered a position at NYU. The bad news is that we have to move to New York."

"Henri, I just got settled in this house. What's going to happen to it?"

"We may have to sell Flora. You were right about Americans."

"O! O! Mwen gen rezon? Ala tris! Kisa ki te pase, yo trete ou move nan Tracey?" (Wow, I'm right? How sad! What has been happening, they treat you bad at work?)

Flora, I don't need an 'I told you so,' from you, this would be a better opportunity for us. Besides, I've been told that New York is more welcoming of foreigners than Massachusetts."

"Okay Henri, is the school system good for JJ?"

"I don't know, if public schools aren't good enough, then we have to send him to parochial school."

Once Henri got the call from NYU, he gave M.I.T, his letter of resignation, and the Cadets put the house up for sale, packed up and moved once again. This time, it was to the "Big Apple."

They settle in the Bronx, on 167th street and the Grand Concourse, across the street from Kent movie theatre. Flora noticed a for rent sign on a commercial property.

"Henri, although there is not much soil in this 'Concrete Jungle,' I am going to make it my mission to bring a little greenery to the neighborhood," Flora said.

With no objection from Henri, Flora rented the commercial property, and opened the floral shop she always wanted. Henri was happy to do this for her, she was going to pick up right where she left off with what she loves so much.

Henri knew giving her back her passion would mean a lot to her. Something that she missed being able to do since the big migration. Besides, he owed this to Flora for all of her unquestionable support of his ambitions.

Not soon after opening the Floral shop, it was an immediate hit. She put her all into the business, ordering exotic plants and flowers from around the world. Flora noticed that the demographic in the neighborhood was diverse, so when patrons shopped at her store, seeing a plant or flower from their home country, resonated with them.

Flora felt right at home for the first time since she and Henri left Haiti. So, the next obvious thing to do was to take up teaching music again. Determined to bring joy and beauty in any way she could, Flora put a sign on the front entrance, "Music Lessons: ages 3-12." She wanted to teach the piano and violin, to bring the joy of learning a musical instrument to the neighborhood children.

It's been four years since Flora and Henri settled in New York. She would often bring Jean-Jacque with her while she conducted her music lessons. Flora soon realized that Jean-Jacque was a prodigy. He could recite what he heard, only after hearing it once or twice. She began to test him with other instruments, like the flute and the harp as well. Jean-Jacque took to music like a fish to water.

He would construct inanimate objects at home to test what pitch or tone it made. He made a xylophone out of several empty toilet tissue rolls, a guitar out of old electrical wire and empty cereal boxes, and he even turned some old leather into a drum set.

Henri observed his son doing this and decided to feed his interest. Henri decided to buy more instruments for Flora's shop, so Jean-Jacque could expand his love for music. One day Jean-Jacque's noticed a shiny-gold instrument hanging on a pedestal in the shop.

"What's that mommy?" asked Jean-Jacque.

"It's a saxophone JJ," Flora replied.

He took down the saxophone, toiled with it for a few moments, he placed his lips around the reed, and he blew into it. An extraordinary sound came out the end of it. Jean-Jacque's eyes lit up and he instantly fell in love with the sax.

Flora gave him private lessons on the saxophone. Astonished

how he mastered the sax by the age of five years old. Determined for him to expand his horizon beyond the scope of their imagination, Henri and Flora applied to the prestigious Cambria Center for The Gifted.

A representative from the school travelled to the floral shop to evaluate Jean-Jacque's musical prowess. He stood outside the floral shop and watched in awe as little "JJ" drew a crowd with his play of several instruments. He didn't bother to enter and disturb the musical genius. The rep. walked down the street to the nearest payphone and called 'Flora's flora shop.'

"Hello Mrs. Cadet, my name is Justin Le, I'm from Cambria Center for The Gifted, and I just saw how poised Jean-Jacque was, as he played those instruments. On behalf of the school, I wanted to congratulate your son on his acceptance into 'The Center…'"

Everything has been going so well for the family. Henri became a respected Professor at NYU, and "JJ" has impressed the administrators, so much so, that they skipped him a couple of grades to the second.

Flora's Floral Shop/Private Music Preparatory Academy has increased in patronage from local businesses for weddings, bar/bat mitzvahs and students taking music lessons, since its inception. Not only is Flora getting business for events–she also has two big contracts from Ortiz funeral home and the photographer next door to her floral shop. His clients loved her unique floral arrangements when he photographed them.

The rumors of her unique arrangements filled the city, and she was in high demand. Flora couldn't fulfill the orders alone, so she had to hire a salesperson. The new hire blended in perfectly into the mystique of the shop; ironically, she was named Rose Gardener.

Rose was a Godsent, she freed up enough time so Flora could add a much-desired greenhouse to the floral shop. Since she migrated to the United States Flora intended to teach the neighborhood kids about Botany, much like back home in Haiti.

They were "Moving on up," the Cadets had realized the American Dream.

One day, after work, the phone rang, and Henri picked up the receiver. "Alo Anri, li te gen yon bon bout tan. Ki jan ou fe fre?" (Hello Henri, it has been a long time. How are you doing brother?) said the caller in Haitian Creole.

"Nou ap fè amann Clyde, tout bagay se jis. Nou te lite lè nou te premye rive isit la, men nou te jwenn wout nou nan obstak la. E ou menm frè? Ki jan madanm ou, ak marasa, se Latrice ak Patrice?" (We're doing fine Clyde, everything is fair. We struggled when we first got here, but we found our way through the obstacle. How about you brother? How is your wife, and the twins, Latrice and Patrice?) replied Henri.

"M ap fè byen frè, madanm mwen ak marasa ap mache byen tou." (I'm doing alright brother; my wife and twins are doing well too.)

"Clyde, nou ap fè byen isit la nan Amerik la, mwen pral voye pou nyès mwen an. Pa gen okenn rezon ki fè yo pa ka gen opòtinite yo menm jan ak nou, ou pa bezwen fè anyen, mwen pral pran swen tout bagay." (Clyde, we're doing well here in America, I am going to send for my nieces. There's no reason why they can't have the same opportunities as us, you don't need to do anything, I'll take care of everything.)

It didn't take long for Henri to handle the immigration process of his beloved twin nieces because of his status in Academia. He didn't wait long, his request for their visa was approved, and Latrice and Patrice came to America soon after.

Henri arrived at JFK international airport, early, and he held up a homemade sign that read: "Byenveni nan Amerik, Latrice ak Patrice Cadet." (Welcome to America, Latrice, and Patrice Cadet.)

The twins walked out of the tunnel and looked over at their uncle and smiled from ear to ear when they saw the sign with their names on it. "Tonton Anri, Tonton Anri, nou tèlman kontan wè ou! Kote Matant Flora ak ti kouzen nou Jean?" (Uncle Henri, Uncle Henri, we're so happy to see you! Where is Aunt Flora and our little cousin Jean?)

"Bonjou bèl nyès mwen yo, Byenveni nan eta yo. Flora

matant ou ak kouzen ou JJ yo tou de byen, men yo nan boutik la flora." (Hello, my beautiful twin nieces, welcome to the states. Your aunt Flora and your cousin JJ are both well, but they are at the floral shop.)

Henri hugged his twin nieces and brought their luggage to the car.

"Tonton Anri, kijan magazen flè a ye? Èske gen kèk pyebwa k'ap donnen la a? Èske ou jwe enstriman mizik tou? Èske kouzen Jean pale kreyòl?" (Uncle Henri, how is the flower shop doing? Are there any fruit trees there? Do you play musical instruments too? Does cousin Jean speak Creole?) said Latrice and Patrice simultaneously.

"Fasil, fasil, ou de kwa egzamine m 'tankou mwen te sou kanpe la nan tribinal la. Pa gen pyebwa ki donnen nan boutik la. Non, mwen pa jwe okenn enstriman mizik, e JJ pale kreyòl," (Easy, easy, you two crossed examined me like I was on the stand in court. There're no fruit trees at the shop. No, I don't play any musical instrument, and JJ does speak Creole,) Henri replied.

Henri drove up to the flora shop and parked out in front. He and the twins stepped out of the car, and they walked into the floral shop. There were several music students practicing their instrument when they walked inside.

Jean-Jacque put down his saxophone and ran into Henri's arms. Henri picked him up and held him in his arms. "JJ, mwen vle prezante ou premye kouzen ou yo, Latrice ak Patrice. Yo se pitit fi jimo tonton Clyde ki soti Ayiti," (JJ, I want to introduce you to your first cousins, Latrice and Patrice. They're Uncle Clyde's twin daughters from Haiti,) Henri said.

"Bonjou Latrice, Bonjou Patrice, mwen kontan rankontre ou tou, de kouzen." (Hello Latrice, Hello Patrice, I'm pleased to meet you both, cousins,) Jean-Jacque said.

Oh, pawòl mwen! Ou pale kreyòl trè byen! Nou kontan rankontre ou tou kouzen Jean, (Oh, my word! You speak Creole very well! We're pleased to meet you too Cousin Jean,) Latrice and Patrice replied in unison.

23

The twins approached Flora with Jean-Jacque in-between them hand in hand. "Bonjou matant Flora, bèl magazen, nou te manke ou anpil! Timoun yo tounen lakay yo akote tèt yo ak lapenn depi ou vwayaje nan Amerik la. Pwofesè a mizik nouvo se pa tankou pasyan jan ou te avèk yo." (Hello Aunty Flora, lovely shop, we missed you very much! The kids back home are beside themselves with grief since you traveled to America. The new music teacher is not as patient as you were with them,) The twins said.

"Mèsi tou de, medam, mwen panse ak elèv mwen yo chak jou. Kouman jaden mwen an mache?" (Thank you both, ladies, I think about my students every day. How's my garden doing?) replied Flora.

"Jaden ou ap mache byen; nou rekòlte kèk fwi anvan nou kite Hati. Li goute bon matant Flora." (Your garden is doing well; we harvested some fruit before we left Haiti. It tasted good Aunty Flora.)

The twins acclimated to their new environment very well, it was no surprise that Henri's nieces would excel. Latrice and Patrice weren't in school very long before it was apparent that they were gifted students. They both excelled in Mathematics and Science.

The twin sisters were placed in an advanced program at the Anderson school that Henri initially enrolled them in. It was a school suited for children with a mind for the arts. So, when the academy called Henri and Flora. It wasn't a surprise when the administrators suggested that they would be better off going to another school geared towards math and science.

Eventually, Henri enrolled them into The Bronx High School of Science. The twins were advance far beyond the Anderson academy level of education had to offer. Latrice and Patrice go on to take college courses simultaneously while in high school.

While everything was going well for Henri's twin nieces, the same couldn't be said for his son. One morning, the phone rang, and Henri answered the call—

"Good morning, how may I help you?" said Henri.

"Good morning, Mr. Cadet, this is the school principal over

at Cambria. How are you doing this morning?" replied the principal.

"Hello principal Grainger, I'm doing well, is everything okay with my son JJ at school?"

"Well, that is the reason for the call, Jean-Jacque has been bullied for some time now. Jean-Jacque has been just rolling with the punches so far, until today. I'll let him tell you the details."

"Good morning, Dad!" said Jean-Jacque.

"JJ, what's going on?" asked Henri.

"Dad, these students were troubling me, I was walking through the halls trying to make it to my next class. When two boys slapped my books out of my hand as they passed me. They, do, it, all, the, time!

"Today they called me; African booty scratcher repeatedly, then they teased me about my accent. These groups of students were partly mixed, but most of them were white.

"I said to them, 'I am not African. Although I am of African descent, I am Haitian. My parents are from Haiti.' I balled up my fists and stood my ground. I got sick of them ridiculing me, Dad."

"JJ, what did you do next?"

"My attempt to appeal to the bullies were futile, so I gave up on appealing to their intellect. I bent down to pick up my books off the floor, and they kicked and punched me with no regard.

"Fearing for my life, I reached out for a stone that held the door open to a classroom, to defend myself with. I stood up, closed my eyes, and swung my arms at anyone that was hitting me.

"I didn't know how many there were at first, but when I opened my eyes, there were two students lying on the ground."

Mr. Grainger grabbed the phone from Jean-Jacque hand. —— "There were only two students that were badly injured. The two boys started with him in the first place. He worked the two with stringent punity. With the tide turned, all those that witnessed the brawl and felt the pressure of siding with the underdog, cheered for Jean-Jacque.

25

"When faculty finally broke through the crowd of students, the only thing they saw was Jean-Jacque towering over them, hitting the boys with a heavy stone, and yelling obscenities at them in Creole.

"So, it's easy to believe that he wasn't at fault, but he was in possession of a deadly weapon."

At that point, Henri and Flora was listening on the call together. "What happened to the bullies, we're they expelled?" asked Flora.

"No, when we found out who the students were, and the extent of their injuries; their parents threatened to press assault charges on Jean." ——

Henri hung up the phone. He and Flora sped to Jean-Jacque's school. When they arrived, they saw the two battered and bruised bullies in the hallway leaving the principal's office, with their parents.

Henri walked into the principal's office and slammed the door behind him. "Why aren't those boys being arrested? Why are they being released before my wife and I got an explanation of why they bullied my son JJ?" asked Henri.

"Mr. and Mrs. Cadet, please sit down," principal Grainger replied.

"Was he tended to by a medical professional? Oh my God! Has he even been seen by the school nurse?" asked Flora.

Flora cried as she touched her child's swollen face. The Principle gave no response to their inquiries. He showed no concern, not even any empathy with them.

"Please, allow me to bring you up to speed," Principal Grainger replied.

Tears ran down Flora's face as she and Henri sat there consoling their son.

"There is no dispute that your son has an exceptional mind. He is a great student and is very kindhearted. After listening to the events that transpired today by multiple witnesses including the other parties involved. I have concluded to proceed with the expulsion of your son Jean-Jacque."

"What do you mean he will be expelled," Henri and Flora replied in unison.

"I don't think that is right, I do not believe that my son is being treated fairly. You have told us all that has happened, but it sounds one sided to me, like you believe that JJ is the aggressor," Henri said.

"No, I have done an extensive investigation and my findings seem to be accurate," Principal Grainger replied.

Henri stood up from his seat and slammed his hand on the desk. "It is impossible for you to find the truth because you're not looking for the truth. You have given me at least three or four versions from different people. All are one sided. So it seems to me like you have already made up your mind because my son had a weapon. It didn't cross your mind that he was defending himself. That may be because the other boys parents are rich and probably donated a lot of money to this school they won't be reprimanded!"

"Listen Mr. Cadet, they want to sue us, and shut the school down if I don't expel Jean. It's unfair I know, but I can't allow that to happen for the sake of the other students in the school. The cards are stacked against him because he used a weapon. For that reason alone, it wouldn't matter who did what to whom. He's wrong, you all would lose this battle even in the court of law. I convinced them not to press charges, only if Jean were expelled and is enrolled in an anger management class. If it's any consolation, everyone involved knows the truth here, we at Cambria Center for the gifted have Jean's best interest at heart."

Henri and Flora looked at each other in disbelief, but they decided to make a hard decision to go along with the terms for the greater good of the school. Henri, Flora and Jean-Jacque all got up, and Henri put his arm over his sons' shoulder. "I am so proud of you JJ. You stood up and fought against those bullies. You pushed back against those who wanted to hurt you. I learned a valuable lesson today:

27

'There is a time for everything, and a season for every activity under heaven: a time to be born and a time to die... A time to kill and a time to heal, a time to tear down and a time to build... A time to scatter stones and a time to gather them, a time to embrace and a time to refrain... A time to be silent and a time to speak, a time to love and a time to hate, a time for war and a time for peace.

'...Whatever is has already been, and what will be, has been before; and God will call the past to account. And I saw something else under the sun: In the place of judgment--wickedness was there, in the place of justice--wickedness was there. I thought in my heart, ...[Ecclesiastes 3 1-12 15-17]

Chapter 2:

Order in the court

Henri was filled with anger and shame for what happened to his son Jean-Jacque. The prejudice he experienced at school was traumatizing enough. Adding insult to injury, the Cadet's had to go to court, to stand in front of a judge. Jean-Jacque may face a higher level of injustice in an unfair court system.

At the same time Henri and Flora were confident in the judicial system, and they hoped that justice would prevail once the evidence was presented that would exonerate their son.

Certain that his son Jean-Jacque would be alright, and whatever happened he would endure it.

When the case was brought before Judge Aaron Black. Jean-Jacque was facing assault charges. Even with a good lawyer, the best that their money could buy, he's at the mercy of the court.

Despite the facts and eyewitnesses to the incident, Jean-Jacques was nervous he might be found guilty.

The Bailiff stood up straight and turned to the attendees in the courtroom. "All rise, Honorable Judge Aaron Black presiding."

Judge Aaron Black climbed up to the bench and sat down. "Court is now in session; You may be seated," Bailiff said.

The judge opened Jean-Jacque's folder, raised his eyebrows above his spectacles, and flipped through the pages. "Well, let's get right to it: Today, it is encumbered upon me to render a verdict that will only be fair for all people involved on the day of this unfortunate incident. Judge Aaron Black postured.

"Go ahead and stand-up son," the judge commanded.

Jean-Jacques stood up tall, and his parents were still hopeful that Judge Aaron Black would do the right thing.

"Although you are one of the good ones, you were wrong on the day in question," Judge Aaron Black said.

The whole room gasped, and there was a low rumble in the

courtroom. Judge Aaron Black banged his gavel a couple of times. "Order in the court."

"I believe that you brought a weapon to school with you that day. Neither the investigators nor I could figure out if you brought the stone with you that morning, or you stashed it in the off chance that if anything happened, you'd be prepared.

"But you see young man, this was premeditated. I do believe you were the target of bullying, but in the same token, you were determined to stand up for yourself, by any means necessary. ——"

"But your honor, my client was brutally attacked by numerous students. There was no way for him to know that things would escalate as they did. I believe that my client luckily found something to use in the fight to defend himself.

"If he didn't find the stone, my client would've been seriously injured and not be standing here in court today.

"Your honor, I implore you, my client is being vilified for merely protecting himself against his would-be attackers. I motion that the assault charge be dropped, and my client released," the defense attorney said.

"Your client is here alive and well, while his so-called attackers are in the New York-Presbyterian Hospital. He should be grateful that those kids' parents aren't pressing assault with a deadly weapon charge against your client.

"Henri Jean-Jacque Cadet, I'm ready to render my verdict. In all my years on the bench, I've never found it difficult to give out a sentence. My verdict is that you will be remanded to Spofford Juvenile Detention Center for no less than one year. Luckily, you're twelve years old and will not be serving your term on Rikers Island.

"Mr. Cadet, you're also to enter in an anger management program and complete 275 hours of community service. Case dismissed, Bailiff, bring in the next case."

Judge Aaron Black pounded his gavel and rendered his verdict.

Outraged, Henri stood up and took off his glasses. "I can't

believe that my boy will be sent away for defending himself. Of all the things to do, you're sending my son to prison. For what? He's innocent!

"Li pa gen pwoblèm konbyen lajan ke yon nonm nwa touche nan peyi sa a, chak chans ke nonm lan blan jwenn raple l 'nan plas li, li pran li," (It doesn't matter how much money that a black man earns in this country, every chance that the white man gets to remind him of his place, he takes it,) Henri said.

Flora put her head into her hands and cried. Her heart pounded loud inside her chest. She wasn't able to move or hear a sound over the breaking of her heart. Latrice and Patrice wrapped their arms around Flora to console her.

Her worst fears came true, the ill treatment of a loved one in this country; all because of deep rooted hatred and bigotry. The only thing a mother wants in life is to protect her child from harm. Unfortunately, that was stripped away from Flora today.

The lawyer turned to Henri to quell his furious rant, but it was too late. Judge Aaron Black banged the gavel, pointed it at Henri. "Mr. Cadet, your inability to contain yourself in my courtroom is grounds for me to find you in contempt.

"Mwen senpati ak sitiyasyon difisil ou, men lalwa a mete an plas pou yon rezon. Pitit ou a te kraze lalwa Moyiz la; tanpri konprann ke Jean-Jacque se fleksib, li pral anfòm." (I empathize with your plight, but the law is put in place for a reason. Your son broke the law; please understand that Jean-Jacque is resilient, he'll be fine,) the judge replied.

Henri raised his eyebrows, looked Judge Aaron in his eyes, took off his shoe and flung it at him. The judge ducked out of the way of the shoe.

"Don't you dare patronize me. Justice was not served here today; my son was guilty before stepping foot in the courtroom," Henri said.

"Mr. Cadet, your outburst didn't help your son's case at all. In fact, it shows where his anger stems from. Bailiff, remove this man from my courtroom," the judge replied.

Flora jumped up with tears still streaming down her face, mixed with emotional distress, pain and make-up. She lunged at Jean-Jacque; the twins weren't fast enough to stop her. Flora wrapped her arms around him. "Le pli vit ke mwen ka vizite put it gas on, mwen pral la. Kenbe ou konfyans ak kanpe fò ak Bondye. Se pou l 'la avèk ou," (As soon as I can visit my son, I will be there. Keep your faith and stand strong with God. May he be with you,) Flora said.

She held on to him tight until Jean-Jacque was pulled away from her clutches by the Bailiff. Jean-Jacque was immediately taken into custody and escorted out of the courtroom.

Flora and the twins waited in the hallway of the courtroom for Henri. "Pa enkyete Aunty, Patrice ak mwen pral etidye lwa, se konsa sot de bagay sa a pa rive nou tout tan anko," (Don't worry Aunty, Patrice and I will study law, so this sort of thing doesn't happen to us ever again,) Latrice said.

Patrice rubbed Flora's back as she cried into her handkerchief. A large wooden door opened, and Henri emerged rubbing his wrist. "Anri, renmen mwen, yo te pran pitit gason nou an lwen tankou yon kriminel komen," (Henri, my love, they took our son away like a common criminal,) Flora said.

"Flora, ki sa ou ap fe toujou ap fe isit la?" (Flora, what are you three still doing here?) asked Henri.

"Oke, ou gen kle machin yo, kle kay yo ak kle magazen yo, ki jan lot bagay nou ta ka jwenn lakay ou." (Well, you have the car keys, the house keys and the shop keys, how else would we get home.)

Jean-Jacque and a dozen other youth offenders boarded a bus waited in the rear of the courtroom. It transported them to Spafford Juvenile Detention Centre in The Bronx. The bus arrived at the facility and he and the other attendees were ordered to alight the bus.

The bus load of adolescent youth walked inside like ants at a picnic. Four C.Os' (correction officers) stood along either side of the walls in the corridor. Jean-Jacques was spotted by a guard, who had

32

taken a notice in him because he stood out like a sore thumb.

"Fresh meat, another group of toys to play with," the C.O thought to himself.

There are two types of kids that come into Spafford, most are juvenile delinquents. They're broken and need to be fixed. These inmates have real problems, and it rarely ever gets addressed. They become repeat offenders until they're old enough to be sent to Rikers Island or any other penitentiary in the country. They usually end up spending most of their adult lives in the prison system.

These lost souls are the forgotten or the people who the universe failed from the beginning. The ones that society cares nothing about, at least no one cares enough for it to matter in their lives, so they end up being callous. Hardened little by little every day until there's nothing left of their humanity. These people can never care one iota for anyone, not even for themselves.

The second type is like the toy you get on your birthday or Christmas. Believing that they're innocent and think they don't belong in "Juvie." They remain nice and shiny for a while, but then

they reach their breaking point. Sometimes you can just snap them back into form, but other times y'all have to use other methods to glue back their broken pieces.

The C.O knew Jean-Jacque was different, he could tell just by the way he carried himself that he came from a loving family. Yet still he had an edge to him. So, compared to everyone else in here, he's a rare gem. Amongst the less sought-after stones and metals.

"Garçon, c'est un joli costume, si votre famille peut se le permettre, elle aurait dû être en mesure de vous trouver le meilleur avocat que l'on puisse acheter pour vous représenter. Comment vous êtes-vous retrouvé dans ce pétrin?" (Boy, that's a nice suit, if your family can afford that, they should've been able to get you the best lawyer money can buy to represent you. How did you get yourself in this mess?) asked the C.O.

"Je ne comprends pas très bien le français, mes parents sont d'Haïti, donc je comprends le créole, je ne parle qu'un petit peu," (I

33

don't understand French very well, my parents are from Haiti, so I understand Creole, I can only speak a little bit,) Jean Jacque replied.

"O! O! Vous venez d'Haïti! Se konsa, ou pale kreyòl, frè mwen an. Non mwen se Jerome, sa se yon kostim bèl, si fanmi ou kapab peye sa, yo ta dwe ve yo te kapab fè ou jwenn pi bon lajan an avoka ka achte reprezante ou. Ki jan ou fè jwenn tèt ou nan dezòd sa a? (Wow! You're from Haiti! So, you speak creole my brother. My name is Jerome, that's a nice suit, if your family can afford that, they should've been able to get you the best lawyer money can buy to represent you. How did you get yourself in this mess?) said the C.O.

"Non mwen se Jean-Jacque, Yo voye m isit la Spofford, paske mwen te nan yon batay nan lekòl la. Mwen defann tèt mwen pou yo pa frape m, lè l sèvi avèk yon wòch ke mwen te jwenn nan koulwa a fè bak yo nan mwen." (My name is Jean-Jacque, and I have been sent here to Spofford because I got into a fight at school. I defended myself from being pummeled by a few guys at my school, by using a stone that I found in the hallway to back them off of me!"

"Konbyen nèg kote ki ge?" (How many guys were there?)

"Mwen pa gen okenn ide. Mwen te twò okipe ap eseye pa mouri. Li te difisil di nan tout mele la. Tout sa mwen konnen lè lafimen an otorize mwen te vivan ak de nan ti gason yo te tap mete sou tè a. (I have no idea. I was too busy trying not to die. It was hard to tell through all the melees. All I know when the smoke cleared, I was alive and two of the boys were lying on the ground.)

"O! O! Ou te fè sa ou te dwe fè men mwen konprann poukisa ou te dwe voye isit la. Ou dwe kite yon bagay deyò paske w ap jistifye nan aksyon ou yo." (Wow! You did what you had to do but I do understand why you had to be sent here. You must be leaving something out because you're justified in your actions.)

"Wi, si sa a te yon mond pafè, epi si mwen te blan ke aksyon mwen ta dwe jistifye jistifye. Oswa si mwen te atake pa timoun nwa. Èske mwen te mansyone ke yo tout te rich?" (Yes, if this was a perfect world, and if I was white that my actions would be deemed justified. Or if I was attacked by black kids. Did I mention that they were all rich?)

34

The guard shook his head, and said, "Woy! Ala tris!" (Yikes! How sad!)

There was a moment of silence between the two as the inmates were processed into the facility.

"Ki jan ou ta renmen li si mwen ta anseye ou Arts masyal. Fason sa a ou ka defann tèt ou nan tout tan, epi ou pa ta gen yo sèvi ak yon zam. Sèl zam ou bezwen depi kounye a se lide ou, kò ou, ak nanm ou. Yon fwa yo nan senkronizasyon, ou pral vin zam nan ultim." (How would you like it if I would teach you martial arts. This way you can defend yourself at all times, and you wouldn't have to use a weapon. The only weapon you need from now on are your mind, body, and soul. Once they are in sync, you will become the ultimate weapon.)

"Pandan ke anba tutèl mwen, ou pa pral gen fè kèk travay lap fè. Ou pral plonje tèt ou nan literati; etidye diferan lang, etidye matematik, tout syans ak istwa. 'Konnen yo pwòp tèt ou,' nan misk nan pi gwo ak pi enpòtan se sèvo ou. (While under my tutelage, you won't have to do menial chores. You will immerse yourself in literature, study different languages, study mathematics, all sciences and history. 'Know they self,' the biggest and most important muscle is your brain.)

"Ou pral bati lide ou nan maten ak travay lekòl la. Nan apremidi yo, ou pral bati kò ou ak fòmasyon masyal Arts. Nan aswè, mwen vle ou etidye diferan disiplin relijyon, meditasyon, ak filozofi. Sa yo ap ede ou gen plis santre,"

(You will build your mind in the mornings with schoolwork. In the afternoons, y'all build your body with martial arts training. In the evenings, I want you to study the different disciplines of religion, meditation, and philosophy. These will help you to be more centered,)" the C.O said.

"Oh monchè! sa anpil! (Oh man! that's a lot!)

"Pa enkyete mwen pral gide ou epi ede ou chak etap nan chemen an. Li ka sanble tankou yon anpil kounye a, men ou pral wè ki jan tout bagay abouti nan fen an. Ou pa gen anyen men tan. Se konsa, li ta entelijan yo ap depanse li amelyore tèt ou, se konsa."

(Don't worry I will guide you and help you every step of the way. It may seem like a lot right now, but y'all see how everything culminates in the end. You have nothing but time. So, it would be smart to spend it bettering yourself, so…?)

The C.O, looked down at Jean-Jacque, and waited for a response from him.

Jean-Jacque was hesitant at first, A few things ran through his mind before he answered: "Why is this guard taking so much of an interest in me? I'm in here for a year, I might as well master something new."

"Wi" (Yes,) replied Jean-Jacques.

He followed the C. O.'s teachings to the Tee. Jean-Jacque studied hard and trained even harder until his release. At first, it was hard, but he continued and didn't give up. Six months into his sentence, an inmate stepped to him during chow time.

"Yo, yuh neva asked me if yuh could sit at this table. I'm big Willie, and I run this facility, yuh been low-key since you got here, so I let yuh live. It's been six months now son, and yuh ain't pay tribute to me or put in work. So, I gotta fuck yuh up!" said Willie.

Willie pushed Jean-Jacques' tray of food to the ground and towered over him.

"Nigga, get up and do something."

Jean-Jacque sprung up out of his seat, and before he could react, another inmate tackled Willie to the ground from behind. The inmate pummelled Willie, and everyone, including the guards stood idly by, and watched the fight unfold.

After a minute, the C.O.'s blew their whistles, and all the inmates laid down on the ground except Jean-Jacque. He stood there panting, with his fists clenched, and looking at Willie with his eyebrows knitted up.

The inmate that interceded in the fight, pulled him down to the ground.

The C.O.'s swooped in and grabbed Willie and the other inmate. As they were being carried away, the inmate turned to Jean-

Jacque and nodded at him. "Yo, my name is Roland Pembroke, any friend of Jerome's, is a friend of mines; aiight! You good in here, nobody won't fuck with you now; I got your back Frenchie," Roland said.

Jean-Jacque was perplexed, how was somebody that he didn't know, willing to fight somebody in his stead.

During Jean-Jacques' martial arts lesson the next day, he wanted to get to the bottom of this. "Jerome, how come that kid fought Willie for me?" asked Jean-Jacque.

"Roland was one of my star pupils, he is a repeat offender, so I stopped training him last fall. I'm not training you to fight in here, I'm training you, so you won't ever have to fight more than once out in the real world. News travels fast once people know that you mastered a discipline. Once you're released for here, I don't want to see you ever again," the C.O replied.

Jean-Jacque took heed to the insight, his stint in Spofford was hard, but in the end, all that he learned from the C.O was more beneficial to him than the anger management program.

Jean-Jacque was released shortly before his freshman year of high school. His parents and his cousins were eager to see him released from Spofford after twelve months in the juvenile detention center.

Jean-Jacque didn't suffer from any infractions while he was in "Juvie," so he was released on time. His father was the first to greet him.

"JJ my son, you're a big strong man now——"

"Almost as tall as your father when he was your age," Flora said.

Jean-Jacque and his parents embraced and there were no dry eyes between the close-knit family.

Before the next school year, his parents tried to get him enrolled into a different private school before his discharge from Spofford, but they were unsuccessful.

As a family they all agreed that it was a field of contention,

37

which was better left alone. As a last resort Jean-Jacque ended up going to Alfred E. Smith High school in the Bronx.

"Being around more people that look like me will make a difference," Jean-Jacque thought on his first day of school.

A few months in school, Jean-Jacque had forgotten how mean kids could be to one another. An occurrence he didn't deal with at Spofford because the guard protected him. Everyone knew that he was being trained by Jerome to be a badass, so no one dared to mess with him.

At the end of his first semester, right before midterms. A senior, named Joshua was bullying a freshman in the hallway. Jean-Jacque walked up to them and intervened. "Joshua, leave him alone, pick on somebody your own size."

Joshua turned to Jean-Jacque, pointed his finger in his chest. "What are you going to do about it, you African Booty Scratcher."

Jean-Jacque saw him going around messing with all the other students. He has grown tired of his bullying the underclassmen. No one else in school attempted to challenge Jean-Jacque because he was so big; he grew almost a foot in a year, 6'-4" to be exact. Joshua didn't care; he was the star forward on the soccer team. Plus, he was the reigning 180lbs all-star wrestler, three years running.

Jean-Jacque thought he might stay under the radar for four years, but all of that flew out of the window when he decided to defend someone else from the star athlete/bully.

"Oh well, so much for maintaining the status quo. When in Rome, you have to do as the Romans do," he thought to himself.

Jean-Jacque used the roundhouse kick maneuver and used the lateral side of his foot to pin Joshua up against the locker with pure poise. He applied pressure with his foot on his throat and said, "Listen, I am not an African booty scratcher. I am not even African, I am Haitian. The last time someone called me that name, they ended up in the hospital.

"So, I would advise you to leave him alone. The next time I hear about you bullying anyone or calling anybody that racial epithet; it's going to be, you, and me.

"I don't want to hear about you messing with nobody, ever again. Do you hear me?"

Joshua was at a loss for words, so Jean-Jacque stretched his legs open more, and he lifted him off the ground slightly. Now, Joshua was on his tippy toes.

"Do I have to repeat myself?"

"No! I got it; I won't do it again."

When Jean-Jacque took his foot off his throat and released him. The big bully wasn't so big and bad anymore.

Joshua dropped down to his knees, rubbed his neck, and coughed incessantly.

Jean-Jacque didn't have to worry about Joshua ever again.

"Yo, thanks man, you were like Jean-Claude Van Damme back there; my name is Jamie by the way. I'm from 167th and College Ave. You look familiar. Does your mother have a floral shop off the Grand Concourse on 167th street?" said the freshman.

"Yeah, my mother's name is Flora, she teaches private music lessons there too."

I knew I recognized you, my older brother Matthew took lessons from her a few years back; before he died, my father used to buy my mother flowers from there every Friday. You were a legend in the neighborhood with how well you played those instruments. Why did you stop?"

"I got into trouble and was sent to Spofford for a year."

"Word, you home now, Jean-Claude, ain't nobody gonna mess with you now since you embarrassed Joshua."

Before long, things went back to normal. After the excitement with Joshua died down, he made a couple of friends, but not too many. Jean-Jacque was careful about who he let in close to his space. Not because he was scared, though, you know how the saying goes, "Once bitten twice shy." He became guarded, wary of people, and fearful of being vulnerable.

He and Jamie became best of friends. Jamie was on the wrestling team, and he attempted to get Jean-Jacque to join after the incident with Joshua, but he wasn't interested. The wrestling coach Mr. Irizarry tried too, but he refused him as well. He signed up for karate class though, to resume his martial arts training.

The pair was thick as thieves when they realized that they had so much in common. A couple of years went by, and things went back to normal. Jean-Jacque reclaimed some of the time that he lost when he was in Spofford.

1996 was the start of a good year, something special for everyone. As a part of his sentence, Jean-Jacque had to complete 275 hours of community service. He bused tables at a club in Manhattan, called Divvy Divvies. This was where a lot of big wigs all over the city congregated, like the Mayor of New York City Rodolfo Meléndez, several other politicians, and V.I.P's from all over the tristate area.

Jean-Jacque had done such a good job, the manager kept him on after he completed his community service.

Club Divvy Divvies was one of the last places in the city where you could listen to live Jazz. This was the place to be if you were a fan. Also, it was known as the place that big deals were made.

On his first day as a part-time employee, Mayor Rodolfo Meléndez and Deputy Mayor Marisol Velasquez, came into the club together, and sat down at their usual table. She was a big deal, the

news reported that Marisol was the first Female Deputy Mayor of New York of Guatemalan descent. Being Hispanic made her an instant legend within the Latin community.

Jean-Jacque walked over to their table and introduced himself. "Hi, my name is Jean, pleased to meet you Sir, Madam."

"I know who you are, I have been watching you for a while now. You've made a reputation for yourself. I like your work ethic, you're like a worker bee. Since you have been keeping your nose clean, I did something for you," Marisol replied.

"What have you done for me, Ms. Velasquez?"

"Since I got into politics. A wise man once told me to get to know everyone around you that you have to see more than twice. You never know who they may turn out to be. More importantly, what they can do for you in the future.

"So, I made it my business to familiarize myself with you including your case. I was the one to get you off of your community service early."

Jean-Jacque raised an eyebrow, he was confused, "Why would she do this for me? Here's another person who's looking out for me for no apparent reason. What do they see in me?" He pondered.

"Thank you, Ms. Velasquez," Jean-Jacque replied.

Humbled by his good fortune, he smiled to draw back the tears that were collecting in the back of his eyelids.

"Here Busy bee, could you take this ashtray away for me, and get me a new one; it has a dead bee in it," Marisol said.

Before Jean-Jacque could take the ashtray away, she put out a Virginia slim in the ashtray. "I know this stuff will kill you, but I can't kick."

Jean-Jacque picked up the ashtray from off the table, and she stuffed a fifty-dollar bill in the left side pocket of his apron.

He continued to work hard and build up a rapport with Deputy Mayor Velasquez. So much so, that she also learned of his abilities to play most instruments. He just didn't have the opportunity to show off his skills for her.

Sometimes the club manager would allow him to fool around with the instruments. Only if it was all right with the resident band members, and only when the club was almost empty before closing.

One day when the club was almost empty. The band was playing a number, and they summoned him on stage to showcase his talent. The Deputy Mayor stayed around a little later than usual.

41

There was an incident earlier, a cop shooting of an unarmed civilian. The racial undertone of the shooting of an unarmed African American man by a white cop made it a particularly bad day.

Jean-Jacque jumped up on stage and played with the piano and the guitar. Out of his peripheral he saw a saxophone case off to the side, close to the speakers. He walked over to it hoping that it wouldn't be empty.

Oftentimes the band members left the case but took the instrument with them. Maybe it was easier for them to carry around. Not this time, he was in luck; the saxophone was in there. When he opened the case, it was shiny and clean. Jean-Jacque didn't hesitate, he took the saxophone out of the case and couldn't wait to play for Deputy Mayor Velasquez.

Marisol hadn't had the pleasure of hearing Jean-Jacque play the saxophone before. This was his favorite instrument, and he played like none other. He harmonized with the other band members, and the melodious sound resonated with the few people left in the club.

"Now that's Jazz," one person said.

The melody that filled the club was more than soulful, it was breath taken. Marisol couldn't believe her ears.

Such sophisticated sounds coming from a young person, as he blew into the sax. He played with such depth and range of emotions. She could feel his life through his song devoid of any words. Marisol hadn't heard anyone play the sax like this before. The notes echoed through her heart and soul.

Marisol approached Jean-Jacque after he wiped down the saxophone and put it back in its case.

"I am completely and utterly speechless, Busy bee," she complimented.

"I had no idea that you could play like that. I am going to have to let the owner know that he has a prodigy on his hands. I want to hear you play more often. I am going to make sure that you play for the club at least once a week. How would you like that?"

said Marisol.

"Thank you, Ms. Velasquez, I would appreciate that very much. I'm going to be here anyway," he casually answered.

Before he knew it, Jean-Jacque was not only playing in the club once a week, but he was also headlining. He was bringing in more and more revenue. Not long, rumors of his talents spread far and wide. People came in from three states away to hear him play the saxophone. He was famous, everyone loved him.

Jean-Jacque traveled from the Bronx to Manhattan more to play with the band. He didn't even have to buss tables anymore. Even his parents loved what he was doing. They worried a little because of his late nights. They didn't stop him because he kept up with his grades, Henri and Flora trusted that he was being safe and knew of his friendship with Deputy Mayor Marisol Velasquez.

One night, after one of his sets, Marisol asked Jean-Jacque to take a ride with her. He agreed, and she took him to her loft in SOHO.

"This is a place that I have set up for young individuals such as yourself. This is a place for "Artists," if you will. This is a brainchild of mind. I am developing a program throughout the city, so artists of all types can hone their skills here," Marisol said.

She showed him around, he was in awe of the concept. Despite his age, he knew the significance of a place like this could mean for someone like him.

"Look, this floor is an area for sculptors, and painters. The first floor is a computer room for writers, and graphic designers. We're setting up a spot in the basement for fashion designers. The best part is, we have a fully functioning recording studio down there already."

"As a matter fact, I know of a group who are recording an album, they are in need of a saxophone player to add their ensemble."

"Do you mean me?" replied Jean-Jacque.

The deputy mayor just looked at him. "No, the sculpture

43

over there of an octopus posing like Bob Marley. Of course, I mean you, silly.

"Wow, that'll be awesome, Ms. Velasquez," he expressed, to her in disbelief.

She then took him to the top floor of the building. This was another open loft with not much furnishing, except for a bed in the center. Which Jean-Jacque paid no attention to? He was preoccupied with the notion of being on an album.

"This is all happening so fast," he thought.

Jean-Jacque watched as Marisol sat on the bed. She slipped out of her shoes then took out a Virginia Slim.

"Come over here and sit down next to me Busy bee. Would you be a gentleman and help a lady light her cigarette, please,"

Marisol said.

Jean-Jacque walked over to her, lit her cigarette, and sat down beside her on the bed.

"Do you know why I like you?! You are smart, you have an impeccable work ethic for such a young man. I admire that about you, Busy bee.

"The other band members have become quite fond of you as well. I've been watching you closely for a long period of time now. I see how confident you're when you play the sax on stage.

"Take off your shirt, Busy bee," Marisol said and caressed his arm and chest.

Jean-Jacque took off his shirt and stood there in front of Marisol awaiting further instructions. "Just look at you, you already have a body of a grown man. Your chiseled chest, and rippling biceps…"

Confused, Jean-Jacque stood up from off the bed like a jack in the box, and the bulge of his erect penis protruded through the front of his pants. He was embarrassed and had no idea of what was about to happen. Filled with mixed-up emotions. Jean-Jacque has never experienced this kind of affection from anyone other than his mother before.

On one hand he hopes that he is about to lose his virginity. On the other hand, if that isn't the case, he'd be both relieved, yet disappointed. It makes perfect sense why she has been so nice to me all this time without asking for anything in return, he thought.

Knowing how the world works, not everyone is going to do something out of the kindness of their heart. Jean-Jacque was young, but he wasn't delusional.

Despite his reservations, Marisol unzipped his pants and pulled them down along with his boxers. Jean-Jacque stood there naked as the day he was born, exposed to Marisol and the luminous moonlight. She reached out and gripped his shaft with her hand, her touch was so soft.

The feeling was unexplainable, strange yet pleasurable like his penis belonged in her hand.

"Has anyone held it other than you before?" she asked.

"Nah, nuh, na, no ma'am," he stuttered as Marisol stroked his cock.

Jean-Jacque was harder than Chinese arithmetic. It was as if all the blood in his body corralled in his penis.

Marisol stood up and pushed him down on the bed on his back, then she finished taking off her clothes. Jean-Jacque looked at her naked body in amazement. She was so beautiful, curves in all the right places. Jean-Jacque was completely mesmerized.

"Have you ever been with a girl before?"

He stammered, but he couldn't articulate the words that were stuck in his mind. The little head was calling all the shots.

"I'll take that as a no."

Marisol smiled, straddled him, and directed his penis inside her. She slid down his shaft, and her moist interior walls gripped it while she flicked her clitoris with her index finger. She kissed him and guided his hands down her back to her buttocks.

45

"What is it you want?" said Marisol into his ear.

"You, I want you," he replied.

"No, not now silly, I can tell you want me. I mean out of life?"

"What?"

"I mean out of life. What do you want out of life?"

Marisol leaned back and rode Jean-Jacque steady like a cowgirl.

"Whatever it is, there is no reason you can't have it. Many young teens throughout the city have benefited from an, ahh…"

Marisol quivered as she orgasms, then she bit down on her lip. Her body went limp, she flopped down on his chest, exhaled.

"An arrangement that when they turn 18, they are set for life. They are able to go to any college of their choice, even if they can't afford it. Or go anywhere they want. So, do you have something in mind, a dream?" asked Marisol.

"Yes, yes, I'll do whatever you want me to do," Jean-Jacque said.

"That's good Busy bee."

She felt his body tense up and heard the anxiety in his voice.

Marisol placed her fingers in-between his and they moved back and forth, up, and down in unison. Panting, sweating, gyrating, and gazing into each other's eyes.

Marisol tried to control the pace as long as she could, but his inexperienced virgin blood boiled over like a bubbling caldron. He thrusts vigorously chasing his first taste of ecstasy. Jean-Jacque grabbed her close to him and clinched his buttocks tight; he'd arrived, and in a few seconds, it was all over.

He pushed her off him, jumped up out of the bed, rushed to the bathroom and closed the door. Jean-Jacque stood there reflecting on all that transpired tonight; to the sound of water running from the faucet.

"That was unbelievable even harder to comprehend," he thought.

She was fond of him. He was enthralled by her essence and her kindness, and by Marisol's feminine wilds.

He cleaned up himself and walked out of the bathroom with a wet rag for her. But Marisol was fast asleep, so he covered her naked body with a sheet, gathered his things and tip-toed out of the loft. Jean-Jacque went into the staircase to get dressed. He ran outside, looked down the street and saw a train station.

Jean-Jacque got on the train and was halfway uptown on the D train before he noticed he'd put on her panties by mistake.

Jean-Jacque continued to go through the events of the night in his head all the way home. He entered his apartment eager to share his first sexual experience with someone, anyone. He walked into the living room, and Henri was asleep on the couch.

Latrice was face down in her textbook on her bed. Patrice was curled up in her bed motionless with headphones plugged into the stereo. His parents' bedroom door was closed, so he walked into his bedroom, and flopped onto his bed.

Getting ready for bed, Jean-Jacque thought about his experience. He wanted to share the news with everyone, but they were all sleeping. What occurred tonight, scattered through his mind all night long.

He smiled and stretched his hands above his head. "I slept with an older woman," Jean-Jacque repeated the sentiment as he looked up at the ceiling fan twirling around in the dark.

"I lost my virginity to the first female Deputy Mayor of New York City Marisol Velasquez," he said until the sun beamed through a seam in the curtains over the window.

"I hope this isn't a one-time thing," he thought to himself, then fell asleep.

Over the next six months, Marisol's secret love affair with Jean-Jacque continued. She groomed him. Teaching him all the ways to conduct himself around the elite socialites of New York.

47

How to speak. How to walk. Even how to hold his drink or carry on a proper conversation. No time was wasted on the young man.

One night, Marisol entered the club and spotted Jean-Jacque before his set. "Come here Busy Bee," Marisol said.

She grabbed him by the arm, planted a small peck on his cheek. "Break a leg."

Marisol waited until he finished his set and applauded his performance as the band exited the stage. She wrapped her arm underneath his and walked backstage with him.

"Hey, I want to be the first to tell you that I'll be taking a sabbatical for a while. I'll be back soon, but I want you to stay in the loft and create music and enjoy the space," she said.

Jean-Jacque took the keys and watched as Marisol walked out of the club.

Marisol was vague with the reason why she had to leave town. He figured maybe she was going out town to deal with something political in Albany or in Washington D.C.

Jean-Jacque listened to her and stayed in the loft that night. The next morning, he called home and Henri picked up:

"Hello, good morning, how can I help you?"

"Good morning, Pops, it's JJ, I just wanted to let you know that I'm okay. I stayed over at the loft last night. Marisol is out of town, and she said I could stay here while she's gone, so I can record music for a new jazz album."

"That's great news JJ, I am so proud of you. Make sure you keep up with your studies."

"Okay Pops, tell mom that I love her."

Marisol came back in town five months after she left, and the two picked up right back where they left off.

Shortly after she got back, she started to teach him how to dress, how to speak using charisma, and how to hold someone's attention during a conversation.

48

Marisol took him to her tailor, Mr. Verona, down the street from the loft.

"I want to get you fitted for suits Busy bee, although the saying is: 'The man makes the clothes, the clothes don't make the man,' I beg to differ.

"Busy bee, did you notice the car key on the ring that I gave you?"

"Yeah, the one with the Chevy logo on it."

"When you get your driver's license It's yours. Only if you pay close attention to what I tell you and fly straight."

They walked into Mr. Verona's Tailor shop, and a well-dressed old Italian man was seated by a small table. He sat by an opened window, with his legs crossed, reading the New York Post; sipping on a cappuccino.

Mr. Verona noticed Marisol enter the shop, he put down the newspaper and stood up. "Donna Molta Bella!" (Very beautiful woman!) Ms. Mayor, to what do I owe the honor?" said Mr. Verona.

"Mr. V, stop it, I'm the Deputy Mayor, and I need to get the kid here fitted for a suit," Marisol replied.

"È lo stesso per me," (It's all the same to me,) Sunny-boy, you heard the lady, let's hop to it. Time is money and money is time," Mr. Verona said.

Jean-Jacque wasn't moved by the old man's dry humor, but he relished every moment that he got with Marisol outside the club. So, he obliged Mr. Verona and held his arms out by his sides as if he was about to conduct an orchestra.

"Hey Sunny-boy, you've done this before."

Mr. Verona took the tape measure from around his neck and stretched it along Jean-Jacque's arms, back, around his neck, his chest, and waist. "Okay Sunny-boy, I'm almost done, turn around so I can take your inseam."

Jean-Jacque turned and faced the old man, then Mr. Verona took his last measurements.

"Give me two weeks, and I'll have a few options for you." Mr. Verona kissed Marisol on the cheek, and he gave Jean-Jacque a handshake.

"Forse la prossima volta potresti suonare il sax per me. Ho sentito così tanto parlare di te, è un piacere conoscerti finalmente" (Maybe next time you could play the sax for me. I've heard so much about you, it's a pleasure to finally meet you,) said Mr. Verona.

"Certo signor Verona, vedo cosa posso fare." (Sure Mr. Verona, I see what I can do,) Jean-Jacque replied.

"Sharp as a tack, not too many high school students your age can speak Italian. Please, call me Mr. V, all my friends do."

Marisol completely groomed him to content with the New York socialites. The caterpillar became the butterfly.

You could barely recognize him. Jean-Jacque walked different; his stride was now accompanied with a certain "Je ne sais pas' quoi." He spoke without an accent. You almost couldn't tell that he was from the Bronx. And not from the upper eastside of Manhattan.

Marisol carried out this training of Jean-Jacque because she wanted to give him the best chance at success.

Someone who, if she was honest with herself, had fallen in love with. Knowledge of this could be detrimental to everyone involved in The Program. It would jeopardize her political career. It would put all the members at club Divvy Divvies in danger, many of whom would sentence to long prison terms. Jean-Jacque would be victimized and shun for being willfully ignorant. All because she couldn't show some constraint.

Chapter 3:

The Routine

Jean-Jacque's life shifted into low gear when Marisol stepped back from their relationship. She explained that it would be best for him to focus on school and finish up his senior year.

Pulling back from the extra time he was spending at club Divvy Divvies wasn't easy, but it was a relief. Even though the extra attention he received from playing with the band and mingling with the who's who of the city was impressive; It was good to hang out with his friends for a change.

Finals were coming up, and everyone in school was stressed out. You could feel the tension in the air. It was thick like 5 o'clock rush hour.

Jean-Jacque along with his bonafide friends had Drama for fifth and sixth period. He loved this class; he took this time to practice his social skills he learned from Marisol. Also, he took the opportunity to fiddle with the instruments here and there when needed for the plays or performances. The teacher recognized his talents and Jean-Jacque had risen to the ranks of student director.

At the end of fifth period one day, the students had a half an hour of free time that they all used to relax, relate and release. Drama was a very strenuous class, and it took a toll out of them. Most times, Jamie, and Bryce went across the street to the projects to smoke weed, but today, Jean-Jacque joined them.

Bryce put a block on the ground to keep the back door open, a kid walked downstairs and immediately noticed Jean-Jacque.

"Frenchie, is that you? It's me, Roland Pembroke, remember me?" said Romain.

"Oh shit, Roland, I haven't seen you since I came home from Spofford, three and a half years ago. When you came home?" replied Jean-Jacque.

"I got expelled from John F. Kennedy High School for breaking a teacher's jaw. I did a stint in Spofford for that. I didn't get sent to "Juvie" for as long as I should've. I thought I would've gone to Rikers Island for real this time.

"Judge Aaron Black signed me up for this Program, and that expedited the process. I just came home a couple of days ago, and they seem to have pull here at Alfred E. Smith because they were the only school in the five boroughs that would accept me."

"Damn Roland, still got that one-hitter quitter, huh!"

"You already know Frenchie. Pardon me, Jean-Jacque."

"Yo, we were about to cop weed from Mikey Dread. Are you interested?"

"Hell yeah, I haven't smoked good weed since I've been home."

"Yo, Jamie, go ahead, get two nicks," said Bryce.

"Nah, man! I always cop, why don't you go?" said Jamie.

"He doesn't sell weed to none of us. He doesn't trust any of us, he only sells to his Caribbean people. That's your man because you used to fuck with his niece Precious," Bryce replied.

"Wait a minute, you're Caribbean too! Roland you're Trinidadian and Bryce, you're Guyanese."

"Yeah, but we were born here in the United States of America, just like you Jamie. And we don't speak that patois shit."

Aight, give me the money."

He crossed the street, walked into the Jamaican bakery, and waited until the customer in front of him left the store before he walked up to the counter.

Mikey dread smiled, got up off his stool and nodded his head at Jamie. "Wah gwan yute, yuh gud?" asked Mikey dread

"Yeh mon, mi cool!" replied Jamie.

He looked around the bakery and noticed that the coast was clear. Jamie dug inside his pants pocket and took out a wad of cash and handed it to Mikey Dread.

"Bumboclot yute, yuh ah gwan wid tings, eeh! Ah dis mi

wan si fram di I, zeen." Mikey dread reached behind the counter and tossed a zip lock back filled with weed at Jamie.

"Yah, gwan wid dis, mek mi kno how dem lakka ih. Cum bac in two weeks' time an mi gi yuh more."

"Yeh mon! Dem tings yeh fresh from yaad eh kno, Fiah. tek time wid it."

"Mikey dread, yuh kno seh mi nah guh bi able fi duh dis nuh more. School kine ah bashy rite ah now."

"Listen mi yute, memba yuh breed off mi niece. Eff mi neva tap mi bredda, him wudda fix yuh biznizz fi yuh. Dawg wudda nyam yuh suppa Suh, nuh bring dat cyaan biznizz tuh mi, zeen. Memba mi tell i-yah, two weeks."

Jamie took the weed, stuffed the zip lock bag under his jacket and departed the bakery. Afterwards, Jamie walked over to Bryce, Roland, and Jean-Jacque, and they all walked to the projects into the staircase. Bryce rolled up the blunts and lit it before they had to go back to drama class.

So, there they were enjoying the benefits of the heavenly smoke, when they were interrupted by some guys.

"Looky, looky, looky, look what we have here! Red and Black, surround 'em and make sure they don't get away from this ass whooping. What y'all doing 'round here? You'll from these projects?" said one of the three guys.

"Nah we're not from 'round here," Jamie replied.

"Oh, really, Yo, Band leader, he said he not from here!" said Black.

"I heard him Black, give me some space, I want to see the whites in his eyes," Band leader said.

"We know that dumb ma'fucker, I'm from here, and I don't recognize y'all. Who told y'all that it was cool to spark up here in the building? You are making the spot hot, fucking up my cash flow. There's two things I don't like people to do, fuck with my money, or my honey."

"Let's whoop they ass just on principle alone," Red said.

"Bryce stood up from sitting on the stairs and stepped down on the landing. "No one told us it was okay; we go to Smith across the street. We figured that it was the safest place to go and smoke some weed. Is there a problem with that?" replied Bryce.

Band leader stepped closer to Bryce, put his finger on his temple, and leaned in closer to his face. "Yeah, we got a problem with that, you Ma'fuckers brought y'all dusty Asses in here to smoke. Why don't you get the fuck out of here with that bullshit?"

Roland jumped up and put his hand on Bryce's chest and pushed him backward. "Chill Bryce, I got this."

Then he turned and faced Band leader and put his hands up with his palms facing forward. "No problem, we can leave, but you didn't have to talk to my man like that, he ain't done shit to you. You could've asked us nicely to leave, and not start with all that rah, rah."

Black stepped closer to Roland with his fist clenched and his eyebrows furrowed "Mother fucker, what? Who the fuck do you think you're talking to? Huh! You think you're tough? Do you know us bitch? We're the Rubber band gang, and this is our turf, punk, ass, ma'fucker," Black said.

"We good bro, we don't want no static," Roland replied.

He put the blunt out on the bottom of his sneaker, and the crew tried to exit the stairwell. Before they could, band leader grabbed Roland from behind after he turned around.

"Motherfucker, don't you ever turn your back on me while I am talking to you. Boy, you must be outside of your rabbit ass mind. You can leave when I tell you it's time to go," Band leader said.

With no hesitation, Roland turned around and hit him with a mean left hook, knocking him out cold.

"Don't you ever put your hands on me again. ——"

"y'all want some too?" said Roland.

Red and Black stood back in amazement. They both put their

hands up and raised their eyebrows. "Nah, we good."

The crew ran out of the project building, went across the street into the school, where they had a block holding the door open. Adrenaline still pumping in their veins after the heavyweight bout that just took place.

Jamie turned to Roland and laughed. "Damn, now I see why yah ass was in Spofford. Is that the reason why you got all those rubber bands around your wrist? Were you down with the 'Rubber band gang' like those guys? said Jamie.

"These rubber bands...? it's an inside thing, you wouldn't understand Jamie," Roland replied.

"Shit, if it means that you collect bodies, then it's well deserved. That guy looked like he was dead."

"Fuck all that, I got that one-hitter-quitter. No one is going to fuck with me like that. Fuck that, no one is going to fuck with us ever again, for this I vow. I pledge my allegiance to this crew, for those who agree, say the Oath with me."

Roland shouted in excitement while the high from the weed and adrenaline pumped in his veins.

"Word, I'm in," Bryce said.

"I'm in too," Jamie said, looked at Jean-Jacque and, shrugged his shoulders.

Jean-Jacque put his hand out and grabbed Jamie's wrist. Everyone else did the same to the person closest to them.

"For this I vow," the crew said in unison.

From then on, they were inseparable. They named the clique the Oath.

The bell rang, and they scurried to six-period to finish drama class with Mr. Loewenberg. Jean-Jacque didn't have sixth-period drama, so he and Roland went their separate ways. Jean-Jacque was the only kid in school who never wore street clothes. He was never in jeans or sneakers. He'd always be in business attire: slacks, button-down shirts, gentlemen, or church shoes, and a felt hat.

He looked like a preacher, almost like Malcolm X or somebody important like that. Jean-Jacque was always mistaken for a teacher and not a part of the student body. He used it to his advantage at times.

Plus, Marisol kept her word. As soon as Jean-Jacque got his driver's license, she gave him the okay to drive the Chevy. He was the only kid who drove a car to school, an SUV, to be exact. It was a two door, mint green Chevy Tahoe with a tan leather interior.

After the sixth period ended, Jamie saw Jean-Jacque in the hallway and ran up to him. "Hey man, what's up? That was some wild shit that happened in the projects earlier, huh."

"Yeah, did those guys ever approach y'all like that before?" asked Jean-Jacque.

"Nah, we always go there; this is the first time Jean-Claude."

"You guys might want to stay away from there from now on. y'all gotta find some other spot to smoke."

"Hey, let me ask you something, how was Mrs. Ortiz's history class?"

"I am not sure; I am a senior; I don't need to take her class anymore."

"Hold up, wait a minute, aren't you like fifteen or sixteen years old like the rest of us?"

"Yes, I skipped a couple of grades when I was in Junior High school. So, I will be graduating high school in June."

"You're too cool for words Jean-Claude. I'll catch you later," Jamie said, shook his head and slapped Jean-Jacque a five.

Jamie stepped past him and saw his girlfriend; she was a fly girl from Watson Avenue. She was fair skinned; some people mistook her for Puerto Rican. But she was half Dominican and half Jamaican. But you couldn't tell unless she told you. Her mom was from the Dominican Republic, and her father is from Jamaica. Most people forget that Dominican Republic was a country that was involved in the slave trade in the past too. So, there is a history of

African descendants mixed with the Spaniard and Taino blood.

Jamie walked over to his girl and embraced her with a tight hug accompanied by a warm kiss. They both walked side by side together. Jean-Jacque stopped dead in his tracks when he saw Jamie's girlfriend.

"Is that your girlfriend Jamie?" asked Jean-Jacque.

"Yeah, let me introduce you——"

"Pardon Me Jamie…"

"Excuse me love, allow me to introduce myself, my name is Jean-Jacque, but Jamie nicknamed me Jean-Claude. You're very beautiful, do you have a sister?" asked Jean-Jacque.

"Thank you, Claude, my name is Asiatic, Asia for short. And you're very handsome yourself," Asia replied.

"Be easy son, stop pushing up on my lady, she's spoken for!" said Jamie.

"Asia, tell him about your sister."

Asia stared at Jean-Jacque, as he held her hand in his. Jamie nudged her with his elbow, and she snapped out of it "Yeah, I have an older sister and her name is Jeneration, Jena for short. She doesn't go to school here; she goes to Jane Addams."

"Asia and I usually take the bus to Jane Addams after school to pick her up," Jamie said.

"This is my opportunity to meet this girl. Especially if she is as half as beautiful as her sister Asia," Jean-Jacque thought to himself.

"Nice meeting you Asia——"

"Yo Jamie, I see you later!" said Jean-Jacque, as he walked to his next class.

Jamie looked at Asia and turned up his lip.

"What? Why are you looking at me sideways?" asked Asia.

"You were all in his grille like he was Keith Sweat, or Al B.

57

Sure or something," Jamie replied.

"Awe, how cute, you're jealous! Baby, you don't have to worry, I only have eyes for you."

After school when everyone got out, there was a commotion across the street by the Bodega. Jean-Jacque, Jamie, Asia and Bryce walked over there to check it out. As they got closer to the scene, they saw members of the Rubber band gang surrounding Roland. Band leader was up in Roland's face. The rest of the gang members surrounded Roland. "That's him, he is the one who snuffed you from behind earlier, Band leader."

Jamie and Bryce pushed their way through the crowd and stood next to Roland. "He ain't snuff you, he gave you just what you was asking for, and you got laid out. It was a one on one. y'all trying to jump my boy! If you want to fight again, let it be one d, let 'em shoot a fair one," they said simultaneously.

The guys from the projects didn't listen, one of them punched Roland in the ear from behind, and the other one punched him in his side. Bryce and Jamie rushed in, to defend their friend, and that's when Jean-Jacque pushed through the crowd to the center of the circle.

The first thing he did was, he took off his hat, then stood in a martial art stance. Seeing someone use fighting skills such as Karate, Taekwondo, Kung Fu, Capoeira, etc. up close. You immediately understand why fighting is referred to as an Art. The way in which he dished out the ass whooping was done tastefully so.

From his set Kung Fu stance, he kicked one guy from one side with his right foot, and another guy from the other side, with the same foot. The onlookers were standing around looking in amazement. No one else matched his martial arts skills, by no one, I mean none of the Rubber band gang members.

Jean-Jacque looked like a Black Bruce Lee out there kicking all of those guys asses. Before long, the guys from the projects were all lying on the ground holding on to their stomachs and heads in excruciating pain.

The Band leader whistled, helped up the other gang members

off the ground. "Let's get out of here. It's Aight though, he's going to get his later on."

They all got up off the ground and ran away. Jean-Jacque picked up his jacket, then he walked over to Jamie and Asia. He stood in front of them for a moment until he caught his breath. "That'll teach 'em not the fuck with the Oath. From now on no one is going to fuck with any of us."

Asia looked at Jamie and shook her head. "There is something that I don't trust about Claude, for some reason my spirit tells me we shouldn't trust him.

"I can't put my finger on it, but he seems devious. Did you see his face while he was beating up those guys? It looked to me like he enjoyed the whole ordeal. History shows that a man with that much power is a dangerous thing. 'Absolute power, corrupts absolutely,' it's a wonder how he's even still standing wielding all that power and strength. He is not right at all," Asia said.

As soon as the words fell out of his mouth. Bryce and Roland walked up to Jean-Jacque and patted him on the back. "Damn dude, that was amazing," exclaimed Roland.

"If you hadn't got in there, they would have fucked Roland up," Bryce said.

"I mean I know the crew jumped in and had my back, but we were outnumbered. Fuck, I still can't believe what happened."

How long did it take for you to learn all that shit?" replied Bryce, as his jaw dropped open in awe.

They all postured with their secret handshake. Roland and Bryce laughed and applauded Jean-Jacque. Jamie was a bit hesitant to react because of Asia's words. On the surface he went along with the crew, but in the back of his mind he felt different.

Bryce lived on 168th street and Findlay Avenue, and Roland lived on 168th Street and College Avenue in the Bronx. "We gotta go and catch the bus fellas, we see you in school tomorrow," both said in unison.

"Damn, with all the commotion we forgot about Jena!

59

"Come on we got to go Jamie, come on hurry up, and let's get to the bus stop," said Asia.

"Where y'all going?" asked Jean-Jacque.

"We're going to the bus stop to pick up my sister from school," Asia replied.

"You know what, we are friends, so y'all rolling with me. Friends don't let friends ride the bus if we can help it. Come on get in, I'll drive y'all there."

"You know what, don't worry about it, we'll take the bus. It's not a problem."

Then she turned and raised her eyebrows at Jamie.

"Besides, Jena won't get into a car with a strange dude."

Jamie pulled Asia to the side and grit his teeth. "Asia chill, you're embarrassing me. Jean-Claude is my boy, I mean did you see what he did for Roland? It could've gone a different way if he didn't intervene. Don't you see that? Roland could have gotten killed out here.

"Those motherfuckers from the projects don't play. He gave them an Ass whooping' and showed them that the Oath are nothing to be fucked with. Come on, give Claude a chance. If he messes up, I'll beat his ass myself. I promise," Jamie said.

"If he fucks up, I will rain down a wrath of vengeance on him myself, the world has never seen. But I'm glad to see that you are willing to have my back. I hope that is not just talk," Asia said.

Asia reluctantly hopped into Jean-Jacque's Tahoe. Asia got into the back of the SUV and looked around. "Wow this is nice. Is this your truck?" asked Asia.

"Yes, it is and it's all mine," Jean-Jacque replied.

"Hmm, how can a young black kid afford a nice car like this? Only people I know who can afford nice cars sell drugs. Do you sell drugs?"

Jean-Jacque was slow to answer. He just put the key into the ignition and started the truck and there was Jazz playing on the radio.

"This is me on the radio Asia, I play the saxophone. That's how I'm able to afford my SUV," Jean-Jacque explained.

"Listen to me Claude, I don't want to go to jail. My mom is going to kill me if it ain't legit," Asia uttered.

"If it ain't, I know some people at the DMV, they're family, so I can get you a legit registration and shit," Jamie said.

"No, no, no, this is mine, all of my paperwork is up to date. You don't have to worry at all because you are riding with someone who is clean. I don't take any chances with the police," Jean-Jacque replied.

On the way to Jane Addams, Jamie spotted two of his homies, Darren and Raushun.

"Hey Claude, pull over, let me holler my boys for a minute. How do you operate this thing? Roll down the window."

Jamie put his head out the passenger side window, and put his arm up in the air., "Yo, what up Darren, what's going on Raushun?" said Jamie.

"What's going on Jamie," the two replied in unison.

"Nothing at all man, I am just here chilling. What are you two getting into right now?"

"We paid for studio time, we were about to go and record some tracks. Jamie, you should come with us," Raushun said.

"Shit, not right now, I am about to go and get Jena from school," Jamie said.

"Who's that in the car with you?" asked Darren.

"That's my boy Claude, and y'all know Asia. He goes to Smith with us, he's a senior," Jamie replied.

"Hey what up Claude, hi miss Asia, how's Jena doing?" Darren said.

"Hi Raushun, Darren, you know my sister don't fuck with

you like that. Don't pretend that shit is forgotten," Asia replied.

"Chill, calm down Asia, my bad damn——"

"Jamie, you better talk to your girl," Darren said.

They were blocking the road, and a car honked their horn at them.

"Listen, we gotta get going, we're obstructing traffic. So, I check you later okay," Jean Jacque said and side eyed Darren.

"Yeah, yeah, yeah, peace, check you later," Raushun replied.

Jean-Jacque drove on, a few miles up the road from Jane Addams High School, a police officer turned on his lights and chirped. Jean-Jacque pulled over.

"You see this shit man. I knew it, we're going to jail. I knew that I wasn't supposed to get in this fucking car. I should've listened to that little voice in my head, it told me not to get into this motherfucking car. I knew that this shit was hot. Listen to me Jamie, I am not going to jail for nobody. As soon as they come," Asia said.

"Yo, Asia chill, I told you I'm clean, the car is legit, relax. I mean that, trust me, I know some important people, everything is going to be alright," Jean-Jacque replied.

Jean-Jacque pulled the truck over on the side of the street. Asia sat in the backseat fidgeting and biting her fingernails. The cops drove right past them.

Jean-Jacque looked in the rearview mirror at Asia and shook his head from side to side. "That's a shame, you didn't know me from a can of paint, but yet you still thought the worst of me."

"My bad Claude, I don't want nobody else's trouble holding me back."

Jean-Jacque drove up the street when he saw that the coast was clear, and he continued driving a short distance, then double parked out in front of Jane Addams. Asia got out of the Tahoe, and Jamie and Jean-Jacque stayed behind.

Asia and Jena walked back to the SUV. Jean-Jacque saw Jena, and whispered to himself, "Oh my, now that is a bad——"

"Claude, I would like to introduce you to my big sister Jena," Asia said.

"Oh really, is she your biological sister, or is one of you adopted?" asked Jean-Jacque.

"What do mean?" replied Asia.

"I mean she's black and you're white."

"Well, we are both products of an interracial union. My father is a Caucasian man from Jamaica, and my mother is an Asiatic black woman from the Dominican Republic," Jena replied.

"Pardon my ignorance, hi Jena, pleased to meet you, my name is Jean-Jacque," he said.

"Asia just called you Claude, which is it?" replied Jena.

"Jamie nick named me Jean-Claude, or Claude for short. You know after the fighter Jean-Claude Van Damme in the movies."

"Oh, so you're a badass?"

"Nah, but I can hold my own."

"Hey Jena, what up girl, can I get some love," Jamie said.

"It ain't nothing you know everything is everything," replied Jena.

She leaned into Jamie, hugged him with one arm and kissed him on the cheek. "How did you all get here so fast? Usually, I would have to wait for you to get off the bus."

"My man Jean-Jacque drove us here from Smith in his whip."

"Whip? you know I don't get into cars with strangers."

"Nah, he is cool. He's different, don't worry. I'll vouch for him. You know how I get down. Ain't nothing going to happen, trust me he's cool."

Asia stood there and didn't say how she felt about Jean-Jacque. Jena knew her sister, so she didn't have to say anything, she sensed it.

63

"Claude, you better not be no axe murderer," Jena said.

They all got into the truck, and Jamie coaxed Asia to the back seat behind Jean-Jacque. Jamie directed Jena to get in the back, and Jean-Jacque looked at him with his eyes wide open, then motioned his head for him to jump in the back with Asia. Jamie got the message and obliged his request, allowing Jena to get in the front passenger seat.

Before she got in, she saw a cd on the seat, and picked it up with her hand. "Hey what do you want me to do with this?" asked Jena.

"Here, let me get it," Jean-Jacque replied.

Jean-Jacque reached out to grab the cd from her, but she resisted, and pulled it away from him.

"Hey, wait a minute is this you? Is this your cd? I see your name on here," Jena enquires.

"Yeah, I'm in a band, and this is our cd. I play a couple of instruments, but my passion is the saxophone. I also play the trumpet. Do you want to hear it?" replied Jean-Jacque.

"Yes, Claude, I would love to, I love jazz. I write and perform poetry at a club called the Nuyorican Poetry Café. When I perform my spoken word pieces, I do it to jazz music. So, go ahead and put it in."

Jean-Jacque complied, and Asia grabbed the back of the seat and leaned forward. "Don't nobody want to hear no old ass Jazz music. Here put this Machiavelli cd in," Asia said.

"Nah, later for 2Pac, put in this Biggie, Ready to Die, cd in," Jamie replied.

"Both of y'all shut up when you hear grown folks talking," Jena said.

"Shut up Jena, y'all ain't grown," Asia replied.

"We're older, and more mature than y'all little asses, ——"

"Excuse my rude ass little sister Claude," Jena said.

"That's okay, I'm used to being around immature people," Jean-Jacque replied.

"Excuse the fuck out of me, y'all not gonna play us like we pickneys in here," Jamie said.

"Shut up Jamie," Jena and Jean-Jacque said simultaneously.

Jena handed the CD back to Jean-Jacque, and he inserted the Jazz album into the CD player. Jena listened to the music intently, as he drove her and Asia home. When Jean-Jacque played any instrument, he did so with passion. He poured his feelings into every single note.

Whether or not you listen to Jazz, you could feel the rhythm. As an artist herself, Jena knew where he was coming from, and she felt it in her bones.

The two were vibing, so Jena felt compelled to share some of her poetry. She reached down into her book bag and drew out her poetry book. "I normally don't do this, but I am going to let you hear some of my poetry. Since you let me hear your album.

Jena turned to a page, and recited a poem to one of his tracks:

'A warm breeze that holds you with a smell so sweet, It reminds you of home sweet home, and sweeps you off your feet.

What's my definition of a man? You ask… Someone who can see where the world weighs heaviest on your shoulders and relieves the weight from dragging you down.

As if he chose the right piece of the puzzle.

Someone who opens the shutters on the darkest parts of your heart, so that the light can touch the corners that spent too much time in the dark.

No sweet talking, web weaving two faced monster, lacking in empathy, honesty, and honor.

Someone willing to dig deep; deep enough to rid himself of the demons he knows he can't keep. Love is the destination that he knows how to seek.

65

A builder, a painter, an architect of sorts, there to fill in the void wherever you fall short.

No judgement, no ridicule, or ego tripping, just a partner, a teammate, prepared for the heavy lifting.

Someone who listens, and doesn't have to be right, a knight who's humble, giving, and worthy of my light.'

Everyone in the car snapped their fingers. "You two should take this show on the road," Jamie said.

The fact that Jena recited her poem with a stranger, was a big deal. She doesn't even do that with Asia, and she is her sister. Asia raised an eyebrow, folded her arms, and sighed. She knew this was bad, and it scared her.

Jamie and Asia looked on in disgust, as Jena and Jean-Jacque bonded over jazz music, and poetry. They both mimicked the different instruments as they played through the speakers. Entertaining one another with their hand gestures.

Asia dug inside her bookbag and took out her Tupac cd. "I can't get into this Jazz stuff. Don't you want to hear the poetic words of Tupac Shakur? He is an artist too, one of the great poets of our times"

She quotes a few of his bars. 'Machiavelli in this, Killuminati, all through your body. The blows like a twelve-gauge shotty, Yuh feel me! And God said he should send his one begotten son to lead the wild into the ways of the man. Follow me; eat my flesh, flesh and my flesh…'

"Shut that Tupac shit down, its Notorious B.I.G all day:

'I got seven Mac-11's, about eight .38's Nine 9's, ten Mac-10's the shits never end You can't touch my riches Even if you had MC Hammer and them 357 bitches Biggie Smalls, the millionaire, the mansion, the yacht, the two weed spots, the two hot Glocks. Huh, that's how I got the weed spot I shot dread in the head, took the bread and the lamb spread,' Jamie replied.

"Ewe, Jamie, you like Notorious P.I.G.! You can't be my man if you do."

"Whatever Asia, go-ahead with all of that noise. We have to agree to disagree, besides I ain't no yes man; 'And if you don't know, now you know.'

Jena looked at Jean-Jacque, then turned she around. "How about you both calm the fuck down."

"Okay, okay, okay, 'Children are seen, and not heard,' we get it," Asia said.

Asia realized that her big sister seemed to be enjoying herself, but she is still going to be overprotective of her big sister. Jena isn't street smart. She couldn't peep game if it came up to her and bit her in the face. Jena was warming up to Jean-Jacque. But Asia doesn't want her to let her guard down too much. Just in case she is right about him.

Chapter 4:

Auditorium

Jean-Jacque drove up to the front of Asia and Jena's apartment building, and there was an undeniable connection between the two. Jean-Jacque knew that he couldn't let her walk away without being able to contact her in the future. He tried to play it cool. But in his experience revealing your hand before you get the chips doesn't always work out in one's favor.

Jena was too pretty for him to let her walk upstairs without shooting his shot. "Hey Jena, can I get your number? Maybe we can get up together and go to the club," Jean-Jacque said.

"Okay Claude, you better call me, it was nice meeting you."

Jena wrote down her number, then she and Asia got out of the truck. Jamie does too. "Yo, Jamie, where are you going?" asked Jean-Jacque.

"I live up the block Claude, I can walk from here."

Asia and Jena hugged Jean-Jacque and Jamie; and the pair watched the girls walk into their building. Jean-Jacque's shook his head in disbelief as he admired Jena's curves before he and Jamie head home.

"Yo, son, I check you tomorrow," Jean-Jacque said.

He opened the driver side door, climbed in then closed it.

"Claude, you live around the way?" asked Jamie.

"Nah, I don't, I live in SOHO with my two cousins Latrice and Patrice. We have this loft down there," Jean-Jacque replied.

"SOHO, you can afford to live in the city. So, what the fuck you are doing going to Smith for?"

"I attend Smith because of the welding program there. That's what I want to do when I graduate high school."

"That's what's up Claude."

"Aight Jamie, I see you in school tomorrow."

The two proceeded to do the Oath handshake.

"Peace," Jean-Jacque said.

"Peace, God," Jamie replied.

The next morning, there was a crowd in front of the Bodega. Jean-Jacque parked his truck and shook his head. "Damn! Ah Shit! Not this again. I hope it ain't none of my boys in trouble again."

He walked over to see what the commotion was and saw a boy being held upside down by his ankles. It was three members of the Rubber band gang; they were going through all his pockets for his money. All his books were scattered all over the sidewalk. They had stripped him down to his underwear. They took his JanSport book bag, his Nuptse North Face bubble Jacket, his Parasuco jeans, and his brand-new Jordan XI's.

Jean-Jacque jumped in to help him. "Give it all back to him?" said Jean-Jacque.

One of them turned to Jean-Jacque and noticed who he was. "Isn't that the dude that we fought the other day?"

"Yeah!"

"Ayo! Let's jump him."

They approached him, and Jean-Jacque knocked out the first guy, then the rest of the gang stopped dead in their tracks and ran away with their tails tucked between their legs.

"Now, don't come back around here and mess with anybody from my school again. If I catch anyone of you jokers around here, it is going to be more of the same," Jean-Jacque said.

The kid was on the ground, really scuffed up bad. He had a bloody nose, a bruised chin, a black eye, the front of his shirt was saturated with blood, and he was nursing his arm. Jean-Jacque checked it, and his arm was broken. Jean-Jacque helped him up, the kid tucked his arm close to his ribs, then he mustered up enough strength to stand up. He was hurt and embarrassed but a little happy because the guys from the projects didn't run away with his pants. The kid limped next to Jean-Jacque across the street toward the school. "Those guys schemed on my stuff for a couple of days. They

69

told me that they were going to rob me, but I didn't believe them. I still brought my .22 with me just in case. But they still got the drop on me. Because one of the dudes yoked me up from behind with a choke hold, after that, I couldn't do anything," he said.

"Listen, you should come with me to my martial arts class and train because I can give you a few pointers on how to defend yourself out here in these streets. I have a brown belt in Jiu Jitsu and a third-degree black belt in Kenpo. I am sure that my sensei would be happy for you to enter his dojo because you need self-defense training," Jean-Jacque replied.

"Sure, I can do that, what's your name?"

"My name is Jean-Jacque."

"Jean? Aiight, my name is Justin. I'll check you later, so that we can build."

"No problem."

The security guards escorted the kid inside, and Jean-Jacque walked over and waited in line to enter the school. This took some time because each student had to walk through metal detectors. Jean-Jacque waited his turn, then he took out his keys, loose change, and his wallet out his pocket, and put inside a tray. He took off his watch, his belt, and anything that could set off the metal detectors. Then a security guard waved a handheld metal detector over his body. Security was tight like it was a federal building.

Fourth period at lunchtime, Jean-Jacque saw Bryce, Roland, and Jamie in the lunchroom sitting at a table. He greeted Bryce first with the handshake, Jamie second, then Roland. Asia was also seated at the table.

"Hello Asia, how's your sister doing?" asked Jean-Jacque.

"She's fine, Claude, all she's been doing since y'all met, is talk about you. Jena can't stop talking about that Jazz shit you were playing in your truck," Asia replied.

"Ha, ha! That's cool, I'm glad to hear."

"You two are too cute for words Claude, I still have

reservations about you Mr. Jean-Jacque."

"Oh word, well I guess I have my work cut out for me, Miss Asia."

"We'll see."

"Aiight, the challenge is set and accepted."

The bell rang and everybody got up and walked out of the cafeteria to go to their classes. At the end of the next period, Mr. Loewenberg said, "Listen students, I'm going to give you guys a break this period. Talk amongst yourselves don't wander too far; y'all have a lot of things to work on for the show on Saturday. I'd advise y'all to take the time to iron things out. I want our performance of "Little shop of horrors" to be picture perfect.

"You won't have your scripts. So, that means that you will have to say your lines properly before show time. Let's get them right, okay. That means you to Jamie, although you're the stagehand/understudy, the fill in for the character Patrick Martin. You don't want to be unprepared on the big day. Those of you who are a part of the play, come to the auditorium after school for rehearsals."

The bell rang, Bryce and Roland, looked at Jamie and shook their heads. "Damn man! What we're going to do? Are you going to get some weed so we can toke up?" asked the guys in unison.

"I don't know about that. I don't want to stir up no more shit," Jamie replied.

"I know huh, but the staircase in the projects was a good spot though," Bryce said.

"Fuck it, we should still go, but let's make sure to bring Jean-Claude with us. So that way if there is any trouble, he'll dead that really quick," Roland said.

"I know where he is at. I think that he is in Spanish class. So, I'll go and get him, we'll meet y'all at the spot," Jamie replied.

He grabbed a blank piece of paper and sprinted out of the auditorium to get Jean-Jacque.

"Perfect, Bryce and I will go and cop the weed," Roland replied.

"Nah, I got it, just meet us there." Jamie ran upstairs to the third floor and walked over to Jean-Jacque's Spanish classroom. He knocked on the door and the teacher Mrs. Maldonado waved Jamie inside.

"¡Hola señora! El director me envió aquí para buscar a Jean-Jacque y traerlo de regreso a su oficina; aquí está la not," (The principal sent me here to get Jean-Jacque and bring him back to his office; here's the note,) Jamie said.

She smiled and shook her head. "Eso no es necesario, está bien, purse or," (That's not necessary, it's okay, he can go,) Mrs. Maldonado replied.

Jean-Jacque got up from behind his desk and walked outside the classroom.

"Yo, Jamie what the fuck was that all about? I didn't know you spoke Spanish," Jean-Jacque said.

"I learned Spanish to impress Asia, and it worked," Jamie replied.

Roland and Bryce went across the bodega and got two Dutch master cigars, then they sprinted to the project staircase and waited for Jamie and Jean-Jacque to come.

Jamie got Jean-Jacque walked in the staircase soon after. "Hey what took y'all so long? We thought y'all wasn't coming. We don't have too much time left we only got twenty minutes. Give me the weed so I could roll up," Bryce said.

Jamie gave Bryce some weed, he rolled it up in the Dutch, lit up the blunt, took a drag, then passed it to Jamie.

"Looky, looky! Who do we have here? It's bad, bad Leroy Brown, the baddest man in this here town. You're not going to get away today because we brought reinforcements. I see y'all came back to the scene of the crime. Y'all thought shit was sweet, huh? The whole crew is here huh! Bruce Leroy, Mojo, and Skinny Minnie," Band leader said.

The other Rubber band gang members that stood beside him, wielded weapons. One had a chain, another had a switchblade, and yet another held an aluminum bat.

Jamie, Bryce, Roland, and Jean-Jacque we're surrounded, facing insurmountable odds. They couldn't talk their way out of this one. The only choice they had, was to fight; win, lose, or draw.

"Why don't y'all leave us the fuck alone? All we want to do is smoke, we're not bothering nobody. Everybody smokes weed in here all the fucking time. I can see cigarette butts and blunt roaches all over the stairs. And I know that we didn't do it. So, that means, other people are smoking in here. So, why do you have a problem with us?" asked Jamie.

"Shut the fuck up Mojo, this is our projects not yours, we can smoke if we want in here. So, y'all need to get taught some manners, that you can't do whatever the fuck, you want to do around these parts. We run these streets," Band leader replied.

One of them swung the chain at Roland, and he put his arm out to protect himself from the blow, and the chain wrapped around his arm. Roland smiled, then he pulled the guy towards him and punched the guy in the jaw knocking him out. He then took the chain and squared off against the guy with the switchblade.

Roland swung the chain at him, and the guy moved out of the way. He swung it at him again and missed, but the guy didn't see the chain swinging back the other way, and Roland knocked the knife out of his hand, disarming him.

Bryce tackled him to the ground from behind, then grabbed his head and banged it on the floor. The other guy with the brass knuckles charged at Jean-Jacque. He was to swift, he side kicked him in the throat, and he dropped to the ground like a sack of potatoes.

Jamie had a difficult time with the last guy standing, he was quicker, and he used his reach advantage to jab him in the face a few times. Jamie furrowed his eyebrows, sidestepped one of his jabs, rushed into his side, bear-hugged the guy and lifted him off his feet, then dropped him down the flight of stairs.

73

Bryce looked down the stairs at the guy and put his hand over his mouth. "Oh, shit Jamie, that nigga ain't moving. I didn't know that you had it in you."

They quickly exited the project building, and re-entered Smith through the side door. Jean-Jacque, Jamie, Roland, and Bryce got inside right on time, before the first bell rang. They walked back into the auditorium; leaving them enough time to change classes before the late bell rang.

The rest of the school day dragged on without a hitch. Classes were dismissed, and the cast for Little Shop of Horrors entered the auditorium for rehearsals.

Twenty minutes later, the cast were all on stage rehearsing a scene, and a crash of glass shattering followed by a loud bang grabbed the attention of everyone in the auditorium. Three guys entered the auditorium and interrupted the rehearsals.

The Rubber band gang members rushed inside and looked around. "Where the fuck is Bruce Leroy?" asked Black.

Mr. Loewenberg turned around from the piano and tilted his glasses with his index finger. "What is the commotion? Who is Bruce Leroy?" said Mr. Loewenberg.

He stood up and walked up the center aisle towards the three guys. "Who do you think you are, breaking into my school? What happened to your face son? It's bruised and all swollen," Mr. Loewenberg said.

Band leader pulled out a gun and pointed it at Mr. Loewenberg. "Shut the fuck up!" Then he shot Mr. Loewenberg in the shoulder. Everyone gasped, some students ran backstage, while others ducked behind the curtains. Only Jamie ran to the aid of the beloved drama teacher. Jamie caught Mr. Loewenberg before he fell to the ground.

Red recognized Jamie and tilted his head. "Yo, that's the dude that was in the staircase earlier."

Band leader turned to his crew and waved his gun at Mr. Loewenberg and the students. "Y'all go ahead and handle my light work," he said.

With no hesitation, Red pulled out his gun from his waistband, shot Jamie in his hip, and he fell to the floor.

"That's what the fuck I'm talking about, now like I said before, where is Bruce, Mother, fucking, Leroy?" said the Band leader.

As soon as he said that Jean-Jacque crept up behind him and whispered in his ear. "Here I am."

Band leader turned around, and Jean-Jacque punched him in the face, knocking him out. He fell down to the floor and Red grabbed for his gun from his waist again. Jean-Jacque pinned Red's wrist to his side and prevented him from retrieving his weapon.

In the same motion, he then threw a punch, hitting Red in the jaw, knocking him over the chair.

As fast as he went down, Black sprung at Jean-Jacque. They wrestled until a loud bang exploded in the auditorium. The two paused, Black shrieked with a blank look on his face, then slide down Jean-Jacque's body to the ground. Jean-Jacque stood there towering over Black's motionless body. With the smoking gun in his hand, a loom of darkness covered Black's face as he took his last breath.

Ear-piercing screams echoed in the auditorium. A female student cried out in terror. "Oh, my goodness, Mr. Loewenberg has been shot, and Jamie has been shot too. What the Fuck is happening here," she cried.

Seeing the carnage was too overwhelming. Shock and terror covered the students like a nightmare that terrifies a young child in their sleep.

A student slipped out of the midst of the battle royal to get help. The emergency responders arrived fifteen minutes later, and they burst into the auditorium pushing two gurneys and medical equipment towards Mr. Loewenberg and Jamie.

The Drama teacher laid on the floor, clutching his chest, covering his wound with his hands. The Paramedic and EMT cut open his shirt and applied a gauze on his gunshot wound to stop the bleeding. They checked his vital signs, put an oxygen mask over his face, and hooked up an IV drip to his arm. Once Mr. Loewenberg was stabilized, the Paramedic and EMT hoisted him up on to the gurney, then wheeled him out of the auditorium.

"Everything is going to be fine; Sir, how are you feeling? Are you in a lot of pain?" said the EMT.

With blood spewing from his mouth, Mr. Loewenberg coughed, pulled the oxygen mask away from his mouth. "Pain?! Pain?! You're asking me about pain! How's Jamie doing? Is he okay?" replied Mr. Loewenberg.

"I think he's okay. From what I saw, he was shot in his hip. He'll live and be on the road to recovery before you know it."

"Good, I hope so, Jamie came to my aid and got shot as a result. I couldn't forgive myself if something ever happened to him."

"Sir, don't you worry about him, okay; my partners are tending to him; I don't want you to raise your blood pressure."

The EMT put the oxygen mask over his mouth, then they whisked him out of the school.

Jamie on the other hand didn't look well, he lost a lot of blood.

"Are you okay?" asked the EMT.

"No! I am not okay, this shit hurts. I'm in a lot of pain," Jamie uttered faintly.

Jamie's voice was shaky, and he coughed. "I feel chilly."

"Take it easy son, we're here to help you, so we can get you to the hospital," the Paramedic said.

The EMT dressed the wound to stop the bleeding before lifting him on to the gurney.

"Ready? 1, 2, 3," the EMT said.

"Oh!" moaned Jamie.

"I know it hurts son, but are you able to turn on your back for me?"

"I don't know, but I can try."

"I need to strap you down; I don't want you to tumble off the gurney while we transport you to the hospital. Let me help you."

Jamie shook his head up and down in agreement, and a single tear streamed down the side of his face. He has never felt so vulnerable. The EMT strapped him down on the gurney, then they rushed him out of the auditorium to the ambulance.

Several police officers, and two detectives walked into the auditorium; one right after the other, accompanied by the school's principal. The detectives looked down at the three guys laid out on the floor. One of the detectives bent down and checked the vital signs of the guy that was shot, and he shook his head in disbelief.

"Officers, Check the other two, if they don't need to see a doctor, mirandize them and take them down to the station. Make sure you get a full statement and do the same for that joker too. It appears as though he's waking up."

The first detective approached the frightened teenagers and flashed his badge. "Hello everyone, I know that this is a terrifying ordeal. I'm Det. Janis Cooper, and my partner over there talking to the other officers is Det. Richard Martins. He will be joining us shortly.

"I really empathize with you, truly I do. So, please bear with me for a little while longer. I need to ask y'all a few questions, so that we can understand what transpired here today. We want to get you guys out of here as quick as possible, so you can go home to your parents, family, and friends. Can any of you tell me what happened here?" asked the Detective.

The crime scene investigators entered the auditorium along with the coroner, who covered up the dead body of the guy, with a white sheet.

Det. Cooper looked away from the students as the police officers secured the perimeter of the auditorium. One student

77

approached the detective and spoke up. "Yeah sure, we were here rehearsing for our play Little Shop of Horrors, we were supposed to perform it on Saturday. When these guys came into the auditorium asking for someone named Bruce Leroy. Whoever in the hell that is, then they shot Mr. Loewenberg and Jamie."

Both detectives were stunned by the name given.

"Bruce Leroy? Wait, are you sure he said that name?" asked Det. Martins.

"Yes, I am sure he said it because he repeated it more than once. Those guys would have killed us if Jean-Jacque hadn't come in and beat them up. I don't know how he did it, but he's a hero," the student replied.

"Okay, thank you I appreciate that, here's my card just in case you need to contact me, or if you remember anything else. What was your last name again? How do you spell that?"

She spelled it out for him. He wrote it down in his little book before he let her go.

Both detectives walked over to the hero of the day Jean-Jacque. Not before giving instructions for the uniform officers to finish taking the statements from the rest of the students on the stage.

Jean-Jacque was sitting down in one of the chairs alone with his head down, one arm on his lap and his other hand holding an ice pack on the back of his neck. Det. Cooper tapped him on the shoulder to get his attention. "How are you doing today?" asked the detective.

"Who me? I am alive is all I can say. I am just happy that nothing worst didn't happen," Jean-Jacque replied.

"That is good. My name is Detective Janis Cooper, and my partner here is Detective Richard Martins. From my understanding of the events that transpired today, you're the hero in this scenario. Can you tell us what happened?"

"Sure, these guys from the projects have been harassing us for the past couple of weeks now. There were four separate occasions wherein I lent a helping hand to my friends after they had run-ins with them. I believe they came to enact revenge."

"Wait a minute… hold on…do you mean to tell me that these guys have been terrorizing you and other students from your school for more than two weeks now. Did you tell anyone who may have been able to help you? Does anyone else know about these guys? A teacher, a counselor, even your principal?"

"No, I hadn't informed anyone about those incidents."

"Someone should've called the police. We do this sort of thing for a living."

Det. Martins and Cooper revealed their side arms and detective badges.

"I didn't, but I am certain that someone else did. Then again, the Police don't usually come to the aid of someone in my community when we call for help," Jean-Jacque said.

"So, you're a vigilante out for justice then? Some sort of crime fighter!" asked Det. Cooper.

"Listen, I heard the gunshots and screaming, so I came to see what was going on. Once I came inside the auditorium, they attacked me. That's when my martial arts training kicked in, and I defended myself."

"You have been through a lot today, here is my card, keep in touch."

We're not going to take up any more of your time; you're free to go. I like for you to go home and get some rest, and when you get a chance, come down to the 44TH precinct tomorrow to make an official statement. Before you come, I would like for you to bring a parent or guardian with you."

Jean-Jacque got up and took the card from Det. Martins and stared at it. Det. Martins took a few steps then turned around. "I'm curious to know, how were you able to fight off, subdue, and disarm all three guys? Funny, you don't look like special forces to me; where did you train?" asked the detective.

"Spofford Juvenile Detention Center, I earned a brown belt

in Jiu Jitsu and a brown belt in Kenpo, at a Dojo in Castle Martins," Jean-Jacque replied.

"Last thing before you go, were you in this auditorium for sixth period?" asked Det. Cooper.

"Yes!" replied Jean-Jacque.

"Did you have this class for seventh period?"

"Huh! No…"

"No?! Then, how did you know they had rehearsals after school?"

"Wait what do you mean?"

Detective Cooper flipped a couple of pages back in his notes and read from it aloud. "I heard the gunshot and screaming, so I came in to see what happened."

"Yeah, so."

"Well, my partner just wanted to know that with the auditorium being way out, how could you possibly hear what was going on? I mean no one else outside the auditorium heard the commotion. So, how did you?" said Det. Martins.

"Well, I'm a student director in this class, so I know the schedule. Wait, am I a suspect here or something?" replied Jean-Jacque.

"No, No, No, of course not, just gathering all the facts. How about you go home, then fill us in tomorrow when you come and make your official statement," Det. Cooper explained.

The principal escorted the detectives to his office and Jean-Jacque sat there in the auditorium, nursing the bruise on his neck with an ice pack.

Jean-Jacque walked out of the school, and he saw Bryce and Roland across the street by his truck. "You see, the Rubber band gang tried to take Jamie out. We gotta roll on these guys before they roll on us again; that's my word!" Bryce exclaimed.

"Yo son, I ain't trying to go out like a rat trying to get a

80

piece of cheese, and that's word to my mother," Roland added.

"So, what are you trying to do?" asked Jean-Jacque, then he threw the ice pack inside his truck.

"Listen, my brother has guns. The only problem is, I can't bring them in the school with all those metal detectors," Roland said.

"Man, you don't need any guns. That is the last thing that you need. All you have to do is train. If you come down to my dojo, you can learn how to defend yourself. Your mind, your hands, and your feet is all that you'd need."

"I disagree, they keep bringing out weapons to get us. First, it was bats, chains, knives, and brass knuckles. Then it was guns, next they might bring a grenade to blow us up. I say we fight fire with fire," Bryce said.

"Those who live by the sword, will die by the sword," Jean Jacque replied.

"That's true, but those who don't have a sword, will die by the hands of those who do," Roland said.

"Yo, we're going to Lincoln Hospital to see Jamie, are you coming?" asked Bryce.

Jean-Jacque looked up the street by the bodega and saw Asia crying and being consoled by another student.

"Nah son, I'm gonna catch up with y'all there later on."

They parted ways after giving the Oath handshake. Jean-Jacque walked over and inched his way to Asia

"Oh, my goodness, Jamie has been shot and I don't how he is doing. I hope he is okay," Asia said.

Jean-Jacque put his arms around Asia and hugged her. "Jamie is going to be okay. I tell you what, I can take you to the hospital after we pick up Jena," Jean-Jacque replied.

"Thank you, Claude, everyone in school is saying that you saved Mr. Loewenberg, and Jamie's lives. If it hadn't been for you, they would be dead right now."

"Asia, 'Believe half of what you see, and none of what you hear.' Come on let's go."

She nodded her head yes and wiped the tears from her face. Asia followed Jean-Jacque to his vehicle. The two got in the truck and he said, "Want me to drop you off at the hospital first before I pick up Jena from school?"

"Nah, I want to be the first to tell her the terrible news about Jamie."

Jean-Jacque sped over to Jane Addams, and Asia got out of the truck when she saw Jena.

"Oh, my goodness, hurry up, we gotta go, Jamie has been shot."

"Asia, stop playing games, Jamie ain't get shot."

"I ain't bullshitting, get in, we don't have any time to explain, we need to get to Lincoln Hospital, now."

Jean-Jacque drove up the block from Jane Addams and made a sharp right turn at the light cutting off a taxicab. Asia was crying hysterically, so Jean-Jacque had to explain what happened earlier.

"Jena, all you need to know is that Jamie is going to be fine, and he got shot trying to save a teacher's life."

"What? Jamie! A hero? I can't believe it."

"Yeah, some guys from the projects calling themselves the Rubber band gang, broke into the school, and shot up the auditorium, and Jamie shielded a teacher from being killed."

"Wow, I hope he's okay; Asia, everything is going to be fine, we're going to make sure of it. Has anyone told his mother that he's been shot yet?"

"Yes, I believe the principal did."

"Damn, I hope we get there before visiting hours are over."

Jean-Jacque escorted Asia over to his truck and he opened the passenger side door. He helped her in and ran around to the

82

driver side and got inside the truck.

Chapter 5:

Get Out of Jail Free

"How could you let this happen? How could you?" asked Jena.

"I didn't do anything; Jamie is my friend," Jean-Jacque replied.

Jean-Jacque paused for a second and exhaled. "Think good thoughts and blessing spirits," he thought.

"I did everything that I could do for him Jena, the guys who did this are in even worst shape. Don't worry about anything, Jamie is going to pull through. I know that he is good because of how I handled the situation today.

"He is strong, we are going to the hospital right now; just sit tight."

Jena sighed, crossed her legs, and folded her arms. She was so overwhelmed by the news that Jena cried. She leaned in on Jean-Jacque's arm and sobbed.

"Come, come now Jena, Jamie is going to be alright." Jean-Jacque put his arm around Jena and kissed her on the top of her head. "Just give me a second, alright, I will get us to the hospital to see Jamie, he's going to pull through," Jean-Jacque said.

Jena gently lifted her head off of him and wiped the tears from her eyes.

Jean-Jacque pulled up in front of Lincoln hospital, and all three of them jumped out of the truck. They rushed inside towards the front desk.

"Hello, how can I help you?" asked the security guard.

"Hi, we are looking for two patients that have been admitted here recently," Asia asked.

"I can help you with that, give me a moment, if they already have a room, then I can point you in the right direction. What are their names?"

"Mr. Loewenberg and my friend Jamie McClymont, they were both victims of that school shooting at Alfred E. Smith High School earlier."

"Yeah, okay young lady, they're in room 225, and 239; here are some visitor passes. Go down that corridor towards the elevators, take it up to the second floor, and the rooms will be over to the right."

"Thank you, sir."

They ran over to the elevator and took it up to the second floor. With their hearts in their hands and their stomach twisted in knots. They attempt to enter room 225, and a nurse stopped them at the door. "Hey, where do y'all think you're going?" asked the nurse.

"Excuse us, we are here to see Mr. Loewenberg and Jamie," they all replied in unison.

"Well, Jamie is being prepped for surgery, and Mr. Loewenberg just got out of surgery. Now is not the right time, go in the waiting room, and wait a bit."

Meanwhile, Mrs. Orlinski was sitting on Mr. Loewenberg's bedside in the room, and she wiped the tears from her blood shot eyes. "I told you we should leave this God forsaken place and go upstate, somewhere safer than here. I told you that you would be hurt by your students one day. These fucking knuckleheads are going to be the death of you," she said.

With tears streaming down her cheeks. Mr. Loewenberg sighed. "Honey, it wasn't my students who did this to me, it was some guys from the projects who broke into the school," he replied.

"It doesn't matter, look at you, just, look at you! You are here in the hospital with a bullet lodged inside your body. All you can think about is the fact that it was not from a student. It was a school shooting! When all I can think about is that I almost lost my husband to gun violence."

"There's too much of this shit going on in this city. Let these people have it, you and I should go somewhere safer than here. A

85

place where these kinds of things don't happen to good people like us."

The students were still in the hallway while they were arguing, and they overheard everything. The nurse walked away, so Asia and Jean-Jacque ran up to the room door.

(Knock, knock, knock) "Hmm mmm, "Mr. Loewenberg we are here to see how you were doing and if you were okay. Is this a good time? If not, we can come back later."

Mrs. Orlinski wiped her tears away from her cheeks; Mr. Loewenberg looked up at the pair, and with his good hand, he waved to the students to enter the room.

"Come here kids," Mr. Loewenberg replied.

They entered the room and walked closer to Mr. Loewenberg's bedside. He grabbed Jean-Jacque's hand and smiled. "I don't know where you learn how to fight like that son but thank you. I'm glad that you were there because those guys had evil in their hearts and the devil in their eyes. They were hard charged and ready to kill. I have to ask son, why were they looking for you in the first place?"

Jean-Jacque stared at the drama teacher with a puzzled look on his face.

"Listen, you don't have to answer that question, you saved my life. So, you are good in my book. But I do remember that movie from the 80's. I got the reference, 'Bruce Leroy' a character from that movie 'The last Dragon.' You are too young to get it or may not have seen the movie in the first place. I could only surmise that you were the one that they were searching for when they charged inside the school earlier today."

Mr. Loewenberg looked into Jean-Jacque's eyes, and not one word was uttered between the two. He nodded his head at the young warrior, and immediately understood the low-down of the goings on.

"Don't worry Mr. Loewenberg, I am glad that I was at the right place at the right time. But I have to go now, I just came by to see you, now we have to go see Jamie."

Asia and Jean-Jacque walked outside of Mr. Loewenberg's room, and Jena was still sitting there in the waiting room. Asia and Jean-Jacque walked by her and summoned her to follow them. They all walked to Jamie's room and he was lying face down on the hospital bed. Asia opened the door and said, "Baby, are you okay? We came as soon as we could. Does it hurt? Did you lose a lot of blood? Don't worry Jamie, we're going to nurse you back to health."

Bryce and Roland walked back into the room with fast-food for Jamie. "Yo, the crew is all here," Bryce said.

"'Damn, it took y'all long enough," Roland said.

"Good looking out fellas, I've been fiending for this food all day, son," Jamie replied.

"My mans is in here with his ass in a sling, I can't wait until we retaliate, son; that's my word," Bryce said.

"Hey Jamie, how are you doing? I have been worried sick about you," Jena said.

"Jena, I don't feel a damn thing, I'm all hopped up on these pain killers. The doctors were supposed to be in here preparing me for surgery. I don't know how y'all got in here but thank you all for coming to see me."

"No problem Jamie, we're family!" they all said simultaneously.

Jamie's mother opened the door and walked into the room. "Wah a gwan in yah suh? Police call me and tell mi seh yuh get shot. Ahuu shoot yuh?" asked Mrs. McClymont.

"Mammy, mi nuh kno ah ahuu dweet," Jamie replied.

"Lawd God Hab Merci, mi wash belly!"

Mrs. McClymont bent down, hugged Jamie and everyone stepped back and gave them some space.

"Hello, Mrs. McClymont, how are you doing?" asked the crew simultaneously.

"Mi thank unuh all for coming to be wit Jamie."

87

"You don't have to thank us, we love him; he's, our boy!"

The doctor and the nurses knocked on the door and walked into the room. "Hello family my name is Dr. Singh, and we're preparing him for surgery, so, please could you leave the room," the Dr. said.

The crew left the hospital room and they walked in the waiting room.

"Hey guys, I gotta go, I need some rest, I'm happy that those two are good. Unfortunately, tomorrow I have to go to the police station to give my statement. I don't want them to come looking for me," Jean-Jacque said.

"I'm staying until visiting hours are over. ——Jena, tell mommy where I am okay," Asia replied.

Jean-Jacque shook hands with everyone, and Jena followed him out of the door. "Hey Claude, I am coming with you," Jena said.

"Okay, I will drop you off," Jean-Jacque replied.

"No, I mean tomorrow to the police department."

"Jena, I have to go by myself. You can't come with me," he answered.

Jena grabbed his hand and looked him straight in the eyes and tilted her head to side. "Please, I know that you are tough and all, but you don't have to do this yourself."

He sighed and looked away from Jena. "Okay, I'm going after school tomorrow."

Jean-Jacque dropped Jena off, and he noticed how she looked at him so intently.

"Bye Claude, I'll see you tomorrow."

"Okay, I'll pick you up from school."

The next day Jean-Jacque picked up Jena from school and he drop straight to the 44TH precinct. He parked out in front of the precinct leaving Jena alone in the truck.

"Hello officer, I am here to give my statement with Detective

Martins and Detective Cooper."

"Sure, no problem son, sit down over there on the bench and the detectives will be out shortly."

His neck was still bruised, and his heart was beating fast. He walked over to the bench and sat down. He saw when the sergeant called the detectives to come up front. Jean-Jacque saw Jena walked inside and sat beside him.

"You know I couldn't sit out there by myself; I came here for moral support and that's just what I'll do," Jena said.

He just shook his head then moved over so that she could sit down next to him. Five minutes went by when Detective Janis Cooper came out to greet Jean-Jacque.

"Hey Jean, where's your parents?" asked Det. Cooper.

"They couldn't come, so I came by myself," Jean-Jacque replied.

"Okay, come step into my office."

Jena stood up to walk inside with her friend, and the detective stopped her. "No not you young lady, stay out here. He will be out shortly, in the meantime, wait right here. There's a vending machine over there, where you can get some snacks or a cup of coffee while you wait," Det. Cooper said.

Det. Cooper escorted Jean-Jacque back to the interrogation room. He sighed and was certain that they were going to pull up his past and use it against him; to send him back to Juvie or worse, prison.

"Alright son, from the little that you told us we could ascertain that you had no choice but to do what was necessary. Especially, since you were outgunned and outmanned.

"Furthermore, with your actions yesterday it helped us put together the missing pieces to a cold case. Those three guys were members of a gang that has been an absolute thorn in the side of the NYPD for some time now.

"The good news is because of you, we're able to make a

89

connection to a bigger criminal enterprise. Details of which we are not at liberty to disgust with you. Just know that you made a real difference with what you did yesterday," Det. Cooper said.

"If we had more individuals like you, the streets would be a better place," Det. Martins said.

Jean-Jacque leaned back in his chair and exhaled. In his experience, the police have never been this nice to him before. He looked at each of the detectives in their eyes to see if they were being disingenuous. The detectives smiled at him, and this made him skeptical that they might have an ulterior motive. "This meeting can't be all good," he thought.

Det. Martins closed his folder and stood up from his chair and said, "So, with that being said, you are free to go. If this case goes to trial, we may need you to testify in court, if need be. So, for now, we would like you to stay in the city."

"Hey, and if you could help it, don't go out doing any more vigilante work. Leave the crime fighting to the police," Det. Cooper exclaimed.

"Oh, yeah, expect to receive a call from the mayor's office. The mayor just called here because they heard about what you had done yesterday. You may even get an award for your valor and bravery kid," Det. Martins added.

"Is that it? I don't know what to say, I only did what anybody else would've, given the circumstances. I understand and hear you both, detectives. But if I find myself in a similar situation; there's no way I would be able to sit idly by while people got hurt. I wouldn't be able to live with myself," Jean-Jacque replied.

"You know what kid, I get that you can defend yourself and you want to help people, I can see it in your eyes. Just be careful because you don't want to become a part of the problem either. So, don't stroll down too many dark alleys. Simply put, just be a kid. Just finish school, date girls, play sports or whatever else you kids do for recreation nowadays. I see that pretty girl you came here with. Is that your girl?" said Det Martins.

"No!" replied Jean-Jacque.

"Well, you should be focusing on your SAT's, prom, college applications, and her. You're a senior, right?"

"Yes!"

"Why don't you ask her to prom?"

Jean-Jacque shrugged his shoulders, shook his head and walked toward the exit.

"Son! Don't forget to tell your parents about today. I am sure that they would like to know that their son is a hero," Det. Martins said.

Det. Cooper took a card out of his pocket and tossed it at him. "Hey, kid, heads up!"

Jean-Jacque caught it and looked at the card. "What's this?"

"That...that is a "get of out jail free card," use it wisely."

"What do I do with it?"

The detective sighed, put his hand on his forehead. "Aye yai yai, for a smart kid, you're not so bright! Son, if you get yourself in a jam, just present that to the arresting officer(s), give them my name, and the situation would take care of itself. So long kid, we'll see you around," Det. Cooper replied.

Jean-Jacque left the interrogation room and saw Jena sitting on the other side of the door eating Funyuns and drinking a pineapple Top Pop soda. He walked up to her and gestured for her to leave with him. She gathered her things and walked out of the precinct.

Jean-Jacque didn't say a word. She figured he's not going to jail, so she held her tongue until she got in the truck. "You're very quiet, what the hell happened in there?" asked Jena.

Jean-Jacque didn't say a word. Once he got far enough away, he dug in his pocket, pulled out the card, then handed it to Jena. She inspected it and shrugged her shoulders. "What is this?" asked Jena.

"I'm trying to fully process what transpired in there myself. That is supposed to be a "get out of jail free card," Jean-Jacque

replied.

"What does that mean exactly?"

"Exactly what you think it means. I figure that it's a thank you for my actions yesterday, apparently, I saved a lot of lives'."

Jena was enthralled by the whole ordeal; she smiled and took off her seatbelt. "Claude, stop the car!"

Jean-Jacque didn't know what she wanted, but he slowed down and found an open parking spot. Jena moved to the back of the truck, she looked at him through the rear-view mirror and opened her shirt. He was intrigued and mesmerized by her beauty as he peeked at Jena through the rear-view mirror.

"Maybe she is going to change her clothes before she goes home," he thought.

"Come! Come back here with me," Jena demanded.

He was fully ready to do all the things that he dreamed he'd do, since the day that they'd met. He got out of the vehicle and jumped into the backseat. Jena grabbed Jean-Jacque by the back of his neck and pulled him close to her and planted a wet kiss on his lips.

They continued kissing and she leaned all the way down on her back and Jean-Jacque pursued her until he was lying on top of her. He motioned his hand in-between her legs, and Jena welcomed his advances. She ran her hands over his back, caressing him, then pulled his shirt over his head.

Jean-Jacque unbuckled his pants, then a police officer tapped on the window of the truck. "Hey, you two get out of here, go get a hotel room, or I'll drag you both downtown for indecent exposure," the police officer said.

They both laughed, got dressed, and Jean-Jacque climbed into the driver's seat and drove out of the parking lot. He waited until Jena got fully clothed, then he went back to Lincoln Hospital to visit Jamie.

They checked in with the security guard at the front desk, and he gave them their visitors passes. "Hey, you two can't stay up there for too long. Visiting hours will be over soon, and only immediate family can stay," the security guard said.

They took the passes and rushed to go upstairs to Jamie's room. Once they got upstairs, they entered the room and saw Asia on one side of the bed and Jamie's mother on the other side. Jamie laid there on the hospital bed motionless. Only the sounds from the medical equipment echoed in the room. Asia looked like she hadn't stopped crying; her eyes were puffy and red. Jean-Jacque moved in closer and saw Jamie's eyes opening.

"Yo! Jamie, what's up, man! Are you awake? I know that you took a bullet to the hip, and the doctors performed surgery on you to close the wound, but what did the doctors say? What's the prognosis? Will you walk again? Are you going to be paralyzed?" asked Jean-Jacque.

Jamie coughed a few times, adjusted the nasal oxygen cannula. "Ha, ha, ha, so funny that I forgot to laugh. No, Claude, I am not paralyzed, the doctors said that I will be okay, the bullet went through and through. It didn't hit any nerves," Jamie replied.

"Thank God," Mrs. McClymont exclaimed.

"I am going to walk again, no problem. I am going to need to do physical therapy. The doctors gave me some crutches and a wheelchair for now if I need it. I should be good, up and running in four to six months. I am thinking maybe sooner if I push myself."

"Jamie, are you serious about pushing yourself?"

"Of course, Claude, I don't want to stay in here with my ass in a sling. Rolling around in a wheelchair, like some invalid."

"Well, I don't want to get your hopes up, I think that I can get you back on your two feet in no time. Possibly I could do it in half the time that the doctors predict."

"How Claude, this sounds like some bull…"

"No, no, no for real, you don't believe me?"

"Hell no, but I'll listen to what you have to say," Jamie said.

"I could teach you what I know. I am into martial arts. With

93

that combined with meditation, coupled by intense training; you could recover in six to eight weeks," Jean Jacque replied.

"Say word!"

"Word!"

The two embraced with the Oath handshake and Jean-Jacque stepped away from Jamie's hospital bed.

Asia and Jena looked at each other in disbelief; no words were exchanged between them. Their facial expressions said it all.

"Jamie, I can't believe that you were up all this time, and you didn't say anything to me, or your mother. I've been by your bedside, crying my eyes out this entire time," Asia said.

"I'm sorry! I was up about ten minutes ago; I was just lying here pondering about all the events of the day. Thinking about my life, my hopes, my dreams, and my desires. I'm young, and I haven't accomplished any of my ambitions. It got me worried that I don't have enough time to do all that I was put here to do. The shooting happened so fast, my life flashed before my eyes," Jamie replied.

Everyone sighed and shook their heads in agreement. "Mi kine ah feel ah way, 'kaaz mi son ah fret bout death. An he too yung fi ah hot up him head bout dat," Mrs. McClymont said.

An overwhelming familiar feeling of dread covered her, like a dark cloud and she felt uneasy. The death of her husband is more than likely the real reason Jamie is contemplating his own mortality.

A nurse knocked on the door and entered the room. "Good evening, everyone, I regret to tell y'all that visiting hours was over an hour ago. Mom, this doesn't include you."

Asia looked at her watch, raised her eyebrows. "Oh my gosh, will you look at the time, I didn't realize how late it was. Jena did you call mom and dad? Did you tell them what happened?" asked Asia.

"Yes, Asia, I told them. I let mommy know that we would be at the hospital visiting Jamie," Jena replied.

"Whew, that's a relief Jena, you know how mommy and

daddy could be hard sometimes. Especially when we don't tell what our plans are after school."

Before the three walked out the door. Asia and Jena hugged Jamie. "Bye Big-head!" said Jena.

Asia leaned into Jamie and kissed him on his lips, —— "Unuh betta mind, mi nuh ready to min no pickney," Mrs. McClymont said.

"I will come see you tomorrow after school," Jean-Jacque said.

All three of them left the room, and Mr. Loewenberg entered right after they left. He was pushing an IV pole with his left hand alongside him. "Hello Mrs. McClymont," he said.

Mrs. McClymont got up from the chair beside Jamie and walked towards the door. "Hello Mr. Loewenberg, mi sorry she yuh get shot. Excuse mi, mi haffi use di bathroom," Mrs. McClymont replied.

"Hey son, how are you doing?" asked Mr. Loewenberg.

"Hey Mr. T, I'm doing okay considering the situation," Jamie replied.

"Well, I just wanted to thank you for your bravery. I'm grateful for that selfless act you had done for me Jamie. You saved my life son."

"Don't get all sentimental on me Mr. T, I am glad to see that you're moving around so soon. You must have some powerful drugs in that IV drip."

Mr. Loewenberg sniffled and looked at Jamie for a moment before he turned around to leave Jamie's hospital room. He used his hand to wipe away the tears that welled up in his eyes. His gratitude was on full display from a man who owes his life to a student. A student that he is glad that he was able to reach. A bond that was formed which solidified a connection between them. Jamie smirked at Mr. Loewenberg's sentiment and felt his appreciation.

Jean-Jacque stopped to get a couple slices at a pizzeria

across the street from the hospital.

"Yo, I haven't eaten all day! What do y'all want to drink?" asked Jean-Jacque.

"Well, we both will have slushies, and get some garlic knots too," Jena replied.

He paid, they got their food, and Jean-Jacque drove Asia and Jena home. Once they arrived Asia got out the truck, ran towards the building. "See you tomorrow, Claude, thank you for the slice," Asia said.

Asia ran straight upstairs Jena sat back down in the truck and nibbled on her garlic knots. The two talked for a while, exchanging sweet pleasantries. As magical as it was, the reality set in and Jena knew that she would have to go upstairs.

"Why don't you come upstairs? I can introduce you to my parents. That is if you don't have anything to do," Jena said.

"Okay cool, I ain't got shit else to do," Jean-Jacque replied.

So, he follows her up to her family's apartment. You would be surprised. He's a skilled fighter. He could easily defend himself, but the thought of meeting her parents still frightened him.

He tagged along behind her to the apartment door. Jena was happy, and eager to bring him into her home. She opened the door, and there was a strong incense aroma in their home. There were lit candles in various parts of the apartment like he had entered a temple of worship.

The girl's mother walked up to them at the door and greeted them as soon as they entered the house.

"Buenos noches, ¿Quién es? ¿Traes chicos a la casa a esta hora? Sabes que no puedes tener compañía después de cierta hora," (Who is this? You bringing in boys in the house at this hour? You know you can't have company after a certain hour," their mother said.

"No, no, no, no se parece en nada a mamá, este es el chico de la escuela. Es el chico del que les hablé que salvó algunas vidas ayer. Si no fuera por él, Jamie no estaría aquí. Mamá, este es Jean-

96

Jacque. Jean-Jacque esta es mi madre Mrs. McCubbin; mamá,
¿dónde está papá?" (No, no, no, it is nothing like mom this is the
guy from school. He's the boy I was telling you about that saved
some lives yesterday. If it weren't for him Jamie wouldn't be here.
Mom this is Jean-Jacque. Jean-Jacque this is my mother Mrs.
McCubbin; mom, where's dad?) replied Jena.

"Your father is asleep in the living room on his favorite
chair. I am pleased to meet you. From what Jena told me, you are a
decent human being. That is wonderful that you were able to save
everyone yesterday. It's so sad that anyone had to experience that. I
guess that is the harsh reality of the world today. I hope that you are
around, if something like is happen again. I hope y'all react
accordingly. My girls are all I have in the world," Mrs. McCubbin
said.

"Sí, lo haré, haré lo mejor que pueda. Te aseguro que estarán
a salvo cuando estén a mi alrededor," (Yes, I will, I will do my best.
I assure you that they will be safe when they are around me,) Jean-
Jacque replied.

Mrs. McCubbin smiled and said, "Hablas muy bien el
español; Estoy impresionado. Gracias por el sentimiento, pero es
una noche escolar, así que Jena tendrá que verte en la escuela
mañana." (You speak Spanish very well; I'm impressed. Thank you
for the sentiment, but it is a school night, so Jena will have to see
you at school tomorrow.)

"I respect that, Mrs. McCubbin; it was nice meeting you."

"Igualmente, Jean-Jacque!" (Likewise, Jean-Jacque!)

He gave Asia a hug and Jena a peck on the cheek, then he
left the apartment and got into his car and drove away.

The next few days were basically uneventfully, bland like
day old bread. It was a nice change of pace for the gang, considering
what's been going on.

Chapter 6:

Key to The City

Bright and early on a Monday morning Jean-Jacque was awakened by the phone ringing. "Hello good morning, is this Henri Jean-Jacque Cadet?"

"Yes," he said half asleep.

"Who is calling me this early in the morning," Jean-Jacque thought.

"My name is Olivia, and I am calling from the mayor's office. Mayor Rodolfo Meléndez would like for you to come down to a press conference in your honor. The mayor would like to present you with an award because of your heroic actions the other day at Alfred E. Smith H.S. The mayor believes that you should be rewarded for your bravery.

"The world should know what you've done for your teacher and classmates. I for one, think that you deserve all the recognition in the world.

"You don't have to worry about transportation because a car has been sent for you, and it should be downstairs waiting out in front, as we speak. So, y'all have approximately twenty minutes to get ready. The Mayor sends his apologies for the last-minute rush, but he only found out yesterday.

"Considering that it hadn't been on the news, there was a slim chance that your story wouldn't have even made it on his radar. If it weren't for the Bronx District Attorney mentioning what transpired the day that you were brought in for questioning at the 44TH precinct; this ceremony wouldn't be happening. Well, let me stop talking, and let you go get ready, so that you can make it on time. I'll see you at the ceremony," Olivia said.

She hung up the phone, and Jean-Jacque cleaned up as fast as he could. He got dressed, sped out the door, but he didn't remember to inform his cousins Patrice and Latrice or his parents about the ceremony. Jean-Jacque was too caught up by the recognition surrounding the incident.

He flew down the stairs, and saw the presidential black suburban parked outside his building. Without hesitation he leaped in the back of the vehicle. The driver then drove behind a police caravan escort to Gracie mansion. They ran all the traffic lights and made it there on time for the press conference.

When he arrived there, Jean-Jacque was escorted inside, and he was met by an awaiting crowd of reporters. lights. The bright lights from the cameras flashed in his face, murmurs and whispers crashed his ears. The reporters were all talking but refrained from asking him any questions.

Mayor Rodolfo Meléndez was the first one who approached him. Jean-Jacque hadn't seen the mayor since the night that Marisol broke it off with him.

Jean-Jacque shook the mayor's hand and shuttered at the notion that this event was solely in his honor. "Was her way to get close to him without raising further suspicion about their tryst. Or at the very least, an attempt to make it up to me for shattering my heart into tiny little pieces," he thought.

He remained stoic, all of his hopes of a reunion with Marisol came crashing down when he looked in her eyes and shook her hand. She was affectless, like she never even met him at all.

"How are you doing today? You are a brave young man Mr. Cadet," Marisol said with the cameras flashing.

Jean-Jacque adjusted his suit and played along with the façade. "I am doing fine today Deputy Mayor Velasquez; I am honored that this is all for me. I was shocked when I received the call at the crack of dawn this morning to come down here," Jean Jacque replied.

"I am glad to hear it, so let's begin."

Mayor Meléndez walked up to the podium then he adjusted the microphone. There was audio feedback from the speaker as he lowered it under his chin. "Hello, and good morning, to everyone here; I have brought you all here today because of a Hero of the

99

hour. Here is the young man who thwarted three gunmen single handedly at Alfred E. Smith High School last week.

"His bravery not only stopped three bad guys who egregiously shot a student, and a teacher, but his actions also allowed police to reopen an unsolved cold case. They are also aggressively investigating the infamous 'Rubber Band Gang.' A gang that has evaded arrest for a long time. The police are now close to bringing them all down. This is all because of the selfless act of this young man.

"This gang has been terrorizing that neighborhood of 151ST Street and 3RD Avenue, for a long time. All the high school students at Alfred E. Smith H.S, and many of the residents in the neighborhood, have many horror stories to tell. Stories about run-ins with this ruthless gang; the harassments, brutality, drug dealings, and utter disrespect by the hands of these thugs.

"I would like to introduce you to Henri Jean-Jacque Cadet. I am going to leave the floor open, so that you may ask him questions before a small award ceremony for his valor," Mayor Meléndez said.

The crowd applauded Jean-Jacque, as he stepped up to the podium to flashing lights flickering in his face like a live rave.

"What did it feel like when you heard gunshots in the auditorium on that horrible day?" asked the first reporter.

"I don't know, I really didn't think; when I ran into the auditorium, I saw three gunmen. I also saw the drama teacher, Mr. Loewenberg, and my best friend Jamie, sitting on the ground, in a pool of their own blood. I just sprang into action, I guess it was attributed to my years of training," Jean-Jacque replied.

"As for your forementioned training, what kind of training is this by the way? It has to be Bruce Lee level training to be able to take down three armed gunmen?" asked another reporter.

"I have a brown belt in Jiu Jitsu and a third-degree black belt in Kenpo, I just reacted how my training dictates. It just came natural to me," Jean-Jacque replied confidently.

"Alright, that will be all, let's not bombard the young man

100

with any more questions. I want to take this time out to bestow this city's hero with a medal of valor and the key to the city," said Deputy Mayor Marisol Velasquez.

As the reporters clamored for their chance to ask Jean-Jacque more questions, she placed the medal around his neck from behind. With the cameras flashing, Mayor Rodolfo Meléndez shook his hand, presented him a small box with a bronze skeleton key inside it.

The sound of the uproarious applause and flashing lights from the cameras queued the media coverage of the event to start. "Reporter Kim Lee here, from channel ten news covering the ceremony honoring Henri Jean-Jacque Cadet. The Mayor and Deputy Mayor presented him with the Keys to the city for his bravery. He single-handedly thwarted a vicious attack on an auditorium bustling with high school students and one teacher, rehearsing for a school play this coming Saturday. The would-be attackers were members of the infamous Rubber-Band Gang. Back to you Bill," she said.

After the ceremony Marisol invited Jean-Jacque to her office. He followed her into office. She let him in first, but before she closed the door, she told Olivia "No interruptions please."

Marisol offered him a seat, and then she went behind her desk, opened the top draw and took out a pack of Virginia Slim cigarettes. She knocked the bottom of the box against the palm of her hand, opened the box, "I'd offer you one, but seeing how this will stunt your growth."

Marisol took out a cigarette, lit it, took in a long drag and exhaled. "I'd rather not contribute to that. Furthermore, it's all around bad for your health," she said.

"Since when did you start back smoking? I thought you quit!" asked Jean-Jacque.

Marisol stared at Jean-Jacque as she waved the lit match up and down in the air. The light flared from the end of the lit cigarette as she took another drag.

"You didn't have a problem stunting my growth when you

101

fucked me and then threw me away like a pot of burnt rice."

Marisol squinted one of her eyes as the smoke bellowed from her mouth and nose like a tugboat.

When the smoke cleared from her face, she leaned forward and put out the cigarette in the ashtray on the desk. "Okay, right to it then. Listen, do you like where you live? You have your own apartment in my building, that I set up for you. How's the sales of your jazz album doing? Well, I presume," Marisol said.

"Yeah! So!" replied Jean-Jacque.

At that moment, Mayor Meléndez entered the office.

"Need I remind you that all three of you all are sitting pretty in a lucrative piece of property, in a swanky part of town. I'm not going to take it away, I'm not an Indian giver. But I am going to need something in return."

Mayor Meléndez walked over to his humidor and took out a cigar. He ran the cigar under his nose then clipped the end of it. He put the cigar in his mouth and lit it. The mayor stoked the cigar and waved the lit match up and down in the air. "I'm sure Deputy mayor Velasquez has briefed you. We're going to need for you to recruit your cousins Latrice and Patrice into The Program.

"Then I'm going to need you and them to recruit more young people to do the same. I don't think that I need to spell it out for you. It would behoove you not to answer negatively, so think really carefully before you answer."

Jean-Jacque was at a loss for words, a myriad of thoughts swirled through his head. "If I don't go through with what they want from me. They're liable to take away everything that I have grown accustomed to. I wouldn't put it past them and their level of influence to revoke my family's status (visas) to stay in the country either," he thought.

Jean-Jacque sighed, and reluctantly agreed to terms before either of them could open their mouths to be more persuasive (lie).

Jean-Jacque understood all too well how things worked. You can't get something from nothing. Marisol is the one who

102

taught him that. One call from her and their whole world can come tumbling down. Influence has more power than money in this city, it's smarter to learn the game than to continue getting played.

"Is that all Mayor Meléndez and Deputy Mayor Velasquez?" asked Jean-Jacque.

Jean-Jacque watched Marisol stare aimlessly at the view of the city's skyline, ignoring his question. He got fed up, kissed his teeth, got up out of the chair. Mayor Meléndez walked over to his wet bar and poured out a glass of cognac. Jean-Jacque walked towards the door to leave the office. But before he opened the door, Marisol turned around in her chair and lit another cigarette. "Hey, Busy bee! Here, you're forgetting something," she said.

"I knew that her hardened shell would crack soon enough, to reveal her soft interior for me," Jean-Jacque thought and smiled.

When he turned around, Marisol took the lit cigarette away from her mouth and put one arm on the desk. "Two things: first, your key to the city," Marisol said.

"And the most important thing is to make sure that you inform your cousins that I can see to it that all of their college scholarships disappear," Mayor Meléndez said.

Jean-Jacque closed the door and left Gracie mansion. He walked to the nearest pay phone. He picked up the phone, searched for two quarters in his pocket, inserted them inside the slot, then dialed his home number. The phone rang twice, and one of his cousins answered the phone.

"Hello," she said.

"Latrice?" asked Jean-Jacque.

"Yes, Jean, from the tone in your voice I can tell something is wrong. What have you gotten yourself into? I heard that you've been running around town pretending you were Batman."

"Nothing of the sort, I haven't gotten myself into anything. Instead, I have gotten us all involved in some shit. Marisol and the Mayor wants me to recruit you and Patrice into The Program that I'm involved in with Club Divvy Divvies and the Mayor's office.

103

She is cashing in on a favor, she's either in too deep, or she's trying to get back at me for something."

"What, like revenge? Explain to me what she could possibly be trying to get you back for, what did you do to her?"

"Nothing, never mind, the most important thing is that they can destroy us if we don't comply to their depends," Jean-Jacque said.

"Listen, I'll do it for your sake, you don't have to explain anything further now, I'm just going to trust that you will tell me everything in your own time, hopefully soon," Latrice replied.

"One thing before your quarter runs out, how could you jeopardize what we got going on? Between the three of us, we had our lives in order for the future. What did you do to risk all we have set up?"

"I'm sorry, but we can't say no to the Mayor. He has the connections to deport you two and my parents out of the country. I can't allow that."

"We can't allow that Jean. Patrice and I won't let that happen. 'Patrice, vin isit la epi koute sa kouzen ti towo bèf nou an te antre nan not, (Patrice, come here and listen to what our bullheaded cousin has gotten us into,) Latrice said.

Patrice got up, and Latrice turned the phone upward, so both of them could listen in on the call. The twins glued themselves to the phone and listened in on the conversation.

"Are you ladies listening?" said Jean-Jacque.

"Yes Jean," the twins replied.

"The Mayor and the Deputy Mayor wants me to recruit both of you into this Program that I'm involved in," Jean-Jacque said.

"What does The Program entail Jean?" asked Patrice.

"It involves you to be groomed by a high-ranking member, who pays for the opportunity to take your virginity before your eighteenth birthday. Then after that you receive the equivalent of one million USD."

"I don't understand Jean, so you mean to tell me that you were pimped out by the Mayor through Marisol, and now you're indebted to her, so you're attempting to do the same thing to us?" asked Latrice.

"Not in no uncertain terms," Jean-Jacque replied.

"All this time we've been living in a brothel, and you are a gigolo!" exclaimed Patrice.

"No, I've only been with Marisol——"

"Wait, what? You're sixteen Jean, when did this happen?" asked the twins simultaneously.

"It was a few months before I moved into the loft," Jean-Jacque said.

"Jean, you were thirteen years old. Why haven't you discussed this with us before? Why didn't you tell your parents? Do you know that you were a victim of statutory rape?!" replied Latrice.

"Yes, Latrice, I'm well aware of the ramifications of our unlawful and unethical union. But I thought she loved me. She has shown me nothing but love since we met."

"Please deposit twenty-five cents for the next three minutes!"

Jean-Jacque inserted two more quarters into the pay phone., "The moment Marisol left town after we had sex and came back months later, she treated me different," said Jean-Jacque.

"Hold on, hold on, Jean, what sort of vices did she have before you two were intimate?" asked Patrice.

"Marisol smoked cigarettes and drank hard liquor," Jean-Jacque replied.

"And months after you had unprotected sex, did her behavior change?" asked Latrice.

"Yes, she stopped drinking, smoking and she couldn't stand to be in the club because everyone smoked there. Come to think of it, I remember her being sick all the time——"

"Oh, shit Jean, you got Marisol Velasquez, The Deputy Mayor of New York City, pregnant?!" replied the twins in unison.

"No, I don't think so, Marisol never told me anything like that."

"And she never will because if this gets out, the shit storm that would involve the Mayor's office, club Divvy Divvies, and the Program would be astronomical," replied Latrice.

"Ladies, it doesn't sound like you're on my side, this is not an interrogation, counselors. I need your help on this matter," Jean-Jacque exclaimed.

"Okay, okay, we'll help you, tell us what we need to know," the twins replied.

"They want me to continue doing what I was doing before at the club with one more addition."

"What is that?" asked Latrice.

"They want us to be recruits. They want us to find young exotic women and men," Jean-Jacque replied.

"What does exotic mean?" asked Patrice.

"They're looking for foreigners; people who are from overseas. More like us, but before we do this; Patrice, I want you to do some searching on both Mayor Meléndez, and Deputy Mayor Velasquez. Find out anything you can, something that would give us a little leverage.

"I don't want to go into this again with my pants down. With that being said, let's garner some influence and make a difference in the lives of the unfortunate. By the way, I'm going to be on news channel ten later on tonight," Jean-Jacque said.

Jean-Jacque hung up the phone, then he turned to the driver of the suburban, "Hey, excuse me, I don't need a ride, I'm going to catch the train," he said.

"What if my cousins were right about Marisol, maybe that's why she was so cold and callous towards me. The circumstances seem bleak, and I don't have any wiggle room right now. Fuck, I

106

had a plan, a ten-year plan, that started when I was fifteen. Now, it doesn't look like that is going to be on hold. This is what I get for trying to be good, trying to save people. I should've stayed out of everyone else's business," he thought on his walk to the train station.

Jean-Jacque cursed and rants aloud on the train like he suffered from Tourette Syndrome, all the way to school.

After he went through the security check, Jean-Jacque saw Mrs. Orlinski stand in as a substitute teacher for Mr. Loewenberg's drama class. She stood next to his classmates in the hallway. Everyone there looked solemn and sad. "I hope that everyone is still going to perform this Saturday. If so, with a lot more enthusiasm than this. I have an idea; we should set up a collection for Mr. Loewenberg and Jamie's parents to help pay their doctor bills. I know that the surgery to repair their bullet wounds was expensive. Come on people, all in favor, say I," Jean-Jacque said.

"I," everyone replied in unison.

The students rallied together to get the word out for their cause. People in the neighborhood were already privy to the upcoming show from the channel ten news report by Kim Lee. The public was receptive of the idea of a fundraiser.

Both performances of Little Shop of Horrors, performed better than anticipated. Jean-Jacque's student directorial debut went on without a hitch. They were able to raise six thousand dollars, more than enough money for the medical debt.

The next week while they were preparing to put on another show. Antonine, a fellow classmate, walked on stage before rehearsals holding a notebook in her hand. "Could I have everyone's attention please, I have a proposition to make. I suggest that we do an impromptu performance of a play that I wrote myself after each show. Mr. Loewenberg promised me before he was shot, that he would put on my play," he said.

Everyone loved the idea and asked for a copy of her script to study. Antonine was a bright playwright, who desperately wanted everyone to perform her plays, so she took the initiative by sharing the directorial duties with Jean-Jacque and Mrs. Pete's, the substitute teacher for drama class.

After school, Jean-Jacque was walking to his truck, when he saw someone in a wheelchair coming towards him. When the person got closer, he realized that it was Jamie.

"Hey! Jamie is that you?" shouted Jean-Jacque.

"Hell yeah, it's me, are you going to let me roll my cripple ass up the street without helping me?" replied Jamie.

Jean-Jacque laughed and helped Jamie to the truck. "How's it being going?"

"I've been doing well, I'm glad to be out though."

While Jean-Jacque helped Jamie out of the wheelchair; Asia saw Jamie from across the street and dropped everything that was in her hands. She ran towards him and screamed, "Jamie!" at the top of her lungs. Asia reached where Jamie was and tackled him; almost knocking him over.

"Ouch, ouch, ouch! Damn girl! Be easy, you're going to put me back in the hospital. I didn't have enough money to pay for the first surgery, I damn sure don't have any money to pay for another one," Jamie exclaimed.

Asia didn't pay Jamie's grouchiness no mind; she kissed him all over his face, "Let me look at you. Are you still in one piece? How was the food?" she said.

She was like a ball of excitement, pressing Jamie with a barrage of questions:

"You look like you lost a little weight while you were laid up. Did you eat any of that hospital food? I may have to make you some home cooking. Are your stitches still in, or did they dissolve? Did you miss me, baby? I know that I missed you," Asia said.

"Easy, easy, easy, Asia, let me catch my breath. Give me a chance girl, just calm down, I am here now, we have all the time in the world to catch up, okay," Jamie replied.

He held Asia close to him and pressed her head on his chest.

Then Jamie used his index finger to raise her chin high enough to gaze into her eyes. He stared at Asia like he was Dracula; then he French kissed her. Their long exchange seemed like an eternity. Asia's eyes were closed, and she was up on her tippy toes. "Wow, if this is what sex feels like, I can't wait to do it," she said.

"Asia, snap out of it! Listen, you left your books across the street. Why don't you go and pick them up before they go missing? Then maybe, Jean-Jacque will take us to Jane Addams to pick up Jena," said Jamie.

Jamie moved out of the way and waited until Asia gathered her things. Afterwards, she got back to the truck, and they drove to Jane Addams. Not soon after they arrived and parked, Jena came out of the school. She was accompanied by a fine, curvaceous strawberry blond.

Jamie and Jean-Jacque saw Jena's friend, and an involuntary cry escaped their control. "Damn son, she's fine as hell," they said in unison.

Asia smacked Jamie in the back of the head in response to his inappropriate catcall. "You better put your eyes back in your head. There's no woman flyer than me. You too, Claude, before I tell Jena that you were scheming on her friend," she said.

When Jena reached the truck, Jean-Jacque hopped out of the car and tongue kissed her. Everyone looked on as they swapped spit. Afterward, Jena wiped the saliva away from her mouth and introduced him to her friend. "Claude, this is my friend Margot, but everyone calls her Blossom," she said.

"Why does everyone call her Blossom?" asked Jean-Jacque.

Margot turned around and showed her butt to him.

"That's why we call her Blossom because her ass is like a flower Blossom. Have you ever seen a booty like that on a white girl?" exclaimed Jena.

"I am not white. I am Jewish; there's a difference. Did you know that many Jews were originally African throughout history? That fact is something that most people don't like to admit.

"So, when I walk down these streets, there is no difference between us. Just because my skin is fair and my hair is straight and red; don't mean shit, we're all the same," Margot retorted.

"Pleased to meet you, Blossom, my name is Jean-Jacque, but my friends call me Claude," he said.

"I see how pleased you are. I damn sure know that is not a gun or knife in your front pocket. Damn boy are you half equidae?" replied Margot.

"Shut up, Blossom, that's a wad of money. At least I hope it is," Jena replied.

"What? Jena, they objectified me when I first walked up, so what's the difference."

"You're lucky you're my best friend, or I would kick your teeth in."

"Is everybody hungry? My treat!" asked Jean-Jacque, after everyone got inside his truck.

"We're all starving, Claude!" replied Jena.

Jean-Jacque drove them to a diner on St. Lawrence, and Westchester Avenue, so they could grab a bite to eat. They sat at the first table that was clean and available. "Hey guys, I got something to tell you. I had a press conference with the mayor, and he gave me the key to the city," he said.

He put the key on the table, and everyone grabbed for it, but Jamie was the only one fast enough to get it first.

"The key to the city, what does that mean?" asked Jamie.

"Well, it means a pass to exclusivity and first-class treatment throughout the five Burroughs," Jean-Jacque replied.

"For how long? And for where exactly?" asked Asia.

"Well, I can't entirely remember the parameters exactly; I don't know it was for a year, five years, ten years, or a lifetime. The main thing is that I can get into certain clubs, museums, Broadway shows, and a slew of places all over the city. Anywhere in the city that New York subsidizes," Jean-Jacque replied.

"Wow! Does that mean food? Will this meal be free in this restaurant?" asked Jamie.

"No, No, No, only if it is owned and operated by the city and state of New York, otherwise, we have to pay. I can bring any number of friends and family with me, and we can get in for free," Jean-Jacque replied.

"Ooh, Mr. Hero! Big man on campus," Blossom exclaimed.

"What are you, Bruce Wayne or something?" Jamie added to the mockery.

"No, come on, it's nothing like that, but when you put good vibes in the ether, you get good vibes from the universe in return. It's the law of karma. Also, Deputy Mayor Marisol Velasquez told me that I could go to any college in the country for free," Jean-Jacque replied.

"That's great man, you can get your family out of the hood. You could graduate and get a job making good money by pushing pencils," Jamie joked.

Jena didn't say anything about the good news. Jean-Jacque noticed and furrowed up his eyebrows. "Jena why are you so quiet?" asked Jean-Jacque.

Jena folded her arms across her chest. "Claude, you never told me about a press conference before it happened," Jena replied.

"Cut me some slack, I didn't even tell my parents or my cousins. Everything happens so fast; I didn't have the time to inform anyone."

"Well then, I think that you should become an engineer."

"I think you should be a lawyer," Blossom added.

"You should study to be an actor or a director. It is the one career that everyone respects. You could be anything you want, and you don't have to worry about anyone fucking with you," Asia said.

"That all sounds promising, but the truth is honestly, I don't have a clue what I am going to do yet. I have time to find out what I am going to do for the rest of my life," Jean-Jacque exclaimed.

111

The waitress walked over to them and put a pitcher of water on the table with five cups. "May I take your orders?"

They each ordered cheeseburger deluxe with fries; everyone had a lovely time, they all ate, laughed, and no one else pressed the issue again.

After they were done, Jean-Jacque paid the check and took everyone home. He dropped Blossom off first at a swanky brownstone in the city.

"This is nice, Blossom; why in the hell are you going to Jane Addams?" exclaimed Jena.

"Jane Addams has the best Nursing program in the five Burroughs. That's what I want to be when I graduate college. I can get a jump on college with the transfer credit that I get from going to Jane Addams," Margot replied.

"I don't think so; I believe it was because your ass is too good. You didn't blend in well with a lot of those proper people in private school. You probably got kicked out of every Ivy League school in the city. I bet any amount of money that Jane Addams was the only school that would accept you, huh!" exclaimed Jamie.

Everyone in the truck laughed.

"Fuck you, you cripple son-of-a-bitch, trying to play me in front of everyone," Margot replied.

"Damn Blossom, why are you so sensitive? It was a joke," Jamie replied.

"I am just fucking with you, Jamie, you know what, I ain't going to lie. I did get kicked out of school for fighting with this bougie ass bitch that acted like she was better than me. So, I had to put her and a few other pigeons in their places. At Jane Addams, everyone seems a little more real.

"They ain't 'bout that bullshit. And since I ain't about that bullshit either, game recognizes game. I can't say the same about students in those Ivy League schools. If I fucks with you, I fucks with you. If not, leave me the fuck alone. I've been here for two years now, and this whole time, I only had one fight.

112

"It's funny because that's how I met Jena—— don't ask; that's a story for another time. I see y'all later, it was nice meeting you guys. Jena, I'll talk to you tomorrow, gurl," Margot replied.

Jean-Jacque waited until she walked inside her house before he drove off. He jumped on the west side highway to bring the girls and Jamie home next. When he got to Jamie's block, he and Asia helped him out of the truck and up the stairs. His mother heard the commotion outside, she came out, and both she and Asia assisted Jamie the rest of the way inside the house.

"Hi Mrs. McClymont!" exclaimed Jean-Jacque and Asia.

"Good afternoon, thank you for bringing Jamie home," Mrs. McClymont replied.

Jena waved hello to Jamie's mother, then Jean-Jacque drove her home. He parked out in front of Jena's building and waited for her to get out the truck. "Aren't you coming upstairs?"

"I am sorry Jena, but I can't stay right now, I will have to take a rain check. I have some business to take care of, so I will see you tomorrow."

"Please Claude, my parents aren't home, come up stairs and keep me company. I don't want to be alone, Asia is with Jamie, and she probably won't be coming back home until later on tonight. His mom doesn't like being at the house by herself, so she appreciates the company. My mother is working a graveyard shift, and my father is out doing him.

"Come upstairs; I can make you a snack or something."

Jean-Jacque looked straight ahead, tapped on the steering wheel with his fingers, and looked at his wristwatch.

"Come on, Mr. Key to the city, you're always doing something nice for everyone else. Let someone do something nice for you for a change."

Jean-Jacque sighed, and he put the truck in park. "Maybe she wants to spend some quality time with me. But I have to take care of some business for Marisol. What a dilemma," he thought.

Jean-Jacque decided to oblige Jena's request, so he got out of

113

the truck and locked it. To the delight of Jena, he knew by the smile on her face that he was gaining brownie points by spending quality time with her.

Jena pulled him up one flight of stairs to her apartment by his hand like a stubborn mule. Jena and Jean-Jacque took off their shoes before entering the apartment. She led him to her room and nudged him onto her bed with her hip. "I'll be right back. Make yourself at home."

Jena turned on the radio and went into the kitchen. She washed her hands before reheating up some leftovers. Then she brought the two plates of food and two bottles of Goya Malta with her, back to the room.

"Here, try this, my mother made some Arroz con gandules last night for dinner. Eat up this is some good traditional Spanish food. It's a lot better than the food that we had earlier. I noticed that you didn't eat all of your food at the diner," Jena said.

After they ate all the food and drinks that she brought, they sat up on the bed together, entwined in each other's arms and watched Video Music Box.

"I'm glad that I decided to come up here with you. I have never spent so much time with someone so cultured like you. You really care about me I can feel that. And I feel the same way. Sometimes when I am at the club I feel like a piece of meat. No one ever tried to get to know me let alone have a conversation with me before, you're the first girl who ever wanted to know me, for me. You're the first girl that I ever met, where I felt comfortable enough to want to share a piece of me with," Jean-Jacque said.

"Awe, so sweet, I feel comfortable with you too," Jena replied.

"Jena, tell me a little bit about yourself."

"Well, my full name is Jeneration, and I am half Jamaican and Half Dominican——"

"Hold up, time out, ya moms named you Jeneration?"

"Yes, and my sisters name is Asiatic; don't interrupt me

114

again, that isn't polite. So, my mother is a midwife, and she grew up in DR, (Dominican Republic) she was told never to date anyone darker than her. That racist stigma stemmed from a long history of prejudice, from slavery times, the Haitian Revolution, through to when President Rafael Trujillo ruled DR. The ruling class perpetuated the stereotype, that blacks were inferior to whites.

"It's ironic that my mother's viewpoint changed when she met and fell in love with my Caucasian father who's a Jamaican-born holistic doctor."

"Your father is white!"

"Yes, he has blond dreadlocks down to his feet, blue eyes, with a deep baritone voice."

"Pardon my ignorance, but is your father a witch doctor? If so, my parents told me about people like that they knew of back in Haiti."

"No, my father is a real medical doctor. He went to medical school; he had a thriving practice and everything. But he told me that at one point, he couldn't keep practicing medicine allopathically. He was conflicted, my father wanted to stop prescribing pharmaceutical drugs to his patients. So, he learned how to treat them the homeopathic way, through meditation, eating natural unprocessed foods and exercise.

"There was this east Indian elder who lived in St. Thomas, Jamaica, a parish where he lived since, he was a little boy. My father asked him for guidance, and the elder taught him the ayurvedic approach to healing the body. When he mastered it, he changed his lifestyle and encouraged his patients to do the same thing. His motto became "Let thy food be thy medicine and let medicine be thy food." –Hippocrates

"Of course, when the medical establishment got wind of what he was doing, they shut down his practice. My father became a holistic doctor ever since," Jena said.

"If your father was born and raised in Jamaica, how did he meet your mother?" asked Jean-Jacque.

115

"My father went to graduate school here in the states, he met my mother while doing his residency in the city," Jena replied.

"Okay, so what did he do to change your mother's perspective?"

"Well, he taught her about Caribbean history from the standpoint of the indigenous people that the conquistadors massacred. When she affirmed the information, she vowed to change the generational curse of hatred and bigotry, hence the name Jeneration. And she named my sister Asiatic as a reminder of who we are."

"Jena, my background story can't top that one."

"Try me, Mr. Key, to the city."

"My parents migrated here from Haiti, and my mother, who was eight months pregnant with me at the time, had me in San Juan, Puerto Rico."

"Now, that's interesting enough in itself. You're a Haitian Boricua. I would've never guessed that combo."

"My father is a math professor at NYU, and my mother is a musician/botanist/music instructor. That's my story in a nutshell."

Flattered by Jean-Jacque being vulnerable, she kissed him. The petting persisted as they intertwined in an erotic dance. Their bodies wrapped around each other like a cocoon and their burning desire steamed up the windows with their heat of passion.

His eyes opened wide when he remembered what Marisol and the Mayor told him. "Jena, we can't do this. Are you sure you want to do this?" asked Jean-Jacque.

"Kind of; I think you're very special and I'm quite fond of you," Jena replied.

"I think we should hold off for now."

Jena shook her head no and put her index finger over his lips. She then slithered her way down to his crotch and opened the front of his pants. Jena pulled out his throbbing semi erect penis and stroked it with her hand. "Damn boy, Blossom wasn't joking, you are part horse."

Jena wrapped her mouth around his cock until it doubled in size. Then she stroked it with both of her hands as she spit and sucked on the head of his penis. Jean-Jacque couldn't muster the strength to last any longer. "Ah! Oh! I'm coming!"

Jean-Jacque ejaculated in Jena's mouth, and she slurped the tip of his penis until there wasn't a drop of spunk left in his shaft. Afterwards, she got up and went into the bathroom to spit out the spunk and to rinse out her mouth with mouthwash.

Jean-Jacque laid there on Jena's bed in a state of shock. When the blood reached back into his head. "Yo, Jena, on the real, where did you learn how to suck dick like that? That shit was borderline professional, let me find out that you do that on the low," he said.

Jena turned off the water from the sink, rushed inside the room and slapped Jean-Jacque in the face. "Is that what you think of me? I ain't no hoe, Claude," Jena replied.

"Chill, chill, I'm sorry, that was a bad joke. Please forgive me."

"Don't try to play me, Claude. Why is it when you men get your dick wet you transform from being sweet to sour?"

"Alright, I said I'm sorry baby! Come here, give me a hug." Jean-Jacque pulled Jena close to him and she pushed him away.

"No, let me go Claude, the last time someone acted like you are now he became verbally abusive."

"Wait, what? Who abused you, Jena?" asked Jean-Jacque.

"My ex-boyfriend Darren, he goes to Smith with you Jamie and Asia," replied Jena.

"Come here Jena stop playing." She put her head down, slumped her shoulders and went over to Jean-Jacque. He wrapped his long arms around her. He sighed and kissed her on the forehead. "Jena, I have a confession to make. I am a part of this Program through the Mayor's office, and I got paid to have sex with

117

someone," Jean-Jacque said.

"Get the fuck out of here," Jena exclaimed.

He looked into Jena's eyes and shook his head. "You're serious aren't you. Eww, get off me, how many women have you been with. I think I'm going to be sick."

Jena got up off the bed and Jean-Jacque grabbed her by the wrist and pulled her back to him. "Come here, let me explain everything to you."

Jena softened up and strolled back over to him and sat down next to him on the bed. "My situation It's not as simple as running the streets landing customers, I'm not a prostitute per say——"

"Do you turn tricks for money?" asked Jena.

"Nah, let me put you on to something right quick. When I was twelve, I got locked up and sent to Spofford for a year for fighting in school. As a part of my sentence, I had to do community service. So, I was assigned to this club in the city called Divvy Divvies, where I used to buss tables at.

"One day, Mayor Meléndez and Deputy Mayor Velasquez entered the club; and I had to buss their table. So, Marisol struck up a conversation with me, and it developed into something more. She groomed me and recruited me into this Program where if you see it through, you earn incentives," Jean-Jacque replied.

"See what through Claude?"

"When you have sexual intercourse with the person who grooms you. You see, there's these rich and powerful people that attend these parties at the club and they seek out young attractive virgins to court. And they pay one million dollars to take your virginity before their eighteenth birthday.

"After the relationship is consummated, you're set for life. You receive a portion of the money up front, half of the money is put into a trust fund, and the rest goes toward any college of your choice in the country."

"So, you went through it already?"

"Yes, Marisol groomed me, she's the only one that I've been with."

Jena raised her eyebrows, exhaled. "Wow, that's some heavy shit Claude. How are you so casual with this type of arrangement?" asked Jena.

"Well, I looked at the bright side, all the perks and incentives of being involved in a situation where you are revered for your purity/innocents and paid a king's ransom for sharing that with one person once. I think that's a great trade off. A good percentage of our people lose their virginities to someone for free," Jean-Jacque replied.

"I don't know if I could go through with that arrangement Claude. I always pictured my first time being with somebody special."

"Jena don't give me a definitive yes right now. Sleep on it and get back to me."

Jean-Jacque got up off the bed and walked to the door. Jena stopped him and said, "Where are you going? My mother and father won't be back until the morning. Sometimes we don't even see her before we leave for school.

"Asia won't be coming back until she's ready to. She might not come home until the morning either. So, you are welcome to stay the night. You don't have to go all the way to SOHO tonight," Jena said.

"I know I would love to, but I have to leave. I have to tend to some business. I'll see you later, think about what we discussed," Jean-Jacque replied.

Jean-Jacque kissed Jena on the forehead and walked out of her room. Jena sat on her bed pondering about the proposition that he just gave her. Jena heard the door slam. She sighed, got up off the bed, and cleaned up her room.

Chapter 7:

Payback

Jean-Jacque woke up in the morning and stretched, but he laid in bed awake waiting for the alarm to sound. 4:59:59 seconds 5:00 am, "Good Morning, Good Morning, Good Morning, Good Morning, Good Morning," the alarm chimed. He reached over and pressed the snooze button on the alarm clock. Jean-Jacque got up for his early morning routine before school.

He went onto the treadmill and pushed the start button. Jean-Jacque ran a mile in the easy setting. After four minutes, he pressed the incline button and increased the speed on the treadmill to challenge himself. He ran another five miles on that setting, then he slowed down the speed, and the incline.

Happy with his run, he stopped the treadmill, got off and walked towards the punching bag. Jean-Jacque struck the punching bag with a jab, then a right cross, then a left jab, and then a roundhouse kick. He continued these combinations for twenty minutes, until he heard the bell ring. He kicked and punched the bag for one last set of combinations. Winded, he hugged the punching bag to stop it. While standing there feeling the energy from the bag, he took a moment to catch his breath.

Jean-Jacque stepped backward, clearing himself from the bag and does a series of backflips. After he landed on his feet, he about faced and walked into the bathroom. He took down his jogging pants and entered into the shower stall naked.

He turned on the faucet and stepped underneath the cascading water. Jean-Jacque allowed the water to beat on his face for a few minutes, then he soaped up his body to a lather with a rag and Irish Spring soap. After he was done, he rinsed the soap off with water, stepped out of the shower, and reached for a towel to dry off his body.

Jean-Jacque got dressed after he put lotion on his body. He put deodorant under his armpits, then he grabbed his book bag, his keys and walked toward the door. He walked downstairs to the lobby, then out of the building. He got in his truck that was parked out in front of the building. Then he drove up the West side highway towards the Bronx and to Smith H.S.

It was only one week of school left, and Jean-Jacque already took most of the regency tests. He took the Math regency, the Advanced Placement English exam, and the Physics Regency exam too. Confident that he passed those exams; he only needed to take the chemistry Regency exam to qualify to get his Regents diploma.

Jean-Jacque entered the class and sat down at an empty desk in the front of the classroom. He got there just in time, while the teacher was passing out the exams.

"Good morning, Jean-Jacque, so nice of you to join us!" said Mr. Downes.

Jean-Jacque didn't respond, he just took the examination and searched his book bag for a number two pencil. He waited until the teacher gave the class the okay to begin the examination.

"Students, you may begin with the exam!" said the teacher in the front of the classroom.

Jean-Jacque read through each question and answered them to the best of his abilities. After he was done, Jean-Jacque saw Jamie from the corner of his eye standing at the door to the classroom. "I'm done," Jean-Jacque said and raised his hand.

He looked at Jamie and motioned with his hand for him to wait, "I'll be there in a second, calm down!" whispered Jean-Jacque

The teacher walked over to him, and Jean-Jacque handed the completed exam to the teacher. He put his book bag on over his shoulder and walked out of the classroom. Jamie was on his crutches, pacing back and forth in the hallway.

Jean-Jacque embraced Jamie, and they did the Oath handshake. "Yo, you ain't heard?" asked Jamie, then he shook his head back and forth.

"Huh? Heard what? Did something happen?" replied Jean-Jacque.

"Yeah man, its Roland man, he got popped, man, someone blew his head off last night. It's all over the news.

"Where you been at, man? I haven't seen you, or fucking Jena in like six weeks now. What y'all been up to man? I see that you and Jena have been getting up close and personal. What y'all fucking now? y'all in love or something? What the fuck is going with y'all? y'all are too busy playing house, all lovey-dovey and shit, to recognize what's going on. They are picking us off, one by one!"

"Jamie, slow down, what is going on? What you mean Roland got shot in the head?"

"Yeah man, Roland got shot executioner style by Bronx Zoo, and the Botanical Gardens. Someone found him with his brains blown out the back of his head. It was a professional hit; one shot took him out. It looked like both of his hands were tied in the front of his body and his feet were tied behind his back. It could've been any of us, look, we gotta skip town, we gotta get out of dodge."

"Nah, kill that noise, we ain't gonna go nowhere. We're not running from no one! I've never ran from a fight in my life, and we are not going to start now. Fuck that, we're not skipping town. Just calm down Jamie, let me make some phone calls and see what happened.

"Trust me I will find who did this foul shit to Roland. That's my word! You already know, whoever did this they're as good as dead. That's on my mom's!" exclaimed Jean-Jacque.

Jean-Jacque walked away from Jamie and ran out of the school towards his truck. He opened the driver's side door and he lifted up the armrest and took out a flip phone and pressed the number 1 twice. The phone rang twice, and a soft female voice answered, "Hello, good morning, this is the mayor's office, how can I direct your call?" asked Olivia.

"Good morning, it's Jean-Jacque, patch me through to Marisol Velasquez please," Jean-Jacque replied.

"One moment please——"

"Hey, Busy Bee, this better be good I was in a meeting,"

Marisol said.

"Marisol, I need you to do something for me, look into a murder that took place late last night uptown near the Bronx Zoo. He was a close friend of mine named Roland Pembroke, who got murdered. Please find out who did it," Jean-Jacque replied.

"Calm down! Give me about an hour and I'll call you right back."

Jean-Jacque hung up the flip phone and he got out of the truck, and he saw Jamie crossing the street with Asia. "Everything is gonna be alright, you gotta calm down Jamie, don't panic, everything is gonna be good. Let me get to the bottom of this. Have you seen or spoke with Bryce?" asked Jean-Jacque.

"Nah man, I haven't seen nor heard from him. I spoke with Roland yesterday after school, we sparked up a blunt and he said he was going to see his shorty. It's like something out of a movie, weird shit keeps happening to us. These demons keep coming out of the woodwork fucking with us. Someone, or something wants us all dead," Jamie replied.

Jamie, Jean-Jacque, and Asia got into the truck and Jean-Jacque drove towards Jane Addams to pick up Jena. Jamie turned on the radio; it was tuned to 10:10 WINS. The theme song played out and the intro played, "Give us twenty-two minutes and we will give you the world."

"This just in, there was a body found in the Hudson River with his head cut off. The hands and feet were bound, and the torso had three gunshot wounds center mass. One moment—— they have just discovered the severed head of the body. They found it with the eyes gouged out, and the tongue was cut out. The police don't have the identity of the victim as yet. We will have the details later at 10:00," The news anchor said.

Jean-Jacque put his hands on top of his head and shook his head in disbelief. "What the fuck is going on in this city?" asked Jamie and Asia.

"Yo! they are picking us off, one by one. I hope and pray that wasn't Bryce. If it was, I think this has something to do with

123

that incident that happened in the projects. This is retaliation for that shit. I hope you have friends in the mayor's office like you said, I hope the Man is your side.

"I thought that the detectives got that scourge off the streets. I thought that they said they arrested everyone involved in gang activities in those projects. This is bullshit, it will seem like they're killing us all over that beef with those mother fuckers from the projects. This shit is deeper than what meets the eye. I ain't ready to die man! I only had sex once, I ain't graduate high school yet, this shit is fucking crazy," Jamie said.

"Jamie calm down, Damn it! I told you I will get to the bottom of this, I got this under control. I am waiting for my contact to give a call and I will find out what's going on. Just chill the fuck out, nothing will happen to the rest of us. I'm on it, I'm going to get to the bottom of this man. You know what I'm saying, don't worry," Jean-Jacque replied.

At that moment, the phone rang, and Jean-Jacque picked up the mobile phone flipped it open. "You see, speaking of the devil."

Jean-Jacque reached for the flip phone in the armrest and answered it.

"What you got?" asked Jean-Jacque.

"I know what happened to your friend Roland Pembroke. I have recovered surveillance footage from the murder scene. I don't think the people you had beef with from that project by the high school was your run of the mill gang members. They seem connected with some paramilitary type mercenaries. If I were you, I would either get reinforcements, or lay low until this shit blows over. These people are professionals, they won't stop, they will come after you with everything they got until everybody involved is dead.

"It also looks as though they're getting help from law enforcement too. There must be some crooked cops in the Police Department. They didn't arrest all of the Rubber band gang members. They're still out in these streets wreaking havoc and they are well connected," replied Marisol.

"Thanks, say no more."

"Oh, I almost forgot to say it, but the body they fished out of the Hudson River was identified as Bryce Benjamin. Was he your high school friend?"

"Yes, he was."

"Sorry for loss, Busy Bee! I'll give you a call back to let you know what the next move will be."

Jean-Jacque looked at the phone and closed it with his chin before he put it back in the armrest. "What happened? What did they say?" asked Jamie and Asia in unison.

"Jamie, you're were right, they are after us, and I just got news that the body the police just found in the Hudson River, was Bryce," Jean-Jacque replied in a somber tone.

"Damn, what's the plan Claude?" asked Asia.

"I don't know yet, let me think first," Jean-Jacque replied.

Jean-Jacque pulled up to Jane Addams and Jena was standing on the sidewalk waiting for them to pick her up.

Jena got in the car, kissed everyone on their cheeks and closed the passenger side door. Jean-Jacque drove off and he was driving for about ten minutes, and nobody spoke a word. All of their attention was preoccupied about what happened and from what Marisol said to Jean-Jacque.

"Why is everyone so quiet today? y'all act like someone died or something," Jena said.

Asia leaned forward and whispered in Jena's ear, briefing her about what they knew so far. Her eyes wondered aimlessly until she heard the bad news. "Oh my God! This can't be happening," Jena said and put her hand over her mouth.

Jean-Jacque dropped them off and barely said goodbye to anyone. He drove down the West side highway towards his loft when the phone rang. Jean-Jacque reached back into the armrest to retrieve the phone and put it on speaker. "Hello Marisol, do you have any good news?"

"Yes, we got facial recognition the person who took the fatal shot in Roland's murder. It is none other than The Rubber band gang leader, named Tuffy. The other shots were fired from the second in command Carlos and a third man was there by the name of Stacy. I have an address, are you ready to write it down," Marisol said.

"Yeah, give it to me!" replied Jean-Jacque.

"First address is 167th Street, 1200 College Ave apt 1C. That is the hideout for Tuffy. I sent you pictures and information on your phone for all of them. Whenever you are ready call #69, and we'll have a team to back you up."

Jean-Jacque changed into the left lane, and made an abrupt U-turn, on the Westside highway, heading back to the Bronx. He knew that he had to put a stop to these individuals responsible for killing off members of his crew, once and for all.

Jean-Jacque dialed #69 after he made the right turn off the Grand Concourse, and left the phone open, so the team could know his exact location.

Jean-Jacque pulled up to 1200 College Ave. and parked out in front of the building. He was going to shut off the truck, but he saw the unmarked inconspicuous van parked across the street. So, he left the truck running, got out, and jogged inside the building.

After he entered, he looked to the right and noticed a Chinese delivery man was about to knock on the very apartment door he was looking for.

He took out some money and told him to give him the food. The Chinese delivery man gladly accepted the money and walked away. Jean-Jacque stood in front of apartment 1C, ready to knock on the door, when the tactical team entered the building in full force.

With a series of hand signals, they mobilized and directed Jean-Jacque to knock on the door, after they got into position. Jean-Jacque pulled his mask over his face, and he put his hand over the keyhole and knocked on the door. "Who is it?" asked a voice from inside the apartment.

"Chinese food!" replied Jean-Jacque in a disguised his voice.

Then he stepped to the side, and he could hear the locks unlocking. As soon as the door opened, the tactical team stormed inside, knocking him down to the ground. They threw in a smoke bomb and a flash bomb as they all raided the apartment, one by one.

Jean-Jacque was the last person to enter the apartment. There was a man inside rolling on the floor in the living room coughing and holding his hands over both of his ears, which were both bleeding.

The lead of the team walked over to him, held a polaroid picture to his face, looked over at Jean-Jacque and nodded that it was a match. Jean-Jacque for the first time in years, felt a bit anxious. He knew that at that point, his life would be changed forever.

He walked over towards the person responsible for killing his friend and Jean-Jacque was handed a nine-millimeter. He cocked it back without hesitation, pulled the trigger and shot Tuffy twice in the head at point blank range. Jean-Jacque handed one of the men standing next to him the gun. He turned around and walked out of the apartment, into the lobby.

Knowing now that he avenged Roland's murder, by killing the person responsible, felt good. But he also knew that it wasn't over yet.

Jean-Jacque walked out of 1200 College Ave, got in his truck and he drove up the street towards the Cross Bronx Expressway north. He looked in the phone and saw the second address, 1023 Manor Avenue, where Carlos's location was. He merged on the highway and got off at the Bronx River Parkway exit. Jean-Jacque got off the parkway at Harrod Avenue and turned right onto Westchester Avenue. He drove down to Manor Avenue and turned left.

Jean-Jacque found a parking spot, and before he could dial #69, he saw a tactical van parked across the street. This time, Jean-Jacque turned off the vehicle, and adrenaline was still pumping in his veins like high octane from before. He looked to see if there were no cars parked in the driveway.

He noticed that the gate was unlocked and the kitchen lights on the 1st floor were on. He walked through the gate and noticed that the basement door was ajar. Jean-Jacque put on his gloves, pulled down his mask over his face and entered the basement through the open door. With low visibility, he tip-toed in the dark; he couldn't see his hand in front of him. Jean-Jacque walked towards a voice singing to loud music he heard playing from the kitchen upstairs.

He climbed the stairs and peeked through the door and saw Terrance. He was in the kitchen wearing a marina and a pair of boxers, singing "Kick in the door by the Notorious B.I.G, aka Biggie Smalls," 'This goes out to you, and you, and you! Uhh! your reign on the top was short like leprechauns As I crush so-called willies, thugs, and rapper-dons Get in that ass quick, fast like Ramadan It's that rap phenomenon Don Dada, fuck Poppa You got to call me Francis M.H White, intake light tokes, tote iron Was told in shootouts, stay low and keep firin' Keep extra clips for extra shit...'

Jean-Jacque waited until his back was turned to him and he rushed into the kitchen. He saw a knife on the kitchen table, picked it up and grabbed Carlos by the neck from behind. He raised the knife up in the air and Jean-Jacque lowered it, plunging it in Carlos's chest. Terrance had a box of cereal in one hand and a half gallon of milk in the other. Everything he had in his hands spilled all over the kitchen floor.

Jean-Jacque held the knife in place until Carlos was no longer moving. Then Jean-Jacque pulled his motionless body down to the ground. "This is for Roland, Motherfucker," he said as stood over Carlos's lifeless body.

Jean-Jacque looked around and didn't see nor hear anyone coming. So, he tip-toed back down the stairs to the basement and left out the side door that he came through. He stepped outside, and saw the tactical team, "We'll take it from here!" said the team's members.

Jean-Jacque got in his truck and drove off. He reached the corner of Ward and Watson Avenue, he looked at his flip phone, and noticed that the 3rd address was 1252 Croes Ave. So, he made a right turn on Watson Ave., drove towards Morrison Avenue, and made a left turn. He drove up Morrison until he reached Westchester Ave., then made a right turn on Westchester Ave. until he saw Croes Ave. and banked a left turn up the street until he saw the number 1252 on the right.

Jean-Jacque pulled into a parking spot, exited the truck and jogged towards the house. He walked up to the front door and tried the doorknob, and it was unlocked. So, Jean-Jacque entered the hallway and didn't hear a sound.

He saw the staircase to the right and a door to his left. Then he heard a pit-bull barking, "Pinky, shut up! Pinky, shut the fuck up! I'm not taking you out for the rest of the night! I fed you already and walked you to! Go in the room and lay down, fucking bitch," a voice said through n the apartment.

Jean-Jacque prepared himself for a struggle with this one. At that moment, he heard the locks unlock, and a man opened the door. Jean-Jacque recognized his face from the picture that was sent to his phone. There they both stood, face to face, like two-gun singers at the O.K Corral

Stacy had a bag of dog food in his hand that he was about to take some out to pour it in the dog bowl in the corridor.

Jean-Jacque didn't waste any time, he struck Stacy in the face with a straight jab, knocking him backwards inside the apartment. Stacy dropped the bag of dog food on the ground, wiped the blood from his mouth with the back of his hand, and put his hands up in a fighting stance.

Jean-Jacque threw another jab, and Stacy side stepped it and punched Jean-Jacque in the face with a right hook. The punch stumbled him back on to the side wall and then Stacy punched Jean-Jacque on both sides of his ribs. Stacy then swept Jean-Jacque's legs from under him, tripping him to the ground. He mounted Jean-Jacque and began to punch downward toward his face.

Jean-Jacque used his elbows to block the attack, then he grabbed one of Stacy's arms, and with his other hand struck him in the throat. Jean-Jacque then used his leg to trap one of his and pushed him off to the side of him. Then he mounted Stacy and drove his knee into the side of his neck and held his arms upward to the ceiling.

Jean-Jacque leaned all his weight on Stacy's neck. He shuffled and wiggled his body as he gasped for air. Stacy tried to push at Jean-Jacque's knees from his neck, but he suddenly stopped. Stacy's hands dropped off to the side, and his body went limp.

Jean-Jacque checked his pulse, and he couldn't feel one; Stacy was dead. Jean-Jacque was breathing in and out fast and looked around. He took a deep breath and saw the dog lying there in the distance in the room panting with her tongue out. Although the dog wasn't chained up, the dog didn't bark or lunge after him while he fought Stacy. "That bastard must have been a real dick to you, huh!" said Jean-Jacque.

Jean-Jacque leaned the open bag of dog food against the wall, took the dog bowl from the hallway, filled it with the bottle of water on the ground, and set it next to the bag. Jean-Jacque backed out of the apartment, shut the door, and exited the house.

Jean-Jacque ran to his truck and saw the tactical team entering the house afterward. He didn't waste any time acknowledging them. He just wanted to get-away fast as he could, without being seen.

Jean-Jacque drove toward 172nd street and made a right turn. Then a left turn towards Bruckner Blvd Expressway south. After he reached the Bruckner, he merged onto the FDR Drive. He heard the phone buzzing, and Jean-Jacque flipped open the phone and read the message: 'Destroy the sim card!!!'

Jean-Jacque took off the back cover off the phone, took out the SIM card, bent it, and tossed it out of the window. He closed the phone, put it back in the armrest and stayed on the FDR until he reached SOHO. He got off the exit, made a right turn, drove a few blocks, then a left inside the parking garage of his loft apartment building. He stepped out of the truck and rushed upstairs, taking the stairs four by four.

After Jean-Jacque made it to his loft, he opened the door,

took off all his clothes, and walked into the shower stall naked. He stood underneath the showerhead while the luke-warm water beat on his body. Jean-Jacque reflected on everything that just transpired, everything that happened leading up to today. Then he pondered about what will occur in the future.

After his shower, Jean-Jacque didn't even put on any clothes. He just plopped down on his bed with a towel wrapped around his waist and went to sleep.

Early the next morning, Jean-Jacque was startled by the phone ringing. "Hello, good morning, who's this?" asked Jean-Jacque.

"This is the office of Mayor Meléndez; please hold for Mayor Meléndez!" said Olivia.

The melancholy sounds of elevator music played on the other end of the receiver. "Good morning, Claude, this is Mayor Meléndez's, I heard you and your friends have been having a rough week. I will put some of my guys on it! Don't worry about anything. Please don't get all vigilant. Besides, I need you to focus on recruitment for the program. How's the latest prospect coming along?" said the mayor

"No word yet, but she's not going to be a problem. I have things under control; you can trust me," Jean-Jacque replied.

"Hey, make sure she keeps up her end of the bargain. I have a suitor that is eagerly waiting to meet her. If things go as planned, Jena and her family will be set financially for life.

Before I forget, my tactical team went on assignment yesterday on some Intel regarding a string of heinous murders going on uptown in the Bronx. Any word on the streets about any big players in the game getting arrested or bumped off?"

"No sir, not that I heard of."

"Hey, does Jena know anyone interested in the Program? I'm sure she knows about 15 or 25 candidates to join The Program; the more, the merrier."

"I'll keep you posted!"

131

"That's good to hear! Keep up the excellent work, Jean-Jacque. The incentives are limitless once you become an elite player. So, you make sure you are honest with people that you recruit, don't leave out any details. Make sure these people are not hot-headed. Make sure they fully understand what they're getting into, and it's a win-win situation for everybody involved. Both parties get what they want, and nobody gets hurt. Besides, free-loving, experimenting, like the swinging sixties. Hey, it is all good for everybody involved."

"Alright, Mr. Mayor, I will be in touch! Is there anything else?" asked Jean-Jacque.

"No, enjoy the rest of your morning. If there is, I'll keep in touch! I know how to reach you," Mayor Meléndez replied.

Jean-Jacque hung up the phone and thought about playing hooky from school. He was reluctant to leave the house after everything that transpired recently. But it's the end of the school year, and he wants to know his test scores. Jean-Jacque couldn't wait to see them. So, he hurried up and got dressed to drive to school. Jean-Jacque arrived just in time; they handed the manila envelopes out to the students in the classroom.

Jean-Jacque saw that he passed all of his classes and his statewide exams too. He was in a prime position to graduate from high school with a highly coveted Regency diploma at 16. His future looked bright; he signed up with a program that provided services to wealthy clientele. All they craved was the company of young virgin males or females.

Jean-Jacque was poised to not only get a good education but have a big bank account to match. Just imagine, his parents came to this country in 1981 with a plan. And in it, one of them would achieve their goal, the American dream. Now, their son has made it become a reality.

Coming from humble beginnings in Haiti, Jean-Jacque's parents knew for a fact that the only way to uplift oneself from poverty is to become educated. Earning degrees in mathematics and botany, his parents made way for themselves to succeed anywhere they were in the known world.

Doing menial jobs to make ends meet to pay for school, gave them the opportunity to change their situation. They set the foundation for the life of their future child. But they never would have thought that Jean-Jacque would grow up to be so brilliant. He's talented, has the discipline and diligence to be more successful beyond their wildest dreams and aspirations.

Chapter 8:

The saga continues

Graduation day, Jean-Jacque adorned a three-piece suit, sharp as a tack as usual. In attendance at his graduation was his parents, Latrice, Patrice, Jamie, Jena and her sister Asia. There was indiscriminate chatter throughout Hostos Community College auditorium, when Richard Applebaum, the principal for Alfred E. Smith H.S, walked out onto the stage. He approached the podium and spoke into the microphone and announced:

"Good morning, ladies and gentlemen, this year's graduating class of 1996, please rise and face the crowd. Everyone, please hold your applause, these diligent young men and women are the future leaders of the free world. What work they do from this day forward, will shape them for an eternity.

"These dedicated students worked and studied hard for four years of their lives. They've achieved what some people have not been able to do. These past 16 to 18 years of their lives gave them insight that helped them journey past this new threshold. Please, know that this is not the end, this is just the beginning of your adult lives.

"Do your very best and be present in the moment at all times, from this day forward. Life is short when you choose to make the wrong decisions, it's only long when you are disciplined enough to make the right ones. It has been my pleasure to guide you all through these turbulent times they call high school. The faculty and I have held you to a higher standard and you not only embraced it, but far surpassed all of our expectations.

"Graduates, please, turn to your neighbor, shake their hands, and tell them congratulations to the graduate of Alfred E. Smith high-school 1996."

At that moment, the seniors tossed their caps in the air, their families and friends in attendance cheered and applauded them. There were smiles, and tears of joy in jubilation throughout the auditorium in support of their achievement.

"Before we go, we're gonna have a speech from Henri Jean-Jacque Cadet, this year's valedictorian. Let us give him a round of applause," Mr. Applebaum said

Everyone in the auditorium cheered as Jean-Jacque approached the podium. He surveyed the auditorium and he saw Marisol standing in the back. He adjusted the microphone to his height and a screeching sound echoed throughout the auditorium from the audio feedback. "Thank you, Mr. Applebaum, Mrs. Orlinski, Mr. Loewenberg and the rest of the faculty. I appreciate you all for being there by our sides, pushing us on the days that we thought that we couldn't move forward. To my fellow graduates who fought the valiant fight and made it to the end of this chapter, give yourselves a pat on the back.

"There is nothing left in the past to do, let us move forward towards our future. We're embarking on a journey that for some of us will be long and hard but be steadfast and determine we will sure get to the other side of the mountain. In the eyes of some nay-sayers who thought we couldn't make it this far, we all have used that negative energy and converted it into positive reinforcements. So, guys and gals, don't let up! Everything we do from this moment forward will determine the rest of our lives, so don't tread softly! Make sure that we do everything in our power to stay positive and motivated to rise to the top. Thank you!" said Jean-Jacque and smiled.

After Jean-Jacque made his inspirational speech, each of the graduating class students walked across the stage and shook hands with the principal. About an hour later, the recent graduates were posing with their families for pictures in their caps and gowns. He noticed Jena standing alone, looking troubled. "What's the matter?" asked Jean-Jacque after he walked over to her.

"I'm having a hard time coming to terms with the idea of allowing a stranger to take my virginity. I mean, I understand that this could be a great opportunity for my family and me. In the same breath, I am having second thoughts. I want to lose my virginity with someone that I love! I want to lose my virginity to you!" replied Jena.

Ignoring that, she told him the L word. Jean-Jacque said, "Listen, you need to relax and take a moment to breathe and understand that this is a great opportunity. What you do afterwards it's up to you. Your birthday is a few weeks away, and you turn 17. After that, follow through with The Program, and become a millionaire.

"By giving up that one thing that you would probably give to somebody for free."

"Please, don't lecture me, or get into semantics with me."

"Come on Jena, imagine, you could afford to live out the rest of your natural life pursuing your dreams and aspirations. You can do something you really want to do; you wouldn't have to worry about money ever again.

"Please just take a breath and think about it! Understand if you decide not to, you will potentially be missing out on a great opportunity if you do not continue with this.

"Relax, come to my graduation party, DJ Frank will be on the ones and twos. Just pass through, smoke some weed, drink some rum punch, or whatever. Wine up yourself to music, and just be easy. Baby, tonight just enjoy yourself and don't even think about making your final decisions yet.

"If you backpedal, just know that these are very powerful people that we're dealing with. If you don't continue with this, they can be very vindictive and they're very thorough! They have people in positions, and they can do harm in more ways than one. So, I urge you to think this through!

"Understand that you will not be hurting yourself if you don't continue on, you would be hurting Asia, me and a lot of other people. They have jackets on everybody as a contingency plan, just in case one person doesn't play ball. They have the power to ruin everybody's lives involved.

"Be easy! come through and we could party it up and hang out, unwind, chill and enjoy yourself. Besides, it is my graduation. This is an important moment in my life, let us celebrate this together."

Jean-Jacque pulled Jena close to him and hugged her. She looked up at him with tears streaming down her face, and he used his thumb to wipe the tears off her face, then he leaned in and kissed her passionately on the lips.

Afterwards, Jean-Jacque walked over to his parents, and introduced them to her.

"Mom, Dad, this is my girlfriend Jena, her sister Asia and my friend Jamie. Babe, guys, these are my parents, Henri and Flora Cadet."

"Pleased to meet you Asia, and Jamie. Jena, how come you're not graduating today?" asked Henri.

"Oh, Mr. Cadet, I don't attend school with Claude —— I mean Jean-Jacque. My sister and Jamie do," replied Jena.

"But you're graduating this year, correct?" asked Flora.

"No, Mrs. Cadet, I will be graduating next year," Jena replied.

"Okay, JJ, will your friends accompany us to Sizzlers?" asked Henri.

"Guys are you coming?" asked Jean-Jacque.

"Hell yah, I am starving like Marvin, Claude," Jamie replied.

"Jamie don't be rude, we'll be delighted, Mr. and Mrs. Cadet," Asia said, then she elbowed Jamie underneath his ribcage.

"Where's my manners, thanks for the invite," Jamie replied and rubbed his side.

"Guys, these are my twin cousins Latrice and Patrice," Jean-Jacque said.

"Hey!" replied Jena, Asia, and Jamie simultaneously.

The twins waved hello to them in kind. They all left Hostos Community College and went out to eat at the restaurant.

Later, that night she went with Jean-Jacque to his party. Jena was a bit reserved at first, until she heard the intro to her favorite song.

'I want to rock, I want to rock, I want to rock, I want to rock right now!' It was "Doo-doo brown" by Luke Campbell of Two Live Crew.

Jena pulled Jean-Jacque by his hand to the dance floor, and she danced to the Doo-doo Brown song with him.

"I am glad to see that you are enjoying yourself," Jean-Jacque said after he leaned in and whispered in Jena's ear.

After dancing to the entire song, Jean-Jacque went to the bar and got a bottle of Canei and a Heineken. While at the bar, Rodrigo approached Jena and grabbed her from behind, "¡Tienes que meterte con un verdadero Boricua! ¡Tienes que dejar a ese Moreno solo y joderme! ¡Sé que eres español! Tú, dominicano, tienes que venir con nosotros," (You need to mess with a true Boricua! You need to leave that Moreno alone and fuck with me! I know you're Spanish! You are Dominican, you need to come with us,) Rodrigo said.

"¡Escucha Rodrigo, ese es mi hombre en el bar y no voy a jugar contigo! Todo este tiempo que hemos estado yendo al colegio yo era el Moreno; ¡Yo era el paria! Ahora lo ves con alguien más, ¡ahora me quieres!" (Listen, Rodrigo, that's my man over at the bar and I'm not messing with you! All this time we've been going to school I was the Moreno; I was the outcast! Now you see with somebody else, now you want me!) replied Jena.

Rodrigo spun her around like a top and grabbed her by the waist with his left hand. He looked deep into her eyes and with his right hand he gripped underneath her buttocks. He brought her in closer to his pelvis to ensure that she felt his bulging erection.

Rodrigo tried to kiss Jena on the lips, but she turned her face away. "Perra, ¿estás tratando de jugar conmigo? ¡Sé que no lo está haciendo bien! ¡Probablemente tenga que comerse este gran culo para hacerte comr! Deja a ese Moreno y jodeme, ¡tengo una gran polla! ¡Podría satisfacerte y asegurarme de que vengas una y otra y otra vez!" (Bitch you trying to play me. I know he ain't hitting it right! He probably gotta eat this big ass to make you come! Drop that Moreno and fuck with me, I got a big dick! I could satisfy you and make sure that you come over and over and over again!) said Rodrigo and laughed it off.

Jena pushed Rodrigo off her and slapped him in the face. DJ Frank stopped the music after he saw the commotion. Jean-Jacque turned around, and saw Rodrigo clench his fists standing in front of Jena after she slapped him. He looked like he was about to hit her.

Embarrassed, Rodrigo threw a punch at Jena's face, but he was too drunk to even have any force behind the punch and missed.

By the time he punched after Jena and missed and fell to the ground. The instant he stood up, Jean-Jacque rushed towards him with the Heineken bottle he got from the bar, spun Rodrigo around and he cracked Rodrigo over the head with it.

"Please don't kill him!" screamed Jena.

Rodrigo dropped back down to the floor and looked up at Jean-Jacque towering over him with a menacing look in his eyes and his eyebrows furrowed up.

"¡Hijo de puta negro! ¡Tu muerte! ¡No eres una mierda! ¡Crees que me lastimaste! ¡Yo como esos! ¡Mis chicos y yo los mataremos a los dos! ¡Este es mi block punk! ¡Este es mi bloque, perra negrata! ¡Estás muerto! ¡Esta perra sabe cómo me deprimo! Tú y toda tu maldita tripulación ya no están a salvo en estas calles," (You black mother fucker! You're dead! You ain't shit! You think you hurt me! I eat those! Me and my boys is gonna kill you both! This is my block punk! This my block you bitch ass nigga! You are dead! This Bitch knows how I get down! You and your whole fucking crew ain't safe no more in these streets,) Rodrigo said.

"Let's go! He ain't gonna do shit! He and his whole crew pussy! Please leave it alone! He had enough, everyone here saw that he was out of line and you defended me. That's it, let us leave it at that," Jena said and grabbed Jean-Jacque by his arm.

Jean-Jacque dropped the broken bottle he held in his hand to the ground and stepped away from Rodrigo.

Everyone left the party including Jean-Jacque and Jena. They both walked outside the building holding hands but stopped on the corner of Boynton and Watson Avenue. Jean-Jacque took out a spliff that he had rolled up from his shirt pocket and lit it up. They both noticed a commotion across the street in front of the NYC chicken spot.

There were members of two rival gangs, Darnel a Crip, and Jaleel a Blood about to get into it with each other.

"Ain't that Darnel! Shit! Let me go over there and stop them from killing each other," Jena said.

Jena took a drag off Jean-Jacque's blunt and jogged across the street towards the chicken spot.

Darnel had his hand by his waistband, where there was a nickel plated .22 sticking outside his shirt.

"Yo! Put that fucking flag away, there's no flagging out here. Watson Ave. is neutral grounds son, you trying to get stomped out here?" said Darnel.

"Ain't nobody gonna do me nothing! I rep my set anywhere I go. So, get the fuck out of my face with that neutral shit," Jaleel replied.

"My nigga, I ain't gonna say it again. I am Crip and I am not representing out here. Respect the code! If you don't know the OG's around here won't have no mercy if they feel like you in violation. They won't hesitate to regulate! So, I suggest you take my advice seriously."

Jena reached over to where they were standing, and she chimes in,

"They won't care about the set you are claiming. Both of y'all families stay around here. If you don't care about your safety, think about their safety," Jena said.

Jaleel pulled out his 9 mm pistol, pointed it at Darnel and looked at Jena. "Shut up bitch! I'm tired of hearing this nigga fucking mouth!" said Jaleel.

He squeezed the trigger, but the gun jammed and Darnel by sheer luck, was able to pull out his own .22 pistol and fired one shot into Jaleel's chest.

Everybody ran away, ducked and hide for cover after hearing the gunshots. The loud bang sent everyone outside into a frenzy.

Jena convinced Darnel to hand her the gun, he relented, and Marques took the firearm from him and started walking away from the scene. Darnel ran into his building, and Jena, still in a state of shock, turned around to run back across the street where Jean-Jacque was still standing.

Jena noticed that a fight was about to happen between Jean-Jacque, Rodrigo and his crew. So, she stepped off the sidewalk and walked into the street. A crackhead walked towards Rodrigo wearing a black hooded sweatshirt with jean shorts and timberland boots. He approached Rodrigo, pulled out a huge knife and stabbed him in the chest two times.

Rodrigo fell to the ground at the feet of Jean-Jacque and his boys chased his attacker into the street. The man ran away from them into oncoming traffic and was hit by a taxicab. The impact sent the man soaring in the air and he dropped on top of the windshield of the taxicab.

Rodrigo's boys, relentless in their pursuit, dragged the man off the car down to the pavement where they began kicking his lifeless body, until they were satisfied that he was dead.

Jena stood there in the middle of the street motionless blocking traffic. Traumatized from bearing witness to not only one, but two murders. After about two minutes of standing in the street shell shocked, she snapped out of her trance and made it across the street. Jena looked down at Rodrigo's lifeless body and she used her right hand to simulate the last rites (the father, son and holy spirit.) And her left hand to clutch her crucifixion pendant on her necklace like a priest's ritual before somebody dies.

Then she grabbed Jean-Jacque by the arm encouraging him to flee the scene. They both rushed towards his truck that was parked on the corner of Ward and Watson Avenue, and drove off down the street towards Elder Ave. Jean-Jacque made a right turn down Elder Ave., then another right turn onto Bruckner Blvd. He took the expressway until he merged on the FDR drive.

Jean-Jacque stayed on the FDR drive until he reached his exit, drove to his building and parked in the parking lot underneath his building. They got out of the truck and walked to the elevator and took it up to his floor where his loft was.

After Jean-Jacque and Jena got inside the apartment, they both took off their shoes., "Where's the bathroom!" asked Jena.

He pointed to where it was, and she made a beeline to it.

After Jena was finished using the restroom, she exited the bathroom wiping the back of her neck with a rag. Then she dried her hands and put the wet rag on the dresser.

"Don't bring anything wet in here and put it on the furniture, do you know water ruins finished wood! Either put it in the hamper, or put it back in the bathroom," Jean-Jacque said.

"So, you don't want anything wet in here, maybe I should just leave," Jena replied.

Jean-Jacque grabbed Jena by the waist and stared at her like a fawn in the forest coming up from a drink of water. He leaned forward and kissed her. Their lips, tongue and breathing intertwined in a moment of pure bliss. "I don't think we should do what both you and I want to do. Because your virginity is worth a million dollars; we're playing with fire here!"

Her eyes welled with tears, and she whimpered, "It won't be worth anything if I don't share it with you!"

Jean-Jacque couldn't resist temptation any longer. He lifted Jena up off her feet and carried her over to his bed and laid her down upon his mattress. He undressed himself as he stood over her lying down waiting for him to mount her.

Jean-Jacque climbed into bed with Jena, unbuttoned her blouse and looked down upon her naked breast in awe. He lowered himself down on top of her; kissed her neck, collar bone, and then her erect nipples one at a time.

His hands hovered over her body at snail's pace, then he lowered her panties down to her ankles. Jena kicked them off across the room, while he unbuttoned her skirt exposing her are naked body. He sat there amazed at how mesmerizing she looked to him au naturel.

Jean-Jacque didn't waste any time, he entered Jena inch by inch; stopping at each increment when she grimaced in discomfort from his bulging penis penetrating her tight, moist, virgin vagina.

Jean-Jacque felt the tension in her body release, he trusts his penis deep inside her until she yelled out in ecstasy. Jean-Jacque stopped trusting and looked down at Jena as her eyes were clinched closed tight and a steady stream of tears cascaded down from them.

Jean-Jacque took out his penis from her vagina and Jena opened her eyes and looked up at him. "What is wrong? Why did you pull out?" asked Jena.

"I want you to ride this dick! It would be less painful if you were on top. Besides, I want to see what your come face looks like as I look up at you," Jean-Jacque replied.

Jena smiled and nodded yes, in agreement to his request. They changed positions and she mounted him slowly but surely. He felt how wet and warm her pussy was as it gripped his cock like a boa constrictor does its prey.

It didn't take long until she found a desirable rhythm and she sat up straight and screamed out, "I'm Cumming!"

Jean-Jacque couldn't hold out any longer, he couldn't pull out fast enough, so he ejaculated inside her. Jena dropped down on top of Jean-Jacque and exhaled. She laid on top of his bare chest panting, sweaty and motionless.

"You know we just ruined your future in The Program!" exclaimed Jean-Jacque.

"I don't give a fuck, I'm in love, and I lost my virginity to my man! If that means I will be poor for the rest of my life, so be it. It was well worth it. You can't put a price tag on a moment like this. It is priceless!

"Besides, how will they find out that I'm not a virgin anymore? What are they going to do to check out if my Hymen is

143

still intact? Please let them try and find it, I bet you they can't because it's all over your dick and these sheets," Jena replied.

Jean-Jacque looked down and noticed that his bedspread was covered with virgin blood.

"Trust me they have ways of finding out that your Hymen is broken. That is something that can't be put back together," Jean-Jacque said.

"Don't worry about a thing, lover boy. Now, could you please take me home, so my mother won't worry about where I am. If you want to be concerned about disappointing someone, be afraid of what my mother might do when she finds out that I won't be a virgin on my wedding day," Jena replied.

Jena got up and walked over to the bathroom and turned on the faucet in the shower. Jean-Jacque got out of the bed and turned on the light in the bedroom. He saw her blood all over his thousand count Egyptian cotton sheets. Jean-Jacque looked for the peroxide, so he could pour it on the stains.

Jean-Jacque found the bottle and began spreading it down on the stains liberally. Then he took the sheet off the bed and placed it in the corner on top of the hamper.

Jean-Jacque walked into the bathroom naked and saw Jena standing there with her back facing him and the water pouring down from the shower head. He snuck in the shower stall behind her and put his hands around her stomach and kissed her softly on her neck.

Jena wasn't frightened at all; she welcomed his embrace, and he took the soap and rag from her hands and began soaping up her body.

After he finished soaping her up, she turned around and reciprocated the same gesture for him. They both finished bathing and Jean-Jacque turned off the water and exited the shower stall. He hands her a clean towel at the same time he took one for himself. They both dry off, walked into the room where they got dressed.

The sound of the elevator echoed throughout the loft. "What is that noise?" asked Jena.

"Oh, that's the elevator! That could only be Latrice, Patrice, or the both of them coming inside the apartment. Come on let's go! They're more than likely going to have some people over, and I don't mingle with their friends," Jean-Jacque replied.

As Jean-Jacque and Jena walked down the stairs from his bedroom holding hands, the gate leading to the loft from the elevator opened. There stood his cousins, Latrice and Patrice. Latrice stepped inside the loft first from the elevator holding a brown paper bag full of grocery items. She looked up at Jean-Jacque and saw Jena coming down the stairs with him. "Kouzen tanpri di m ou pa t '" (Cousin please tell me you didn't!)

Patrice entered the loft, closed the gate behind her and glanced up at her cousin. She walked over to the kitchen where Latrice stood and placed her bags of groceries on the counter next to the rest of them.

The twins stood there in a state of suspended animation; frightened by the sight of their cousin coming downstairs with a new prospect in The Program.

Jean-Jacque walked over to his cousins, wrapped his arms around both of them and whispered, "Please don't make a scene, I'll explain later!"

The twins pushed Jean-Jacque off of them and kissed their teeth. "Non, eksplike kounye a!" (No, explain now!) exclaimed the twins simultaneously.

Jean-Jacque turned around and told Jena, "Meet me downstairs by the truck, I'll be there in a minute. I have to speak with my cousins for a moment."

Jena turned to the elevator, and Jean-Jacque stopped her.

"Where is my manners, ladies this is my girlfriend, Jena. And baby, these are my favorite cousins Latrice and Patrice," Jean-Jacque said.

"Hello, pleased to meet you, Jean has told us nothing about you," Patrice replied.

Latrice folded her arms across her chest, and her lips twisted

145

to the side in disbelief. She was steadfast in her reservations of the situation as it unfolded.

Jena entered the elevator and before she closed it, Jean-Jacque said, "I won't be long."

His cousins looked at him with disgust, as the elevator went down. Latrice pulled Jean-Jacque's arm from around her and slammed her hand down on the counter. "How could you? You just ruined that girl's life, and the lives of everyone else around her. Mayor Meléndez is going to come after you! How could you be so irresponsible?" asked Latrice.

"You mean to tell me that this girl is so important to you that you're willing to throw everything we worked for," Patrice said.

"You are a selfish, fucking bastard. I should shoot the both of you myself and save Mayor Meléndez the trouble of enlisting his henchmen to do it. Patrice and I had to fuck that nasty Russian Diplomat. Lucky for us that he didn't pop our cherries because he wasn't well endowed. ——"

"What's your point Latrice?" asked Jean-Jacque.

"Her point is, that we all been through The Program, we have almost made it through law school at St. John's University. We are one semester away from achieving our degrees.

"After we passed the bar both Patrice and I, will be lawyers. I am not willing to throw all that away because you couldn't keep your fucking dick in your pants!" exclaimed Patrice.

"Ladies, I know I fucked up! I don't know what I was thinking! It was a lack of judgment on my part, to allow myself to succumb to a temporary weakness of the flesh. I don't know what I should do. The deed is done, and I will have to face the consequences of my actions on my own," Jean-Jacque replied.

Jean-Jacque couldn't wait for the elevator to return back upstairs so he raced down the steps to meet Jena in the parking garage. Panting like a dog trying to cool himself down on a hot day. He motioned his fingers in the direction of his truck, giving himself time to catch his breath.

"Come on, let's go!" said Jean-Jacque.

He opened Jena's door first and helped her into the truck. He jogged around the rear of the truck to the driver's side and hopped in.

Jean-Jacque put the key in the ignition, started it up, pulled the lever down from park to drive, and drove out of the building into the street. He was focused on the traffic, avoiding the inevitable explanation to Jena of what just happened.

She crossed her leg over in his direction and folded her arms across her chest. Jena stared at Jean-Jacque until he glanced over at her—— "You know that was rude as hell Claude! What was that about with your cousins? Why did you have to speak with them in private? Were you three talking shit about me behind my back?" said Jena.

"Yes, we were! At least they were, I just listened. Believe me, I was just as perturbed as you are right now. But they're just looking out for our best interest at hand. All of our well beings! They both went through The Program and are both reaping the benefits. They're just worried about me," Jean-Jacque replied.

"Well, they don't have to worry about a thing! I'm a big girl, and I can take care of myself; Thank you very much. I understand their concerns, but I made up my mind and I don't regret what I decided to do. Are you regretful of what we shared together, Claude?"

"No, not really! I know what can happen if Mayor Meléndez ever found out what we've done together. If you and I aren't concerned now, trust me, we will be."

"Are you scared Loverboy? Give me your hand, I promise, I will protect you!"

For the first time in his life, Jean-Jacque felt like someone else other than his parents and Jerome, finally loved him. He gripped her hand tight, put it up to his lips, kissed the back of her hand. "Jena, I feel safer already!"

They sat there holding hands listening to his jazz music the entire ride back to the Bronx. After Jean-Jacque dropped off Jena at home, he drove up the street where everything transpired earlier that day.

Jean-Jacque parked on Watson and Boynton Avenue, got out the truck and slammed the door behind him. He walked over to a group of people standing at the spot where Rodrigo was stabbed and killed earlier that day. He approached the group and noticed that Jamie, Darrelle, Marques, and Raheem were there paying their respects to Rodrigo.

A few females from the neighborhood placed some lit candles on the sidewalk. Some of Rodrigo's boys put down a few unopened bottles of his favorite drink, Bacardi Limon, down beside the candles.

Marques opened a bottle of his own Bacardi Limon and pour it out on the sidewalk. "This is for my nigga who ain't here, he left us too soon! We miss you Bro!" said Marques.

Jean-Jacque shook hands with all the guys there except for Marques, who was busy pouring out liquor on Rodrigo's behalf. "What the fuck you doing here? This ain't your hood, you might be cool with Jamie, but you ain't no friend of mine! Didn't you have beef with Rodrigo?" asked Marques.

Jean-Jacque moved through the crowd like a shark swim through water towards its prey. Marques smashed the bottle of Bacardi Limon on the ground and met him halfway. They stood toe to toe, and everyone around them tried to intervene, but he waved them off. "Nah, let him speak!" replied Jean-Jacque.

"I should fuck you up for what you did to my boy!"

"Maybe you should fuck me up, but know that I did what I had to do to defend what your boy did to my girl! If Jena was your girl, and he groped her and tried to snuff her. What would you do?"

"That wouldn't happen to me, niggas know not to fuck with nothing of mines! I'd body a nigga first! They know how I get down! Trust!"

"You see! So, why are you in my face like I violated your

man's for?"

"Cause you not from around here!"

Marques pulled out a 9 mm pistol, cocked it back and pointed it Jean-Jacque's forehead. Darnel ran towards them and stepped in-between the two men and put his hands on their chests.

"What the fuck are you doing Mark, chill! Everyone saw Rodrigo violate Jena! He did what any of us would do! Besides, I wanna thank y'all for holding me down earlier! I should be locked up right now, but people vouched for me, and now all I have to do is make a statement down at the precinct," Darnel said.

"I got weed and blunts! Let's go up to Darrelle's roof and get high as fuck!" said Raheem.

Everyone left standing there all agreed and walked down the block to Darrelle's building. On their way up to the roof, Darnel started beat boxing and Raheem started free styling.

"It is I, the dead living guy, with red eyes, 16 bar Jedi, I leave tracks with a led line. Me and my team's motto is 'Get dough or die.' We puff lah, 'til our eyes cry blood, half thug half gentleman, millennium man. Rah 2k, me and PR touchdown on bitches like the squeeze play! N.F.L" (Niggas for life), Raheem said.

Everyone went into a frenzy. "Yo, you are nice man! You should pursue that rap shit! represent Watson Avenue! You need to put the Bronx back on the map!" said Darnel.

Raheem sparked up the blunt and passed it to Marques, he slapped it away from him and furrowed his eyebrows. "Get that laced weed shit the fuck away from me! We heard from the grapevine that you smoke wet, nigga! I ain't on that shit!" said Marques.

Raheem lunged at Marques, swung a fist at his face and missed. "You know how much money I spent on that weed? You better give me back my money!" replied Raheem.

Jamie and Darnel held him back, and Marques dug in his pants pocket and tossed a hand full of money at Raheem. They let him go, he bent down to pick up the money off the ground.

149

"You lucky I'm in a good mood Mark," Raheem said.

Darnel brought weed that he already rolled up. He sparked it up and passed the blunt around to everyone there.

Twenty minutes later, Darrelle found the blunt that Marques slapped from Raheem's hand and he picked it up. He lit it up and took a long drag off the embalming fluid laced blunt. Darrelle's eyes rolled up into his head, he stumbled backwards and fell over the side of the roof onto a parked car.

Everyone else left on the roof ducked down and looked over where the loud bang came from. They all ran over to the ledge and down at Darrelle laid out on the roof of the parked car.

"Oh shit, Darrelle dead son!" exclaimed Marques.

"Nah, look, he's still moving! He's still alive!" said Jamie.

Marques punched Raheem in the face and knocked him down to the ground. "I told you stop fucking with that wet shit! Now look at what you did! You almost killed Darrelle," said Marques.

They all raced downstairs, but by the time they got there. A crowd already surrounded Darrelle on the roof of the car. A few people help take him off the roof and put him down on the ground. He was bleeding out from his mouth, ears and nose. Darrelle also had blood running from the back of his head. His mother and older brother ran out the building asking questions, but nobody there knew what had happened.

The police and ambulance arrived a short time after everyone made it outside. The cops immediately made all the men there assume the position soon after they arrived on the scene. They checked everyone's identification and pockets.

Marques didn't have any ID, but he had a loaded gun on him, so they handcuffed him and put him in the back of the squad car.

"Arrest them too, they're all responsible for hurting my baby!" said Darrelle's mother aloud.

She walked over to Raheem, slapped him across his face,

and Darrelle's older brother grabbed her from behind.

"If I find out that you had something to do with this, with that, that laced weed of yours; I am gonna hunt you down and kill you myself!" said Darrelle's mother.

Darrelle's older brother held her back, and the police put handcuffs on Raheem Jamie, Darnel, Jean-Jacque, and put them in squad cars too.

The Paramedic and an EMT, worked on Darrelle and got him hooked up to an IV drip. They put him on a gurney, rolled it into the back of the ambulance and drove off with him. The squad cars holding everyone else the cops arrested, sped off afterwards.

They all watched Darrelle's mother crying hysterically on the sidewalk as they all rode inside the backs of the police cruisers.

While at the precinct, before the cops fingerprinted anyone. They brought all of them into different interrogation rooms. Jean-Jacque was handcuffed to a table when a plane closed officer walked in and closed the door behind him. He held a folder in one hand and a hot cup of coffee in the other.

The cop dropped the folder down on the table and crime scene photos spilled out from the murders of Terrance, Stacy, Tuffy, Rodrigo and Jaleel from earlier. This was the first time that he saw the dead bodies of these men. Surprised, Jean-Jacque sat up straight in his chair.

"My name is Det. Dudley; do you know who did these murders?" asked Det. Dudley.

Jean-Jacque hesitated to answer at first, then the detective stood up and tossed the cup of coffee over Jean-Jacque's head at the wall. "Answer Me, God Damn It!"

Jean-Jacque didn't look at the photos, he shook his head no. "If you don't release me right now, y'all be in Alaska writing people parking tickets by the end of the week," Jean-Jacque said.

The detective lunged at Jean-Jacque and grabbed him by the front of his shirt and pulled him close to him. "What the fuck did you just say to me?" asked Det. Dudley.

151

At that moment the door opened, and a female officer walked in and interrupted the interrogation and said, "Detective Dudley that's enough!"

She leaned into the detective's ear and whispered to him, then walked out of the interrogation room. The detective sighed, walked over to Jean-Jacque and unlocked his handcuffs.

"You must have friends in high places, you're free to go!" said Det. Dudley.

"What about my friends? How's Darrelle doing?" asked Jean-Jacque.

"They're going to be released too! Rest assured we're gonna get y'all soon! Your luck is going to run out one of these days, trust me!"

"Remember, by the end of the week you will be in Alaska. So, dress warm!"

As Jean-Jacque walked past the interrogation rooms where his friends were held in, they all walked out one by one except for Darnel.

"What about Darnel?" asked Jean-Jacque.

"No, can do; this kid is on video shooting and killing someone earlier today! He's going to need a lawyer! An excellent lawyer, to help him beat this murder rap!" replied the police officer.

Determined to face the challenge, Jean-Jacque looked at the officer and smirked. "We'll see about that!"

"Yo, I got you, son! You are coming out soon! You're gonna beat this! I promise you! That's my word!" said Jean-Jacque.

Chapter 9:

Out on Bail

Walking out of the 43rd precinct, Jean-Jacque noticed detectives Martins and Cooper in another interrogation room. He had hoped never to ever cross paths with those two again. Jean-Jacque looked up at the clock in the precinct and saw that it was 6:00 am. He realized that he and his friends were down at the police station all night long.

After he stepped outside, Jamie, Marques, and Raheem followed soon afterward. "Damn! Now I have to walk back to Watson Avenue to get my truck," Jean-Jacque thought to himself.

Marques walked off the steps of the precinct and headed straight up the street., "y'all niggas just gonna stand there? If you stay, they might tell you to come back inside because you fit a description. Then you mother fuckers would be here all day! C'mon, let's go! We gotta walk across the bridge back to the block," He said.

"Yeah, let's go to that diner over on Morrison and have some breakfast, I'm buying," Jean-Jacque replied.

"Breakfast! His treat! You ain't gotta tell me twice!" said Jamie and Raheem in unison.

All four of them walked towards the overpass that stretched over the Bruckner Blvd Expressway. This highway did two things: one, it gave motorists, a pathway through arguably the roughest part of the Bronx to Manhattan. Two, it helped keep the street kids from Watson and Sound View separated.

This rivalry between the two neighborhoods is much older than many people who live on either side of the Bruckner. It was like the feud between Hatfields and the McCoys. But the people that live there still participate in the senseless tradition 'til this day.

Much to his amazement, Marques checked his pockets and found a blunt. He turned to the guys and raised it in the air.

"Look what I found!" said Marques.

He also located a book of matches and sparked up the blunt he just found.

"Where the fuck you hid that at? I hope you ain't boof that L!" replied Raheem.

"Even if I did, smoking a blunt with shit residue on it ain't half as harmful as the embalming fluid laced weed you smoke. You stay fucking with that wet!" said Marques.

"Can't we all just get along!" replied Jamie.

Everyone laughed.

"Anyone heard that Ironman album yet?" asked Jamie.

Marques and Raheem shook their heads no, as they continued to walk towards the bridge, passing the blunt around, amongst themselves.

"Well, I have the CD, and I have these booming speaker headphones too! y'all about to hear it now!" replied Jamie.

Jamie pressed play on his portable Sony Discman, CD player of Ghostface Killah's: Ironman album. It wasn't even available in the stores yet. The guys shared the blunt and listened to a masterpiece of American hip-hop, by the Wu-tang clan.

Before long, they reached the diner, and the establishment was empty. The waitress offered them a booth that accommodated all of them. She put four menus down on the table.

"Good morning, fellas, can I take your order?" asked the waitress.

"Yeah, we want two stacks of pancakes, a big plate of scrambled cheese eggs, six sausages, a dozen crisp bacon strips and home fries," Marques said.

The waitress wrote down the order, put the notepad in her apron. She picked up the menus off the table and Jamie grabbed her wrist.

"Hold up, I want to order a slice of cheese pizza and mint tea," Jamie said.

Everyone at the table, including the waitress looked at him funny. Wondering why he would order lunch or dinner food at breakfast time.

"Fuck y'all, I'm hungry and I want pizza!" exclaimed Jamie.

The waitress picked up all the menus after the table's order was filled. She walked away from the table and Jean-Jacque got everyone's attention at the table.

"Listen up, it's only a matter of time that one day either one of you catches a case, like Darnel, or we end up dead. We gotta switch shit up. I got a plan; give me a few days to hash things out and I'll lay it on y'all soon. Trust me!" said Jean-Jacque.

The waitress returned to the table with a pitcher of water, some empty cups, and glasses filled with orange juice for everyone, except Jamie. He ordered mint tea.

"Hold on, we didn't order orange juice," Raheem said.

"I know, it's on the house; we recognize Mr. Cadet from the news. We here at this diner want to extend our gratitude," replied the waitress.

The staff tipped their hats at Jean-Jacque's and he nodded his head in acknowledgement. Not long after, the food they ordered was placed on the table. It resembled a continental breakfast at a five-star hotel. Jamie got his pizza, then reached for the saltshaker. He didn't realize that the container he reached for was sugar. He poured it all over the slice, and the entire table erupted in laughter.

Marques was the first to ridicule Jamie.

"Yo! You ain't know that was sugar? We gotta start calling you sugar slice!" said Marques.

"Fuck you Mark! Or should I say, Baby Huey!" retorts Jamie, as he scraped off the sugar granules from his slice.

The entire diner erupted in an uproar. It sounded like Def Comedy Jam, live and uncut.

When the laughter subsided a bit, Marques retorted with a zinger.

155

"Fuck you, Jamie! That's why you look like Mojo from the X-men!" said Marques.

Now the waitress, the cashier, and the cooks in the kitchen laughed and held their sides.

Jean-Jacque took some money out his pocket, dropped it on the table to pay for the food. "I ain't fucking with y'all, I am walking back to the block to get my truck, I'm gonna bounce! Besides, I gotta make a few phone calls to get Darnel a Defense Attorney," he said.

After everyone at the table gave Jean-Jacque dap. He walked out of the diner by himself, while the rest of the guys stayed there and finished eating their breakfast.

Jean-Jacque took in a long breath of fresh air to clear his head. He was unsure if he wanted to continue to walk towards where his truck was parked or take the train. He stood at the train station at Morrison and Westchester Ave. for a few moments when he could hear the 6-train barreling down the tracks from a distance. The train stopped at St. Lawrence, so he only had a few moments to decide if he wanted to take the train.

Jean-Jacque looked down at his shoes and said, "Feet don't fail me now!"

After forty-five minutes of walking in dress shoes, it can be murder on a person's feet. So, he ran up the steps to the platform, flashed the teller the identification he acquired from getting the key to the city. One of the perks of being a Good Samaritan.

The teller buzzed him through the gate, and Jean-Jacque ran up the stairs leading up to the platform where the oncoming 6 train just pulled into a screeching halt. After the doors opened and passengers alighted the train, he boarded the train and stood by the doors.

The train car was filled with passengers heading off to work or school. It was rush hour, in the city that never sleeps, at any given hour there's loads of people moving throughout the city, especially on public transportation!

Jean-Jacque got off the 6 train at the Elder avenue station.

Which was just one station up from Morrison Avenue station. But, that quick trip saved Jean-Jacque a twenty-minute walk. As the train doors opened, he got off and hurried down the stairs outside on Elder Avenue. Jean-Jacque knew that he still had to walk up one more long New York City block. He had to get to Watson Avenue, where his truck was parked.

He made it to the truck in no time, opened the driver's side door and hopped inside. Before Jean-Jacque started the truck, he reached inside the armrest, took out the flip phone and called Marisol. The phone rang twice before she picked up the phone.

"Good morning, Busy bee, to what do I owe the pleasure?" said Marisol.

"My friends and I were arrested last night. Most of us got released, but the police held on to one of my friends Darnel. He was involved in an altercation last night that resulted in him shooting someone in self-defense. The police claim to have surveillance footage of the entire incident. He needs a defense attorney, could you please set him up with one!" replied Jean-Jacque.

There was a long silence on the other end of the line.

"Hello! Hello! Did you hear anything I just said, Marisol?" asked Jean-Jacque.

"Yes, Busy bee! Who do you think bailed you and your friends out in the first place? I already sent a reputable attorney to the precinct where Darnel is being held. Don't worry about it! I got it covered," Marisol replied.

Jean-Jacque relaxed a moment and sighed in relief, that his friend was going to get representation that he desperately needed. At least now he will get a fair trial, and possibly even beat the murder case.

"Thank you, Marisol! But how did you know I got brought down to the precinct for questioning?" asked Jean-Jacque.

"You're not the only one who has friends in high places. I'll talk to you later. Have a great day. You should go home and get some rest. After all, you've been out all night long!" replied

Marisol.

Marisol hung up the phone, and Jean-Jacque sat there in his truck wondering how the hell she knew about his whereabouts. It kind of creeped him out, it seemed as if he was under surveillance, like she's been keeping tabs on him. If he is indeed under surveillance. What else does she and Mayor Meléndez know about who or what he had been doing lately.

Summer was in full swing, and Jean-Jacque has been trying to stay low key. It has been about a month since everything transpired on his graduation day. Jean-Jacque landed an internship at the mayor's office, under the tutelage of the Deputy Mayor, Marisol Velasquez.

With his new internship, Jean-Jacque thinks that acquiring a degree would only be to appease his parents' wishes for him. Jean-Jacque received acceptance letters from prestigious universities like Georgetown, Princeton, Northwestern, Stanford, and NYU. He also got one from M.I.T, but that's out of the question on account of what calamities happened with his father during his tenure there.

Jean-Jacque decided to go to school at NYU to study Political Science. Per the advice of his mentor, Marisol. He hasn't told his father about his decision yet, but he knew he would be proud. After all, his dad was the head of the Mathematics Department there at the University.

Jean-Jacque hadn't seen Jena since he dropped her off that night of his graduation. He won't admit to it, but he misses her. Jean-Jacque has grown quite fond of Jeneration. She's beautiful, both street and book smart, sophisticated, and multi-faceted, much like himself.

It was Friday night; Marisol and Jean-Jacque went down to club Divvy Divvies. Jean-Jacque was headlining, and there will be some new talent performing there. Mayor Meléndez entered the club and was seated directly upfront next to Marisol at his usual table. Their drink orders were taken and brought over to them. Jean-Jacque made his way backstage and greeted the rest of the band before curtain call.

The velvet curtain opened to a packed ballroom. Jean-Jacque initiated the performance with a few notes from his saxophone. Then the pianist fingered the keys of the piano. Then the cellist, strung up the bass and the trumpets flared, capping off the intros of each instrument.

The melodic sound of the ensemble playing Jazz, filled the ballroom. The smell of cigarette smoke, whiskey, and the indiscriminate chatter of people inside club Divvy Divvies, filled the room.

After the number was done, the curtain closed to the patrons' loud applause in the ballroom. The MC grabbed the 1940s style microphone with a lit cigarette in the same hand as a short glass of cognac.

Jean-Jacque made his way off stage and sat at the table with Mayor Meléndez and Marisol.

"Our next performer is not only new, but she's going to do something that's never been done here at club Divvy Divvies. Give a warm welcome for Jeneration, and she will be reciting poetry here for the first time!" said the announcer.

People applauded, and some began to snap. Jena walked over to the microphone, griped it with her right hand and pulled it closer to her mouth. "Goodnight, ladies and gentlemen, my name is Jena short for Jeneration and this piece is titled:

"I forgot

For a moment, I forgot about the power I felt when I discovered love. I forgot the joy that moment brought me, I forgot the scars that it helped to heal. I forgot those dreadful tears it finally dried. For a moment, I'd forgotten about the power of love.

"I forgot the lives that it saved, I forgot the shelter that it gave to those lost and troubled souls seeking refuge. OMG, how could I have forgotten about the power I felt when I first found LOVE. Love is something that so many people spend a lifetime searching for, yearning for, crying for, and praying for love to rescue them from obscurity.

159

"So many hearts worn on sleeves, so many souls have gone out on a limb like leaves, only to be left out in the storm alone and slowly dying inside. For a moment, I forgot about my first love. Profoundly enough, that it was only for a moment. Thank you!"

The crowd snapped as Jena stepped away from the microphone and walked off the stage. Jean-Jacque got up and headed backstage to greet her. As they both saw each other, they embraced, and Jean-Jacque kissed Jena on the cheek.

"You look amazing! You did amazing! Do you hear the announcer complimenting your performance! I am moved, that was beautiful!" said Jean-Jacque.

Jena stepped back away from Jean-Jacque and asked him, "Where have you been all summer? I've been hanging around a man named Arthur Rosenbaum for a couple of weeks. He claimed that he was grooming me. I don't know what that means, but he seems well connected in the city.

"I see why you like being around these people, there are people here who are movers and shakers in New York. If you get in good with them everything is smooth sailing," Jena replied.

"Do you want to get out of here?" asked Jean-Jacque.

Jena looked at Jean-Jacque with love in her eyes and nodded her head yes. Jena and Jean-Jacque walked side by side through the ballroom and exited the club. Much to the chagrin of Marisol, and Author Rosenbaum who noticed them walking out the club together.

The valet drove up his truck after he gave him the ticket. Jena and Jean-Jacque got into his truck, she crossed her legs and folded her arms.

"Where are we headed?" asked Jena.

"You'll see when we get there!" replied Jean-Jacque.

Jean-Jacque drove a short distance and he parked the truck in a parking spot. Her eyes lit up when Jena looked at where they were and noticed that they were outside the Nuyorican Poets Café.

"What are we doing here?"

"You'll see!"

He got out of the truck, closed his door, walked over to her side, opened Jena's door, bowed and said, "Madame!"

Jena exited the truck, and they bypassed the line and walked inside the club hand in hand. The bouncer opened the door for Jena and Jean-Jacque and gave them both a nod. Jean-Jacque escorted Jena to a table and whispered to her, "I will be right back," he said.

Jean-Jacque walked towards the stage as a performer finished their piece. The announcer snapped his fingers, grabbed the microphone with one hand and said, "Ladies and gentlemen you are in for a treat! This talented young man who's about to touch the stage, is a Jazz Musician. He needs no introduction, he's a regular here at the Nuyorican Poets Café. Please give it up for Claude!"

Jean-Jacque grabbed the microphone and adjusted the mic stand up to his height. "Give it up for the host of the show!"

Everyone snapped their fingers and Jean-Jacque smiled. "I am going to do something different tonight. I will be reciting poetry. This piece is titled:

"Foreigners: Bound by Honor, Betrayed by Trust!
While my blood is put on fire during the overhauling of my country of origin
As this "shystem" crumbles, I don't know how or when I will be whole again.
My people were prematurely harvested from our land. And directly trekked across an ocean for the use of our hands. Most of them, lay in shallow graves under the ocean floor.
Chained to each other, like paper cut out origami.
Stretching from shores of home to the shores of the unknown.
From Sierra Leone, to Saint-Domingue, with sweat dripping from our brows. And blood oozing from whelps on our backs. We bear this perpetual burden like Sisyphus.
Knees deep in the trenches, sustained only by bonbon te'
Protected by a shield gilded from pride. And mixed with tears streaming out of our eyes, covered by a cloak conjured by the practice of vodoun.
Those enslavers, tried to work us to the brink of our humanity.

161

Much like the indigenous people of Hayti before us. But our will,
wouldn't give out.
They devised a plan to conquer us, with biological and
psychological warfare.
Through racism, classism, and colorism but our immune system is
stout.
On August 22, 1791, led by Toussaint Louverture,
we started to revolt and fought our way out from underneath
subjugation.
Jean Jacque Dessalines aided in securing victory,
declaring independence after the revolution, on January 1, 1804.
Trodden down the beaten path through perdition, yearning for
restitution.
From the clutches of our captures, with our stolen legacy in tote.
The Colonizers sealed the fate of some when they wrote their
constitution on stolen land.
We survived the 1937 Parsley Massacre, propagated by
Rafael Trujillo, from the onset of xenophobia.
We won't wait in vain for our salvation.
Whenever, if ever the rapture, comes to fruition," Jean-Jacque said.

The crowd including Jena snapped their fingers then
transitioned to a standing ovation. Jean-Jacque exited the stage and
Jena waited for him with opened arms. Jean-Jacque led Jena out the
club into a dark alleyway. He forcefully kissed her as the
momentum pushed her against the building next to the Nuyorican
Poets Café.

Jean-Jacque turned Jena around and reached under her skirt
and ripped off her panties with one grab and swipe. He zipped down
his zipper and took out his penis. Before Jean-Jacque entered Jena
turned and threw up all over the side of the building uncontrollably.
This definitely killed the mood, and Jean-Jacque just held back
Jena's hair as she spewed lunch all over the alley.

With his flaccid penis still exposed, Jean-Jacque attended to
Jena's sudden sickness. He discreetly put his penis back inside his
pants. Jena was toppled over and felt bad and embarrassed for
ruining the moment.

They both walked out of the alley towards his truck. Jean-

Jacque asked the obvious question, "Are you ok?"

Jena nodded, yes, while she held her stomach and leaned over on Jean-Jacque's shoulder for support. As they reached the truck, Jean-Jacque opened the passenger's side door, and helped Jena inside the truck. Jean-Jacque walked out in front of the truck and entered the driver's side of the truck. After he started the ignition, Jean-Jacque drove Jena to the Bronx where he intended to drop her off at home.

The entire truck ride back uptown was quiet because Jena was fast asleep. Twenty-five minutes later, Jean-Jacque pulled up in front of Jena's building. He put the truck in park and nudged her awake, "Your home baby!"

The sound of his voice uttering those words of endearment, made her feel much better than she did previously.

Jean-Jacque escorted Jena into her building and guided her up one flight of stairs to her floor. He helped Jena to her apartment and checked her pockets for the house keys. Asia was in the kitchen; when she heard the ruffled noise from the hallway and opened the door.

"Is she drunk?" asked Asia.

"I assume so!" replied Jean-Jacque.

Asia shook her head in disappointment as she aided Jena the rest of the way inside the apartment. Jean-Jacque barely said goodnight, as Asia closed and locked the door on Jean-Jacque.

He stood there alone in the drafty hallway and assumed the worst about Jena's condition. He knew for a fact that she wasn't drunk because underage drinking is not allowed in club Divvy Divvies. The majority of the people who frequently go to the club, are either government officials, lawmakers or work in law enforcement. So, either she had food poisoning or she's pregnant.

Jean-Jacque shuttered at the thought of the latter. So, he sighed, about faced, walked back downstairs one step at a time, and sauntered along. With his shoulders and head drooped down, he shuffled his feet out of the building towards his truck. Jean-Jacque unlocked the door and entered the truck.

After he got in, Jean-Jacque sat there for five minutes, mulling over the possibility of Jena being pregnant. He banged his palms on the steering wheel; and blurted out a few expletives. Knowing first-hand the consequences that would ensue if she is.

Several weeks went by, and the phone rang, while he was interning at The Mayor's office.

"Hello good morning, who do I have the pleasure of speaking with?" asked Jean-Jacque.

Jamie, Asia and Jena called him on three-way, and they laughed at Jean-Jacque's proper phone etiquette. He remained astute and didn't react to them taunting him.

"What can I do for you?" asked Jean-Jacque.

"Good morning, Mr. Key to the city, we were all wondering if you wanted to accompany us to the Labor Day Parade on Eastern Parkway in Brooklyn?" asked Jena.

"What day is it?" replied Jean-Jacque.

"It's the first Monday of September; I know you are busy doing important things, but take a day off to unwind," Asia said.

"Yeah Claude, enjoy some Caribbean music, eat some island food, and celebrate our West Indian culture," Jamie said.

"That sounds like a plan! I'll pencil you in for that date, see you then," Jean-Jacque replied.

He hung up the phone and continued to assist Marisol attend to an important city ordinance issue that needed to be rectified or the plans to erect a commercial property won't be approved.

The first Monday of September rolled around, and it was Labor Day. This national holiday pays homage to all the workers who labored the entire year. It also unofficially marks the end of summer, the beginning of fall, and the beginning of a new school year.

Jean-Jacque kept his word and showed up at Jena's house around eight am in the morning. He tooted his horn and Asia poked her head out the window. "It's about time! We've been eagerly awaiting your arrival, Mr. Key to the city!" said Asia.

Asia ducked her head back inside the apartment and Jean-Jacque walked over to the entrance of the building. He leaned up against his truck and waited for Jena and Asia to come downstairs. Jean-Jacque's smiled when he saw that Jamie accompanied them. He met them halfway as they all walked out of the building to greet him.

Jamie and Jean-Jacque embraced for a moment. He stepped aside and Jena was standing there as stunning as always, wearing a colorful ensemble, commemorating her Dominican and Jamaican heritage with pride.

"Everyone looks so festive with their outfits," Jean-Jacque said.

"Yeah, we're reppin' our Caribbean culture," Jamie replied.

All three of them sported what seemed like touristy attire. But it was all about representing your culture, your heritage that day! The one day where black and brown foreign nationalism is celebrated and not despised. People from all over the tristate area, had intentions on letting everyone know where they were originally from.

The Irish have St. Patrick's Day! The celebration of their patron saint who gained notoriety from his role in dispelling the Twa from off the island.

Mexicans have Cinco de Mayo! The celebration of Mexican nationals commemorating their four father's victory over the Spanish on May 5, during the colonization of Central and South America.

Black Americans have Juneteenth! The celebration of the last state of the confederacy, Texas; recognizing the emancipation proclamation freeing the slaves on the 19th of June 1869.

This parade is the equivalent of Carnival, in the Caribbean, but here in the states. It is all about celebrating freedom from slavery and honoring our ancestors who endured through it.

165

Jamie dug in his back pocket and presented Jean-Jacque with a Haitian flag. He took it and tied it on his head, like one would do with a bandana. He then walked to his truck, opened the trunk and pulled out a large Haitian flag and he tied it around his neck and allowed it to hang off his shoulders like a cape.

Asia laughed, as Jamie and Jena saluted him for his self-expression of Haitian pride.

"What are supposed to be, super negro?" said Asia.

Nobody acknowledged her insensitive, inappropriate joke. Jena just embraced Jean-Jacque and planted a long-anticipated kiss on his lips.

"I missed those lips, Claude. Are you ready to go?" said Jena.

Jean-Jacque closed the trunk and ushered everyone to get inside, but Asia, Jamie and Jena, all declined.

"Nah Claude, we are taking the train; It's tradition!" said Jamie.

Their small tight knit group of four people made their way up Morrison Avenue, to the 6-train station. Upon their arrival on the platform, Jamie, Asia and Jena made their way to the ticket book to pay their fare. Jean-Jacque just took out his badge and the teller buzzed the gate.

"C'mon guys, we're going to miss the train!" said Jean-Jacque.

They all put their money away and hurried up the steps because the train was entering into the station. As the group entered the train, it was packed with passengers heading to the parade. Caribbean and American people were on the train representing their respective countries with flags, colorful outfits, or different color dyes in their hair.

Everyone heading to Eastern Parkway had to transfer at Times Square to get the 4 train. Then they took it out to Brooklyn, where the stop for Eastern Parkway was. After an hour or so of riding the train, they finally arrived at the stop for the parade.

Hundreds of people got off the train and moved up to street level. Vendors were setting tables and the police officers putting up barricades. Everybody eagerly awaited the start of the festivities.

Jean-Jacque ushered everyone towards the Grand Army Plaza entrance, located by Prospect Park Zoo and the Brooklyn botanical gardens. This is where the floats that were going to drive around Prospect Park, and Eastern Parkway, were setting up.

"What float would you like to board for the parade?" asked Jean-Jacque.

"Burning Spear!" replied Jamie, Asia, and Jena in unison, without hesitation.

All West Indian day parade-goers love this highly coveted float. Due to the Roots & Culture music, and good vibes by the respected Reggae Band. Anyone following the float, enjoy endless dancing all day long. Or, as long as the float moved down Eastern Parkway and around the park.

The parade started promptly at 11 am sharp. So, Jean-Jacque wasted no time in getting the group on the float before it departed. He flashed his credentials to the person who seemed to be in charge, then Jamie, Asia, and Jena boarded the Burning Spear float. They did so, just as the clock struck 11:00.

The abrupt movement of the float startled Jena, and she held on to Jean-Jacque's arm as the truck picked up speed. Females we're down on the street, both young and old, wearing bikinis and elaborate costumes. It was adorned with feathered headdresses, blooming like a male peacock during mating season. Others had on their countries flags and some were covered in flour while some men's bare chests were covered with black grease.

As the acoustic sounds from the steel drums serenaded everyone on the street. The aroma of island cuisine filled everyone's noses. Traditional food like jerk chicken, fritters, or pork. Roti, filled with curry chicken, goat, or shrimp. Oxtail, rice, and peas, escovich fish and fried dumpling.

On every corner the float past were different vendors selling food, souvenirs, and or beverages. Mostly Caribbean drinks like

167

Irish moss, roots, ginger beer, ting, cola champagne and coconut water. Sorrell and a wide array of tropical fruit juice like pineapple, guava, passion fruit, soursop, and carrot juice were available too.

Riding along with the band on their float made the group feel like celebrities. The girls were moving to the Soca, and Reggae Music by gyrating their hips to the rhythm. Hours went by, dancing to the rhythm made the group hungry and thirsty.

The moment they decided to get off the float to buy some food from the vendors, four men walked on the truck holding bags of food and a variety of beverages. Perks of being a Good Samaritan.

The group on the float ate and drank until they had their fill.

"We can't be distant from the people dancing on the streets in the parade. We're missing out on the best part," said Jamie.

They all agreed with Jamie to get off the float and party alongside everyone else in the parade. They all said their goodbyes to the band and the other people on the float and thanked them for the food and drinks.

As they all made it to the street, Jamie started dancing with one of the females wearing a costume. Asia didn't seem bothered by the site of seeing her man dancing with another girl. She just joined in on the action and danced behind Jamie.

Jena stayed extremely close to Jean-Jacque as the group walked and danced along with the people moving with the floats. They witnessed two Rastafarian men wielding sharp machetes, one in each of their hands, move through the crowd unabated. Then a small group of people moved through the crowd swiftly throwing ice cold milk around at everyone they passed by.

Jena leaned in towards Jean-Jacque, pull him close enough to her, and whispered in his ear, "My 17th birthday is coming up in two weeks. My parents are having a party for me. I also got into UNLV, so we are celebrating that as well," said Jena.

Jean-Jacque turned to Jena, lifted her up, twirled her around in the air. "Congratulations! I know your parents are proud of you. I have good news too, I got into a university too. I am going to NYU," he replied.

After about a few hours of dancing, walking, and listening to music. Everyone was very tired, so they decided to get on the train. They located the train station nearest to them, and Jean-Jacque flashed his credentials at the teller, after they cleared the stairs that led them to the subway.

Then the group walked through the open gate toward the platform. The train took about ten minutes to arrive. This gave the foursome plenty of time to couple up and canoodle.

The train arrived and everyone boarded the express train to Times Square. The four train only made a few stops before arriving at their stop that they needed to transfer to the six train that went to the part of the Bronx where they lived.

The train ride was long, and people were quiet during the ride. Everyone was beat from all the dancing at the parade. Before long the Morrison Avenue stop was next, and the group prepared themselves to get off the train. Tired and weary from the long day. They dreaded the long walk back to Jena and Asia's apartment building.

"Finally! I don't want to use my feet to do anything else for at least a week!" said Asia.

Then others shook their heads in agreement. Jean-Jacque and Jamie didn't even attempt to follow the ladies upstairs to their front door. They both just kissed each of their girlfriend's goodbye and made their way towards Jean-Jacque's truck.

Jamie put his hand out attempted to say his goodbyes to Jean-Jacque, but he pushed his hand away and said, "Nah bro! Get in! I'm going to drop you off at your house. We walked enough today don't you think." Jamie shrugged his shoulders and got back into Jean-Jacque's truck.

He drove up Watson Avenue towards Manor Avenue where he made a left turn and continued towards the Bruckner Blvd. Claude waited patiently until the traffic let up, then he made a right turn and drove one block, then turned up Ward Avenue and stopped

169

in front of Jamie house.

Jamie slightly opened the door then looked back at Jean-Jacque.

"We had mad fun today! I'm glad you came with us! We're going to be reminiscing on this day for the next ten years!" said Jamie.

Jean-Jacque and Jamie dapped each other's fist together and Jamie closed the truck door behind him. Claude beeped the horn twice as Jamie opened the gate to the front of his house.

Two weeks had passed, and it was the day of Jena's party. Jean-Jacque stood in his bathroom checking himself out in the mirror, when Latrice walked inside his room and said, "Hey cousin, looking good! Where are you going tonight looking so debonair?"

"Don't you two ever knock? I'm going to Jena's birthday party! Would you and Patrice like to come?" replied Jean-Jacque.

"No, I don't chaperone kid parties, besides Patrice and I are going out for drinks with these twin brothers we met last week."

Jean-Jacque sighed, turned, and faced Latrice. She noticed how nervous he looked.

"What's wrong cousin? Are you nervous about meeting her father?!" said Latrice.

Jean-Jacque shook his head yes.

"Good for you! If you didn't fuck that girl and took her virginity, you wouldn't have to be nervous. I don't feel sorry for you at all. You made your bed, now lay in it!" retorted Latrice.

"Thanks cousin, I rather enjoyed your pep talk!" replied Jean-Jacque's.

He shut off the light in the bathroom and walked downstairs and headed towards the front door of the loft. He saw Patrice in the kitchen drinking from a bottle of water and nodded is head at her.

"Take care cousin! Don't do anything that I wouldn't do!" replied Patrice.

Before she finished her quip, Jean-Jacque was already out of the apartment. He took the stairs to the parking garage and walked towards his truck. He got inside, started it up and forgot to take the gift he'd bought for Jena, plus the bouquet of flowers.

As he was going to turn off the truck engine. He saw in his rear-view mirror Latrice and Patrice holding the flowers and the box with the gift in their hands.

Jean-Jacque got out of his truck with a huge smile on his face.

"Did you forget something?" said Patrice.

Jean-Jacque kissed them both on their foreheads and hugged them both. "Thank you very much, you're a lifesaver!"

"Goodnight, Jean, we will see you in the morning," They both said and placed the items in the back seat of the truck.

Jean-Jacque hopped back into his truck, closed the door and drove towards the FDR Drive East heading to the Bronx. Traffic was light, so the drive wasn't that long. He arrived in front of Jena's building and found a parking spot nearby.

Without delay he pulled his seat forward so he could retrieve the flowers and the gift he had brought there for Jena. He made sure not to damage the box or mess up the beautiful floral arrangement.

As Jean-Jacque entered the building, he heard Spanish music blaring from the second floor. He walked up the stairs following the music emanating from Jena's apartment. When he arrived on the landing the door was open and there were people standing around talking amongst themselves, while holding plates of food and alcohol in their hands.

Asia noticed Jean-Jacque outside trying to navigate through the crowd. She walked over to him and greeted him at the entrance. "Goodnight, Mr. Key to the city! Nice of you to make it," she said.

She kissed him on the cheek and escorted him inside where Jena, her mother and father were standing in the kitchen talking amongst themselves.

Jena noticed that Jean-Jacque was standing there, and she

171

smiled. "Mom you've met Claude before, but dad this is my boyfriend, Claude," she said.

Jena's mother kissed Jean-Jacque on the cheek and took the flowers from him. "Those are beautiful flowers Jean; how did you know that daisies and chrysanthemums were my favorite?" asked Mrs. McCubbin.

Jean-Jacque stood there with a bewildered look on his face as Jena's mother took the flowers from his hands.

"I'm going to put this in some water right away!"

"Jean-Jacque this is my father Dr. Augustus McCubbin, but people call him Mr. Easy. Maybe you two should talk, I am going to help mom with the flowers."

Before she walked away Jean-Jacque handed her the present he got for her, and her face lit up. "Thank you, I didn't expect anything from you Claude," Jena said.

Jena gave Jean-Jacque a big hug, then she hurried over to where her mother was tending to the flowers.

Jena's father extended his hand and gripped his hand tight around Jean-Jacque's hand. "Boyfriend! How cums dis a di fos mi ah hear bout boyfriend!" asked Mr. McCubbin.

Jean-Jacque grimaced and struggled to pull his hand away from Mr. McCubbin's clutches. "I am not sure sir!" replied Jean-Jacque.

"Jeneration! Cum yah tuh mi! Cum, Cum taak tuh mi!"

Jena stopped what she was doing and walked over to her father.

"Now tell mi sumtin' yuh mean fi tell mi seh, yuh an dat bwoy deh together? All di try mi an yuh madda try fi raise yuh and Asia right. Yuh a go tell mi seh, di two a unuh hav boyfriend. Next yuh a go tell mi seh yuh a hab baby!" said Mr. McCubbin.

Jena stepped back away from both her father and Jean-Jacque and held both of their hands

"Well, I wasn't going to say anything now to either of you,

but Dad, Claude. I'm pregnant!" said Jena.

"Bumbaclot! A joke yuh ah mek!" replied Mr. McCubbin.

He turned to Jean-Jacque and kissed his teeth.

"Yuh fuck and breed off mi sixteen-year-old daughter?" asked Mr. McCubbin.

Mr. McCubbin slapped Jena across the face and pointed his finger at her to scold her.

"Yuh ah big ooman now eeh! Well den, mek di bwoy mash up yuh life. Mi dun wid yuh. Tek yuh things an cum outta mi yaad, now!

Mr. McCubbin grabbed Jena, but Jean-Jacque put his hand in the way. Mr. McCubbin swept Jean-Jacque's hand away from him and chopped Jean-Jacque in the throat. He bent down on his hands and knees, then karate swept him off his feet down to the ground. Jean-Jacque was shocked that an older 5'-6" tall, white Jamaican man had the abilities to do what he did.

Before he could even begin to retaliate, Mr. McCubbin broke a beer bottle over his head, knocking Jean-Jacque out cold. Jena dropped down to the ground to aid Jean-Jacque.

"Daddy, what did you do? I think he's hurt badly," Jena said.

Mr. McCubbin, then grabbed a sobbing Jena by her shoulder off the ground beside Jean-Jacque and ushered her towards her bedroom. Everyone at the party was in shock from the spectacle that had transpired before their eyes.

"Melba, guh fi di suitcase an bring tuh mi. Dat gyal yah, a go need ih. Shi cyaan liv unda fi mi roof, an ah hav belly at seventeen. Shi didn't even finish high skool. Cyaan even pee chriet, much less," Mr. McCubbin said.

Jena pushed her father's hand off her shoulder and slapped him across his face.

"How dare you embarrass me like this in front of everyone. I've been respectful of you and mommy's rules my entire life. I am a good person! I will not allow you to degrade me nor disrespect my boyfriend anymore. Claude didn't know that I was pregnant, he just found out. He will be just as disappointed about this as you are now. He didn't deserve that," Jena said.

Surprised, Mr. McCubbin rubbed his cheek with one hand, then rushed Jena like a defensive back.

"Ah wuh yuh jus do? Eeh, ah defend yuh ah defend di bwoy ova yuh fada?" said Mr. McCubbin.

He pulled his open hand back to strike Jena again and her mother and Asia intervened. Jena stood up in front of Mr. McCubbin, with fury in her eyes, her fists clenched tight and ready to fight.

"If you don't want me in your house, fine! I'll get out of your life too! I don't need anything you bought for me either, since you are going to disown me anyway. My baby and I will make it on our own," Jena said.

Jena stormed out of the apartment as Jean-Jacque began to regain consciousness. Jamie and Asia helped him up onto his feet from off the ground and he stumbled outside the apartment looking for Jena. By the time he had got outside, she was nowhere to be found. He drove around the area a few times to no avail.

Jean-Jacque circled back to Jena's building and noticed that Jamie and Asia stood outside of the apartment building. "I can't find her anywhere!" said Jean-Jacque after he rolled down the glass and poked his head outside the driver's side window.

"We know where she's at!" said Jamie and Asia in unison.

Jamie and Asia got inside the truck and directed him to drive to Jamie's block. As he pulled up to his house, he saw Jena sitting on Jamie's porch. Jean-Jacque got out of the truck and walked over towards Jena. She was sitting there sobbing uncontrollably.

He reached his hands out toward Jena to console her and she shrugged him off. "I bet your mad, and don't want me in your life either right!" exclaimed Jena.

Before he could even respond, she stepped past him and tried to avoid the confrontation.

Asia stepped in front of her path and directed her to go back to talk it out with Jean-Jacque. After she agreed, Jamie and Asia then walked into the driveway to give them their privacy. Jean-Jacque hugged Jena and she sobbed into his chest for five minutes, nonstop.

After she calmed down, Jean-Jacque looked her in her eyes and kissed her on the lips. "Can we go talk in my truck, so we could have some privacy?"

She nodded her head yes and they both walked over to the truck. Jean-Jacque opened the passenger side door for Jena and she got inside the truck. He walked around the front of the truck and entered it from the driver's side.

Jean-Jacque and Jena sat there in the truck with the doors closed in silence for about a minute before Jena looked over at Jean-Jacque's.

"I'm sorry my father hit you over the head with a beer bottle. Oh my Gosh, you're bleeding! I'm sorry that we're in this predicament with me being pregnant and all. I know that I am in violation of the program rules. But I am in love with you, I want us to be together as a family and I want to have this baby," Jena said.

Jena took the Haitian flag Claude still had in the truck from the West Indian Day parade and put it against the gash he had on his head. Jean-Jacque's grimaced, jerked his head to the side and took the flag away from Jena.

"You don't understand Jena! These people don't care about you and they don't care about me. When they find out, we're all dead. You won't know who will come after you, or how it's going to happen. But rest assured, they're coming after us," Jean-Jacque replied.

"I don't care about these mother fuckers, either! They are your peoples', Claude! For all I know it's you that wants me dead. If you knew how dangerous it was to be intimate with me, then why did you fuck me? Why didn't you have more discipline, Mr. Karate man? I didn't expect you to be on board with this, but I thought that you cared about me Claude!"

175

With tears welled up in both eyes, he looked straight out the front of the truck windshield without blinking.

"I do love you! That's the problem, these people are powerful, and they won't rest until we're all dead!" replied Jean-Jacque.

"I guess we have a fight on our hands! I expect you to do your very best to defend my honor, and the life of our unborn child. I expect you to fight for us, like you have been doing so far for me. I hope one day we could be a family and never have to look over our shoulders," Jena said and got out of the truck.

Jean-Jacque didn't look at Jena, blood and tears streamed down the side of his face. He just kept his head forward and put the truck in drive.

"That will never happen, they won't allow it," Jean-Jacque replied.

Jena slammed the truck door and she watched as Jean-Jacque sped off up the street. She stood there crying until his truck turned the corner and was out of sight.

Chapter 10:

Re-group

Jean-Jacque laid in his bed, wondering what he had done with Jena—knowing that there will be consequences and repercussions for their temporary lack of judgment and weakness of the flesh. His actions will be detrimental to their safety and the safety of their families.

Jean-Jacque fell asleep after hours of lying awake in bed, going over what happened between him and Jena. He never felt this way for another person other than his mother before, and he is struggling with how passionate he feels for her. He struggles with the notion that; he now has to be the best person imaginable to Jena in the world.

They can't go public with their affair. Jean-Jacque understood that some influential people wouldn't approve of their relationship. He needs to keep his relationship with Jena secret because he still has the thing going with Marisol.

In retrospect, that relationship is complicated. But the public doesn't know about that secret love affair that has been going on since he was 13 years old. Jean-Jacque and Marisol continued sleeping with one another while he was supposed to recruit in The Program.

Jean-Jacque fell asleep at 3:00 am. The alarm sounded, and with his eyes still closed, he reached for the snooze button on the alarm clock. A stranger's hand grabbed his wrist. Startled, Jean-Jacque gasped, opened his eyes, and all he saw were four men standing in his bedroom.

The men surrounded his bed wore black masks, covered in a full suit of black regalia from head to toe. The one closest to him that grabbed his wrist covered his head with a black burlap sack. Two other men used zip ties to bind both of his hands behind his back. They overlapped his feet, one on top of the other, and tightly wrapped them together.

The fourth man clubbed him in the head with the butt of his

Ar-16 assault rifle. The four mysterious men dragged Jean-Jacque down the stairs of his loft apartment building, carried him outside and tossed him into the back of a van.

The van doors all closed simultaneously, his chest hit the bottom of the cold van floor, knocking the wind out of him. All Jean-Jacque could hear was the steady breathing of his would-be kidnappers, the engine running, the stench of cigar smoke, and cheap cologne.

The men took Jean-Jacque to an undisclosed location; nobody uttered a word. Struggling to breathe and going in and out of consciousness, Jean-Jacque tried to keep his composure. Remembering his training, he focused on his Ujjayi breath while figuring out who knew where he lived.

Who in their right mind would break into his house? What crime syndicate kidnapped him and why? While he was going down his list of possible suspects, the van's driver was driving recklessly, swerving in and out of traffic.

His body moved about the van indiscriminately, and Jean-Jacque lost his train of thought. But then a strange feeling washed over his entire body. "This van, those trained swat type soldiers, this has Mayor Meléndez written all over it. If so, The Mayor might have me killed for having sex with Jena before she went through the process of The Program," Jean-Jacque thought.

The van stopped abruptly, and the door opened, and Jean-Jacque was dragged out of the van and carried inside a building. Jean-Jacque was thrown to the ground, and he heard a door slamming, bam! One man pulled Jean-Jacque up to his knees and dragged the burlap sack off his head.

The room was spinning, his ears were ringing, and he couldn't entirely focus. Suddenly, he was face to face with Mayor Meléndez.

"You know, I know about everything, fucking piece of shit. You brought that bitch to The Program, and she agreed to terms. Jena was supposed to give her virginity to the person who purchased it for one million dollars. Now, it's too late, son, you know what you did, you took her fucking virginity.

"How could you do this? You know the rules! Now I am in the hole a million bucks. This guy fronted me the money, and he wants his money back. I don't have the money, everything is gone. I put that money inside an offshore account for Jena, that is all tied up and inaccessible.

"The rest of the money paid for her college tuition in full. There is no more money! I cannot pay that money back, so what he wants is Jena's severed head and all of your fingers and your toes. If you would have just kept your dick inside your pants, none of this would be happening right now.

"Hold him down, Jean-Jacque there's no need to struggle, you know what you did, and you knew the consequences of breaking the rules. You were in this very room, you bared witness to the others in the past that broke protocol for not going through with The Program after they signed on the dotted line.

"So, what's about to happen is no secret. ——"

"You, cut off those zip ties and put his hands on the table. You, give me that butcher knife over there," Mayor Meléndez said.

One of the men got a butcher knife and he handed it to Mayor Meléndez and stood over Jean-Jacque and he put one hand over his hand and the other over his forearm. The mayor then raised the knife into the air to chop off Jean-Jacque's hand, and the phone rang.

While the Mayor was distracted by the call, Jean-Jacque took his chance and moved his wrist back, elbowing one man in the face who was behind him. He made a fist, arched his back, and flipped the man into the air and onto the desk. One of the men grabbed Jean-Jacque from behind, and he motioned his head backward and hit him in his nose, breaking it.

Then he clenched his fist, hit him in the balls and used the other hand to uppercut him in the face. Jean-Jacque kicked Mayor Meléndez in the chest with both feet, and the butcher knife dropped. He picked it up and cut the zip tie from his ankles.

179

Jean-Jacque turned the butcher knife around and clunked Mayor Meléndez in the back of the head knocking him out cold. He then took the same butcher knife and threw it at the crotch of one of the four men sitting on the floor.

"Without those zip ties on my hands and my feet, none of you in this room have a chance. I'm sure The Mayor briefed you on my abilities and I doubt that any of you in this room can withstand an attack for me without a gun.

"Even if you had your firearm, I still have a good chance of taking out everybody in this mother fucker. So, I suggest everybody to back to fuck up and leave me alone. Get out of my way and allow me to walk out of this room. If you align yourself with this man all of your lives are going to be in danger.

"We have evidence on The Program and we're going to expose Mayor Rodolfo Meléndez, and anybody who is associated with him will face jail time. I suggest you guys either go home and think things through or change your career path. If you are a police officer, continue to be a police officer and if you're a goon, be a goon for another crime boss.

"Forget this ever happened and if you don't, I'm going to take my time and go after each and every one of you. I heard glass shattering while you had the mask over my face. I'm more than certain that you broke something of value in my house. If you don't walk away right, mother, fucking, now, I promise you all of your lives are over," Jean-Jacque said.

Everybody left standing, backed up, Jean-Jacque clenched his fists, but he noticed that the men stepped aside. He walked to the office door, kicked it open, and walked through it. Jean-Jacque looked at Olivia and told her, "The mayor won't be taking any calls today."

Then he stormed out of the building and ran to the nearest subway station. Jean-Jacque hopped the turnstile, ran up the stairs barefooted, and boarded the train.

The train car was filled with people, Jean-Jacque looked around, and no one even alluded to the fact that he was bloody and wearing only his boxers and a tee shirt. "Typical New Yorkers," Jean-Jacque thought.

He reached his stop, and he ran out of the train and hurried outside. He took a moment to gather his thoughts, took a deep breath, and laughed to himself. He regained his composure and entered his building.

Jean-Jacque walked gingerly over the glass and took the steps to his apartment two by two. Latrice met him at the landing. She had a fat lip; Patrice had a bloody nose and a black eye. All three of them embraced, and Latrice said, "I thought you were dead! We heard when they came inside the house, and we tried to defend ourselves, but we couldn't. The four men overpowered us, and there was nothing we could do to stop them ——"

"Shh! Shh! Shh! don't worry about it, I got them back for everything they have done to us. Everything is going to be alright from now on. We're going to turn state evidence against the current mayor for all the sex crimes he helped orchestrate. Marisol will be the acting Mayor.

"She's going to bring Mayor Meléndez to justice, and we're all going to be ok. As long as I pledge allegiance to her, she's going to take care of everything. She's going to clean this stuff up, and everything should be alright," Jean-Jacque replied.

Two months past and the trial of Mayor Meléndez was underway. The former Deputy Mayor, now the acting Mayor Marisol Velasquez, had overwhelming evidence exposing Mayor Meléndez and his involvement in The Program. She had both audio and video of governors, lawyers, doctors, and CEOs of Fortune five hundred companies, involved with these underage children. Proving their guilt for the entire time that Rodolfo Meléndez was The Mayor of New York City.

"It's Kim Lee here with channel ten news reporting outside the courtroom of the trial for Mayor Meléndez. The judge wouldn't allow cameras in the courtroom to cover the proceedings, but what we know so far is that after the prosecutors and the defense attorneys presented their cases, the jury went to deliberate.

Kim Lee looked down and put her hand up to her ears. "One moment, this just in, the jurors found him guilty of all counts of sex trafficking. He was charged with racketeering, reckless endangerment in 30 cases, 30 counts. The judge sentenced him to 25 years in prison. The doors to the courtroom just opened and The District Attorney just walked out to make a statement. From the looks of the attendees of the courtroom, it was filled with all the parents of the victims involved in The Program. The DA is about to address the media.

"Today, the real scourge was brought to justice by the DAs office. The Program, led by supposed respectable men and women was exposed. An underage sex trafficking ring was uncovered and the individuals that was supposed to protect everybody in this city was the face and the mastermind behind this criminal organization.

"Next, those individuals that were involved will be brought to justice and The Program will be null and void. We have closed down club Divvy Divvies. To the parents of the victims involved, our sincere apologies, we will do our very best to make things right. These kids' innocence could never be restored but rest assured that they won't be preyed upon in the future to come. I'm a mom, and I couldn't imagine the pain and—" The District Attorney choked up, cried and stepped away from the podium. "Please, no more questions, no more questions, please the DA gave her statement, and do with it as you will, have a good afternoon," the chief of police said.

Marisol and Jean-Jacque were in the mayor's office watching this on the news. "You know that that was a multi-million-dollar program that is now turned to shit. All because you couldn't keep your fucking dick in your pants. What now? How are we going to make money?" said Marisol.

"I have an idea, instead of exploiting unsuspecting foreigners for their virginity, we revamp The Program. We should go to third world countries and recruit the top students and give them an opportunity to receive a top-notch education, here in the states. We will call it, The Helping Hand Initiative.

"This program would not only bridge the gap between our

182

country and these third world countries. It would help jump start their economy and possibly help restructure the government as well. This bridge will help a lot of countries come out of poverty. The only catch is that when they finish their education, they have to move back to their homeland.

"While there, they have to set up a school or something that could benefit the people there. Think about it, this is a win-win situation, that everyone involved could benefit from. What do you think about that Marisol?" replied Jean-Jacque.

"I think it's an awesome idea, that is something that we could definitely do with all the money that the government has seized. We could subsidize those funds into this program.

"Busy bee, I hope you don't hate me, but I have something to tell you. We have a four-year-old son together. I know you might be thinking that he's not yours. But all these years, you've been the only person that I've been intimate with. I thought that keeping this a secret might help you in the long run.

"I mean me sleeping with an underage boy, isn't exactly an ideal situation. All in all, I'm sorry."

"You don't have to apologize, what you've done for me is more than anybody could have done. The man that is standing in front of you today is because of you! You said that we have a beautiful son together, right?

"Yes," Marisol said.

"Well, even though our relationship in the eyes of the law was illegal, you took care of me!" replied Jean-Jacque.

Marisol and Jean-Jacque kissed, and he undressed her, and he put her on top of the mayors' desk. Jean-Jacque and Marisol made love. After they both climaxed, they both laid on the desk facing the ceiling and reminisced on past moments that they had together.

"I remember when I first met you at club Divvy Divvies. You were just this young man that I saw and didn't know was 13 years of age. You were bussing tables; you were very polite, and your Haitian accent was so thick. You came to my table, and I could tell that you spoke Creole.

"So, to break the ice, I began to speak French to you to make you a little bit more comfortable. But, by your posture and your demeanor I could tell that you weren't innocent. You were this vibrant young man, that was confident in his own skin.

"You certainly didn't need me to make you feel comfortable. I guess it was just my ploy to get an in with you so that we could have something in common. Our relationship grew from me coming down to club Divvy Divvies and sitting at the table in your section.

I remember you bringing me my favorite drinks, sex on the beach, ankles in the air, cum in my panties, and leg spreader. I was floored that you never picked up on me being flirtatious and giving you hints that I was attracted to you. I was surprised to know that such a young man could play the saxophone so well.

"Later, I realized that you played the trumpet as well. Introducing you to Ted, one of the record execs and a friend I knew from college, was the least I could do for you. He helped you start a career in the music business. You were playing your instruments and having your jazz album.

"Going from bussing tables to being a headliner at the same club that I first laid eyes on you. It was a beautiful sight to witness. I have seen you grow from a bright-eyed young man into an honorable one that the city declared a hero.

"I said that to say this, what happened today will usher in a new era, a bright future. If our plan works, we will change the lives of millions of people. I truly respect and love you the way you carry yourself, and hopefully, someday, our son will be the same way as you," Marisol said.

Marisol leaned over and kissed Jean-Jacque on his forehead. "By the power vested in me, by the city of New York, I unofficially deputize you." She continued to kiss him on his cheek ever so slightly and again on his collarbone ever so gently.

Jean-Jacque lifted her chin with his fingertips, kissed her on the lips, she pushed Jean-Jacque backward on the desk, and then she mounted him. They go at it again, but this time a lot slower and more passionate. Jean-Jacque took his time as he thrust his penis inside Marisol, and she screamed out in ecstasy.

Their shared intimate moment lasted what seemed like a lifetime. It ended when they both came together. Afterward, they both put on their clothes and walked out of the office side by side. They both noticed that Olivia's face was a bit flush.

The sound of the office door closing echoed on the intercom on her desk. That only meant that Olivia was listening to the whole ordeal that transpired between them in the office. They must have pressed the intercom button while they were rolling around on the desk. Their sexual escapade was on display for Olivia, and whoever else was in the room.

Olivia adjusted herself and said, "Good morning, Mayor Velasquez! I heard everything! I mean, I saw everything on the news! Congratulations!"

Marisol put her hands on Olivia's desk, leaned over and looked her square in the eyes. "You heard nothing, and you saw nothing, capeesh," Marisol said.

Olivia nodded her head yes in acknowledgement to the obvious threat from the acting Mayor.

Jean-Jacque went downstairs and looked for the nearest payphone and he put two quarters in, and he called up Jamie. (Ring, ring, ring, ring,) "Yo! Yo! Yo! Jamie, Yo rally the troops man we gotta meet up on the roof," Jean-Jacque said.

"For what Claude? You know that roof is hot," Jamie replied.

"Get everybody together and I'll tell you about everything when I see you. Let's meet on the roof of Darrelle's building."

"Bet, say no more."

Jean-Jacque got in his truck, raced up the FDR drive and got off at the Willis Ave. bridge exit. He merged on the Bruckner Blvd expressway. He then turned off on the service entrance and made a left turn off Bronx River, and an abrupt right turn on Watson Ave.

185

Finally, a short right turn onto Colgate and parked in front of Darrelle's building.

Jean-Jacque got out his truck, locked the doors and walked upstairs to the roof.

"Good, everybody is present and accounted for! Yo, wat up Rah and wat up Mark, wat up Darrelle!" said Jean-Jacque and embraced everybody one by one.

"Ok everybody is here, so the reason why I asked you all here today to have this meeting is as follows: Darnel has been locked up for a couple of months now. Mayor Meléndez got locked up and Deputy Mayor Velasquez is now the acting Mayor of NYC. I got an in with her, so I can put specific bugs in her ear, and things will happen. I got a little bit of pull in the city right now.

"First things first, I have to get Darnel's sentence reduced because the situation that he had with that blood was self-defense. His defense attorney proved that in a court of law. Although a jury of his peers charged him, he was charged with involuntary manslaughter. Those charges can be overturned. The one thing that I can't get reduced is the time that he must serve for the unregistered firearm. That's something that's out of my hands. I can't do anything about that. So, he could serve anywhere from 3 to 7 years for the illegal firearm that he used. He can even serve less if he went to this program that trains him to become a grief counselor.

"If he tried to get individuals who are involved in gang activities to get away from gang culture. If he does that and finishes the program successfully, he could get his sentence drastically reduced.

"Darnel could come home within three years, and he could then get out and continue that program out here on the streets. Ultimately becoming a motivational speaker/gang counselor. Where he goes into different communities and get these Crips and Bloods in the communities to refrain from being a Menace to Society.

"That program could help stop these gangs from terrorizing citizens in these communities. He could basically turn CRIP back to do what community leaders initially sought out to be, Community

Revolution in Progress. Those founding members set to protect and serve the community because the police and the white people around would prey on people in our neighborhoods back in the 50s and the 60s.

"The law wasn't helping us, they were hurting us, so they had to form these gangs to protect themselves from the attack from outside entities. Hopefully, with Darnel, we can get it back to what it was originally supposed to be.

"Much like the Guardian Angels did back in the 80s, I want to make certain that community unity is top priority. Hopefully, with this program we could continue where the Black Panthers left off back in the 70s. Forgive me, I am going off on a tangent.

"That's neither here, nor there, I'm here to present to you guys an opportunity to be wealthy. I know that you have your own things going on and we could definitely make a change in that. I wish to make everything and everyone legitimate businessmen.

"With organizing this new program, I have an opportunity to atone from my involvement in the old program that got Mayor Meléndez locked up. Although whatever I was involved in yielded me a lot of money, and I helped ruin a lot of lives in the process. It was all illegal, and the government swooped in and they saw to it that The Program ceased to exist.

"Now in the aftermath of what that program represented, we are starting this Helping Hand Initiative. After we forge relationships with leaders by going into different countries setting up medical clinics, food banks, providing fresh water and other sustainable resources.

"We plan to ultimately set up satellite schools for students who would typically not be able to afford to go to school and get a proper education. After these students finish the satellite school in these third-world countries, they would get to come here and attend any college across the nation.

"Former students already here will help mentor new students so that they won't feel different in a strange place. This would reduce bullying tremendously. This would allow staff and faculty

187

better understand other cultures and empathize more with foreigners in general.

"When these students come out of high school, they would have earned a place within the school system. You have MIT in Boston, and you have Brown in Rhode Island. You have NYU or Columbia here in New York. Rutgers University in Jersey, Yale in Connecticut. And the list goes on.

"So, I know you were doing your hand-to-hand hustling out here in the streets. So, what I want you all to do is to stop all that illegal shit. If you join, the government will scrutinize who we associate with from here on in. If you guys are involved in any criminal activity whatsoever. That could look badly upon me, and worst, the mayor's office.

"My idea is for each of you to do what you were doing before but do it legally.

"Darrelle, I know you got your hands and heroin, so we're gonna do is send you to school to be a pharmacist. So, you could learn the business on a corporate level. Instead of peddling heroin in the streets, you're going to run a company that sells opioids, oxy cotton, Percocet, methadone. All those other prescription drugs that come from poppy seeds. Darrelle, you gonna make your money five times over, but legitimately.

"Marques, you sell weed, and you got your gun running thing going on. I'm not mad at you, but what we are gonna do is, any record that you have, we got to erase all of that shit. Marques, you're gonna get your federal firearm license, and you will be able to have a gun store.

"In that gun shop, you will sell legal guns to patrons that have their permit and their license to carry a firearm. Trust me, you will make money hand over fist. Instead of selling weed illegally, we will open up a dispensary in Colorado. I know you have some family members that do baking and sell food, you could have a Cuchifrito, shit, you could have them all over the city and call them Alejandro's, you know what I'm saying, and y'all make your money hand over fist.

"Of course, since I'm the one who started up all these companies legally, we are going to have a partnership. The management company behind all of this is going to be called, Partner's Collective.

"I will have a small percentage of these companies. I'm going to have you guys put in some money per week inside a pot. At the end of the month, you take a hand from that partner. Or roll it over until the end of the year.

"Whatever you do with your cut is up to you; spend it how you see fit. Whatever hand that you leave in The Partners Collective, we will use that money to invest in different companies across NYC, in our neighborhoods.

"After that, the nation. Raheem, people on the street are saying that you're fucking with those wet blunts. You got to go to rehab, brother. When you come out, you are going to be a Mortician. We will give you a Funeral Home.

Eventually, those funeral homes will expand across New York City. We can make sure this money is made between all of us, and we're gonna start this partnership from here. Is everyone here all in?" said Jean-Jacque.

"No objections, we all in," the crew said, and everybody placed their palms down on top of each other's hand.

Chapter 11:

The shootout

A few months had gone by, including the holidays and the new year. The guys haven't seen much of one another since Darrelle fell off the roof. Jean-Jacque had to get ten stitches in his head after getting knocked unconscious by Mr. McCubbin.

The crew has followed the advice of Jean-Jacque, urging everyone to stay low after the incident. He didn't want anyone risking getting locked up by the police again. If they did, it would seem like he was taking advantage of his relationship with Marisol. Or seem reckless and ungrateful for her bailing them out after they'd gotten in trouble.

Jean-Jacque was suspicious of the capabilities of The Program and their tactical team of henchmen. Even though former Mayor Rodolfo Meléndez was locked away in jail awaiting his appeal hearing; he was still a powerful and well-connected man.

Against their better judgement, everyone was getting cabin fever and went outside like a bear out of hibernation. Jean-Jacque missed Jena, so he went against his advice to the crew and contacted Jamie from his flip phone.

"Yo Jamie, meet me at the park of Monroe High School," Jean-Jacque said.

"For what, I thought we were supposed to lay low," Jamie replied.

"C'mon Jamie, let's smoke a blunt, you could give me an update on Jena and the baby."

"Aiight, I'll meet you there in twenty minutes."

Jean-Jacque drove up to the front of Monroe H.S, and he spotted Jamie standing there, with a lit cigarette in his hand. Jean-Jacque tooted the horn and Jamie opened the passenger door and closed the door after he entered inside the truck.

"What's good Claude? How are you doing man?" said Jamie

"Doing well man! But on the real, you can't smoke that

190

cancer stick inside my car! Since when you smoke boges?" replied Jean-Jacque.

"Aiight bet! We're going to have to walk and talk then because I need this bogey! I'm under a lot of pressure!" said Jamie.

Jean-Jacque shut off the truck and got out the truck and he and Jamie began to walk down the street together towards Bronx River Ave.

Jean-Jacque scratched his head and was puzzled by Jamie's statement.

"What pressure? What you Asia started fucking and you worried about her being pregnant too? You know Hispanic girls get pregnant easily, one touch and they're with child," Jean-Jacque replied.

Jamie took in a long pull off the cigarette and flicked it onto the sidewalk, blew some smoke in the air, while shaking his head from left to right. "Nah, you know you and Jena fucked that up for me. Asia's scared about getting kicked out of the house like her sister if she does. I mean the fiasco between you, her, and her parents. From that day on, she has been in the backroom in my basement. I've been hiding her from my mom's ever since that day, she hasn't been back home. Luckily, my moms don't go downstairs that often, and my older brother's done moved out.

"One is in the military, one lives in the South Bronx, and the other moved to Connecticut, to be with his daughter and her mother. I got Jena staying in his room, but she is eating me out of the house and home. My moms spazzed out on me a few times, saying shit like, "Bwoy yuh craving bad! How yuh ah nyam suh? Yuh ah nyam fi two eeh? Nuh mek mi find out seh yuh have sumbody in yah suh ah live!" said Jamie.

"Ha, ha, you sound funny as shit impersonating ya mom's Jamaican patois. I bet if she heard you mocking her like that, she'd kick your teeth in."

"That shit ain't funny man! I'm taking care of your responsibilities man! My mom's gonna kill me if she ever finds out

Jena is living in the basement."

Jamie reached in his pocket, pulled out a blunt, lit it up and handed it to Jean-Jacque. "Here, this shit is purple haze and hydro from Briggs. This shit might bust our heads wide open."

"Word, I hope it will make you forget about all that shit you're worrying about! I want to thank you for doing this for Jena man! Jamie, you are a great friend!"

Jean-Jacque reached inside his coat pocket and pulled out a wad of money and handed it to Jamie. "Here take this, buy some groceries and make sure Jena goes to the doctor to get checked up," Jean-Jacque said.

Jamie inhaled the weed smoke, took the cash, and put it inside his pocket. "Good looking out man! I think she's already been going to see her OBGYN, she goes once a week. She's not going to school anymore, she's about five months pregnant and doesn't want to be ridiculed at school. Especially by those females that she had beef with at school.

"Asia and I had to go to Jane Addams and tell her teachers the truth, and they were real understanding of the situation. They gave us her schoolwork, so she could finish up school and graduate on time in June," Jamie replied.

Jean-Jacque and Jamie continued to walk side by side, stride for stride but weren't paying attention to their surroundings. A black unmarked, Astro van with presidential tint, has been shadowing the pair. As soon as they both stepped off the sidewalk into the street, the van sped up. Jamie was positioned closest to the van. He turned and saw the van barreling down on them full speed ahead.

"Oh Shit! Watch out! said Jamie.

Jamie pushed Jean-Jacque back onto the sidewalk and jumped on top of the hood of the van. His back hit the windshield, then he rolled off into the street as the Astro Van sped off down Bronx River Ave. Jean-Jacque quickly got up off the sidewalk and ran into the street where Jamie was sitting there holding his right arm.

"Yo Jamie, you aiight?" asked Jean-Jacque.

"Yeah, I'm good! Lucky thing I'm fat and have on this Triple Fat Goose Coat, or I wouldn't be," Jamie replied.

"Damn son, you still held onto the L after all of that?"

"Hell yeah! This is Jekyll and Hyde! This shit hard to come by."

Jean-Jacque didn't remember that he drove to Monroe High School, so he and Jamie continued to walk towards Watson Avenue and Evergreen, where Marques' block was. After they arrived, Marques and Darrelle were standing outside of his building with some other guys they didn't recognize at first.

As they slapped fives and gave dap to everyone who was there. They noticed that it was Raphael and Marvelous who were accompanying Marques and Darrelle. Jamie and Jean-Jacque were surprised to see Darrelle after the incident that happened on his roof.

"Yo son, you good? I haven't seen you in months. You know your moms would not let us come see you while you were laid up in the hospital right. She blamed all of us for your accident. I don't blame her though, my moms would have had the same reaction," Jamie said.

Darrelle shrugged it off and put his hands up in the air.

"I'm alright man! You know me I be Maintaining! I broke my collar bone, fractured a few ribs, and ruptured my spleen. But all in all, I survived the fall. The Paramedic and the Doctors seem to think that the tree broke my fall, and that is the only reason why I didn't die," Darrelle replied.

"Yo, fuck all that! Marv, tell Jamie about what you just told me about Raheem," Marques said.

"Yo, I saw your mans' out here looking like a zombie for real! Like Thriller or Night of The Living Baseheads! That nigga been fucking with Black and Bilal, and those two peddle that weed laced with embalming fluid. That wet shit is dangerous Yo! It's like a step down from smoking crack or shooting up heroin. That's your mans', y'all need his help! Get him off that shit. Word up!" replied

Marvelous.

Jamie shook his head in disappointment as the same Astro Van that almost ran him, and Jean-Jacque down earlier sped down the street. The passenger side window and the rear door slid open, and the men inside opened fire on the group of men standing there. Marques and Marvelous pulled out their firearms and returned fire. Everyone else ducked down for cover behind the parked cars in front of the building.

The Astro Van, sped down the street towards Bronx River Avenue and made a left turn towards Bruckner Blvd.

"Yo, everyone aiight?" asked Marques and Marvelous.

Panting and still crocheting down behind the parked cars, everyone nodded their heads, yeah!

"We're good, and nobody got hit!" replied Darrelle.

"What the fuck is going on? Who the fuck was that?" said Raphael and Darrelle.

"That same Astro Van tried to run us over earlier. We don't know who the fuck they are, or why they're trying to kill us!" replied Jamie.

"I have to find out what's going on, I need to make a phone call," Jean-Jacque said.

Jean-Jacque checked his pants pocket and pulled out his car keys. He looked around for his truck and realized that he had left it parked in front of Monroe High School. Minutes later, a man holding his arm, ran towards the group of men. Still anxious from the drive-by shooting, Marques and Marvelous pulled their guns out and pointed them at the would-be attacker.

Marques noticed who it was and lowered his gun.

"Marvelous! Hold on, don't shoot! That's my man Kingston!" said Marques.

Marques put his hand on Marvelous' gun and lowered it. The injured man reached close enough to them and stopped.

"Police ah run mi dung, mon! Mi haffi luk sumweh fi go,"

194

Kingston said.

He wasted no time exchanging pleasantries with anyone outside the building. He just ran inside Marques's building holding his bloody arm.

After Kingston ran inside, a squadron of police cruisers swarmed in front of the building. A slew of police officers hopped out and approached the men out in front of the building.

"Anyone seen a short man come this way? He has been shot and he's armed and dangerous. Anyone?" said one police officer.

Everyone shrugged their shoulders and shook their heads no.

"I hate this code of the streets bullshit! No snitching, false sense of loyalty fuckry! That piece of shit shot and killed the number one draft pick in the NBA, Herman Brentwood, just twenty minutes ago. In case you fucking foreign bastards didn't know. You'll come here to this country and fuck up everything here. Go back to your country, and fuck that up!" said the police officer.

The Sargent grabbed the irate officer by the arm and ordered him to get back. About six other officers ran into Marques's building. While the other officers stood outside and looked around the area with flashlights. They searched for possible clues that may point them in the right direction of the assailant.

"You think you're not a foreigner officer! The last time I checked, none of us here are indigenous people. So, you should watch who you ridicule officer O'Reilly. We've all played a part in fucking up this country, some of us were forced into doing it. But the fact remains that we're all culpable in the biggest crime against humanity, colonization!" said Marvelous.

"Enough now, we're looking for an accused rapist and a murder. If any of you should see him, please contact the authorities," The Sergeant said.

The officer handed out his card with his contact information on it, then ordered the officers back into their cruisers. The officers that ran into the building, came out soon after and followed suit. Then the entire fleet of cop cars drove off.

After the cops left, Marvelous turned to Marques with a blank look on his face.

"You heard that, your mans committed murder and rape in our hood! I should have shot him when I had the chance. Make sure you get that mother fucker off the block. It's open season on his ass! If he's alive he has one hour to get out of Dodge," Marvelous said.

Marques nodded his head in agreement and dapped Marvelous.

"Say no more! I'll take care of it!" replied Marques.

Marvelous and everyone else started walking up the street towards Ward Avenue, where Herman Brentwood lived. Jean-Jacque stopped when he saw a payphone at the smoke shop.

"y'all go ahead without me, I'll catch up! I gotta make a phone call!" said Jamie.

Jean-Jacque dug inside his pants pocket, took out two quarters and inserted them into the payphone. The phone rang twice, and Marisol picked up the phone.

"Hello Busy bee, Thank God you're okay. I'm watching on the news and there has been a murder in the area where your friends' lives. Please tell me that you weren't involved with the incident!" asked Marisol.

"Of course not, why would you even think that I could've been involved in such a heinous crime," Jean-Jacque replied.

"Good, that's a relief, did you know the victim? From what the news is reporting, he was a big deal. I feel sorry for his family, I could only imagine what they might be going through!"

"Marisol, all of what you said is accurate, but I wasn't involved at all. I didn't know the guy who was killed. He lived on my friend Jamie's Street. The reason for the call, was to ask you if you know of a contract out for me and my friends.

"We were almost run over by an Astro Van, and the people who were in that same van shot at me and my friends. What the fuck is going on? I thought the mayor was locked up and you were in control of everything!"

"Calm down Busy bee, the only other person who has the authority to orchestrate anything like that would be Arthur Rosenbaum. He's a Venture Capitalist, who handles the accounts of several major players in the state of New York. This is the very man who was grooming Jena and is out one million dollars. I'm sure he is pissed off and is the person responsible for the attempts on your life.

"Be very careful and warn your friends too. Tell Jena to leave town if she wants to live. I'll see if I can convince Arthur to call it off or dig up some dirt on him and blackmail him. I'll talk to you later!"

Jean-Jacque walked up the street towards his truck, abandoning the idea to go where the crime scene was on Ward Avenue and to see Jena. Walking up Colgate Avenue, he heard sirens blaring in the distance heading towards Watson Avenue. People in their homes and the storefronts, were watching the report of the tragic news of the fallen basketball star.

Jamie and the other guys who walked to Ward Avenue, saw the yellow crime scene tape blocking off the middle of the street. A white sheet covered the body, the news media personnel, crime scene investigation team, and the first responders were already there on the scene. A few officers, set up barricades to ensure that the crime scene was not tainted.

"Clear the area," said one of the detectives on scene.

The onlookers from the neighborhood gathered along the sidewalk, the crowd swelled, and several people spilled over in the street. Jamie pushed his way through the crowd, and a beat cop attempted to stop him.

"I live down the street!" said Jamie, as he flashed his identification at the cop.

The officer allowed Jamie to pass through the blockade, but the other guys with him weren't so lucky. Jamie saw Meadow, Herman's sister, being escorted into the back of a fire department ambulance. She was distraught and the side of her face was bruised,

197

bloody, and swollen.

Jamie saw Herman's parents and his little brother Anderson, talking with a reporter about the events that transpired earlier. EMT's were working on a man who appeared to be injured; he was being escorted to the back of an ambulance as well. A number of his neighbors were in the street sobbing and holding each other in their arms in solidarity.

Witnessing everything as it unfolded brought on a range of emotions for Jamie and his eyes welled up with tears. Sam, Herman's next-door neighbor, saw Jamie and walked over to him and put his hand on his shoulder. With tears cascading down his cheek as well, he wiped his face with a handkerchief.

"It's going to be okay son! We all have to be strong for the family. We also can't allow the bastard that did this, get us all too," Sam said.

"What happened?" asked Jamie.

Sam cleared his throat trying to fight back tears.

"Nobody knows, all we are sure of is that a rising star is gone from this world and on to the next. He's with Jehovah now! May peace be upon his soul!" replied Sam.

Jamie hugged Sam and started walking towards Jena who was standing there off to the side sobbing and rubbing her belly. As he got close to her, Jena grabbed Jamie, they hugged and cried in each other's arms. After a few minutes, Jamie led Jena back to the house.

"You shouldn't be out here! This shit is too sad! I don't want you to go into premature labor," Jamie said.

As Jamie and the rest of the neighborhood mourned the loss of one of their own. Jean-Jacque finally got to his truck. He had been walking for at least twenty minutes in the cold. He had on thin dress pants with no long johns underneath them.

Jean-Jacque turned on the truck and the heat as soon as he entered the truck. He sat there for a few trying to thaw off a bit, before he called Patrice and Latrice.

Jean-Jacque finally got the feeling back in his fingers, he reached inside the center console and retrieved his flip phone. He dialed the house phone and Patrice picked up. "Hello! Who's this?" asked Patrice.

"Patrice it's me, do me a favor, call Rachel over at club Divvy Divvies and ask her if you could view the surveillance videos of the back room. Tell her that Marisol needs to view the footage right away," Jean-Jacque replied.

"Why would she trust me to view footage from that room? I'm quite sure it is under lock and key and not for prying eyes."

"Trust me, she has to follow protocol and oblige any requests from the mayor's office. I'm looking for the identity of Arthur Rosenbaum. Marisol told me that he is the person set to groom Jena and her and has been cozy with each other."

"So, why is he so important to you?" asked Patrice.

"That mother fucker ordered the tactical team to take out my friends and me. They tried to run us over with a van, and unsuccessfully did a drive-by shooting as well," Jean-Jacque replied.

"Damn Jean, Is everyone okay?"

"Yeah Patrice, everything is fine. Thankfully, nobody was hurt, but I need that footage. Maybe there's some incriminating evidence that could further implicate former Mayor, Rodolfo Meléndez and his appeal could be denied. I want to put this bastard in jail where he belongs."

"Jean, this better be good! Are you sure you want to go up against these titans? I mean The Program and their empire spreads far and wide and dates back decades. There's no telling how many people are involved in this, and who's willing to do everything in their power to stop you from trying to reduce the empire to rubble."

"Well Patrice, we as foreign nationals have a responsibility to protect our own. We must prevent any more of us from being taken advantage of anymore. I must empower these powerless unsuspecting immigrants, there's strength in numbers!"

"I hope you know what you're doing Jean. Take care of

yourself."

Patrice hung up the phone and Jean-Jacque sped off down the street towards the Bronx River Ave to the Bruckner Blvd expressway.

Meanwhile, Marques grew tired of waiting for Kingston to come back out of the building. "He must have found a good spot to hide because the police couldn't find him," Marques thought.

Marques went inside the building to go to his apartment. He wanted to get a bit to eat before he walked up the block where everyone else was.

As he entered the lobby, Marques saw the elevator door open up but there was no elevator. A bloody hand reached up from the shaft and Kingston pulled himself up on the lobby floor.

"Wow, the police were looking all over for you! You're the main suspect in the murder of Herman Brentwood. Please tell me you didn't kill him!" said Marques.

Kingston was visibly fatigued and out of breath. He looked up at Marques towering over him and reached out his hand for help.

"My yute, gib mi a hand nuh! Help mi git up!" replied Kingston.

Marques hastily helped him get up on his feet and Kingston continued...

"Hear mi now, my buck up pon a gal wah day yah an mi tek har out pan a date, zeen. Afta, mi drop har off bac. She tell mi fi falla bar inna har yaad. Mi feel seh ah di cocky she waan, ah fuck she waan fuck. Boom, we deh inna di hallway an mi a feel har up an ah fingga har pum pum. She tek out mi cocky and tun round an tell mi fi push it eena har. As mi shoob in my cocky now, she baal out loud!

"Har brudda cum out fi si wah gwan, an si seh mi fuck him sistah. An him cum downstairs pan mi an push mi off har. So, mi chuck him back! Him hall off an box mi dung a grung, den throw two kick pan mi.

"So, mi git fed up now, back out mi gun, an shot him inna

200

him chest. Him dung boof pan di ground, di gal start baal and rush mi, so mi use di gun and butt her inna her face.

"Mi run outside an a try jump inna di cyar now, an one ol man lick shot afta di cyar. So, mi lick shot afta him bac an miss. Him shot mi inna mi arm here suh. Mi tek foot up di street an shot two more time after him. Mi sure seh mi kill him, cause all mi memba is wen him drop dung ah grung, an mi run wen," Kingston said.

"Damn son! You're a real gangster for real! But you hot man, you gotta get off the block, quick. If these niggas round here catch you. 'You ago end up in the morgue yuh Bumbaclot," Marques replied.

Marques gave Kingston dap and walked upstairs to his apartment. Kingston lost a lot of blood from the gunshot wound, stumbled outside, and managed to get away unseen.

Jamie walked Jena back to his house to prevent her from getting overly excited. She stopped and handed him a manila envelope.

"What is this?" asked Jami as he took the envelope from Jena.

"Just open it!" replied Jena.

Jamie opened the envelope and took out a paper that turned out to be a sonogram.

"What am I looking at? Am I even holding it up right?"

Jena spun the photo right-side-up and Jamie got a better look at it.

"Is this what I think it is? Am I looking at two figures here?" asked Jamie.

"Yup, twin girls to be exact!" replied Jena

"Congratulations!" This is the best news I've heard all day. I just saw Claude and we almost got ourselves ran over by some people driving an Astro Van. Then, we walked over to Marques's block and the same people in the van tried to gun us down in a drive-by shooting. Luckily, Mark and Marv shot back at them, so they drove off."

"Damn Jamie! Are you okay? I was wondering why your clothes were all dirty!"

"Forget all that! Let's go inside, away from all this madness. I wanna be able to hold my nieces when they're born."

Jamie assisted Jena upstairs inside his house, and she sat down at the kitchen table and held the side of her stomach and grimaced in pain.

"What's wrong Jena? Is everything okay?" asked Jamie.

"I think it's just cramps, they've been moving around a lot lately. I better eat something, or they're liable to burst through my belly. I hope they don't come early. I'm only seven months pregnant," Jena replied.

Jamie opened the fridge and took out a loaf of bread, mayonnaise, cheese, ham, and mustard. He put the stuff down on the kitchen table and walked over to the kitchen sink, washed his hands, and grabbed a butter knife from the draw. As soon he finished making one sandwich and Jena grabbed it and took a bite of it. The doorbell rang and Jamie put the bread and the butter knife down on the table and went to answer the door.

As he arrived at the front door, Jamie saw his mother standing in the doorway with a bunch of grocery bags on the ground by her feet.

"Son, mi glad yuh cum, mi seh di roadblock off! Di police officers neva waan let mi pass. Mi stan up di road fi ten minutes before smaddy tell di officers seh, ah dung di street mi live. Ah few ah dem bwoy deh, carry mi bags dung yah fi my," Mrs. McClymont said.

Jamie grabbed all of the grocery bags a few at a time and brought them inside the kitchen. Jena finished making the sandwiches, cleaned up the table, and put everything back inside the fridge. As Jamie walked into the kitchen, she saw Jena and they both greeted one another.

"I neva know seh nobody else did eena yah! Jamie! How many times mi ah go tell yuh seh mi nuh waan nuhbadi inna di house, wen mi nuh deh yah, ehh!" said Mrs. McClymont.

"My fault Mommy, I wanted to get her off the road. Besides, Jena needed to use the bathroom," Jamie replied.

"So, tell mi something young lady yuh ah breed fi mi son? Jamie, ah she yuh hav a live downstairs inna yuh bredda room. Unuh think seh mi stupid! Yung lady, if yuh ah breed fi mi son, nuh sleep downstairs, tan inna dat room deh. Unnu cyaan tan inna di sed room doah, cause unnu nuh married yet," Mrs. McClymont asked.

"Ma! She's not pregnant by me, she is Asia's sister!" replied Jamie.

"Den she cyaan tan yah! Think ah shelter mi ah run. Cum, cum go bac ah yuh yaad!"

"Ma, her parents kicked her out of the house when she told them she was pregnant."

"So, how long she deh yah?"

"About two months!"

"Kiss mi nek bac! Yuh hav har ah liv anda mi nose, all dis time. An yuh neva have di decency to ask mi if she cyan tan yah! Young lady, you have to go! Tek up yuh tings dem an lef mi yaad now! Unnu outtah auduh bad man! Mi should tek something an clap yuh inna yuh head Jamie. Tek dat gal outtah mi yaad now! Or dem ah go charge mi fi murda!" exclaimed Mrs. McClymont.

"Aiight Ma, damn!" replied Jamie.

Jamie and Jena went downstairs and as he closed the door behind him. His mother took off her shoe and threw it at him, but the door was already closed. The loud sound from the impact of the shoe hitting the door startled Jena and Jamie's mother continued to yell and scream indiscriminately as they walked towards the room in the basement.

Jena packed her clothes in a knapsack she had, and Jamie paced back and forth. "Jena, I'm sorry for my mother! What are we going to do now? Where are you going to go?" asked Jamie.

"Don't worry about me Jamie, I have family in Bridgeport, CT. I will call them, then go out there until the babies are born," Jena replied.

"That could be any week now! After that what are you going to do?"

Jena shrugged her shoulders and sighed.

"I start school in August, so I will just head out there. I got a full scholarship plus room and board. If the school won't allow me to stay on campus with my girls, I have the 100k from the program that the government doesn't know about. I could use that to get a place off-campus.

"I might have to stay at a hotel at first, but I'll manage. Jamie, thanks for everything you've done for me and my babies. I will always love you for doing this for us," Jena replied.

Jena approached Jamie and kissed him on the lips, then used her finger to wipe away the remnants of her lipstick off his lips. Jamie picked up her bags, then dug his hand inside his pocket.

"I almost forgot, here Jena, Claude just gave me this money to buy groceries for you and the girls. So, take it, it's yours. How are you getting to Connecticut?"

"I'm going to take a greyhound bus!"

"How are you gonna get to Penn Station?"

"I'm going to take the train, Jamie!"

"Jena, there are people who are trying to kill all of us. You have to be careful, you gotta take a gypsy cab."

Jamie went into the other bedroom in the basement and dialed the number for a dollar cab that people in the neighborhood frequently use. He rushed back into the room where Jena was and grabbed her bags from off the bed.

"C'mon let's go! The taxi will be here in five minutes, we have to walk down to the Bruckner so you can catch it. With Ward Avenue blocked off, the cab won't be allowed to pass through it,"

Jamie said.

Jamie and Jena exited the basement through a side entrance to his house. As they both walked out onto the sidewalk, there were still hordes of people there. The outpour of the community in the wake of this tragedy was tremendous. They made it to the corner not a moment too soon, the taxicab was waiting there. Jamie directed the driver to open the trunk and he put Jena's bag inside.

Jamie closed down the trunk and hugged Jena.

"I am going to miss you! Call me when you've arrived in Connecticut."

"I'm gonna miss you too, Big head. You better take care of my sister."

Jena got inside the taxi, and it drove off down the Bruckner Blvd expressway.

"Where to?" asked the driver, while Jena was sitting in the backseat.

"Port Authority!" replied Jena.

The driver put the car into drive and pulled out when traffic was clear.

"You're leaving the city huh! I don't blame you! Especially with tragedies like what happened today. It's kind of makes you wonder why people are so violent. Some wealthy people blame all the crime and mishaps on foreigners. They claim that the influx of immigrants in the city caused a spike in the crime rate. What do you think?" said the driver.

"I don't know what to think anymore! Please could you please turn the radio station to W.B.L.S?" replied Jena, after she sighed.

The driver obliged her request and Jena took out her book that she writes poetry in and turned to the page where she had an unfinished piece titled:

"My life is like a mixed tape!

"My life is like a mixtape, and it's filled with only good shit

Funk from the '70s, Soulful sounds from the '80s, the rawness of the '90s, and the sleek style from the '60s.

"Light fairy feels of Cee Cee Penniston, smooth melodic tones of Anita Baker and Sade. Thought-provoking tunes from Bob Marley and Illmatic lyrics from Nas.

"Smiling while my hips slowly swayed from side to side after hearing, 'double trouble,' by Beres Hammond."

Jena looked out the window and daydreamed about her crazy life.

'Damn! I truly miss my mom and my sister! I know my dad was just trying to protect me and he was only concerned about my future. But he overreacted! I'm not a little girl anymore! I'm not the innocent kid he used to bounce off his knee. Like it or not, he's going to be a grandfather. I hope he comes to his senses and accepts me and my babies back into his life. I miss him too!' thought Jena.

Jena looked down on the page and wrote the next stanza of the poem:

"Bopping my head up and down listening to gangster rap from Ice Cube.

'But today wasn't a good day!'

A single tear streamed down her cheek and she wrote:

It was all a Dream, R.I.P Biggie Smalls best rapper of all time."

After Jena wrote the last stanza of the poem, she closed the notebook and listened to the radio. It was a familiar song that reminded her of her childhood, cleaning up the apartment with her mother and sister on Saturday morning. The song was fitting, given the current events that recently had taken place in her life and in the lives of people she knew in the neighborhood. It was a song by Anne Pebbles 'I can't stand the rain.'

Tears rushed out of her eyes as she sang the lyrics to the song while reminiscing about her past as a child. Jena thought about Jean-Jacque, about her father, about the school, about The Program, and her babies.

Before she knew it, they were in front of Port Authority. The driver got out and retrieved her bag from the trunk and helped Jena out of the car. She dug inside her handbag and handed him a ten-dollar bill.

"Are you going to be, okay? Where are you going?" asked the driver, as he took the money from Jena.

Jena nodded her head yes, turned around, and entered Port Authority terminal.

Jena stood in line and waited for the person in front of her to finish his transaction. The older man wearing a ten-gallon hat, cowboy boots with spurs; turned around, recognized Jena.

"Jena? Aren't you Raheem's friend, Jena?" asked the older man.

She nodded her head yes.

"I'm Raheem's Grand-Uncle, Jasper. I saw you at his house a few times with that Haitian boy Clyde," he said.

"You mean Claude!" replied Jena.

"Yes, that's the boy! I see that you're pregnant! How far along are you, girlie?"

"I'm almost seven months now!"

"Wow! Do you know what the gender of the baby is?"

"Yes, female! And it's twins, so it's babies!"

"Well, congratulations! Are you leaving town for the weekend?"

"No! My parents kicked me out of the house after I told them that I was pregnant. So, I'm going to Connecticut to stay with some family members until I have the babies. Then it is off to school in Nevada," Jena replied.

"I'm sorry to hear that! I tell you what, instead of burdening someone else. Why don't you stay here in the city? You can raise the twins while you go to school. A big plus, and you won't have to

207

attend summer school. That way, your parents can see the girls, before you head off to college," Uncle Jasper said.

"That sounds like a great idea Uncle Jasper, but I don't have anywhere to go! My friend Jamie's mother just kicked me out of their house, after she found out I was staying there without her permission," Jena replied.

"I have an idea Girlie; you could stay at my house!"

"Excuse you, it ain't that type of party Uncle Jasper!"

"No, not with me, but at one of the houses that I own in the city. The place is empty, it's quiet and it's in Mt. Vernon, not too far away from your folks. C'mon, what do you say? You're a city girl, trust me you won't like Connecticut," Uncle Jasper replied.

"Uncle Jasper, what are you buying a bus ticket for?" asked Jena, after she agreed to stay in his house.

"Girlie, I wasn't, my daughter works here! I pulled some strings to get her the job. She was on drugs a few years ago once she got here from Monserrat. She got mixed up with the wrong crowd and became addicted to heroin. But I was able to get her into rehab and she has been clean for three years now. She has turned herself around, she is working here and is doing well."

"Good for her! I'm glad to hear it, Uncle Jasper!"

"Girlie, shall we go?"

Uncle Jasper was a military veteran, who served in the Vietnam war and the Korean War. He used his GI bill to invest in real estate. He owned over seventy properties in the tri-state area.

Uncle Jasper drove to the house in Mt Vernon with Jena.

"Here we are Girlie! This is it; you can stay here for as long as you need to. He opened the front door and turned on the lights inside the house. It was fully furnished but everything was covered with white sheets.

"If there's anything you need from me just let me know. I live by Jane Addams High School in the Bronx. My phone number is in the Rolodex by the telephone in the kitchen," Uncle Jasper said.

208

"Thanks for doing this for me! I need one thing from you, I attend Jane Addams high-school and if you would be so kind as to get my schoolwork for me and when it's midterms in a few weeks, take me there for my exams!" asked Jena.

"Sure Girlie! It would be my pleasure! Just make yourself at home. I know it needs a little TLC, but it's all yours. I will stop by shortly with some groceries for you," Uncle Jasper replied.

Jena dug inside her purse and tried to hand Uncle Jasper some money. He pushed her hand away and waved his hand out in front her.

"No Girlie, I own a dozen West Beef supermarkets, the groceries are on me! Just focus on you and those babies," Uncle Jasper said.

As promised, Uncle Jasper returned with groceries for Jena. He did so every three days like clockwork over the next month. He also helped Jena keep up with her schoolwork. One day Jena was at the house, and she thought it would be a good idea to visit her mother and father before she gave birth to the twins. She called the same dollar cab that dropped her off at Port Authority, and she went over to her old apartment to see her parents.

After the taxi arrived, Jena dug into her purse, took out some money and handed it to the driver.

"Here's a fifty-dollar bill, I'm gonna be here for two hours tops. I will call you when I am ready to leave," Jena said.

As she walked inside the building, she noticed a tinted Astro Van parked out front of the building. Jena thought nothing of it.

As she entered the building and walked towards the staircase that led to her parent's apartment; four men wearing tactical gear ambushed her. One of them put his hand over her mouth from behind. Another man took out a picture and compared it to Jena. He nodded his head up and down and two men, grabbed her legs, and the men hoisted Jena off her feet. All four men carried Jena in their hands, back outside of the building with them.

Jena bit the man's hand that covered her mouth and

screamed out loud. Another man put a huge knife to her stomach and leaned in close, so she could hear him.

"I wouldn't hesitate to cut your baby out of you, stomp on its skull and leave you both here for dead if you don't shut the fuck up," one of the henchmen said.

Jena's scream alerted The Super, who was mopping the hallway on the third floor. He went back into his apartment and called the police. The commotion scared Jena so bad that her water broke, and she fainted. The tactical team hurried up and put her inside the Astro Van parked out front.

By the time the men carrying Jena in their hands got outside, the place was swarming with police officers. After the incident on Ward Avenue with Herman Brentwood's murder, there has been a police trailer on Ward and Watson Avenue ever since. So, it didn't take them long to respond to the call of a kidnapping in progress.

"Freeze! Put down the girl, we got you surrounded!" exclaimed the police officers.

The tactical team was caught red-handed, with Jena in tote. The hench-men couldn't deny anything. The Astro Van door was slid open and there were two more members of the tactical team in the van. They were waiting for the other four henchmen to return out of the building with Jena.

The cops searched the Astro Van after they ordered the hench-men out of the van and handcuffed them. The officers discovered that the van had bloodstains in the back and the windshield was cracked.

"This Astro Van fits the description of a hit and run, and a drive-by shooting that was reported a month ago. It was the same day that kid Herman Brentwood was shot and killed on Ward Avenue. I don't give a fuck if you sons of bitches are ex-military, connected to the city somehow. You're going down!" said the police officer.

The other officers noticed that Jena was pregnant, unconscious and the front of her dress was wet. An ambulance arrived minutes later and The Paramedic and the EMT'S hopped out, the officers yelled: "Hurry up, I think she's going into labor! I think her water broke!"

The medics didn't waste any time. They strapped Jena in the gurney and hooked her to an IV and an oxygen mask. They put her inside the ambulance and rushed her to the nearest hospital. The paramedic looked inside Jena's purse for her ID and saw the information from her last OBGYN visit.

"Oh shit, she is pregnant with twins! Let's get her to a hospital stat."

The FDNY ambulance weaved through traffic with the sirens blaring and got Jena to Montefiore Hospital by Southern Blvd. The Paramedics radioed the Emergency Room ahead and as they arrived it wasn't a moment too soon.

Since Jena was unconscious and lost some blood. A natural delivery wasn't an option. So, the doctors opted to perform an emergency C-section on her to deliver the twins. They needed to save Jena's life and the lives of the babies. The doctors were able to deliver the twins and successfully stabilized Jena before it was too late.

Chapter 12:

Afterbirth

The morning after Jena gave birth to the twins; she saw a pamphlet on the nightstand about adoption. Jena read the information and contemplated putting the babies up for adoption. She laid in the hospital bed feeling defeated and alone. Jena understood that she wouldn't be getting any help from her family or her babies' father. The decision weighed heavy on her heart like a sumo wrestler before a bout.

There was a knock on the door.

"Come in," Jena said.

A familiar figure entered the room, placing her at ease. Perfect timing, she had been putting up a resistance but had no real plans to make it out.

"Girlie, how are you doing?" said Uncle Jasper.

"I'm not doing too bad Uncle Jasper, thanks for visiting," Jena replied.

No relation to Jena, but might as well have been, he always looked out for her like a real Uncle would have.

"You know, you're the first person to visit me since I had these babies."

Uncle Jasper came with two arms full of gifts.

"Thank you so much, you brought me flowers and so much…"

Before she could finish, she became too choked up to articulate what it was she wanted to say.

"Words alone can't express how much this all means to me. I truly appreciate everything that you done for me so far," Jena said with tears streaming down her cheeks.

"No worries, Girlie, everybody needs a little support in their life. No one is an Island. Everybody deserves some love and support," Uncle Jasper replied.

Jena stretched out her arms toward Uncle Jasper, and they had a long embrace. Her heart filled up with joy, knowing that she isn't wholly forsaken, and not alone in her journey through this "Hard knock life." For a moment, she forgot about everything. No doubt it was her emotions, with her hormones raging out of control, and all. The neonatal nurse walked in with her twins in a bassinet, for a feeding.

"Am I interrupting? Here are your beautiful little darlings. They have been checked and cleaned. Are you ready to feed them?" said the nurse, with the sweetest little voice.

"Yes, yes I am. I'm in all sorts of pain and dead dog-tired, but bring them in, I am prepared to be there for my babies," Jena replied.

"That's good. If you like, I can take the babies back to neonatal care, after your feeding, so that you can get some rest," the nurse said.

"Awe! Look at those babies? What are their names? I can hardly tell them apart, although one looks a little darker than the other," mumbled Uncle Jasper.

"I hadn't noticed," Jena replied.

"Oh, my goodness! It looks like one has blue eyes and the other has light brown hazel eyes. The dark one has curly hair, while the other one has straight blonde hair. Is the baby's father Caucasian?" said Uncle Jasper.

"No, he's Haitian; my father is, Uncle Jasper," Jena replied.

"Those are some beautiful babies, Girlie. You did an awesome job."

"Thank you, Uncle Jasper."

"What are their names, Girlie?"

"Well, Uncle Jasper, the little chocolate one here, her name will be Amanirenas Nzinga. And my little sugar cube there will be

Tiye Khalifa."

"Beautiful names, Girlie, you named them after African warrior queens. Who's the father?"

"Don't ask Uncle Jasper. It's a long story, and that is a road that I don't want to go down anymore. And quite frankly, I would rather not have that individual in our lives. My daughters and I are better off going down the path of least resistance."

"Say no more Girlie, I don't want to pry, I am impartial and here to support you with whatever you need; I am here to help. As a matter of fact, consider me Switzerland. From this day forward, I will block whatever phenomenon you want out of your life.

"It's hard enough out here to take care of yourself much less having two little mouths to feed. Now Girlie, I've heard some things about you," Uncle Jasper said.

"What have you heard Uncle Jasper?" asked Jena.

"I've known for some time now; how hard you've had it during your pregnancy. I've kept my distance but rest assured that I will be here for you through thick and thin, Girlie."

He hugged Jena; it was an edifying one that gave her some reassurance. Something that she has very little of, at this point.

Two nurses entered Jena's room to do their rounds: check her vitals, change the gauze on her C-section stitches, and to see if the girls have been fed properly.

"Hey Jena, we're here to make sure everything is copacetic. My name is Laura, and this is Lisa. Do you need anything? Do you want any ice chips? Do you need any more medication? Are you feeling any pain?" said nurse Laura.

"I would like some ice, otherwise I'm feeling okay. The medication hasn't worn off from the last dosage I got a few hours ago," Jena replied.

Before the nurses conducted the examination of Jena, they asked Uncle Jasper to step out of the room.

"Ok Jena, first, we need to look at those stitches, are you

214

feeling any abdominal pain?" asked nurse Lisa.

"Not while I'm on all these pain killers," Jena replied.

"Ok, the stitches look good, no sign of infection. We're going to change those gauzes, and bedding. Could you stand up for a minute while we change your linens," nurse Laura said.

Jena climbed out of bed and grimaced a little when her feet hit the floor. The impact sent a jolt through her body.

"Thank you, Jena, so far so good, everything is coming along nicely. Is the breast milk coming in yet or is it still colostrum?" said nurse Lisa.

"I think the milk is in, my breast is throbbing, and it's engorged up to my neck," Jena replied.

Jena pulled down her "johnnie" and showed the nurses her breasts.

"Yeah, the milk is in; are the girls latching on properly? If you need one of us to show you how to get them to latch on to your nipples, let us know," nurse Lisa said.

"I think I'll be fine, there is nothing to it but to do it," Jena replied.

"If you need anything, don't hesitate to ask. You are still young, so you should bounce back quick," nurse Laura said.

"Here's some forms that you can fill out for state aid, it's not much, but every little bit helps. I wish I knew about this program when I had my twin boys. You do know that you qualify for two thousand dollars, a month in government aid. This is not WIC, welfare, public assistance or anything like that. This is due to the fact that you had those twins after a specific term in your pregnancy. Consider this a consolation prize, for having these beautiful babies. It is financial backing if you need it to support these precious little girls. Assuming the father isn't in the picture that is," nurse Lisa said.

Nurse Lisa paused for a moment because she could see that Jena was a bit uncomfortable with her intrusion.

215

"I must confess that I overheard a bit of the conversation that you had with that older gentleman. I don't mean to pry, but we women must stick together, especially us women of color, 'entiéndeme," nurse Lisa said.

Jena shook her head in agreement and the nurse continued...

"A bond of sisterhood through knowledge and moral support in the absence of a paternal presence, is important. I'm compelled as a nurse, and as a mother to share my wealth of knowledge of the system.

"The government assistance is so you know that there will always be food on the table, clothes on you or your babies' back, and a roof over your head."

Nurse Lisa continued talking, and nurse Lisa folded her hands out in front of her, nodding her head in agreement. Jena listened to the information intently, and the twins fussed and squirmed in the bassinet.

"I don't say this because I presume to know you or your predicament. Frankly my dear, it's the exact opposite. If you are in need of any assistance, you should take it; you deserve it."

Jena continued to nod her head up and down but realized that the nurses' wings had been clipped before, so she did not interrupt her, Jena allowed her to release her truth.

"Mothers are the crop of this planet. And Men... Men are nothing but the fertilizer.

"Their contributions are what landed society in the predicament we're in, right, now. We mothers are responsible for more than giving birth. We're responsible for nursing, healing, teaching, and imparting our acumen to the next ——"

Nurse Laura stepped on nurse Lisa's foot to shut her up. She stopped talking, cleared her throat and took a breath.

"Anyway, I just wanted to let you know that before you say no to the assistance that you need. Think more about what it takes to raise a child, much less twins. And forgive me for listening in on your conversation with the older gentleman. When I heard you say that you didn't want the father in these girl's life, I had to let you know what I knew. More importantly, how, and where you can get help if you need it," nurse Lisa said.

She handed Jena some forms in a folder.

"Look these over, if you have any questions, I can send a social worker in here to give you a hand. If you need anything, just press that button and one of the nurses on staff will come in right away!" exclaimed nurse Lisa.

Before Jena could thank her, nurse Lisa smiled at Jena and walked out of the room.

"I'm so sorry, Mrs. Lisa can lay it on pretty thick, I'll send in your uncle. Tiye, and Amanirenas are beautiful names, congratulations Jena. I hope y'all have a good day. I will be on until 5:30, but I'll see you before the shift change," nurse Laura said.

Nurse Laura opened the door, held it open, and told Uncle Jasper that he could come back inside the room.

Uncle Jasper stepped back into the room, took off his ten-gallon hat and smiled at nurse Laura.

"Girlie, are your parents or your sister coming? Is anybody coming to see you at all?" asked Uncle Jasper.

"No, Uncle Jasper, unfortunately they didn't agree with my relationship with my baby's father. So, they don't want to have anything to do with me. My mother and my father don't care about me at all," Jena replied.

"Girlie, I don't think that's entirely true."

"According to them, I am a statistic: A young teenage girl who barely finished high school, got pregnant out of wedlock, with no aspirations of going to college any time soon. They made me feel like I am a disappointment. My parents pretty much cut me off. My father expressed his concerns, and my mother didn't defend me."

"How are you planning to take care of yourself and these babies, Girlie?"

"Listen to me, I'm going to divulge something about the

217

father of these twins, that I haven't told anyone. He's in this situation with the mayor's office, specifically the deputy mayor. They had a sexual relationship when he was much younger, before he was of age. As a result, they have a son together.

"Mayor Meléndez has this program, where they wanted Claude to recruit virgin girls and sometimes boys. He would lure them down to this club in Manhattan, called Divvy Divvies. While there, they would pledge their virtue to these rich influential people all over the state of New York. I'm talking doctors, lawyers, CEOs of Fortune 500 companies, so on and so forth," Jena said.

She told him everything she knew, while she nursed the twins. Uncle Jasper wasn't entirely surprised, but he was intrigued with what Jena had to say.

"I could only imagine that 'For unto whomsoever much is given, of him shall be much required,' (Luke 12:48) Uncle Jasper replied.

"Well, Claude, told me that they would pay upwards of a million dollars. They would give one hundred thousand dollars upfront, and the rest of the money would be incentives to the teenagers. They got to attend any college in the country of their choice. All-expense paid full room and board. Could you imagine what that can do for a kid from our neighborhood? Just think how alluring that is for a kid in the inner-city."

"Yes, I sure do, makes me wish that I still had mine to sell, Girlie."

"Oh! That's not all, Uncle Jasper. this could make your undies chafe you." If your family has any outstanding bills or financially strapped at all, they will take care of all that stuff as well."

Jena looked down at the twins and adjusted them as she fed her babies.

"I wish I'd never agreed to join 'The Program in the first place. But the devil is in the details, and Claude sold me on the details. I trusted him you know."

Jena looked away from Uncle Jasper and a single tear ran

218

down her cheek.

"It's alright Girlie," said Uncle Jasper.

"I have to take responsibility for my role in all of this. I was enamored by his rugged good looks, his charm, and that gorgeous smile of his. I must admit, he did warn me about the consequences if I didn't follow through. I was supposed to be pure for the individual who paid for my virginity.

"I just wanted to be next to him and do anything he asked me to do. I was getting too cozy with Claude, and that didn't sit well with the people that ran the program. It was fun at first, until..."

"What went wrong Girlie?"

"Something just didn't sit well with me, Uncle Jasper. I probably was just blinded by my love for Claude. Even though he recruited other people in The Program, I felt special. I just didn't feel comfortable with giving myself to somebody that I didn't care for. I didn't see myself enjoying the moment.

"At the time, I didn't think about the ramifications of my actions. I didn't consider the fact that I'd lose out on all that money. Mmm, mmm! Look at me now, two babies, no Claude, no million dollars, I'm in fear for my life, and the lives of my family," Jena said.

"Is your family, okay? Is Claude alright? Is that the reason he is not here with you and these beautiful babies?" asked Uncle Jasper.

Jena looked at Uncle Jasper and shrugged her shoulders.

"I want to believe that Claude still cares for me," Jena replied.

"Let me ask you a question? Weren't you careful? I mean you knew what the situation was and that these people do not play when it comes to their money," Uncle Jasper said.

"Yes, we were Uncle Jasper, they just put two and two together, I guess. It wasn't hard to figure out, we were inseparable."

"Wow Girlie, you just said a mouthful. It's kind of unfortunate that you had to go through what you did. You know I can see how you've sacrificed. You only did what you thought was the right thing."

"Thank you for listening to my story Uncle Jasper, I really truly appreciate you. You don't know what that means to me, there are not many people, in the world I can trust. I thank you."

Jena couldn't contain her emotions. Maybe because of all what she went through or maybe because she just gave birth. Either way, she was full of mixed emotions. Her eyes welled up with tears.

At that moment, the door opened, and the nurses returned to take the twins back to the neonatal care unit.

"I think I'll be leaving now Girlie, I'm gonna get the apartment ready for you and the twins. You get some rest," Uncle Jasper said.

Uncle Jasper left Jena and the twins to get some rest.

Jena fell asleep and rested for two hours until she was abruptly awakened by a knock on the door.

"Hello Jena! Hello! Wake up! The twins have been causing a raucous, they're starving," nurse Laura said as she wheeled in the carts with the twins inside the room.

"Yeah!" replied Jena, still half asleep and groggy from being awakened by the nurse.

"Are you awake?" asked nurse Laura.

Jena's eyes closed, and nurse Laura snapped her fingers.

"Come Jena, the babies want to be fed," nurse Laura said.

"Jena, we notice that they are losing their color when we did the thumb test."

"What is the thumb test?"

"When we pressed our thumbs on their skin with pressure, and their skin color doesn't return as quickly as it should. We also did a light test."

"Oh my gosh, is something wrong with my babies?"

"Let me help you get them latched on your breast properly before I go into any further details."

Nurse Laura propped up two pillows on the bed next to Jena and put each baby down one at a time. She placed their bodies underneath Jena's arms, and their heads facing forward latched on to each nipple.

"Whew, now that's settled. Well, to answer your question not necessarily. It's caused by a buildup of bilirubin, and likely jaundice," said nurse Laura.

Jena sat up in the hospital bed and cried uncontrollably. The nurse rubbed her shoulder, to calm her down. Nurse Laura gave a more in-depth explanation:

"There is no need to worry yet. But we discovered that their bilirubin levels are higher than normal. Normal indirect bilirubin would be under 5.2 mg/dL within the first 24 hours of birth. But many newborns have some kind of jaundice and bilirubin levels that rise above 5 mg/dL within the first few days after birth."

"What do you mean? what is, what is bilirubin?"

"Well, Bilirubin attached by the liver to glucuronic acid, a glucose-derived acid, is called direct, or conjugated, bilirubin. Bilirubin not attached to glucuronic acid is called indirect, or unconjugated, bilirubin. All the bilirubin in your blood together is called total bilirubin. Basically, what I'm saying is that the babies may have jaundice," replied nurse Laura.

"Will they be alright?" asked Jena.

"Sure, in an infant, high (usually indirect) bilirubin and jaundice can be very dangerous and may be caused by several factors. There are three common types:

"The first is physiological jaundice. Within two to four days after birth, a brief delay in the functioning of the liver and is not usually serious.

"The second is breastfeeding jaundice. During the first week of life, caused by a baby not nursing well or low milk supply in the mother," nurse Laura said.

Jena hung on to every word the nurse said. She feared that she's responsible for her baby's condition. Jena held on to every statement, anticipating a solution.

"The third is breast milk Jaundice. After two to three weeks of life, this is caused by the processing of some substances in breast milk. All of these can be easily treated and are usually harmless if treated. Some more serious conditions that cause high bilirubin and jaundice in an infant such as sickle cell anemia.

"Oftentimes the baby and the mother have different blood types. In those cases, your blood cells are attacking and killing off all of the blood cells that you both shared in-utero called erythroblastosis.

"Because their livers are not strong enough to get rid of all of those blood cells. They accumulate in the system. We are waiting for results from a blood test which could tell us more. I'm afraid if we don't do something about it soon, then it will be too much for the babies' systems. They could suffer terrible damage to their organs," nurse Laura said.

The feel of dread and despondency overwhelmed Jena's poor heart as the nurse continued describing her twins' disorder, she heard no remedy.

Nurse Laura put her hand on Jena's shoulder and rubbed it gently.

"They may develop liver failure and brain damage, if we don't do something now," nurse Laura said.

"What is it?" asked Jena.

"Fortunately, Phototherapy is a therapy that can be administered to them for the high levels of bilirubin," nurse Laura replied.

"What is Phototherapy and how can it help?" asked Jena.

"Phototherapy is treatment with a special type of light. Placing the baby in a Bili-light bed which helps to breakdown the bilirubin levels in the blood. Photo-oxidation adds oxygen to the bilirubin, so it dissolves easily in water. Therefore, bringing down the levels could be passed out through their stool and urine," nurse Laura replied.

The news of the treatment pulled her from the brink of complete despair. Granted, the therapy works, and their issues is not that severe.

"You will have to feed them Jena. So, the collection of meconium that they have in their bodies can be broken down," nurse Laura said.

"Please speak to me in layman's terms. Instead of using all the technical terms that I don't understand," Jena replied, as she looked up at nurse Laura.

"Okay, breast feeding the twins will help them. The light therapy treatment will do the rest to help push the bilirubin out through their stool.

"After everything is said and done, I just wanted to let you know this is the situation. Where the probability of your babies being fine is high. I just would be remiss not to give you all of the facts. Before I leave, I just want you to remember your breast milk is the best thing for them. So, give them as much as you can. It will help them pass the bilirubin buildup in their system.

"Meanwhile, we'll shoot them over to the neonatal care unit, put them under the Bili-light, and everything should be fine. It wasn't my intention to scare you, I want to let you know the severity of the situation."

"Oh my God, you scared me for a moment," Jena said, and put her hand over her chest.

Jena closed her eyes, took a deep breath, and exhaled. The Ujjayi breathing exercise calmed her anxiety, but she wasn't fully settled.

"Does this mean that after I breast feed them, they will be out of danger? What about the blood test?" asked Jena, after she opened her eyes.

"Listen, I have been a nurse for a long time. My professional

223

opinion, I believe that they'll be fine. Although, if anything changes, I will let you know. Okay!" replied nurse Laura.

"Thank you, Laura, I'm glad you guys caught this in time. I would've never known about the symptoms until it was too late."

"You're welcome, Jena, that's what we're here for. I'm going to leave now, and I will see you in a couple of hours to do my rounds. Just let me know if you have any problems with them latching on."

"O.K. thank you Laura, I appreciate it."

"If you need anything you press that button. Everything will be ok, alright Jena."

Nurse Laura left the room, and the phone rang. Jena reached for the phone on the side table and picked up the receiver.

"Hello!" said Jena.

"Hey Jena, this is Margot, how are you?" replied Margot.

"Hey Blossom!"

"How are you doing gurl? Asia told me that you were in the hospital having a baby."

"Yeah, I had twins."

"Congratulations gurl, I gotta come see you. What did you have?"

"I had two girls; my sister told you?!"

"Yes, she did, that's why I am calling you. I had to talk to my gurl, and make sure you were alright. Initially, when I heard you were in the hospital, I thought you was seriously injured or some shit like that. I heard it through the grapevine that some people kidnapped you."

"From whom?" said Jena, as she picked up the twins one by one to breast feed them.

"Jamie said that you went to Bridgeport, Connecticut. Word on the street is that you were in trouble, and that you were on the run. I didn't get details of what happened. Does it have to do with

Claude? You know Asia never trusted his black ass. I assumed the worst that he tried to hurt you or worse."

"No, no, gurl, Claude didn't try to hurt me. That's not funny at all."

"Jena, I know about 'The Program,' so you don't have to beat around the bush. I never told anyone this, but when I was younger, I was forced into joining. I couldn't completely go through with it. I was groomed by Mayor Rodolfo Meléndez and believe it or not my uncle recruited me. He was mad that I didn't complete my initiation."

Jena didn't say a word and adjusted her body to a more comfortable position.

"Hello, Jena, are you still there?" said Margot, as she waited for a response.

"Yes, I'm feeding the twins and talking to you at the same time; give me a sec—— I'm trying to wrap my mind around what you just told me. What was the initiation?" replied Jena.

"I had to give him a blow-job. I started to, but I stopped and ran out the room. My Uncle was in the hallway, and he chewed me up and spit me out. I ran out of that club of theirs, Divvy Divvy's, and I never looked back."

"Oh, my goodness gurl, how come nothing ever happened to you?"

"My Uncle who's a judge must have sorted something out with the other members."

Jena paused again and put down Tiye in the bassinet because she fell asleep. Margot could hear the shuffling through the phone. Jena sat back in the upright position, then sighed.

"Claude recruited me into 'The Program,' but I gave him head. Someone else named Arthur Rosenbaum was set to groom me. I'm so confused Blossom," Jena replied.

"Don't worry, that shit ain't important gurl. The only thing that matters now, are those babies."

"I'm afraid that they will continue to send goons after me until I'm——"

"Hush don't think like that Jena, nothing won't happen to you. Especially since you didn't take any money."

"That's not entirely true," Jena said, then she paused.

"You took money? Oh, my goodness, did you receive the first installment?" replied Margot.

"Um—— Yeah."

"Oh shit, you have to get out of town. They're serious about their money. That means Arthur Rosenbaum already paid "The Program" a million dollars."

"I believe now that I have to leave New York. I disrupted the whole program, I was supposed to give it up, but I couldn't go through with it. I don't regret doing what Claude and I did. My life changed when I discovered that I was pregnant. I thought about getting an abortion, I couldn't go through with it. I even thought about giving them up for adoption, but I couldn't do that either.

"The first time that I looked in their eyes and held their little hands; I saw their futures, and I wanted to be there. I can't, I can't do this all by myself though, but I gotta do what I gotta do. I'm 17 years old going on 18, this is a blessing from God. I have to take care of my responsibilities."

Margot was sniffling and crying on the other end of the phone. She took a deep breath then wiped the tears from her cheeks.

"I hear you girl, I'm proud of you. I'm gonna be there for you through thick and thin. I'm going to be those babies' godmother," Margot said.

Jena and Margot both laughed and cried together.

"I can see us fighting me over who loves these babies more."

"Yup, you know I would win too. Hey, does Claude know that you gave birth?"

"I don't know, I haven't spoken to anyone. I really don't think I should tell him. I should just let sleeping dogs lie. Besides, he's capable of taking care of himself. I remember when Rodrigo grabbed my ass at Claude's graduation party. He beat him up in front of everyone for disrespecting me. Plus, do you know my ex-boyfriend, Darren?"

"I think I do," Margot replied.

"Well, he used to be abusive to me. I made the mistake of telling him that he slapped me in my face swelling up my jaw. Lord knows if Claude will confront him. Darren is a semi-pro martial arts fighter in that "Knuckle up Fight Club," in The Bronx. But he doesn't care, he'll fight anyone."

"I never trusted Claude Jena, he seemed dangerous."

"He is, I saw a dark side of him. If you see Claude Margot don't tell him anything. The less he knows the better," Jena said.

"I hear you girl," Margot replied to reassure Jena that she wouldn't talk.

"I think "The Program" is over though. The FBI arrested Mayor Rodolfo Meléndez and charged him with sex trafficking. The Deputy Mayor Marisol Velasquez and Claude are working together to revamp "The Program." As a path toward redemption to find people who wants a chance to come to America to have a better future. In this new program, they recruit top students from third world countries. Then they give them student visas, scholarships in the hopes they could come here and get a good education.

"Eventually, they would go back to their countries to help their communities where they're from. It's a good program, it's called "The Helping Hand Initiative."

"I heard that is an amazing program, and they are in all kinds of countries all over the world. Israel, Africa, Australia, Papua New Guinea, Cuba, India, parts in Eastern Europe, Asia, South America, and they're in every Caribbean country you could think of. They are in every third world country in the world. Now, these students have a real chance to compete on a global stage. Otherwise, they would've wallowed into obscurity.

"It is a good thing. This program is not like when you and I

227

were coaxed into giving up our virginities. Instead, they opened the program for people to benefit from it," Margot said.

"Were you paid money for your involvement in "The Program?" asked Jena.

"No, what I got was hush money, I have a family member who was the ADA at the time, and they didn't like my uncle. In the long run the ends justify the means. I'm using that money for good. I'm going to be a gemologist. I'm going to make money the old fashion way, by earning it with jewelry.

"Everybody wants to be remembered, I plan on making a name for myself as a world renown professional jeweler."

"Hey, Blossom, you go out and make that money."

"Yeah, thanks gurl! Whenever you're ready to come out of hiding, you let me know. Here, I'll give you my number. I am going to be a phone call away. I don't know if you want me to visit at all because you know they might have a trail on me or something like that. I don't want to jeopardize you and the twins, cause their still mad about their money. So, I might just stay away from the hospital. Call me when you get a chance, so that I can know that you're alright. Get a pen and paper and write down my number."

"Okay give me a sec. I have to put down the baby, she fell asleep."

Jena was suspicious of Margot; she really wasn't sure of her true intentions. Jena hadn't spoken to Asia in months. 'How does she know so much about me in such great detail,' Jena thought.

"I got a pen and paper, give me the number," Jena said when got back on the phone.

"The number is 347-555-4646," Margot replied.

"Ok, that is 3 4 7 5 5 5 4 6 4 6."

"Yes girl, that's it"

"I'll give you a call when I get settled. We haven't talked in like forever."

"Alright, take care, I love you."

"Love you too gurl, bye."

Jena stayed in the hospital for a week. The hospital needed to monitor the baby's bilirubin levels. Jena counted down the days until Tiye, and Amanirenas were ready to leave the hospital.

(Knock, knock, knock) "Jena, this is it, the babies bilirubin levels are normal. Their bodies seem to be functioning well. Take care of yourself and those darling twins," nurse Laura said.

"Thank you, Laura, let me make sure that I filled out all of the paperwork. I don't want to forget anything. I got my keys, got my wallet, got everything," Jena replied.

"Let me walk you to the neonatal care unit."

"Yay, I couldn't wait until this moment came. I'm so ecstatic, I need to get my babies."

Nurse Laura escorted Jena out of the room slowly. Then they made their way to the next floor, to check the babies out of the hospital.

"Thank God it is all good. I'm going home," she sang happily to herself as she entered the neonatal care. "Hello," she greets the nurses in the bay where all of the babies were that had to have extra special care.

"Hey, mom," one of the nurses responds. "Y'all ready to go?" asked one of the nurses.

"Yes, I sure am. I am ready to go. It has been a long stay," Jena replied.

"Do you have a car seat?"

"No, I don't have no car seat."

"You're gonna have to have a car seat for the babies to bring them home."

This dilemma put Jena in a moment of desperation, she was posed with questions that she couldn't quite answer, or remedy now. 'What they gonna do keep my girls if I don't have a car,' she thought to herself.

"I'm not driving, so, what if I wanted to go on the train with them? Does that mean that I can't take my girls home? What if I don't have a car? Are you going to buy me one? This doesn't make any gosh darn sense—— I don't have no gosh darn car seat! I didn't know I needed a car seat!" said Jena as she pounded her hand on the desk.

Uncle Jasper walked into the neonatal unit smiling from ear to ear. His smile turned upside down after he heard the commotion.

"I didn't know that was the situation, I want to speak with the shift supervisor!" said Jena.

"It's just policy, Mam, could you please keep your voice down," the nurse replied and pumped her palms downward trying to calm Jena down. If she got any louder the neonatal care will be like a zoo filled with crying newborns.

"Hey Girlie, what's going on here?" asked Uncle Jasper.

"Uncle Jasper, this lady told me if I didn't have a car seat, then I couldn't take the twins," Jena replied.

"There's no need to get worked up, look at what I have."

"Is this a stroller equipped with car seats for the twins?"

Sam brought a double stroller built for twins, with detachable car seats.

"Right on time, I thought I was going to have to get ghetto up in here."

"I see, I didn't know you and the twins were going to get released today. I wanted this to be a surprise. I knew you didn't have a stroller and car seat for the girls. So, I'm here, I said that I got you. Everything happens for a reason Girlie."

"I have a car seat now Miss, can I take my twins home please?!" Jena said.

"Yes Mam, you have to understand that it's protocol, the hospital's policy is set in place to ensure the safety of every newborn that gets discharged from this hospital," the nurse replied.

Jena rolled her eyes at the nurse as she signed the release

forms to get the twins.

"Uncle Jasper, you are a lifesaver, I don't know what I would do without you," Jena said.

"Yeah, it's alright I told you I will support you, we're family. Bring these babies on, put them in the car seats and we will be on our way," Uncle Jasper replied.

After Jena packed up the twins in the stroller, they walked to the elevator, and got off in the lobby of the hospital. Uncle Jasper's car was parked out in front of the hospital.

"I thought you said you didn't know that the twins and I were getting discharged Uncle Jasper. Why are you parked here?"

"I know the security guards' father, I told him why I was here, and he let me park here as a courtesy. That's neither here nor there Girlie, lets focus on the now and secure these babies on the car."

In no time Uncle Jasper, Jena and the security guard were able to secure the twins in the car. Uncle Jasper tugged on the straps one last time, making sure the twins weren't going to fly over the back seat as he drove on the cross Bronx Expressway to his house.

"Got it, this is harder than it looks, Girlie. A taxi driver wouldn't have been able to secure these car seats Girlie."

"Uncle Jasper, thank you so much. I really appreciate everything you are doing for me."

Jena got in the front passenger side of Uncle Jasper's Oldsmobile station wagon. As she strapped in her seatbelt, the belt parted her now 36 double D breasts.

"Girlie those breasts are huge. Are they swollen or is it all breast milk?" asked Uncle Jasper.

"It's milk, and they hurt too. I hope they won't sag down to my waist after all this. It's all for them and well worth the anguish, these girls eat round the clock," Jena replied.

Traffic was light on the cross Bronx expressway, it didn't take long to make it back home. They got out of the car and Uncle

Jasper took the double stroller out the trunk. Jena put the twins in the stroller, and they walked a few steps towards the house. Jena reached for her keys to open the door to the basement apartment.

"I got something better for you," Uncle Jasper said, and turned to Jena.

"What do you mean, this is enough for me, it is a warm roof over our heads for the time being," Jena replied.

"No, up here Girlie, you're not living down there anymore. You're going to need more space than that. So, I am going to give you the 1st floor apartment."

"Uncle Jasper, I can't afford the rent, I don't have any money."

"There's no rent whatsoever, Girlie, remember I said I'm going to support you, with no questions asked, I'm Switzerland, remember. I know y'all pay whenever you can, but for now, I'm going to be there for you. It is not about the money for me, it is about doing the right thing."

"There is no way, I can repay you, for your kindness Uncle Jasper. Thank you very much."

Tears ran down her face faster than the Bronx River. It was tears of joy, shame, and desertion. This should've been quality time where Jena, her baby's father, and her immediate family should be celebrating this occasion. Exchanging pleasantries, showered with gifts, patience, tenderness, and love. Instead, Jena was forsaken by everyone except for this kind man. Who is asking for nothing in return, at least not yet? In the back of her mind, she knew that this arrangement was temporary.

Her mind settled on her faith, and she came to the conclusion that only God could send Uncle Jasper into her life, when she's so vulnerable. He has implanted a luminous smile on her face and an eternal warmth in her soul. Jena felt safe around Uncle Jasper. He opened the front door to the apartment, and Jena followed behind him, pushing the stroller.

Jena entered the first-floor apartment and said, "Oh my Goodness! This apartment is beautiful. It's nice and spacious too. Look at these hardwood floors; they are amazing. I love it," she said.

Just for a moment, Jena felt like a princess in all of those fairytales most girls read about when they're little. Uncle Jasper showed Jena the kitchen, the bathroom, and the two bedrooms. The apartment was furnished with a crib for the twins, a futon for the living room and a bedroom set.

"It's way more than I could ever dream of Uncle Jasper, you got me ——"

She paused when she looked in the second room.

"Wow, they have their own room," Jena said.

Her voice echoed throughout the apartment. For most people, starting a family is planned. First you have a strong bond with a mate, you profess your love and adoration for them in front of friends and family. Then you consummate the relationship, and nine months later a baby boy or a girl.

That was her fantasy since she was a little girl. Jena thought she found prince charming with Claude, but it was just a façade.

'This would've been really nice for Claude, the twins and I,' she thought. Wishful thinking, not a bad setup for a single teenage mom with twin girls. This is definitely a huge deal. In some ways it's more than what she feels she deserves. Especially looking back at her moral slips.

"Here Girlie, I got you and the girls some things to tie you over while you get settled: Diapers, blankets, wipes, clothes, bottles, towels sheets for the room, and there's food in the refrigerator. If you need anything else let me know. I'm going to let you tend to those babies, I'll see you soon Girlie."

In all the excitement, she missed feeding time. So, Jena brought the twins inside their room and breast fed the girls. Jena burped them, changed their diapers, wiped them off and put the twins down to sleep in their new crib.

Over the next couple of weeks, Jena got into a routine

but was tired from lack of sleep. Feedings every two hours don't leave one enough time to rest.

"How can I pay Uncle Jasper back for all he has done," Jena thought, one day while cleaning the apartment.

Jena picked up the phone and called Uncle Jasper.

"Hey, Uncle Jasper, could you stop by the house when you get a chance?" asked Jena.

"Sure Girlie, is everything okay?" replied Uncle Jasper.

"Yes, everything is fine, I want to show you something."

"Okay Girlie, I'll be right over…"

Uncle Jasper opened the door and entered the apartment. "Jena it's Uncle Jasper," he called out.

He slowly entered the dimly lit apartment.

"How are you doing Girlie? Where are you?" asked Uncle Jasper.

"Why is it so dark in here? Why are there so many lit candles?" thought Uncle Jasper.

"I'm in the bedroom just come back here, I'm feeding the babies," shouted Gina, from the back of the apartment.

Uncle Jasper took off his shoes, and he walked through the apartment to the twin's room. It was empty, so he walked over to Jena's room and knocked on her door.

(Knock, knock…)

"Come in," Jena commanded.

Uncle Jasper slowly entered the room, it was dark, and there were sticks of lit incense throughout the room.

"Girlie, why are the lights off?" asked Uncle Jasper.

Jena had jazz music playing, she was wearing a satin robe, and a multi-colored pillowcase was draped over the lamp. The soft iridescent light illuminated the dark room.

The candles kindled and Jena's silhouette danced on the wall from the flickering of the flames like shadow puppets. Uncle Jasper walked closer to Jena, she stood up from off the bed and took off her robe revealing a taut negligée. The moon light struck her young voluptuous body, exposing her bare breast to him. Sam averted his eyes.

"I just want to repay you for all you have done for us. So, I'm offering myself to you, do what you want with me, anything you want, I'll do for you. This is my way to thank you. You have been so supportive," Jena said, in a sultry voice to the backdrop of the jazz music playing in the background.

"Girlie, this is not what I want, why would you offer me sex? This is not my motivation for taking care of you. I wouldn't dare put that pressure on you. Go ahead, put your clothes back on," Uncle Jasper replied.

Uncle Jasper turned around and waited until Jena put back on her robe. He sat down on the bed once she was fully clothed.

"Sit down Girlie," Uncle Jasper said, and he directed Jena to sit beside him.

"My oldest daughter fell for the allure of the fast life. When she first migrated here from Monserrat, she ran with the wrong crowd, and got seduced by a pimp, and he forced her to turn tricks. My daughter became addicted to heroin to cope with the extraneous circumstances, and one day she overdosed.

My daughter was a smart girl with potential. My little girl could've been anything she chose to be. A true pillar of the community. People envied her, but most people looked up to her. She was my 'She-ro.'" Sam stood up and gazed at the full moon.

"I blamed myself for years because I couldn't protect her from the streets. I blamed her pimp for taking my little girl from me ever since she overdosed. I used to ask myself, 'Where did I go wrong? Did I not give her enough attention?' I worked too hard to provide my family with the things I couldn't have when I grew up in Monserrat. I realized that it was all her choice. She was a prostitute, a drug abuser and in the end she overdosed. A sickness so many of us fall victim to in this community. I did my best, but it was not enough."

"So, you don't have to offer me your body. All I want to do is take care of you. Girlie, you are helping me cope with my pain and the torment of losing my daughter, and my wife. My family has been in disarray after their deaths. That's why I help you, or anybody else I can," Uncle Jasper said, as he wiped the tears off his face with a handkerchief.

"I feel so embarrassed, I am so sorry for this Uncle Jasper. I didn't know about your daughter, or your motive. But you can't help everyone though, sometimes I feel like a lost cause," Jena replied.

"There is no reason you shouldn't make it because she didn't. I realize I am trying to make up for not being able to save her. So, whatever I can do to help, is satisfactory for me. It is an honor to lend a helping hand."

Jena put her arm around Uncle Jasper as he continued to use his handkerchief, to wipe tears from his eyes.

The next day while resting with the twins in the bed, the phone rang. It was a loud rotary phone, and it was on the other side of the bed. So, she wrestled the sheets in haste and maneuvered over the twins to quell the loud phone from waking them up. Jena answered the phone and the voice on the other end said:

"Hello Jena, it's me Asia, your sister."

"Asia, what's up?"

"How are you doing? Did you forget about me? I know you didn't." Asia said joking around.

"Oh, my goodness, how did you get this number? Won't you get in trouble for consorting with the likes of me? I thought mom and dad forbade you from having anything to do with me, Claude, and my babies. You're an aunt by the way, I know you figured that much."

"I ran into Uncle Jasper the other day in "Western Beef," and he gave me this number to call you. You already know, Daddy and Mommy have their hands, eyes, and ears on every aspect of my life.

I had to go to Jaime's house to even make this phone call. Daddy forbade me to even have any contact with you whatsoever, he said, 'Mi nuh wan Jena whoring ways fi run off pan yuh,' Asia said.

Jena kissed her teeth and rolled her eyes. "Anyways, I'm happy to hear your voice. You're my sister either way. I know how our parents can be. You could never stand up to them anyway. Asia I can't talk about this shit right now, I was just asleep. A luxury I have not been able to enjoy these days. You know that you almost woke them up. These girls don't want to sleep long for nothing," Jena replied.

"Hear me out, okay ——"

"No! I don't have time to ease your guilt, I have real shit going on in my life right now."

"Don't be like that Jena, I could only imagine how hard it has been for you. I just feel like there is much that is up in the air between us, we should address them when you calm down. I want to come and see you now, but I don't even know where you live."

"It's alright Asia, you don't have to do me any favors. I'll talk to you later."

"Wait, wait, wait, Jena, what are their names and sizes?"

"Well, if you must know, they were born premature, so buy newborn or one month old clothes. I named them Tiye and Amanirenas. I was gonna name one Eighsza and Aphrica because these girls are grandma's eighth and ninth grandkids. So, I merged the number eight and Asia."

"Awe, you were gonna name one of them Asia after me? I love you too big sis."

"And, you know how I love Greek mythology and African culture, so I was gonna merge the name of Aphrodite and Africa together."

"Those names would've been very unique Jena."

"But I decided to name them what I did because I felt slighted."

"Jena, I love you, you're my big sister and I adore you. I want to see you, where do you live?"

"Well, if you must know, when Blossom visits me, you can come along with her. I'll talk to you later, peace."

Jena a hung up the phone on Asia, but the call lifted her spirits a little, knowing now that her baby sister still cared for her, meant the world to her.

"Thank you for letting me call my sister, but if you tell my parents I spoke with Jena or where she's at when I find out; I won't ever forgive you. As a matter of fact, I would tell my uncles that you hit me, so they would fuck your shit up," said Asia, then she put down the receiver and turned to Jamie.

"Chill, Asia, damn. Don't worry, I got you, Jena was my girl way before Claude even came into the picture. You ain't gotta worry 'bout nothing," replied Jamie.

"Thank you, baby, I love you for this. I thought we were close, but I didn't know that you cared about my sister and I that much," said Asia, then she smirked, looked Jamie in his eyes, put her forehead to his and kissed him on the lips.

"Of course, you think I would've been taking buses, being overprotective, and even sneaking Jena in my crib if I didn't care. Come on now, you should've known me better than that Asia," Jamie said.

"Good answer," Asia replied, and she smiled at Jamie.

Asia pushed Jamie's shoulder down on the bed, mounted him, and kissed him on the forehead. Asia entwined her fingers with his and kissed his eyelids, nose, cheeks, earlobes.

"I'm ready, I'm ready for you to make love to me," Asia said.

"You for real? No bullshitin'?" replied Jamie, as he stretched his eyes wide open.

"Yes Jamie, do you have a condom?"

"Hell, yah I got a condom."

238

"Shit, which one do you want me to use?" replied Jamie, then he whipped out a Magnum from one pocket, and a Long Love from the next one.

"I don't know Jamie, pick one, I'm a virgin I don't know about condoms. Wait a minute, why did you have immediate access to condoms Jamie? You thought you were gonna get some pussy, huh!"

Asia punched Jamie in his chest and leaned back from his face, but still straddled his pelvis.

"Nah, Nah, Nah, I'm a dude Asia, I gotta have these things, my older brothers taught me to always be prepared because you never know."

Jamie grabbed Asia by her wrist and pulled her back down on his chest.

"Stop trippin' you are the one who said, 'I'm ready for you to take my virginity.' Relax, it's me, I love you, Asia," Jamie replied.

"Awe, you love me, Jamie?"

"Yes, Asia, I loved you from the moment I met you."

Jamie grabbed Asia by her waist and pulled her in closed to him and French kissed her. She was wearing a schoolgirl uniform, so it was easy access, he removed her panties, Asia unbuckled his belt, unbuttoned his pants, pulled down his zipper, and his erect penis peaked out the front of his boxers.

"Oh my… I didn't know you were packing like this Jamie, why is it so warm?" asked Asia.

"Because all of the blood in my head is inside my dick," Jamie replied, and he smiled.

Asia giggled, and he unwrapped the magnum condom, took it out the wrapper, and pulled it down the shaft of his erect penis. He caressed Asia's buttocks, then motioned his hands up her back, over her shoulders, then down the front of her blouse. Jamie unbuttoned it while they continued to kiss each other revealing her bra covering Asia's 32 double D breast.

239

The latch was in the front where the underwire laid, so he pulled it, and Asia's bare breast flopped down on his chest. Jamie pulled her knees up closer to his ribcage, then Asia reached down in between her thighs and grabbed his erect penis and placed it at the entrance of her pulsating vagina.

Jamie thrust his throbbing member inside Asia's wet, welcoming virgin vagina. She moaned and grabbed the bed sheet as he motioned his penis in and out of her. Jamie bit Asia's bottom lip, then kissed her chin. He licked the side of her neck, nuzzled her collar bone, then Jamie used both hands to grab her breasts. He plunged his face in between them and continued to thrust inside Asia. Jamie licked, then sucked her nipples one after the other.

"I want you to fuck me harder," Asia said.

Jamie grabbed Asia by her shoulder and moved her down to the bed onto her back. He obliged her request and thrust his penis inside her faster, faster until she wrapped her arms around his neck, her legs around his waist.

"I'm coming, I'm coming!" screamed Asia.

"Ah, me too!" yelled Jamie.

They both ejaculated simultaneously. Asia and Jamie laid there wrapped in each other's arms panting and sweating. Jamie looked down at Asia and kissed the top of her head.

"Are you okay? Did you enjoy it?" asked Jamie

Asia looked up into Jamie's eyes and nodded her head up and down. "I love you," They both said in unison and smiled.

"You owe me a Pepsi!" exclaimed Asia.

Jamie smiled and eased back off Asia and saw that her crotch was bloody, and so was his.

"Oh shit, it looks like a crime scene, my sheets are saturated with blood."

"Jamie, get me a towel or a rag, don't leave me here like a stuck pig."

He smiled and walked out the room towards the bathroom

and put two rags underneath the faucet, turned on the hot water, wrung it out, then brought them back inside the room. Jamie gave one to Asia, and they both cleaned up themselves. Jamie removed the soiled fitted sheet from off his mattress, brought it downstairs, and put it in the washing machine. "Shit, I hope these blood stains will come out these sheets, or my moms gonna kill me."

Jamie walked back upstairs with a new fitted sheet and made the bed back up. Asia and Jamie both laid down next to each other and fell asleep.

Two months later, Jena laid in her bed fast asleep, and the doorbell rang.

(Ring, ring, ring, ring) The doorbell rang non–stop, until Jena woke up, and walked toward the front door. "Who the hell is this ringing the doorbell like a mad person. They better have a real good explanation of why they're being such assholes," she retorted to the incessant doorbell ringing.

The doorbell continued to ring nonstop until Jena reached the front door. "Who the hell is it?" said Jena in a stern voice.

"It's Uncle Jasper, Girlie, open the door," he replied.

Jena unlatched the chain on the door, unlocked the locks, then opened it.

"Hey Uncle Jasper, what's going on? Is everything okay?" asked Jena.

"Yeah Girlie, everything is fine," Uncle Jasper replied.

"Okay, come on in."

Uncle Jasper stepped forward, then two masked men armed with assault rifles, pushed their way inside the apartment. One of the men used the butt of his gun and hit Uncle Jasper in the back of his head, sending him to the ground, knocking him unconscious. The other man punched Jena in her face, put a knapsack over her head, and caught her limp body before it hit the hardwood floor.

He zip-tied her hands behind her back, carried her limp body into the kitchen, and put her down on a chair around the kitchen table. Jena woke up five minutes later to the sound of her twins

241

crying, and the sound of high heels walking on the hardwood floor toward her. One of the men pulled the knapsack off Jena's head, and she opened her eyes only to see the two masked men holding her wailing twins in their arms.

"Please don't hurt my babies. I'll do anything you want, just leave them alone," Jena said.

Out of her peripheral vision, Jena noticed Marisol seated at the other end of the kitchen table.

"You had to fuck Busy bee! You couldn't resist?! You just, couldn't, follow, protocol. You know that the stunt you two pulled, ruined a multi-million-dollar operation. Here is what's going to happen. You are going to leave town and never come back to New York again or my men here are going to crush those babies' skulls underneath their boots. Then we are going to pay your parents a visit and torture them. If you think I'm bluffing; Try me, bitch!" said Marisol.

Marisol looked Jena in her eyes, pulled a nickel-plated desert eagle out of her purse, and placed it on the kitchen table.

Jena sat on the chair with her jaw swollen, blood trickling out of her nose, and her hands zip-tied behind her back.

"Okay, please, please, leave us alone, I'll leave New York, please put my babies down," Jena replied, while crying hysterically.

Marisol looked over at the two men, nodded her head, and they both walked back to the bedroom. Marisol took up the gun, put it back in her purse and stepped past Jena. The men walked out of the bedroom, and one of them took a knife from his waistband and cut off the zip ties from Jena's wrists.

Jena ran back to the bedroom where the twins were, and they were in one crib side by side consoling each other.

"Tiye, Amanirenas are you okay?" asked Jena.

Jena pulled down the front of the crib, hugged the twins.

"My babies, my babies," Jena screamed.

Marisol and the two men walked out the apartment past

Uncle Jasper's body lying there in the doorway unconscious.

Jena ran to the front door and saw Uncle Jasper lying there on the ground motionless.

"Oh, my goodness, Uncle Jasper, come on wake up! Don't you die on me."

Jena ran back inside the apartment, grabbed the phone, and dialed 9-1-1.

"Hello police, my uncle was attacked, and he's not moving. Please, send help before it's too late," Jena said.

"Okay Mam, what is your location?"

"I'm at 401 Warwick Avenue in Mt. Vernon, please hurry!"

Jena hung up the phone, ran back to her bedroom, and put on some clothes. She walked into the twin's room and put clothes on them too. Jena put the girls inside the stroller and rolled them into the living room. She took a throw blanket and put it over Uncle Jasper's body on the floor.

Ten minutes later, the ambulance pulled up in front of the house. The Paramedic, and EMT rolled the gurney to Uncle Jasper. They checked his vital signs, performed CPR on him, then strapped him to the gurney.

"Mam is he your grandfather?" said the Paramedic.

"No, he's my uncle," Jena replied.

"Well, we found a pulse, but it was faint. We got him stabilized, but we have to get him to a hospital ASAP. Are you okay? Do you need medical assistance?"

"I'll be fine, please tend to my uncle."

"It won't take long, just come with us inside the ambulance?"

"I don't know if I would fit, I have my twins with me."

"Okay, I understand, well, we will be transporting him to Montefiore Medical Center, on 233rd Street in the Bronx. It's not too far from here. When you get ready, come down and see him in the hospital."

"Will Uncle Jasper, be, okay?" asked Jena.

"It's hard to say, he sustained a head injury, doctors would have to do a CAT scan to determine the extent of his injuries," the Paramedic replied.

The Paramedic walked away, got inside the ambulance, and it drove down the road with the sirens and lights blaring. Jena walked inside the apartment and packed the baby's clothes in their diaper bags, and she put her things in her suitcase.

Jena looked inside the top dresser draw and saw a manila envelope inside. She opened it, and there was ten thousand dollars in cash and a letter addressed to her:

"Dear Girlie,

I left you this to help you out whenever you decided to go out on your own. I figure you won't be here forever. We all need to forge our own alliances and walk down our own paths to wherever it may lead us.

I know I told you about my daughter that worked at Port Authority. But she wasn't my daughter. My daughter died of a drug overdose some time ago. What I didn't tell you, was that she fell victim to that very same program that you got involved in. I remember how obnoxious she became after she was recruited, and that, that rich man groomed her.

She had all these expensive gifts, and when I asked her where she got it from. She told me to mind my business and that she had access to more money that I could ever have. She grew to be too disrespectful, so I kicked her out of my house.

One year later, some news reported the discovery of a young woman's body, found dead in a dumpster. They said it was an apparent drug overdose. I suspected foul play, I hired a private investigator, and they found out what really happened to my daughter.

Government officials were involved, and they were members of an elitist group. I sued the group and the city, and they settled out of court for an undisclosed amount. That was back in 1982, I used to have hair back then, and I was fit as a fiddle.

I accepted the settlement and used the money to buy houses all throughout the tristate area, trying to help unsuspecting girls like my daughter, avoid the lure of The Program.

I hope I was able to help you, take care of yourself and those babies. Be careful and remember that you mean the world to me.

Sincerely, Uncle Jasper"

Jena held her hand over her mouth and cried like a baby. She folded the letter and put it back in the manila envelope. Jena called a taxicab, rolled her twins in the stroller, along with her luggage through the apartment. She locked the front door and waited outside the house for the taxicab to arrive.

Her usual driver pulled up ten minutes later, got out the car, grabbed Jena's bags, and put it inside the trunk. She took the twins inside their car seats out of the stroller, and the driver folded the stroller, then tucked it in the trunk. Jena secured the twins in the back seat, sat down beside them, and let out a sigh of relief.

Visibly shaken, and her face was swollen like she was in anaphylactic shock.

"What's going on Jena? What happened to your face? Is everything alright?" asked the driver.

"No, I was attacked, and my uncle is in the hospital in critical condition. I need to get there now, please. The Paramedic took him to Montefiore Medical Center on 233rd street in the Bronx, could you hurry," Jena replied.

"I'm sorry to hear that Jena, I hope you both will be alright."

The driver made it to the hospital and grabbed the driver-side door handle. Jena put her hand on his shoulder and stopped him.

"Here, keep the meter running, will ya, I need to go to the airport after this."

Jena handed the taxi driver a $50 bill, then she attempted to unbuckle the seatbelts off the twins and their car seat.

The taxi driver put his hand on Jena's shoulder and shook his head back and forth.

"Leave them with me, you go ahead, get yourself checked out and see your uncle. I will look after them until you get back," the driver said.

Jena knitted up her eyebrows and stared at the driver, then continued to unbuckle the twins.

"I don't know about that," Jena replied.

"Trust me, I have kids of my own, it won't be a bother for me."

Jena fastened back the seatbelts over the twin's car seats and kissed them on their foreheads.

"Mommy will be right back," said Jena, then she exited the taxicab.

The lobby of the hospital was crowded with doctors and nurses tending to patients, and people seated in the waiting room with their ears open for their names to be called by a nurse. Jena walked up to the information desk and the nurse pushed a clipboard at her.

"Please fill out these forms," the nurse said.

"No, no, no, I'm here to see my uncle, he was admitted in here about twenty minutes ago," Jena replied.

"Name?"

"Jasper——"

"African American elderly male with blunt force trauma to the head?"

"Yes!"

'He's in intensive care, room 203. Here, take this badge with you. Tell the nurse, Gladys sent you up, she will let you in to see your uncle."

Jena thanked the nurse, took the badge from her, and walked toward the elevator.

"Take the stairs, that elevator is out of service."

Jena opened the door to the staircase and walked up the steps to the 2nd floor. She opened the door, and it was just as chaotic as the lobby. The nurse spotted Jena as she entered through the doorway.

"Are you here to see the old man?" asked the nurse.

Jena nodded her head up and down and flashed the badge that the nurse at the front desk gave to her.

"Gladys sent you, huh! He's over there in room 203," the nurse said.

Her eyes never made contact with Jena's. The nurse was too focused on a computer monitor, and her fingertips clicked and clacked on a keyboard.

Jena walked into the room and saw Uncle Jasper, laid there on the bed hooked up to numerous machines. His eyelids were taped shut and a tube was hanging out the side of his mouth. Every time his chest moved up and down there was a beeping noise.

"Excuse me, are you next of kin?" said a voice, coming from behind her.

Jena turned around and a doctor stood there with a clipboard in his hand.

"Yes, he's my uncle," Jena replied.

"Well, he's been placed in a drug induced coma to take down the swelling of the brain. He's on life support, we're not sure if he's going to make it through this. Are you okay? Have you been checked out? What happened to you two?" asked the doctor.

"I'll be fine, and I wasn't with him. When I got to the house the neighbors told me he was in here," Jena replied as the tears streamed down her swollen cheek.

"If his condition doesn't improve, somebody has a decision to make."

"What do you mean doctor?"

247

"Someone has to decide whether or not to keep him on life support. I'll give you some privacy, I have to make my rounds."

The doctor walked out of the room and closed the door. Jena walked over to Uncle Jasper's side and picked up his hand.

"I'm so sorry Uncle Jasper, this should've never happened to you. Please fight this, you have so much more love to give. Don't die Uncle Jasper."

Jena put her head on his chest and listened to his heartbeat. It wasn't beating strong, and he was kind of cold to the touch. Jena looked up at Uncle Jasper's face, and she leaned in and kissed him on his lips.

"I love you, but I have to leave town. I don't want anybody else getting hurt on account of my screw up. Take care, and thanks for everything," Jena said.

The doctor in the hallway watched Jena walk out of the room and enter the staircase. He stood there with a blank look on his face and stared at the door slowly closed behind her.

Chapter 13:

Out of town

Jena arrived at the JFK International Airport at 7am in the morning. The taxi driver got her luggage and the double stroller from the trunk. Jena managed to take out the two car seats from the car, as the driver placed her luggage and the double stroller on the sidewalk. Jena slightly exhaled, then reached inside her purse and handed the driver a twenty-dollar bill.

"Take care of yourself, those girls, and have a safe flight," the driver said.

Jena was approached by a man who worked for American Airlines, and he grabbed her luggage.

"What is your flight number?" asked the curbside assistant.

The curbside assistant looked at Jena and noticed the swelling on her face. "Oh, my goodness mam, are you alright? Your face is all swollen."

Jena ignored the question and continued to take out the car seat from the taxi. "I have not purchased a ticket yet!" replied Jena.

The curbside assistant piled Jena's luggage onto a cart, then he reached for the car seat in Jena's hand.

"Would you like me to help you put those car seats on the stroller?" asked the curbside assistant.

Jena barely heard a word he said, she was still in a state of shock from what happened at Uncle Jasper's house. She was beside herself about being kicked out of town.

Jena snapped back into reality and accepted the offer by nodding her head up and down. After the curbside assistant helped Jena, they both strolled inside the airport. Jena thanked him for assisting her by giving him a five-dollar bill. She looked up at the board and located the flight to Las Vegas, then she joined the line to purchase a plane ticket.

After waiting in line for ten minutes, Jena was next up to see the front desk clerk. There weren't a lot of people at the airport, those of whom purchased their tickets and were moving along accordingly.

The airline attendant raised her eyebrows and cleared her throat after she took one look at Jena. "Good morning, how could I help you today?" asked the airline attendant.

"Good morning, I want to buy a plane ticket, please!" replied Jena.

"Ok, where do you want to go? American Airlines goes to over 125 countries all over the world. What class would you like to fly? First class or economy?"

"Economy, I am going to Vegas! Do you have seats left for that flight? I need to get as far away from New York as possible. I gotta get out of the city, pronto!"

"One moment please!"

The airline attendant looked at her computer screen and checked the system.

"I have a flight here that lays over in Chicago for four hours before you get to your destination; do you want that one?"

"Do you have any non-stop flights? I have twin infants, and I don't want to carry around these car seats and luggage more than I need to."

The lady looked over the counter and saw the twins and smiled.

"Gotcha! Ok, I have a straight flight here to Vegas at 8:30am, but it's 1st class, do you want this flight? First class tickets to Vegas are discounted tickets, it's off-peak pricing, so y'all get them at the same price as a normal economy class ticket. There's two seats available and I could sell them to you for $378," the airline attendant asked.

"Yes, put us on that flight," Jena replied, and she took out the Manila envelope that Uncle Jasper gave to her. She took out four hundred dollars and gave it to the airline attendant.

"No, mam it is $378 plus tax and fees for your luggage, that comes up to $448.79!"

Jena took out another fifty-dollar bill and gave it to the front desk clerk. The clerk asked for her ID and the names of the girls.

After she put Jena and the twin's information in the system, the clerk printed out the tickets. She handed her the tickets and her change and prompted her to fill out the tags for her luggage. A different man took Jena's luggage and put them onto the conveyor belt.

"Thank you for flying with American Airlines! Have a safe flight!"

Jena smiled and pushed the stroller with the girls towards the gate.

Jena reached the security check and started searching for the tickets and her ID. The diaper bag dropped, and everything spilled out. The abrupt sound startled the twins and they wailed at the top of their lungs. Jena didn't panic, she just sang "Twinkle, twinkle little star," [by Jane Taylor] for them, and that calmed them down.

A guy helped her pickup the stuff and put them back inside the diaper bag.

"Thank you!" said Jena.

"No problem, I saw you struggling! You know everybody here got some place to go, if we all lend a helping hand when it's needed, we all can get to where we need to be in a timely manner," the good Samaritan replied.

Jena handed the tickets to the security agent. He inspected the documents, then handed them back to Jena and pointed where she needed to go next. Jena put her documents inside the diaper bag and pushed the stroller towards the other security check.

The security agent checked Jena's diaper bag and allowed her to pass. Jena looked at her ticket and saw that she needed to be at gate 17. She walked down the corridor pushing the stroller towards the gate and the man that helped her earlier, spotted Jena and flagged her down.

"Hey! Excuse me! Wait up!"

The man ran up to Jena holding a briefcase in his hand.

"My name is Ted! What's your name miss?"

"It's Jena short for Jeneration!"

"What kind of name is Jeneration? Your mother called you Jeneration?"

"Yes, she saw these commercials about "Generation X" and how they were going to change the world. So, that's why she named me Jeneration, Jena for short. Plus, she told me when I was little that I was supposed to stop the generational curse that befalls black people."

"Well, that is cool! I like that! My name is just plain old Ted. But I overheard you singing to quiet your babies, you have a nice decent singing voice. Are you a recording artist or a stage performer?"

Jena tried to hold back her laugh, but it came out anyway.

"No, I mean I always had a passion for performing on stage, I recite poetry at clubs here and there. The only other stage acting I've done was bit parts in small plays in the village. But I haven't done anything major. I rather enjoy the reaction I receive after I have showcased my talents on stage. It's intoxicating to receive a standing ovation after a performance," Jena said.

"That's great! I am a producer for stage shows in Vegas and I think you should try out for the part in one of the plays. It is in pre-production obviously, but I think you have the presence and attitude we're looking for," Ted replied.

"Okay, but I have to warn you that I am a simple New York girl, and I have only done small stage shows you know like high-school plays, BCBG's, Nuyorican café, other spots way off Broadway. Just things like that, I've never done anything too big, or nothing paid for that matter."

"OK that's cool! The part is perfect for you! The main character is from a small town, and she found herself in the big city. While there, she discovered that her big personality was a perfect fit for life outside of her hometown. She has always been a big fish in a small pond. So, here's my card; my number is on the back. Give me a call when you land in Vegas. After you get settled in, you could come down to the studio, read the script and try out for the part. I will be expecting a call from you!"

Ted extended his hand, and Jena shook it.

"OK, that sounds good! Thank you, Ted!"

Jena put his card in her purse, and she sat there and waited for her flight number to be announced.

"Now boarding at gate 17, flight to Las Vegas, Nevada, flight number 334. Flight to Las Vegas, boarding first-class passengers, and anybody with small children, please come up to the front to board now."

Jena went up to the front with the girls in the stroller, and she gave the clerk her ticket. The attendant tore off a portion of the ticket and gave her back the bottom portion.

"Mam, the baggage handlers will check the stroller and car seats before you board the plane. They will be available for you after the plane arrives at your destination."

Jena pushed the stroller towards the plane entrance and unbuckled each baby from their car seats. One of the flight attendants walked over to Jena and picked up one of the twins as she picked up the other one. Jena grabbed the diaper bag and adjusted it over her shoulder. Jena and the flight attendant entered the plane with the twins in tote.

"Where are your seats?" asked the flight attendant.

"I am seated at 1e and 1f," Jena replied.

Jena sat down first then the attendant gave her back the other twin.

"Mam! those babies are so precious! If there is anything you need from now on. My name is Mary, and I will be assisting you today," she said.

"Thanks Mary! I am Jena! Could I get a bottle water and

some hot water in a cup, please? I gotta make a bottle for these girls," Jena replied.

"Sure thing, I'll be right back, just sit tight."

Jena seated the girls down next to each other and buckled them in, as she was rummaging through the diaper bag for the girl's bottles, bibs, and formula. Ted walked in the plane and winked at Jena and gave the twins one lollipop each.

"You don't mind if they have these do you?" asked Ted.

"Nope not at all! Thank you!" replied Jena.

Ted continued to walk down the aisle until he reached his seat. The flight attendant returned with the water for Jena, and she immediately started making the bottles. She used two ounces of hot water, four ounces of bottled water, three scoops of formula and one scoop of cereal for each bottle.

Jena shook them up, to thoroughly mix the formula, placed the bibs around the girl's necks, tested the temperature of the formula on the back of her hand, then gave each of them their bottles.

"Here little ones! Mommy loves you!" said Jena.

Jena kissed Tiye and Amanirenas on each of their foreheads as they drank their bottles. She closed up the containers and put them back inside the diaper bag.

Jena let out a big sigh, after she closed the diaper bag and tucked it under the seat.

"That was tiring! Vegas here we come! I don't know nothing about Vegas, shit, truth be told, I don't want to know anything about Vegas either. But I got these two babies, and I can't afford for anything to happen to them. I am running from the stress that New York has put me under. God, please take the wheel!" thought Jena.

Jena closed her eyes after she noticed that the twins fell back asleep. She put her hand over her eyes, then she heard the flight attendant's voice. "Do you want tea, coffee or a glass of champagne?"

Jena nodded her head from left to right, then fell asleep. Jena slept through the safety announcements, and through most of the flight. The flight attendant covered both her and the girls with a blanket and adjusted the recliner; so, they would be more comfortable.

About two and a half hours into the flight, the flight attendant announced on the intercom:

"We will begin our descent! Please put your trays up and your seats back to the upright position. The pilot will be landing in Las Vegas momentarily. Please stay seated with your seatbelts fastened until the sign goes off. The local time is 8 am, Atlantic time. Thank you for flying with American Airlines, I hope you enjoy your stay here in Nevada."

Jena woke up and followed the flight attendant's instructions. The twins were still asleep, so she just wrapped her arms around them as the plane landed. Everyone on the flight applauded, after the plane touched the runway safely. After a few moments the seat belt sign went off, and then the passengers shuffled around getting their things ready to get off the plane.

Jena got up and put the diaper bag around her shoulder and bent down to pick up one of the twins. Ted walked up behind her and stretched out his hands to pick up one of the twins. ——

"I'll give you a hand! Come here little one!" said Ted.

Ted picked up the baby then allowed Jena to walk in front of him.

"After you!" said Ted.

Jena walked out in front of Ted, and he stared at her from behind admiring her buxom figure.

"So, are you going out to Las Vegas to a family member's house?" asked Ted.

"Nope, I am staying at a hotel," Jena replied.

"Did you book a room already?"

"No Ted I haven't yet! I figured I would book one in the

airport when I got off the plane."

"You do know if you didn't book anything yet, you just may be staying in the seedy part of town. I tell you what, I got some pull here in Vegas. I could get you a room in a great hotel, it won't cost you anything. Like I said, I'm something like an important guy out here! I'm pretty much a big deal."

"Ok Mr. big shot Ted, lead the way!"

Jena's stroller and car seats for the twins were placed in the corridor outside of the plane. Ted and Jena put the twins inside their car seats, and they secured them both in the stroller.

"Whew, Jena, you need an award for mastering this contraption. I don't have any children, so I never had the pleasure of dealing with this in my life."

"Lucky you! I will have to agree with you, that it is a daunting task dealing with a baby, let alone two."

"You seem to be doing a great job Jena! You have managed so far, may I ask, what happened to their father? Why is he not in the picture?"

"Don't ask Ted! He is still back in New York, and that is where he needs to be."

"Did he do that to your face Jena? Is he the reason why you're traveling so far away from home?" asked Ted.

"Ted, you're an inquisitive S.O.B aren't you! I said that I don't want to talk about it," Jena replied.

After they collected their luggage, Jena, the twins, and Ted walked outside the airport where a car service was waiting to pick up Ted from the airport.

"Good morning Mr. Brown! Will this young lady be accompanying you to your destination," the driver asked.

"Yes! Good morning, Justin, could you please collect her luggage!" replied Ted.

"Right away sir!"

Ted and Jena unhooked the car seats from the stroller and put the twins inside the van one at a time. They secured the twins to the seats with the seat belts. The driver packed away the luggage and stroller in the back of the van. Then he walked up towards the driver side door and entered the van.

"Mr. Brown, are we heading to the Balangao hotel?"

"Yes Justin!" said Ted.

The driver nodded his head, then put the van into drive.

"Very well, Sir!" replied the driver.

Ted grabbed a briefcase he had in the van, opened it up and handed Jena a folder with some papers inside it.

"Here Jena, this is the script for the play that I want you to read for. Give it a once over and get familiar with the highlighted sections. You will be reading for the part of Phyllis," Ted said.

Jena took the folder, opened it up and read the script. About twenty minutes later, they drove to a swanky hotel, and Jena picked her head up from the script with a smile on her face.

"Ted, I love the story! You didn't tell me that this was the lead role!" replied Jena.

Jena looked outside the van window and noticed how extravagant the hotel was.

The driver put the van in park, got out and walked towards the back. He opened the doors and took the luggage out. He placed them on a cart that a bellhop pushed to the van. Ted flipped open his mobile phone and answered a call. He gushed over Jena to the caller, of how she would be perfect for the lead in the stage show.

Jena was kind of overwhelmed by everything so far. Ted, Jena, and the twins entered the hotel lobby and were immediately greeted by the front desk clerk. "Good morning, Mr. Brown."

"Good morning, Jennifer! This is Jena, get her into the Roosevelt suit, and set her up with a babysitter for 9 am tomorrow morning!" replied Ted.

257

"Right away Mr. Brown!"

Ted turned to Jena and looked at his watch. "Jena, get some rest, be here in the lobby at 9 am sharp. Justin will take you to the theater. I will see you then," Ted said.

Ted kissed Jena on the cheek, then walked away from her. He put the mobile phone up to his ear and continued to speak with the person on the other line. He didn't even wait until Jena responded to his instructions.

Jennifer gave Jena the room key and smiled at her. "Welcome to the Balangao hotel, your suite is on the 32nd floor. The bellhop will take you there. Good luck on your audition!"

Jena took the keycard and followed the bellhop to the elevator with the twins in tote. The elevator arrived and they all entered, and the bellhop pushed the button for the 32nd floor. The elevator door closed, and it abruptly shot up, Jena gasped and held on to the railing.

The bellhop smiled, but still stood up straight as an arrow. "It takes some getting used to! I did the same thing when I first got into the elevator," he said.

After the elevator reached her floor, the bellhop pushed the cart towards the suite, took the keycard from Jena, opened the double doors and pushed the cart inside.

Jena walked inside and was in awe of how fancy the suite was. Jena pushed the stroller inside the living room and looked around as the bellhop took her luggage off the cart.

"Mam! If you need anything else, my name is Timothy, ask for me when you call the front desk," he said.

"Thank you very much Timothy," Jena replied, and reached inside the manila envelope and tried to hand the bellhop a ten-dollar bill. He shook his head from left to right and put his hands out in front of him.

"That won't be necessary, everything is complimentary while you and your beautiful twins stay here."

The bellhop put the key card on a desk in the foyer, pushed

the cart out of the suite and closed the door behind him.

For the first time in a long time, Jena felt relieved. Not knowing how long this feeling will last for, she took charge of the situation and did exactly what Ted wanted her to do. Jena put her luggage in the sprawling bedroom. She carefully took the twins out of their car seats, laid them on the bed and changed their diapers.

It's been a couple of hours since they had a bottle so, Jena picked the twins up and carried them both towards the kitchen. She looked around and noticed an oversized playpen in the room.

"Hmm! That's convenient!" thought Jena.

Jena put the twins inside the playpen, walked over to the stroller, picked up the diaper bag and walked into the kitchen. She put the diaper bag on the counter and opened the refrigerator. Jena noticed that it was stocked to the gills with groceries.

"Wow! It's almost like they expected someone to come here," Jena said.

Jena didn't think anything of it, she just shrugged it off and prepared two bottles for the twins. She put on the tea kettle and waited for the water to boil. After a few minutes, the kettle whistled like a train leaving the station at high noon. Jena poured the hot water in each bottle, then offset the temperature with cool bottled water. She tested the temperature of the formula on the back of her hand, then brought the bottles over to the girls.

They were sitting up in the playpen playing quietly amongst themselves. Jena smiled, put on their bibs, then gave each of the twins their bottles. Jena walked into the living room, picked up the script and started studying it.

After about an hour her eyes got heavy, and she felt tired. So, Jena put down the script, walked towards the playpen and saw Tiye and Amanirenas cuddled up with each other. Jena smiled and walked into the bathroom towards the bathtub and turned on the faucet. Jena put her hand underneath the water ensuring that the temperature was just right. She walked back into the living room and picked up each of the twins one by one, undressed them, and carried both of them in the bathroom.

The tub was a quarter of the way full, and she sat the twins inside the tub and turned off the faucet. Jena took off her shoes and the rest of her clothes and climbed into the tub with them. There were tiny bars of soap on the ledge of the tub, so she grabbed them and soaped up herself, then the twins.

After they were all soaped up and rinsed off. Jena let out the soapy water from the tub, reached for a towel and gathered the twins up in her arms. She walked over to the bedroom; still dripping wet and put them down on the bed. Jena dug into the diaper bag that was on the dresser and searched for the baby's lotion. The girls were crawling on the bed, so she rushed back to them and applied lotion to each of their bodies.

While applying the lotion to each part of their bodies, Jena named each body part in Spanish and English.

"Arms (brazos), hands (manos), chest (pecho), stomach (vientre), legs (la pata), feet (el pies), butt (culo), back (espalda), neck (cuello) and head (cabeza)."

The twins giggled, and Jena put on their clothes. She picked them up and put them back inside the playpen. Then rolled it into the bedroom so she could watch them and tend to herself. She didn't waste too much time applying lotion to her body. She only paid close attention when applying shea butter to her C-section scar.

Jena put on her clothes and climbed into the king size bed. She planned to read more of the script before bed, but she was suffering from jetlag, and fell right asleep.

The entire day passed by, and Jena woke up abruptly after hearing the twins crying. She looked at the clock and it was 6 am. Jena got up, put pacifiers in each of their mouths and walked towards the kitchen to make bottles for them. Standing there in the dark yawning, while the pot boiled on the stove. Jena rolled her neck around in circles. "It's been a while since I spoke with my parents or Asia. I bet my parents don't miss me!" thought Jena.

Jena sighed, then the tea kettle whistled, so she turned off the stove. She rinsed out the bottles in the sink, before filling them up with cereal, formula and hot water. She opened the fridge and took out a bottle of water and brought it over to the counter and poured water in the bottles.

Jena shook each of the bottles, mixing the contents; then she tested them on the back of her hand, to make sure they were the right temperature. She walked back into the room and gave the twins their bottles.

Jena knew she didn't have much time to waste, so she picked up the phone and called the front desk to confirm if they really had a baby-sitting service. The phone rang twice, and someone picked up the phone.

"Good morning, front desk, this is Jennifer, how can I help you?" asked the front desk clerk.

"Good morning, Jennifer, my name is Jena, and I'm in suite 3202; I was told that this hotel has a babysitting service. If so, I'm going to need to use that service," Jena replied.

"I understand mam! Yes, we do provide the service you seek. Whenever you are ready, bring the babies down to the lobby, and we'll have somebody to take care of your kids for you at no additional charge. This service is included with the suite that you have here at the hotel. Just let us know how long you need, and we will take care of it."

"Okay thank you!"

Jena hung up the phone, walked into the bathroom, then turned on the faucet in the tub. After a quick five-minute shower, Jena walked back into the bedroom with a towel wrapped around her torso. She took each of the twins from the playpen and put them on the bed one at a time. Jena unzipped her suitcase, grabbed two outfits, then changed the twins.

Jena put the twins back inside the playpen, she looked at the clock and it was a quarter to eight. She put lotion on her body, put on deodorant and perfume that she got from her suitcase. Then put on her under garments and a simple sundress over it. She gathered the twins from the play pen and put each of them in their car seats. Jena looked inside their diaper bag to make sure there were enough diapers, wipes, formula and change of clothes.

Jena picked up the room's keycard and backed out of the room. After the door slammed shut, she pressed the elevator button. After the elevator door opened, She and the twins entered. Jena pressed the lobby button then braced herself for the abrupt drop. Before long, she and the twins were in the lobby and the hotel personnel were patiently waiting for her arrival with the twins.

Jena walked up to the front desk, smiled and put the brakes on the back of the stroller with her foot. "Thank you so much for this! I won't be long, here's their diaper bag. Everything is in there, and they are good babies, they won't give trouble," Jena said.

Jena bent down and kissed Tiye and Amanirenas on their foreheads and stood up straight. "Mommy will be back soon! You two be good while I am gone!"

Jena shook the hand of the woman who would be babysitting the girl's hand and smiled. "Thanks again!"

"No problem, Jena, my name is Felicia, and I'll be taking care of these beautiful girls of yours. What are their names?" asked Felicia.

"Well, the darker twin's name is Amanirenas, and the lighter twin's name is Tiye," Jena replied.

"Those are beautiful names Jena. We're going to get along just great."

Jennifer smiled back and pointed out towards the parking lot.

"Justin, your driver, is outside waiting for you! Good luck with your audition!"

Jena went outside and saw the driver out there waiting for her. Jena squinted her eyes at the sun glaring directly in her face. Justin reached inside his suit pocket and handed Jena a pair of sunglasses while holding open the van door.

"Good morning, Miss Jena," Justin said.

"Thank you, Justin, Good morning, to you too," Jena replied.

The driver took her to the theater where the auditions were

located. Jena saw Ted outside the entrance of the building as the driver pulled up to where he was standing.

"Good morning, Jena! I'm glad you could make it. There is no time to waste, the other producers are ecstatic about seeing your audition for our show, The Strength Within. I've been gushing about you since yesterday. Here is a copy of the script, I will be seated up front and we'll be assisting you, as you read the part you're auditioning for. Good luck, and remember, just be yourself," Ted said.

"Ted, I read the entire script and although I am bilingual. I am not Mexican; my mother is Dominican, and my father is Jamaican. This story is about a teenage migrant worker who organized a revolt against a system that exploits migrant workers. Her strength and ability to mobilize all of the Mexican migrant workers to strike and protest all over the country; was awe inspiring.

"All of their efforts were not in vain, the revolution exposed how American companies offer migrant workers a path to citizenship; then allow immigration to raid the camps and deport them before they can go through that process. How did you and the other producers come up with this story?" asked Jena.

Ted smiled, blew on his fingers, then rubbed his fingernails on his chest.

"I will explain it to you later! Now, let's just get through the audition!"

About an hour went by and the driver stood outside smoking a cigarette when Jena and Ted walked back outside from the theater. Ted had his hand around Jena's waist, and he had a lit cigar in his mouth.

"Jena, you killed it in there! This show is going to be great. The other producers of the show and the other actors for the show, loved your audition. Everybody applauded and you got a standing ovation for that singing voice. I am blown away! Your range, that pitch. This was just practice; I can't wait for the real thing. I see you soon! Enjoy Vegas! Justin will take you anywhere you want to go. In two weeks, we start rehearsals; practice those lines."

Ted kissed Jena on the cheek, and she entered the van feeling like a million bucks. The driver took Jena back to the hotel and she walked inside the hotel lobby floating on cloud nine.

"Hey, where are the twins?" asked Jena, with a huge smile on her face.

Jennifer pointed to a room adjacent to the front desk. Jena walked over to the door and opened it and saw the twins seated on the floor playing with blocks and the babysitter was down there with them.

"Back so soon! I'll be on the clock for the next three hours. So, if you want, I can keep them until then. There's still breakfast being served in the cafeteria, if you didn't eat yet; go and have some breakfast. Tiye, Amanirenas and I are getting along just fine," Felicia said.

"Okay Felicia, I see that you have things under control here. I'm going to take you up on that offer," Jena replied.

She was impressed with how everything was going so far. Almost too good to be true. She smiled and nodded her head at Felicia. Jena walked towards the cafeteria for breakfast. She looked at the sprawling buffet, took a tray and grabbed an orange.

Jena took a plate and shared herself a spoon of eggs, took a muffin, poured a cup of hot water and grabbed a teabag; then sat down at an empty table. Jena took her time and ate breakfast, she even went back for a bowl of oatmeal, and a few strips of bacon. Feeling tired, Jena thought it would be a good idea to get a nap in before the twins came up from the sitter.

Jena put her tray away and walked over towards the elevator and pushed the button. After getting into the elevator, Jena twirled around the elevator stall and looked at herself in the mirror.

"Today is the first time since Tiye and Amanirenas were born that I've been away from them. Am I a bad mother?" thought Jena.

Jena reached over to press the lobby button, but she stopped herself and allowed the elevator to go up to the 32nd floor. Jena used the key card to open her suite and walked towards the bedroom, before she climbed into bed, she took off her sundress and laid down.

A few hours went by and there was a knock on the door. Jena woke up right away, she put back on her dress and walked over to the front door of her suite. She looked through the peephole and saw that the babysitter was with the twins in the hallway. Jena wiped the crust out of her eyes and opened the door.

"Hello there, I was fast asleep! Were you standing out there long?" asked Jena.

Felicia shook her head from left to right then let go of the stroller. "These girls were a pleasure to spend time with. Anytime you need a sitter, don't hesitate to ask," she replied.

Two weeks passed by and rehearsals for the show The Strength Within, started to rave reviews. Over the following three weeks, Jena went to the theater for rehearsals every morning from 9 am to 12 noon. The staff at the hotel was monumental in their assistance during that transition period.

Three months has past and although Jena didn't have a place to stay yet, she was able to stay at the hotel. Ted has put her and the twins up, since she has been in Las Vegas. The show was a smash hit! Jena and the entire cast garnered rave reviews.

The theater was packed every night and she made a decent amount of money but had a feeling that something was fishy about this situation, and she wanted to make as much money as she could and save so she could move on to the next stage of her life.

School was going to start soon, and Jena was going to have to figure out a way to do both at the same time. Luckily, the shows were at night, so that gave her all morning to attend classes. Besides, Jena didn't want to continue to rely on somebody else's help.

After an entire year of going to school at UNLV and doing the show, The Strength Within. One night after another sold out show, the entire cast and crew went out to eat to celebrate. Everyone at the table was talking amongst themselves and Ted leaned over to Jena, then whispered in her ear:

"Psst! Jena, a big-name Hollywood producer, was in the crowd tonight. He loved your performance; he wanted you to fly out to Beverly Hills and try out for a pilot he's pitching to a television network. What do you think about that? This could be the break you need in showbiz, kid!"

"Wow Ted, that's great news! But, what about Tiye, Amanirenas, school, and the show?" asked Jena.

"Don't worry about that Jena. If you're interested, we could take the first flight out to Los Angeles, you can try out for the role."

"Ted, that's amazing news!"

Jena's eyes lit up like a Christmas tree, and she was filled with glee.

"That's cool Ted! You really got some pull, I kinda thought you were bullshitting, but you really know some people."

"What can I say! All I know is that good people deserve good things. So, Jena, what is it gonna be?"

"What time is the flight, Ted?"

"We could fly out there today, Jena! How long would it take for you to get ready?"

Jena hugged Ted and excused herself from the table and left the restaurant. The driver took her back to the hotel. Jena stopped by the front desk and called over the clerk. She ushered Jena into the room where the twins were; the lights were off and as soon as they stepped inside. The lights turned and Felicia yelled "Surprise!"

"It's the twins first birthday, and we thought that it would be nice to get them a birthday cake," Jenifer said.

"Oh, my goodness I was so caught up that I totally forgot. Thanks, you guys," Jena replied.

The twins grabbed a handful of the birthday cake and mashed it in their mouths. Jena, leaned in close to Felicia and whispered:

"Felicia, I landed an audition in Los Angeles, could someone watch Tiye, and Amanirenas for a few days?" asked Jena.

"Yes, that is fine we love the girls! It's been a year now since you've been staying here, they're like family, like our little sisters. I hope when you baptize those babies, y'all consider us to be their God parents," Felicia replied.

"Of course! Felicia, I was thinking about that the other day. But I haven't been to church since I've been out here in Vegas. I wouldn't even know where to go, or who to ask about that sort of thing."

"Listen Jena, don't worry about that girl, I got this, I can ask my grandmother to talk to The Pastor at our church and we can get this setup, Ok!"

"Thanks for everything Felicia, you've done a lot for us since we've been in town. I couldn't have been able to manage without you and Jennifer's help."

"You are very welcome, just focus on that audition."

"California! I've never been there; I hope I get the part for this role for a pilot. Ted told me about some producer friend of his out there that plan to pitch the pilot to the studio. I am crossing my fingers, hopefully, I can get the part!"

Felicia raised her eyebrows, shuffled in her seat and crossed her legs.

"Jena, I know Ted has been real kind and generous to you and the girls but be careful about this LA trip. Ted means well, but his associates have some influence over him at times. He meets a lot of pretty girls everywhere he goes at airports, train stations etc. He tries to impress them with all of his Hollywood connections and offers them stardom. But his friends don't play nice, if the girls don't play ball after they audition——

"Let's just say that they always leave this hotel earlier than they should. I'm sorry to be the bearer of bad news, but I needed to give you a heads up. I don't know if you have already gone down that road with Ted already! If not, he might not yet feel as though he has gained your trust yet. So, just be careful, these guys out here don't do anything for nothing, if you catch my drift. Okay Jena! Good luck and hopefully they want you for your talent and they don't want to know how talented you are in other ways," Felicia said.

Jena paused for a moment and stood there with a look of dismay on her face.

"Ok gurl, I will see you soon! Thanks for the heads up," Jena replied.

Jena got into the van and the driver took her to the airport. He didn't drop her off at the commercial airport; the driver took her to a private hangar.

They arrived at the airport and Ted was already there. The driver opened the van door and Jena got out and leaned into the driver and hugged him.

"Thank you for taking care of me," Jena said.

"It's my pleasure, Miss Jena," Justin replied.

Jena walked towards Ted with an overnight bag in tote. He was standing in front of the jet smoking a cigar, wearing sunglasses. He had a blue blazer on, a white T shirt, blue jeans and flip flops. He gave Jena a one-armed sideways hug; to avoid blowing cigar smoke in her face.

Ted grabbed Jena's bag and gave it to the baggage handlers.

"Are you ready to go? Are you pumped? Are you ready to kill this audition? In my opinion you were made for this role. This is going to be something a lot different than 'The Strength Within.' I know you got the chops for this; you're going to blow this out of the frame!" asked Ted.

"I'm as ready as I'll ever be Ted," Jena replied.

Ted walked alongside Jena, and they both walked up the steps into the private jet. Jena stepped inside the plane, and Ted entered afterward. The pilot pulled up the stairs and closed the door.

They both sat down, and Ted was ecstatic.

"The producer loved your performance! He was in attendance at the last three shows. His name is Sasha, and he gave you a standing ovation at the end of each of your performances.

Sasha loved your cadence, how you moved on stage and how you sang the songs. Sasha was tickled by your sassiness and what you brought to the character. He told me that you would be perfect for this role.

"They are in pre-production on this new pilot that he is producing. I don't have too many details about the program, but what I do have, is the script. Here Jena, read it and see if you like it. It is about an hour and a half flight to Los Angeles, and I told him that you were a quick study.

"Jena, Sasha wanted a fresh take on this role. Although it's such short notice; you should have enough time to put your own spin on it. Make this character your own! Hopefully, you have the fresh look that he's looking for," Ted said.

Jena took the script and skimmed through the first couple of pages. She read that it was about two sisters from South Africa that got kidnapped by some rebels. They sold the sisters to Arab slave traders, and they took them to France. En route, one of the kidnappers tried to rape one of the sisters. She fought him off as much as she could, but she was killed during the struggle. The lone survivor ended up escaping her captors by stroke of luck. Afterwards she spent weeks in the wilderness without proper food or shelter, living in fear for her life.

"She was on the brink of dying of exposure, her clothes were tattered, and she was mangy. Luckily, a camper found her sleeping under a rock and she was taken to get medical treatment. Her story was headline news and a tip, helped the authorities arrest the human traffickers. She stayed in the country for a year during the trial period. After the prosecutors found the men guilty; the French government gave her a visa and a work permit..."

Jena looked up from the script and she yawned.

"Mmm, this is interesting!" thought Jena.

The plane began its final descent and Jena closed the script. Ted looked over at Jena and put his sunglasses down the bridge of his nose.

"Well, Jena, what do you think?" asked Ted.

"Ted, I'm intrigued, I need to read through it more. But so far, the story is very interesting," Jena replied.

"Everyone please stay seated, fasten your seat belts; we are making our final descent. If you look over to the side, you will see the Hollywood sign. Welcome to Los Angeles," the pilot said over the intercom.

After the plane landed, a limousine was there at the hangar awaiting their arrival. Jena and Ted exited the airplane and walked over to the luxury vehicle. The driver opened the door and they got inside.

"Ted, a girl could get used to this, and I like the journey of the main character. This reads as if it was based on true events. It's lovely! I love it! I want this role," Jena said.

"I told you! This role is yours for the taking. When the writers wrote this script, they were considering you for the role," Ted replied.

The limousine pulled up to this sprawling Beverly Hills estate; Jena and Ted got out of the limousine, then walked up to the mansion. Before they reached the front door; a man opened the door.

Ted with his unlit cigar hanging from his mouth put his hands up in the air and took the cigar out of his mouth.

"Hey Sasha! This is Jena, short for Jeneration. Sasha, this is the girl that I told you about, she's the girl from my show, in Las Vegas. I gave her the script and she loved it. Please don't let anybody else audition for this part! This is the girl!" said Ted.

Sasha stepped back away from the doorway and welcomed the pair inside.

"Come in! Come in! Where's my manners!" replied Sasha.

Jena entered the mansion and Ted was a step behind her, when his phone rang. —— "I'll be right in, you guys go ahead start without me," Ted said.

Ted answered the call and walked back outside with his

mobile phone at his ear. Sasha and Jena took a few steps inside and Jena was impressed by the Beverly Hills home. She looked around and saw that there was a fountain inside with tons of Koi fish at the bottom of it. She saw a Fabergé egg and immediately walked over to it.

"Is this real?" said Jena, as she gasped.

"Yes, it is!" replied Sasha.

"Yeah right, so that is an original 'ninth wave' by Ivan Aivazovsky too, I presume?"

"Jena, I'm impressed!

"I don't limit myself to just performing arts. I am a bit of an art connoisseur. I like the Malachite pieces you have here in this room, and I'm going to also presume that the chaise lounge chair, is also from the late Russian empire."

"A bit presumptuous, but Yes! Let me save you the trouble of asking again; every art piece I have here in my home are all originals. Shall we go to my theater."

A Butler stood in the foyer holding a tray with three pre-poured glasses of champagne on it. There was a small table beside him with a bottle of Dom Perignon and an assortment of hors d'oeuvres on it. Jena took a glass of champagne, grabbed a hors d'oeuvre and bit into it. With a mouth full, she attempted to gush over how she loved the script. But having a mouth full of food put a damper on that.

Jena placed a napkin over her mouth and finished chewing the hors d'oeuvre. Then she drank some champagne to wash it all down.

"Excuse me, I am sorry about that! What I was trying to say was that I loved parts of the script that I've read so far. it's very different from what is playing on television right now. This show, if it got picked up; will be better than all other stuff that's on TV."

Jena drank the rest of the champagne in her glass and directed the butler to pour her another glass. After she grabbed a few more hors d'oeuvres, they went inside the elevator. Sasha closed the

271

gate, pressed a button and the elevator slowly lowered them down to the basement. Sasha opened the gate, exited the elevator, and he flipped on the light switch. He offered his hand to Jena, she took it and stepped out of the elevator.

She looked around and she was blown away by the space. Sasha had retrofitted his basement to resemble an old turn of the century theater. It was equipped with plush tufted maroon seats that were arranged in a semi-circle adjacent to the stage. There was a thick velvet curtain draped in front of the stage.

Jena's eyes and mouth opened wide, and she surveyed the theatre. "Wow, you have all this stuff inside this place!"

Jena walked down the aisle and slowly walked on the stage. Sasha pressed a few switches that opened the curtains and turned on the spotlight illuminating the stage where Jena stood. She cleared her throat, placed the champagne glass on the floor and read from the script.

Sasha held a copy of the script in his hands, put on his reading glasses and waited for his character's part to come. They read back and forth for a few lines. Then Sasha put up his hands and stopped her.

"I love how passionate you are while reading this part. I can't wait until I could film your portrayal. I don't need to see anymore; you got the part," Sasha said.

Jena closed the script and walked down off the stage. Sasha stood up in the aisle and applauded Jena's performance. He took out a small metal case from his shirt pocket, opened it up and snorted the contents up his nose with a straw. Jena reached where Sasha was standing and saw what he was doing.

"Do you want some coke?" asked Sasha.

Jena shook her head from left to right, so Sasha draped his arms around her. Jena hugged him back, then he caressed her, and inched his hands down to the small of her back. Sasha smiled, grabbed her ass, then pushed his tongue in Jena's mouth.

Jena pushed Sasha off of her with all of her strength and

wiped away Sasha's saliva from her mouth with her forearm.

"What the fuck are you doing? I didn't come here for this shit!" said Jena, repulsed by the gesture.

"Look sweetheart if you want this role this is what you have to do," Sasha replied, unfazed by Jena's rejection.

Sasha stepped back away from Jena, unbuttoned his pants, pulled out his penis and pointed at his crotch. "Now get down on your knees and suck my dick!"

Jena looked down at his flaccid penis, walked closer to him and kicked him in between his legs. Sasha slumped over and dropped down to the ground in agony. Jena pulled his shirt over his head, used her knee to hit him on the bridge of his nose. Sasha wallowed on the ground and Jena tossed the script at him.

She stormed up the aisle, entered the elevator, closed the gate, then insistently pressed the elevator button. The elevator slowly moved back up to the main floor. After a few moments the elevator stopped on the first floor and Jena ripped open the gate and shot out of the elevator like a bat out of hell. Clearly upset, her mascara ran underneath her eyelids. There was blood all over her right knee, and her stocking was tattered.

The butler looked at Jena and rushed to her aid.

"Ma'am, what happened? Are you Ok? Did you fall?" asked the butler.

"Yeah, I fell!" said Jena, sarcastically.

Jena slapped the tray with the champagne glasses out of his hand and stepped past him.

"You know Goddamn well what happened to me! You mother fuckers must have violated a multitude of females here! But you fucked with the wrong one today!"

Jena flipped the table with the hors d'oeuvres on it over and walked out of the front door. She saw Ted, he closed the flip phone, turned toward Jena and opened his arms up and smiled.

"Hey, did you kill it?" asked Ted, sounding giddy and

exuberant.

"No mother fucker, I didn't kill it!" without warning, she grabbed the lapel on his blazer with one hand and punched him in the face with the other hand. Surprised from the unprovoked attack; Ted held his jaw with his hand and Jena went berserk. She charged Ted, grabbed him by his shoulders, dragged him forward and downward, then she kneed him in the solar plexus.

Ted dropped his mobile phone as he hit the ground. Jena stood over him huffing and puffing with her fists clenched.

"That's what you get! This is what you and your cronies do? Huh! Is this what you've been grooming me for? Huh! You thought you were gonna just pawn me off to somebody else, so that they could get me to give up my pussy? Huh! Why? Is it because you couldn't get in my panties? I am not a whore, Ted!

"Did I ever give you an inkling that I wanted you to fuck me? Mmm! Did I ever try to suck you off? Huh? Have you ever seen me use any drugs or anything like that? I'm not some cheap prostitute, you came to me in the airport, you approached me with an opportunity; that you said was a great opportunity.

"You said that this was going to be a great opportunity. You said that this script was going to be fresh and innovative; and it was. But I'm not that type of girl Ted. I'm from New York, you mother fuckers tried the wrong one! Sasha told me that if I didn't suck his dick, that I wouldn't get the role," Jena said.

After Jena's tirade, Ted gathered himself off the ground and put his palms out in front of him facing Jena.

"I had nothing to do with that! My God, man!" replied Ted.

Ted put his hand on his chest and one hand on his mouth and adjusted his jaw.

"Ouch! I think you broke my tooth! Jena, c'mon, think for a sec! Did I ever, ever try to seduce you? I have never tried to do anything to disrespect you or your daughters. Give me a moment, let me fix this, let me fix it! You stay right here. I can fix this."

Ted got up off the ground and took a handkerchief out of his sports jacket pocket and wiped the blood out of his mouth. He ran towards the mansion, and Sasha met him at the front door. Sasha stood in the entryway with blood cascading from his nose.

"Bitch, you are dead! Don't you know who I am? You'll never work in this town again!" exclaimed Sasha.

Jena bent down and grabbed a handful of dirt from the ground. Ted couldn't hold Sasha back. He managed to slip away from him and charged Jena. She waited until Sasha was close enough, then she tossed the dirt in his face. Sasha was momentarily blinded, he struggled to wipe the dirt out of his eyes.

Jena karate tripped him down to the ground, used her right foot and stepped in his groin. She kicked dirt in his face as he wallowed on the ground in agony.

"Nah, ma'fucka, yuh don't know who I be, son?! I'm from New York. I'm not to be fucked with, Sasha. I will fuck your shit up, before you even and think to do anything to me," Jena said, in her New York accent.

¡Hijo de puta! Tratando de que tenga sexo conmigo sin mi consentimiento!" (You son of a bitch! Trying to have sex with me without my consent!)

Sasha tenuously conceded to Jena, trembling, and on the verge of tears.

"Ok! Ok! just let me up! just let me up! just let me up!" said Sasha, begging for mercy.

Jena stepped back from Sasha to assure him that she no longer posed a threat to him.

"Piece of shit! Don't you ever, in your life, come at me like that again!" replied Jena.

Ted stepped in between Sasha and Jena and extended his arms out separating the two combatants.

"I'll fix it Jena!" said Ted.

"Aargh!" replied Jena.

Jena shook her head, threw her hands up in the air and

walked away.

"Jena, wait up, wait up! C'mon I'll take you back to the hotel! Let me square things away! I'll take you back to Vegas! Don't worry about anything, you don't have to worry about Sasha anymore. He's a low-level producer in this pilot anyway! I'll talk to the director, and I will let him know what happened today. I could guarantee that he will give you the roll anyway, just on principle.

"You are good money! You are Golden! I'm telling you Jena; you are good for this role! Fuck Sasha, that's not even his mansion, that's the director's mansion. When the director hears about what Sasha did; he is finished in this town!" said Ted, as he chased after Jena.

Jena stopped, turned around and slapped Ted in his face.

"Felicia at the hotel warned me about you and your cronies. She said that you all played this kind of game all the time with young women; eager to get a break into showbiz. Most girls get star struck and are naive and give in to you or your cronies advancesbecause they don't know no better.

"I bet you didn't anticipate that I would be strong enough not to succumb under pressure and put you in your place. Take me back now! No more talking Ted, I am done with you!" replied Jena.

"Ok Jena! Ok, Ok!"

Ted and Jena got inside the limousine, and it took them back to the hangar where the private jet was. Ted cleaned up his face with some tissue, put some ice in his handkerchief and put it on the bridge of his nose. Ted sat far away from Jena on the jet. Jena was clearly pissed off; she had her arms folded across her chest and her legs crossed.

She just sat there quietly the entire flight back to Las Vegas, just shaking her leg up and down repeatedly. Jena shook the entire hour and a half flight from Los Angeles to Las Vegas.

The plane landed safely, and Jena got off the jet, got inside the van and the driver drove Jena back to the hotel without Ted. The driver felt the vibe and didn't bother to ask what had happened. He just assumed that she was okay because she didn't have any defense wounds on her body, just offensive ones.

The van pulled up to the entrance of the hotel, Jena got out and stormed inside. She frowned and went up to the front desk breathing heavily with her nostrils flared upward.

"Goodbye gurl! I gotta go, you were right about Ted! You were totally right! But I had to regulate on those fools. They didn't catch me slippin' trust me; they thought shit was sweet," said Jena.

Jena looked up at the ceiling in a failed attempt to stop herself from crying. With tears cascading down her face she looks back down directly at Felicia and placed both hands on her chest.

"I have to thank you for warning me, Felicia!" said Jena.

"Damn Jena, I am so sorry that you had to go through that. I just had a feeling that would happen. Ted has brought in all kinds of females through here with dreams of making it in Hollywood. Then he flies them to Los Angeles to that big ass mansion. The other producers feed them all kinds of lies, give them drugs and alcohol. Then boom, they fuck 'em and bring 'em right back here to the hotel.

"A few days later, they tell 'em some cockamamie story; that they went with somebody else with more experience. It's like a revolving door, and the turnover rate is high. Those ladies always come in here happy; then they leave sad. I see it all the time. The furthest those females ever got in Hollywood was in that mansion," Felicia replied.

"I don't understand; Ted was so nice to me, Tiye and Amanirenas! I would never have thought that about him. He seemed very respectful of the other females in the cast and me."

"I'm sorry Jena, men are dogs! But listen to me, what are you gonna do now? Where are you gonna go? Where are you gonna stay? What are you gonna do now?"

"I don't even know, Felicia, I can't go back home—— I really can't go back home! I guess I'm gonna see if I could find a place out here in Vegas. I still have school; after I graduate UNLV, I will figure out what my next move is from there."

"So, this is what I propose! I have a big house with lots of room, enough room for you, Tiye and Amanirenas. It's just my grandma living there and me. Would you consider coming and staying with us? It would be temporary until you figure things out.

"My grandmother loves kids. You could stay as long as you like. My shift ends in 20 minutes, stick around and wait for me to clock out. Don't worry; I ain't gonna try to have sex with you or nothing like that," Felicia said.

Jena grabbed a few Kleenexes from the counter, wiped away the tears from her face, and blew her nose.

"Ok, gurl! Alright! How could I say no! You've been there for me since day one," Jena replied.

Oh Jena, I forgot to tell you that I live in LA. I drive out here on Sunday nights, I stay in Vegas until Friday afternoon, then I drive back home."

Damn gurl! You do that every week?"

"Yup! Three weeks out of the month, I'm off one week of each month. Jena, I make it work, the pay is good, I save a lot of money on transportation, and room and board."

"I hear that, I'll be in the rest area after I go upstairs, pack and get the twins."

After about an hour passed by, Jena came back downstairs with her luggage. Felicia waited in the rest area watching the news and played with the twins. When breaking news flashed across the TV screen:

"This just in, breaking news out of the Bronx, New York; the FBI have uncovered an illegal Fight Club. One fighter was critically injured during a bout. The FBI has indicted the owner, Raphael Rodriguez, on charges of operating an illegal, underground, bare-knuckle fighting ring," the news anchor said.

Jena recognized the fighter's face that was injured, and she opened her eyes and mouth wide open and yelped.

"Oh, my goodness! I knew him. His name was Darren," Jena

said.

Jena shed a tear and Felicia handed her a tissue and put a hand on her shoulder. Immediately, Jena had an eerie feeling that Claude had some involvement with this incident. Although the news didn't show the picture of the other fighter involved, she knew with every fiber of her being down to her soul that it was him.

Jena stood there in shock at the terrible news. But she remembered that she told Claude that while she dated Darren, he was mentally and physically abusive. If Claude had something to do with Darren's death, in a twisted way, it lets her know that he was still thinking about her.

"Shit!" said Jena, out loud.

"It's been so long since I had any concerns about anyone coming after me. I hope and pray that this is not a prelude to what's about to happen. I'm not prepared mentally for my world to come crashing down again," Jena thought.

"Are you going to be okay, Jena?" asked Felicia.

"Yes, Felicia, I am going to be just fine," Jena replied.

Felicia grabbed the diaper bags and swung them over each shoulder. Jena pushed the stroller towards the parking garage, and Felicia directed her to where her car was parked. Both Jena and Felicia unlatched each car seat from the stroller and secured them in the car's back seat. Jena folded the double stroller, then put it inside the trunk. Felicia got inside the driver's side and started the car as Jena slammed close the trunk. She walked to the passenger side and got inside.

Jena put on her seat belt, and Felicia reversed out of the parking spot. She drove out of the parking garage towards the highway on the two-hour trek to Los Angeles.

Jena and the twins fell asleep one hour into the journey. Felicia felt a bit fatigued, so she pulled into a gas station to stretch out her legs and get herself some coffee.

"Hey, Jena!" said Felicia, then she nudged Jena awake.

Jena opened her eyes and looked over at Felicia.

"Hey, do you need to use the restroom? The girls might need a diaper change and a bottle. I'm going inside the gas station to get something to keep me up; did you want anything?" asked Felicia.

Jena stretched and kindly shook her head from left to right. Jena has been awake since earlier that morning. It has been a very long day. After Jena took a moment to wake up, she got out of the car and attended to the twins one at a time. Jena took Tiye out of her car seat first, then took her to the front seat and changed her diaper.

She did the same for Amanirenas, and all three of them stood up around the car and waited for Felicia to get back from the car. Jena checked the diaper bag and took out two juice boxes and toddler snacks for the twins to nosh on. All three of them stood up outside the car to stretch out their legs.

Felicia walked out of the gas station with a plastic bag filled with goodies and a cup of coffee in her hand. When Felicia got closer to Jena, and she smiled at the twins standing up on their own.

"Are you ready to go?" asked Felicia.

"No, I have to use the ladies' room; first, I feel a bit queasy," Jena replied.

Jena put her hand over her stomach as she grabbed her pocketbook, then walked towards the ladies' room on the side of the gas station. Jena entered the restroom and luckily found an empty stall. She pulled down her underwear to sit down on the toilet and discovered that she had started her monthly cycle. She sighed in relief that she caught it before she made a mess of Felicia's car seat cushion.

Jena finished tidying up herself the best way she could; given her surroundings. Then she joined the rest of the girls outside in the parking lot. She got inside the vehicle and Felicia was singing nursery rhymes with Tiye and Amanirenas.

At that moment Jena realized that everything was going to be alright.

"The wheels on the bus go round and round, round and

round. All 'round town!"

Jena joined in and everyone sang nursery rhymes until the twins fell asleep. They both stayed down for the duration of their journey to Los Angeles.

Forty-five minutes later, Felicia pulled up to the house and let out a sigh of relief.

"This is it; we're here! Welcome home!" sad Felicia.

"Oh wow, this is a big house! This is nice! Oh my God, this is beautiful! How could you afford this house working at the front desk at a hotel?" replied Jena.

"This house has been in my family for generations. Before the first prospectors came out west panning for gold, and even before the Hollywood land sign was up. My family was the first set of black people to settle in Los Angeles, way back when California was still Mexico.

"My ancestors were mestizos and mulattos; very proud Californio people. Did you know California was named after an indigenous black warrior queen by the name of Calafia or Califia! Well, at least that is the legend according to the 16th-century romance novel "Las sergas de Esplandian.""

"You know Tiye's middle name is Khalifa! But I spelled it the Arabic way, though!"

"That is ironic, Queen Calafia was a Moor. And more than likely her name was spelled that way."

"That's very interesting Felicia, I will have to look that up. But how can you afford the upkeep on this place? It must be expensive gurl," Jena asked.

"I run my own business, gurl. I am a masseuse. My grandmother collects her pension checks from when she was a nurse; she also collects my grandfather's pension too. He passed away a few years back. I work at the hotel to pass the time, meet new people, and I get hella clients like that; you know what I mean.

"Most of the time, I go out to their location and massage them there. I make pretty good money. I have a good life here, I

281

don't have any kids or anything, and I finally start school soon; so, I can better myself even further. I've been saving up most of my money; I plan to earn my bachelor's degree," Felicia replied.

Jena and Felicia continued talking as they unpacked the car and the twins.

"What did you plan on earning your degree in?" asked Jena.

"My next step is to become a lawyer! I wanna help people. I would be a criminal defense attorney or study family law," Felicia replied.

"Lawyer! Hmm, I never considered studying law before. I always thought I would become a performance artist of some sort. But studying law seems interesting."

"After I finish my studies at UNLV, maybe I'll take up law in graduate school. Since I've been here, the only money I spent was on the plane ticket out here. Let's see how things play out first. That sounds like a great backup plan," Jena thought.

"Nana, I'm home!" said Felicia, as she opened the front door.

"Felicia, I hear voices. Do you have some company with you?" replied Felicia's grandmother.

Felicia's grandmother sauntered over to the foyer to greet her granddaughter and to investigate who she'd brought inside the house without her consent.

"Nana, this is a friend of mine from work, Jena, and her twin girls Tiye and Amanirenas."

"Pleased to meet you, baby, my name is Josephine," Nana said.

"Nana, her husband, is tripping, and he kicked her out the house. She doesn't have anywhere to go; is it okay if she stayed here with the girl?" asked Felicia.

"Let me see these babies. Lord have mercy! Why would a man kick a woman out with these babies? Come here, baby, hug me! How are you doing? These men nowadays don't know how to treat a woman. Back in my day, my husband, my husband Garfield, God rest his soul.

"He was the sweetest man ever; he went out and worked two jobs. He would come in after a hard day's work with flowers underneath his arm every Friday. Sometimes, when the mood struck, he would bring candy too. Honey child, from time to time, he'd give me loving. We were compatible. I love and miss him so much.

"Garfield was the only man that I ever loved. I have never known another man since my husband passed away. These little boys nowadays don't love themselves, let alone talking about loving a woman. They don't know nothing about nothing. They have their trousers hanging halfway off their asses, showing the world their underwear! They don't have any sense," Nana replied.

"Ok, Ok, Ok, Nana! Let me take Jena and the girls to their room. When we get back, you could tell us all about Grandpa Garfield," Felicia said.

Felicia took Jena's bags and ushered her and the twins to their room. Felicia opened the room door and turned on the light.

"It's not much, gurl, but it's free, and the best could do on short notice. This is it gurl, and there's an on-suite bathroom in here too. I know you and the girls might need privacy. Now, you don't have to worry about sharing a bathroom," Felicia said.

Felicia walked over to the window and pulled open the curtain.

"Also, this room gets a good amount of natural light Io n here," Felicia said.

"Wow, this room is huge, Felicia! Thanks again for your hospitality!" replied Jena.

Jena wrapped her arms around Felicia and squeezed her tight.

"So, you were telling me about studying to become a lawyer. Since you haven't started going to school yet. Would you possibly have any books or anything here? If not, is there a library close by that I can go and get some books?" asked Jena.

"Oh, okay! You're interested in studying law too? Come to think of it, I do have a few books lying around here. Make yourself at home, why don't you get settled and I'll look in my study for those books for you. If there is anything you need here, don't hesitate to ask. Jena, we're family, mi casa es sue casa," replied Felicia.

Felicia walked out of the room, closed the door and went to search for those books. Jena unstrapped the twins, lifted them out of their car seats and put them on the bed. They were both still asleep, the drive in from Vegas tuckered them out. Either that, or all the nursery rhymes everyone sung in the car, on their way to California.

"Mommy loves you both! You girls are so good, you don't give me any trouble at all. You two are so peaceful; I hope one day you both could meet your Abuelo Augustus, your Abuela Melba, your Tia Asia, and your Padre Claude too!" said Jena.

Jena looked at them passionately, as the twins laid on the bed sucking on their pacifiers. Felicia came back into the room clutching the books under both her arms.

"Jena, these are the only law books that I have, study these and when you're ready; we could go to the library. It's not too far from here, we can go there and get some more books.

"There's a college campus not too far from here, also. The next semester is coming up soon, I'm not sure if you were planning on continuing going to UNLV, or transfer to school out here. Whatever you want to do, you have options girl," Felicia said.

Jena took the books, opened the cover of a few of them, and nodded her head up and down.

"Sounds like a plan! I will explore my options. I will take my time and study these books," Jena replied.

Jena turned on the lamp and sat down on the rocking chair next to the window. She shuffled through the books and stopped at the one on criminology. Jena put away the rest of the other books and opened the book on criminology. She opened the book and she read the first page:

"Criminology is the study of crime and deviant behavior.

Criminology is an interdisciplinary field in both the behavioral and social sciences, which draws primarily upon the research of sociologists, psychologists, philosophers, psychiatrists, biologists, social anthropologists, as well as scholars of law."

Jena continued to read until the fourth chapter, then she grabbed a bookmark and put down the book on the nightstand. After reading those chapters, she was intrigued and considered becoming a criminologist.

"If this criminology thing pans out; I could work with the District Attorney's office back in New York. I could help prosecute those people involved in 'The Program' once and for all," thought Jena.

Jena continued to study and before long, she managed to read all five of those books. Jena was intrigued about the study of the criminal mind. A few months went by, and she settled in quite nicely. Felicia and Nana was a godsend to her and the twins.

School started back up and Jena decided to travel back and forth with Felicia to Vegas to attend classes. Everything was going on well; she got to study, and she didn't have to worry about a babysitter. Nana agreed to take care of the twins while she attended school. She was so blessed to have met Felicia. Jena took the time that God gave her to focus on her studies.

One Sunday while she was in the room reading, she heard a knock on the door. Jena closed the book that she was reading, walked over to the door and opened it. It was Nana and she was all dressed up in her Sunday best for church.

"Baby, we're gonna go to church this Sunday, are you coming to church with us? You know, all this time you've been staying here; we've left you alone to get to your studies. But you gotta get to church now, you gotta get some God in you. He has blessed you with those girls, he has blessed you with life; so, you gotta get to church now!

"These babies gotta get baptized, you have these babies out here without being filled with the Holy Ghost. We're gonna make sure that we do something about that. Jena, baby, you can't continue having a man be your only motivation. God has to be the only motivation in your life. Now, get up and get yourself and these babies dressed because you all are going to church this Sunday," Nana said.

Nana shut the door and Jena didn't have the chance to accept or decline the invitation.

"I guess I'm going to church today!" replied Jena, to the back of the door.

She put down her pencil, put away her books and hopped in the shower with the twins. While she was bathing, Felicia entered the bedroom, knocked on the bathroom door and opened it.

"Are you done washing off the girls yet?" asked Felicia.

"Yes!" replied Jena.

Felicia walked into the bathroom, took a towel and got the twins from Jena.

"Nana and I will get the twins ready!" said Felicia, as she wrapped up the twins in a towel.

Jena finished bathing a few minutes later, toweled off, hurried back into the bedroom and searched for a dress that she had in her bag. She found it hung up neatly in the closet. Jena thought that she would never get the chance to wear it. Jena got dressed in a hurry and walked downstairs as Nana, Felicia and the twins were walking outside the house.

Everyone got into the car, and Felicia drove a few city blocks to where the church was. After Felicia parked in a spot by the entrance, the Deacon of the church helped Nana out of the car. Jena and Felicia took each of the twins and got out the car with them. They all entered the church and the usher escorted them to an empty pew.

Church service was underway when they sat down. Everybody's hands were clapping, thimbles were clanging, the organist was playing the organ like he was filled with the holy ghost. The drums were thumping, and the guitarist strung the bass guitar like Sly from the family stone. People praised God by extending their hands over their heads, opening their minds, their bodies and souls to blessings that they hope to receive. Those in attendance who could, stomped their feet to the instruments playing. The choir sang various hymns and Amazing grace, filling the church with the holy spirit. After fifteen minutes of singing, The Pastor stepped up to the podium and the Deacon commanded everyone to be silent with a few hand gestures.

"You shall be seated!" said The Pastor.

Everyone sat down, and The Pastor paced back and forth then grabbed hold of the microphone. "Good morning, church! There's those of us here that are living in the past. ——

"y'all don't hear me! There are those of us here in the present, that can't leave the past in the past. Then they wonder why they can't move along gracefully into the future.

"Never forget what transpired in the past, try not to make that what you've done or was done to you demotivate you and ruin your chances of receiving your blessings.

"Don't focus on the negative, you gotta take the positive out of the negative, and always put God first!" said the Pastor.

Jena stood up with tears cascading down her face and raised her hands in the air. "Preach, yes, yes, lord!"

The Pastor stopped his sermon and located Jena standing up with her hands outstretched like the sun pose in yoga.

"My child, come up front, God is telling me to lay hands on you!" asked the Pastor.

Jena picked up the twins and carried them up to the front of the church with her. The Pastor put his thumb in some anointed oil and placed it across the foreheads of all three of them.

Then he urged the members of the church to bow their heads with a hand gesture.

"On this day, I am going to fill these vessels with the holy ghost!"

The Pastor's body jerked back, and he spoke in tongues.

Then he prayed over all three of the girls and at the same time the Deacon brought out a tub of water and The Pastor looked at Jena and nodded his head.

"Are you ready? Are you ready to give yourself over to God?" asked The Pastor.

Jena didn't hesitate to answer the question, she trembled and squeezed the twins tight in her hands.

"Yes, Lord, I'm ready!" replied Jena.

"Yes lord!" said everyone in the church simultaneously.

The entire church applauded and held their hands high above their heads. A few of the elder females in the church offered to take Jena in a back room to change. Jena shook her head from left to right.

"No, I want to get baptized with my girls just the way I am!" said Jena.

A few people got filled with the Holy Ghost, as the organist played. The Deacon ran to aid one old lady who fell down, as she got filled with the holy spirit. She rolled around on the ground speaking in tongues, and they took out a white cloth and waved it over her, to give her some oxygen.

Jena, stepped inside that tub with the twins in her arms fully clothed. The Pastor stepped in the tub with her and didn't change his clothes either. The Pastor prayed and he took each of the twins one at a time. He prayed over them individually, then he scooped up a handful of water and poured it over their foreheads. After he finished, he handed them back to Jena. After he baptized the twins, two elders took the twins away from Jena. The Pastor held the back of her head and Jena held her nose. Then the Pastor dunked Jena underneath the water.

The portrait of Jesus getting baptized by John the Baptist was the relief on the stained-glass window; after Jena opened her eyes. Jena immediately knew that it was the right time for her, Tiye and Amanirenas to be baptized.

Felicia and Nana were given towels and they both took each

of the twins out of the tub. As the girls were being taken out the tub The Pastor continued to pray over Tiye and Amanirenas individually. Jena and The Pastor walked out of the tub of water together, and they were assisted to the back, where they dried off.

After fifteen minutes, Jena returned from the back wearing different clothing and she furrowed up her face to Nana and Felicia after she reached where they were seated.

"You guys had this all planned out, huh!" asked Jena.

Nana hugged her and the twins, then they all sat down.

"No way, I didn't! It was the will of the lord; we are just the messengers we just carry out God's work! It is God's will baby, don't fight it! Don't fight the creator," Nana replied.

After church, they all walked outside and Jena was beaming like a fluorescent light bulb, as they got into the vehicle and Felicia drove them home. They arrived at the house, and Josephine's family was already inside. Felicia introduced Jena and the twins to her family, then she went upstairs to change clothes.

Nana and a few of the other women at the house prepared the food. Felicia and Jena set the table, then everyone sat down and enjoyed Sunday dinner. The night ended on a good note, Jena felt at peace. She had a new perspective on things, a new way of being, a different way of thinking. She shifted her mindset to not only succeed but prepared for the hereafter as well. She can't continue to think about her only salvation; but lead by example for others to follow.

It was clear to her what she must do, she now knows that her drive must be to help protect not only her kids, but other people who need guidance and assistance. Jena understood that it's going to be a bumpy road, but the road less traveled always is. It's up to her to pave the way for others to have an easier road ahead.

Chapter 14:

Partner

It has been a year since Jena left town and Jean-Jacque has been focused on performing his duties at the mayor's office under the acting Mayor of New York City, Marisol Velasquez. Jean-Jacque attended NYU, majoring in Political Science, and a minor in Business Management. His hard work has led to a training program at a brokerage firm.

Jean-Jacque has been biding his time, until he could get in a position where he's outside of the reach of Marisol and the rest of her cohorts. All the while he has been getting some major backing from some key people in prominent positions in education; that could ensure his vision for the "Helping Hand Initiative" would be successful.

He took his role as the assistant to the acting mayor very seriously, and all the power of influence that came with it. Jean-Jacque organized an outreach program for former criminals, who want a new lease on life. Atoning for their past transgressions, by being an asset to society and not a destructive force in their communities.

This outreach program helps attendees with literacy, finance, and business training opportunities at brokerage firms. Which helps them gain real world experience in various industries. Participants of the training program will build relationships with industry leaders, earning the respect they deserve as professionals in various industries.

The only thing that is certain is, when a person has the proper tools, confidence and means to succeed; leads them down the right path of being a productive member of society. Leading a life of crime is not as attractive in comparison to being a leading man or woman in your profession.

Jean-Jacque was in the mayor's office one day and thought to himself, "I haven't spared with anyone in a long time." So, he picked up the phone and decided to call Marques.

(Ring, ring, ring) "Hello, who's dis?" asked Marques.

"Yo, it's Claude, I heard about that underground fight club that Raphael started. Could you give me his number, I want to spar in an upcoming match," Jean-Jacque replied.

"Say no more Claude, I got you. There's a fight every Friday and Saturday night in the gymnasium behind Darrelle's building. Let me find out that you're trying to turn in your suits for boxing gloves," Marques said.

"The man makes the clothes Mark, not the other way around."

"Chill Claude don't get your suspenders in a bunch. The fight starts at 7pm, show up an hour before the bout and sign up to fight. I'll see you Saturday."

Marques hung up the phone and Claude smiled, cracked his neck from side to side with his hands.

"All work and no play have made me a dull boy, a little weekly exercise should help restore the edge I once had," thought Jean-Jacque.

One week has past and Jean-Jacque drove to the Bronx, right after work. It was a quarter to six in the evening; Raphael, Darren and Marvelous were all standing outside the Gym. Jean-Jacque parked his truck and walked up to them.

"Oh shit, look it's Claude, Mark told me you wanted to spar. I thought he was bullshitting me, but here you are," Raphael said.

Jean-Jacque shook hands with everyone and unbuckled his blazer.

"Yeah, he told me I could fight if I signed up an hour before you started," Jean-Jacque replied.

"Yeah, c'mon we were just about to set up, pay the two-hundred-dollar fee and give your information to Marvelous. If you win tonight, you get the purse; it will be you and Darren in the main event, his opponent couldn't make it."

"Ok, cool, let me get my bag from my truck."

291

Jean-Jacque grabbed a duffle bag from his truck, signed the release forms and put down the money on the table. He went to the locker room and the trainers briefed him on the rules of the ring. They taped his hands and helped him warm up before the match.

The noise from people entering the gym echoed throughout the locker room. The three undercard bouts ended sooner than expected. It was 8:30, a half an hour before the scheduled main event. The announcer grabbed the microphone and read from the Q-cards the introduction of the bout.

"Hear ye, hear ye! Now, it's time for the main event at Friday night fights at double up or knuckle up fight club. In the red corner we have the fan favorite, undefeated golden gloves at the junior Olympics, Muay Thai fighter, Darren 'Sly Mongoose' Lyn," the announcer said.

The crowd stood up from their seats and cheered for Darren. The announcer switched the Q-card, adjusted his glasses and pointed at Jean-Jacque.

"And in this corner, a new corner, a brown belt in jiu-jitsu and a third-degree black belt in Kenpo; Jean Claude 'Body Slam' Cadet!" exclaimed the announcer.

The two-fighters walked to the center of the ring and the referee stood in between them. Then the people in the crowd clamored to place their bets for the first round.

"This fight is scheduled to be three, two-minute rounds. It is a no holds barred bare knuckle fight, the only rules are no hitting below the belt, no eye gouging, stop fighting when the bell rings and when I say break. Now, you two, touch knuckles," the referee said.

Darren stared at Jean-Jacque the entire time the ref discussed the rules. Jean-Jacque smirked and jumped up and down in place.

"Fighters are you ready?"

Both combatants nodded their heads up and down at the referee.

"Knuckle up!"

The men approached the center of the ring and Darren threw

the first punch. Jean-Jacque, side stepped it and threw a hook to his body. The crowd booed when Darren grimaced from the body blow. Jean-Jacque stepped back and threw an upper-cut at Darren. He missed and Darren took two steps back and kicked Jean-Jacque to the side of his head.

Jean-Jacque stumbled to the side but kept up his defensive stance. Darren attacked him with a front knee to the chest, and Jean-Jacque sidestepped the flying knee, then countered with an overhand left to Darren's ear. He dropped down to one knee and the ref ordered Jean-Jacque to stand back.

The crowd was in a state of shock, seeing their fighter on the verge of his first loss. Darren's ear was bleeding, and he was disorientated. Jean-Jacque smirked and noticed that Darren's arm was covering his right side.

The bell rang and the two men went back to their corners. Darren's corner worked on him frantically to stop the bleeding from his ear. People in the crowd placed their bets for the next round. Darren stood up from his stool and jumped up and down in place. Jean-Jacque spit water into the bucket and stood up from his stool.

The bell rang and Darren dashed to the center of the ring toward Jean-Jacque with a flying superman punch. He blocked it and punched him in his side. Darren dropped down to one knee, Jean-Jacque jumped in the air, elevated his foot and lowered his heel on the back of Darren's neck knocking him out cold.

Darren's head bounced off the ground when it hit the ground and the referee waved off the fight. Darren's corner men rushed to aid their fighter and the crowd was speechless. The referee checked his pulse and shook his head from left to right.

Raphael stood up from his seat and rushed to the center of the ring.

"Yo, somebody call an ambulance," Raphael said.

Darren laid on the ground motionless in the same position that he fell in. Jean-Jacque walked over to his side and took a knee. Five minutes later, the medics ran inside the gym with the gurney and an IV drip. The ref, Darren's corner men, and Jean-Jacque, moved out of their way. The Paramedic checked Darren's pulse and took out a neck brace to secure it in place.

"His pulse is faint, we have to get him to a hospital, stat," The Paramedic said.

The medics transferred Darren's limp body over on the gurney, secured him to it and hoisted him out the gym to the ambulance.

Jean-Jacque unwrapped the tape off his hands, ankles and walked over to Raphael counting out the take for the night. He put a stack of money in an envelope and handed it to Jean-Jacque.

"Here is your cut for winning the fight. I have to get to the hospital and see if Darren's alright," Raphael said.

"Nah, you keep it, take the money with you to the hospital and use it to pay for Darren's medical bill. I'll be pulling for him to make a full recovery," Jean-Jacque replied.

Raphael looked at Jean-Jacque as he walked out of the gym barefoot with his duffle bag over his shoulder.

Over the next few weeks, the FBI caught wind of the incident and shut down Raphael's underground fight club. They indicted him for running an illegal fighting circuit. Darren was on life support and his chances for survival was slim to none.

Jean-Jacque has dedicated the last few years of his life in atonement mode. For all the wrongs that he's done in the past as a young man. And now he must make amends for what happened between him and Darren. So, he decided to set up a meeting with Darren's parents at The Mayor's Office.

The phone rang in Jean-Jacque's office, and he picked up the phone

"Yes?" said Jean-Jacque.

"Mr. and Mrs. Chan are here to see you," Olivia replied.

"Alright Olivia, send them right in."

The door opened and Mr. and Mrs. Chan entered the office. Jean-Jacque stood up from behind his desk and buttoned his blazer.

"Please, Mr. and Mrs. Chan, have a seat, I'm glad you two could make it on such short notice, please sit down. My sincere condolences for what happened that terrible night awhile back, when your son and I fought each other, and he suffered some serious injuries," Jean-Jacque said.

Darren's parents and Jean-Jacque sat down, and he unbuttoned his blazer.

"Would you like some tea or coffee?" asked Jean-Jacque.

"No thank you!" said Mr. and Mrs. Chan.

"OK, the reason why I asked you two to come down is, I want to open up a Community Center in Darren's honor. This Community Center will teach self-defense in all forms of martial arts. I want to make sure that all the inner-city youth, especially the foreign ones; to have a place to go to build confidence and discipline. With all the negativity in our neighborhoods, I want to make sure there's something positive that the kids could do other than sell drugs and join gangs."

Mr. Chan slid back in his chair and kissed his teeth. "Mi nuh like it! Mi nuh ovastan how afta all dis time, yuh waan cum sawf we up wid a likkle building in ah mi son name. Unnuh cyan bring bac mi son, nuh matta wah yuh duh!" said Mr. Chan.

Mrs. Chan put her hand on Mr. Chan's shoulder and moved forward in her seat. "Honey, come now, be reasonable. It has been very hard for us to deal with. You must understand how we could perceive this as a cheap attempt at making amends for what happened. But I do appreciate the idea of the city actually doing something constructive in the inner city that would be beneficial for the youths that reside there," Mrs. Chan replied.

Mr. Chan stood up and pushed all of the papers that was on Jean-Jacque's desk.

"Mi nuh truss di bwoy yah, ah fuckry dis yuh ah taak! Fram wah mi know, yuh neva luv mi son fram lang time. Eh luk lakka kill, yuh di waah kill mi son. Mi hab half a mind jus shot yuh a bloodclot bax!" said Mr. Chan.

295

Jean-Jacque stood up with his hands outreached defensively in front of him.

"Please Mr. Chan, calm down! It wasn't anything like that. We fought in the ring; Darren was a willing participant. In fact, he was undefeated in that arena at the time. It was an unfortunate set of circumstances, either of us could have been hurt. Before we got into the ring, we understood the risks we were taking. I am truly sorry about what happened, but I want to honor your son on what he dedicated his life to, and that is martial arts," Jean-Jacque replied.

Mr. Chan stood there with his bald up fist on the desk snarling at Jean-Jacque. "Wollah unnuh think yuh slick, but if yuh slip, yuh ah go slide; if dis ting is jus a way to eat a food offa mi son name," Mr. Chan said.

"Sir, I assure you that it's nothing like that. I understand what your position is, given the severity of the situation. But if you permit us to carry out this venture, there would be nobody benefiting from it other than the youths that are enrolled in the program. The program would be free for everyone in each facility that we open in this city.

"They all would have Darren's name on it, we would want you two and his siblings to be there at the grand opening of each facility. I will have my secretary give you my contact information, and when you are ready to sign off on this; then we would break ground and start building."

Mrs. Chan stood up and offered her hand to Jean-Jacque, and he shook it.

"It sounds like a great idea, but we have to discuss it more. We will be in touch!" said Mrs. Chan.

Mr. Chan stared at Jean-Jacque the entire time as he walked out of his office. After the door slammed behind Mr. and Mrs. Chan, Jean-Jacque sat down and exhaled with a sigh of relief.

"That went well!" thought Jean-Jacque.

Jean-Jacque looked at his palm pilot, then picked up the phone and dialed up all of the guys. It's been a good while since they agreed to start legitimate businesses together. Each week they all got on a conference call to give a progress report on their ventures. The phone rang, and one by one, each of the guys answered the call.

"Fellas, what's up? Marques, how's things out there in Colorado? I'm going to assume the Marijuana dispensary you got is generating some good dividends," Jean-Jacque said.

"Yeah man, the weed dispensary is pretty cool man!" replied Marques.

"I know you fucked a few snow bunnies out there, Mark!" said Raheem.

"Ha, ha, ha! Nah man, I brought wifey out here with me. Besides, I can't mess up sure money, for no snow bunny! This dispensary out here is legit, I am learning the business on my end, Jean-Jacque, I hope you and your politician friends are trying to bring the idea of making cannabis legal through to legislation in New York; so, I won't be out here in the cold Rocky Mountains, for too long," Marques replied.

"Marques, we are working on just that, so Mark, when I come out there the company will be a full-fledged Corporation?!" asked Jean-Jacque.

"No doubt, it's already on a bigger scale operation than what it was when we first started."

"That's great news, how are the other business ventures going? How's the Barber shops, the Cuchifrito, and Alejandro's clothing stores out here in the Bronx?"

"Business is booming! My mother and my sister are both making sure of that. We're making a lot of money, so much so, that we'll be opening up three new locations soon. It's going to be one of each of those businesses uptown and we're planning on opening a super center in Spanish Harlem."

"So, Darrelle, what's going on with the pharmaceutical company? How's everything going on with that man? Was that a good move for you?" asked Jean-Jacque.

"At first, I didn't like being stuck in a laboratory learning the chemistry aspect of the business, and the logistics of it all; It was an eye-opening experience to say the least. But I realized over time, how lucrative starting a legitimate pharmaceutical company can be. Pharmacists earn one hundred thousand dollars per year by themselves. It's very gratifying to be the Boss of my own corporation and distributing drugs to a lot of establishments across the nation, legally. I don't have to carry a piece anymore; I am not looking over my shoulder for any unsuspecting people gunning for me. This is a nice change for the better. I have plans of traveling to Panama where my parents are from and buying some land there. I want to set up Castillo Industries there. I feel like I am in position to give back to my fellow countrymen," Darrelle replied.

"That's great news Darrelle! ——"

"Raheem how's the funeral home going? I know back in the day, anyone who had a loved one who passed away in our area, went to Ortiz funeral home. Since Knight Funeral Home opened, I hear business is booming! You must be doing pretty good for yourself," Jean-Jacque said.

"I really wouldn't say yes because I still have my doubts about this whole being a mortician thing. I can't get used to seeing all those dead bodies, the mourning family members, and the smell. The funeral home generates great business, I just don't want to experience anyone waking up on me," Raheem replied.

Everyone laughed, and Jean-Jacque waited a few moments until the guys settled down.

"You shouldn't have to concern yourself with that aspect of the business, you should have a staff of professionals that deals with that. What you should focus on is the logistics, and make sure these mourning families keep using your funeral home for burying their loved ones.

"The main goal is for everyone to be extremely savvy with the numbers of their respective companies. All the extra money you earn, you should buy more and more shares in your companies from The Program, and slowly but surely be the majority owner. Then, the scrutiny from shareholders won't be a concern anymore. You will be the H.N.I.C, and you all will be calling all the shots," Jean-

Jacque said.

There was dead silence on the call, Jean-Jacque cleared his throat to interrupt the awkward silence on the phone.

"I have been corresponding with Darnel in prison, and he's been doing well considering his situation. He completely made a one-hundred-and-eighty-degree turn around. He has completed most, if not all the programs he needs to, and he has started his own gang reform group. Darnel and I has partnered up and we plan to give gang members an option to get out the life.

"So, when they're released from prison, they have real options. The business relationships that were forged through our organization, carries over on the outside. All we ask is to volunteer their time for the outreach programs in their communities.

"So, the next Jeneration of youths doesn't have to join a gang in the first place for validation; they would have better options. When Darnel gets out in a few years, he will be on pace to be an asset to our community. He is on the verge of earning his bachelor's degree, and he is already an influential motivational speaker in jail," Jean-Jacque said.

Jean-Jacque stopped speaking for a moment to drink some water; he looked down and saw an important email that came in on his palm pilot.

"Excuse me fellas, I am proud to call all you my friends, and we are currently business partners as well. Trust me when I tell you, things are changing in the city. The wealthy people are planning to gentrify the inner city, one borough at a time. They're looking to start in downtown Brooklyn, a lot of investors are buying up most of the properties there. The plan is to attract more people from a higher tax bracket to follow suit. So, if you have any extra money, now is the time to invest in real estate.

"We always boast by saying things like, 'this is my block,' let us invest and literally buy the block. When you have ownership in your neighborhood, you have the power to make decisions about what happens in your neighborhood. The police would no longer oversee what you're doing, their job would be to protect and serve you, your family, and your property.

"The world is changing; we have to be savvy enough to change with it. The way things are going, I bet there will be an African American president elected soon," Jean-Jacque said.

"Get the fuck out of here! There would be a woman president before a black man was elected president. Next, you might tell us that Trump is going to be president one day," the guys said simultaneously.

"I'm not feeling nothing of what you're saying man. The rich or privileged are going to stay where they are. They're not going to invest in the slums Jean-Jacque. For decades since the government built the projects for working class white Europeans, Jewish community and anyone who could afford to live there.

Since segregation became a thing, they have been doing everything in their power to keep a safe distance from the us in the ghetto. Once the powers that be noticed that the poor whites were intermingling with the poor blacks and brown folks; they started red lining in the inner cities to keep the ethnic groups separated.

"So, the privileged would not be coming up in the Bronx, Brooklyn, Queens, or Harlem. Investors won't be spending a dime in the slums; they won't gentrify nothing in the hood. You know I mean; they're not trying to live next to nobody or move inside any building that is infested with rats, roaches, base heads, homeless or shit like that. Uppity folks from Scarsdale or Connecticut, are not used to smelly ass cab drivers, and pissy hallways.

"The term gentrification definition is to fix up one house, one building, one business, in one neighborhood anytime; to increase the property value and drive up the cost of living there. That would intern make it too expensive for poor people to live there; they would have to move out, then more wealthy people could come in to live.

"After the tactic of driving out the current element out of the hood, it becomes safer for a more desirable element to replace them in the hood. This makes it more attractive to investors to invest money, turning it into a neighborhood; bringing all the money and more investors to follow the blueprint," Marques replied.

"Marques, that's all true what you're saying, but investment opportunities shouldn't be limited to people outside the 'hood. We have the means to reap all the benefits of these ventures. If we buy now, when the cost is low; we get in on the ground floor and buy up all the vacant lots, dilapidated buildings, or anybody who's upside-down in their mortgage. We'll be in prime position when investors want to start buying up the property in the 'hood," Jean-Jacque said.

"When that happens then I'll be on board," Marques replied.

"Now is the time you can't try to invest in buildings when everything is all fixed up and nicer; it is going to be five or six times more expensive. Listen to what I'm saying, buy it now and just hold it until the market goes up, when real-estate investors start investments in the 'hood. They are going to have to buy it from you who owns the property; trust me on this, I have the inside track, I work for the city, this is inevitable.

"Fellas, the best way to gain power of influence is to own property and have political affiliations with the people that govern your community. You gotta put your money where your mouth is; we need to be more involved in the process. Think about it, and we'll discuss it more on our next call. I have to go; I will talk to you all soon," Jean-Jacque said.

Jean-Jacque ended the conference call, leaned back in his chair and sighed.

It was clearly apparent to him that changing his friend's circumstances doesn't mean that they're evolving as individuals. He pressed the speaker button on the phone and dialed up Raphael. The phone rang a few times before he answered the call.

"Who dis?" said Raphael.

"Hello, this is Claude!" replied Jean-Jacque.

"Who? I don't know nobody named Claude."

"Raphael! Don't hang up, I am the one that fought Darren at your Double up, put 'em up, or knuckle up Fight Club man!"

"Man, you got some nerve calling me after what you did.

301

You know the FBI raided my spot, I'm facing charges, I lost a ton of money and you killed Darren. They shut down everything that I built; I should slap the shit out you man, all of what I worked for has gone down the drain."

"Listen, listen to me Raphael, I know a way where you can start Put 'em up, back up."

"Word, I'm listening!"

"I have connections, I know how you can start your own federation with professional martial arts fighters. You won't have no worries about the government raiding your spot, no more illegal underground Fight Club. This will be legit man, you would be as recognized as boxing is with the WBA, WBC, and the WBO. I'm gonna front you that money, so the little bit of money that you said you lost, y'all get all that shit back, plus interest.

"Give me two years, and after those two years, what I want you to do is before the beginning of that third year of operation; I want you to go public with your company. After you go public with that company, in the matter of months, maybe less; you're gonna be a billionaire. Trust me, mixed martial arts is big business all over the world. You know movies like, Blood sport, Street Fighter, and even Mortal Kombat; showcases the way these fights are in real life.

"Investors, and fighters all around the world have been trying to bring it out here in the states. Because it is kind of like bare knuckle fist fighting in the street; the governing body that regulates professional fighting, didn't want to legalize it here for years. Plus, not a lot of people really know about it, they have to be guaranteed that it's going to be lucrative first, before they bring it here. Do you have the footage of the fight between me and Darren?"

"Yes, I have footage of all those fights."

"Good, make copies of each of them on DVDs, like banned from TV, you know. We got to get people interested in that kind of stuff again. Get the streets talking, and once there's enough buzz about the old fights; fans will show up at the arenas. That's where you can sell merchandise, food and beverages. We'll have a meeting and I'll give you the contract, then we go from there," Jean-Jacque

said.

"This shit sounds too good to be true, I will have to see it to believe it; this shit better work or I'll come after you myself," Raphael replied.

Raphael hung up the phone and Jean-Jacque sat back in his chair and contemplated his next move. He thought about Margot and decided to give her a call. Jean-Jacque dialed her number, and the phone rang.

"Hello, this Margaret, how can I help you?" said Margot.

"Hey Blossom, how are you doing?" replied Jean-Jacque.

"Claude? Hey, how are you doing? I haven't heard from you in a long time."

"I'm doing well Blossom, the reason why I called is, I see what's going on with you, and your jewelry company. I read that your company generated fifty million dollars last quarter. I would love to align with you and your company."

"Well Claude, I am impressed, I don't know if I should take your sudden interest in my business as a compliment; or hire a security detail!"

"Blossom, it's nothing like that, trust me. From what I understand, you're not just mining for precious minerals in these third world countries. You're helping the local people that live in the areas where you mine as well."

"Yeah, at my jewelry exchange company, Gem to Gem. We pride ourselves on understanding how mining for metals like, silver, gold, platinum, and gems like rubies, sapphires, beryl, and diamonds could devastate the ecosystem and disrupt how people live. So, we try to limit our carbon footprint, and partner up with the local residents. We offer them an opportunity to not only work in the mine, but train to be geologists too.

"I also devised a way where after people are trained and understand everything there is to know about the process of mining and jewelry; I would relinquish my majority stake back to the people, and I would just be a buyer. I know how all those other jewelry companies do business, that go in these third world countries, exploit them and decimate the local economy; further plunging the people into poverty."

"Blossom, how did you become so ambitious? That last thing that I remember about you is that you wanted you to become a nurse after you graduated from Jane Addams. What made change your plans?"

"Claude, after I graduated high school, I moved back to Israel to join the IDF (Israeli Defense Force.) I wanted to have an experience outside of my comfort zone and learn some discipline in the process. Through the Mahal program, I was able to enlist in the Israeli army because my parents were from Israeli. In retrospect, I don't know if I would've turned out the way I am now if I didn't join the Israeli military. I probably would have remained loud and obnoxious. Having a worldly perspective gave me the insight need to venture the world and strive to make a difference."

"Blossom, that's why I want to partner up with you. I recently started a program called The Helping Hand Initiative, where we partner with different underdeveloped countries and recruit under privileged students to come here to the states to receive a top-notch education. If it goes well, we will build schools in that country; where students would get to learn right there at home."

"That sounds good, Claude, how would my company be of service," Margot asked.

"You have ties with different governments all over the world; I would love to have you as my liaison to help me pitch this plan to them. Once they see that your company backs it, they will be more inclined to join. We could bridge the gap between here in the States and foreign countries, cultures, and languages of other people. Hopefully, people would be able to understand where somebody else comes from and not be so quick to judge them.

"What you're already doing is perfect, the concept of The Helping Hand Initiative has already been introduced in these countries with your valiant efforts. Helping reverse the lasting effects of colonialism, is the only way these countries can have sturdy footing. With the money that they earn, they could build up infrastructure in their country. So, no corporation could go into these countries and continue to take advantage of the local people who don't understand the importance and value of their natural resources," Jean-Jacque replied.

"That sounds ingenious Claude, I am on board! I will be flying into South Africa in a few months, why don't you fly out here, and we can discuss this further over dinner. We'll have to catch up with each other; you can't be all about business. I'll give you a call soon!"

Margot hung up the phone, and Jean-Jacque leaned back in his chair and gazed out the window at the view of the city.

"South Africa? I don't know about that, did Blossom just flirt with me?" thought Jean-Jacque.

A few months had gone by, and Jean-Jacque traveled to South Africa. He and Margot were on her yacht sailing around the Cape of Good Hope, in South Africa. He was drinking champagne with Margot and enjoying the view.

"I am glad you decided to fly down to meet with me, I can definitely say that I made a good decision by pairing up with The Helping Hand Initiative. I think you should change the name to hand to hand; it's more inviting," Margot said.

"I considered that name but was not exchanging goods or services for money. The revamped program is a non-profit organization," Jean-Jacque replied.

"My company has operations across the world, and I'm not just making money, I am making a difference. Aside from educating and empowering people, we are making breakthroughs in the medical field. My company has modernized by reverse engineering ancient discoveries of natural cures for diseases from plants; that could help people across the world."

"I am glad I came to Blossom; I appreciate the invitation, I am eager to get started, with both of our minds together and your influence, this initiative will be a success."

Margo has been drinking champagne and was a bit tipsy. She leaned into Jean-Jacque and tried to kiss him on his cheek–but because she's drunk, she slipped, and kissed his lips. He was caught off guard and Margot fell over. He caught her in the nick of time, stopping her from falling and hurting herself. A simple friendly gesture of respect turned into a passionate kiss.

Margot's face went flush with embarrassment, but Jean-Jacque looked into her eyes and kissed her back. They tossed their champagne glasses to the side and Margot led Jean-Jacque downstairs below deck. After she walked in the bedroom, she laid down on the bed. Jean-Jacque took off his shirt, and Margot looked at his chiseled frame glistening under the moonlight shining off the surface off the ocean.

Jean-Jacque laid on top of Margot and he stroked her hair with his hands, and he put it behind her ears. He kissed the nap of her neck, then her collar bone. He put one hand around her turn neck and ripped open her blouse with the other hand. He kissed her chest, took off her bra, licked and sucked her nipples.

He went down past her stomach and undoes her skirt, and he pulled her panties down to her knees; he lifted up both of her legs in the air and gently kissed her clitoris. Margot grabbed the sheet on the bed, and she went wild. He stopped suddenly, then took her panties down to her ankles as he licked the back of her thighs along the way.

Jean-Jacque sucked her toes as he undid his pants at the same time. He laid back down on top of Margot, spread her legs and entered her. She moaned and groaned as if she came from girth and length after he penetrated into her vagina. She creams all over his cock and the bed, she trembled as he continued to thrust faster, and faster.

He took her legs, put them over his shoulders and continued to thrust in and out of her vagina and she screamed out in ecstasy.

"I'm coming, I'm coming!" exclaimed Margot.

"She grabbed his head and pulled it toward hers and kissed his lips. Jean-Jacque then came inside Margot and rolled off to the side of her on the bed, and they both fell asleep.

Jean-Jacque was awakened by the sound of Margot taking a shower. So, he got up and joined her. Afterwards, she steered the yacht back to shore, Jean-Jacque accompanied Margot in one of her mines, and he saw firsthand how she ran her operation. After two weeks, he flew back to the states and continued working with Margot to establish more relationships with different governments all over the world.

A few months have passed since Jean-Jacque left South Africa. Margot noticed that she was experiencing a lot of morning sickness and she had to cancel a lot of meetings. Just out of curiosity, she took a pregnancy test; and it was positive. Sitting on the toilet in the bathroom, holding the pregnancy test; she screamed out loud and tossed the test in the sink.

"What am I going to do with a baby? Oh my God, I am pregnant with Claude's baby. Jena is going to be so mad at me. What am I going to do now?" thought Margot. She rushed out of the bathroom and plopped down on her bed face first into her pillow. She laid there and cried herself to sleep.

Chapter 15:

The big payback

Jean-Jacque had a number of wheels in motion, in preparation for his endgame. During the plane ride back, instead of doing what every other passenger was doing on board; he decided to reflect on how his plans were coming to fruition. Jean-Jacque wanted to jot down what his next move was going to be, so he took the complimentary pen and pad from the seatback in front of him in first class.

Jean-Jacque wrote down a plan to have his parents direct for the Helping Hand Initiative headquarters in Haiti. He wrote: 1. My mother would love to have a garden big enough to grow different species of plants and flowers there. 2. She would need a greenhouse or a classroom to instruct students in. 3. She's also going to need instruments for the music lessons she would conduct.

The flight attendant tapped Jean-Jacque on the shoulder and offered him a glass of champagne. He took the glass from her and placed it on the tray table; then continued to write out his list. "I know my father would want to play more of the role of Chief executive officer; he might want to teach Mathematics, or even American English. I would have to discuss it with him when I arrive back in the states."

Jean-Jacque wrote down a three pages long to-do list. Although he had several things in place, in order to be totally independent from Marisol, the program and The Mayor's Office. He had to have other Avenues in which to go down. Dealing with Marisol over the years, she always lived by a code of ethics, and she always had a contingency plan. The one thing that resonated with him over the years was her "Things to do list:"

"Never make friends with someone who can't help you in the future. Always expect the unexpected and don't ever get too comfortable, or complacent. Ambition and determination are two qualities that would ensure a clean break from The Program. You must have a way out. Otherwise, you would be indebted to it for

308

life."

The flight attendant made the announcement that the plane was going to land. So, he put away the notepad in his briefcase, and fastened his seatbelt to prepare for landing. After the plane touched down on the tarmac, all of the passengers applauded in relief for a safe landing.

Jean-Jacque exited the plane and walked outside the airport where the taxi stand was. He noticed that everything and everyone appeared different to him now. The ground was harder, the air seems to have traces of dread and the remnants of underachievement; all throughout the atmosphere. It wasn't as clean as South Africa back in New York, and the people seemed smaller; not smaller in stature, but in principle.

The people here had a pretentious sense of entitlement to them, smug even. Walking around projecting their shortcomings upon others who they feel are less fortunate. But they're the ones who need help.

Jean-Jacque understood immediately after his trip to South Africa, that the answers to life's questions were not solely going to be answered in America anymore. There was an entire world to traverse, forge a path, and make his mark on the world. For the time being he had Blossom to rely on, to show him the way.

Jean-Jacque didn't waste any time making the moves necessary to start on his journey of being independent. He called a meeting with all of the guys and asked them to meet him at a restaurant on city island in the Bronx.

Jean-Jacque was the first person to arrive at the restaurant with his lawyer. They both sat at the private table he'd reserved for the meeting. He and his lawyer waited there for over an hour. Then, one by one, the guys entered the restaurant and were directed to the table where Jean-Jacque was by the maître d'.

He noticed that Marques brought Raphael and Kingston with him, and they brought two other people each inside with them. Darrelle brought a young lady with him, and Raheem came in alone. Realizing that the initial plans for the meeting had changed; Jean-

Jacque devised a quick strategy to cut this meeting short with the guys.

After everyone sat down, the waitresses brought over pitchers of water, as well as bottles of champagne to the table; and filled everyone's glasses with water and champagne.

Jean-Jacque stood up, with a champagne glass in his hand and tapped on the side of it with a spoon.

"Fellas, I am glad you could make it on such short notice. I just came back from a much-needed trip to South Africa. While I was in the motherland, I discovered that the way in which I've been leading my life has been misguided. We all have been friends for years, and some of us even started businesses together. I'm proud to have called most of you here my friend. Those of you who trusted my vision and invested in real estate; it worked out tremendously in your favor. You all have earned millions of dollars because of it.

"But I want to pretty much cut ties with all of the material aspects of life, and I want to take a religious pilgrimage for one year. After I get back, I should have a better perspective on life. I told everybody here that eventually you guys were going to be in control of your own companies one day; that day is today," Jean-Jacque said.

Jean-Jacque's lawyer passed out folders for everyone at the table.

"Gentlemen, these envelopes that my lawyer handed out to everybody are the contracts. It states that I, Henri Jean-Jacque Cadet, relinquish all of my shares in your companies. After signing these documents, you will own eighty five percent of your companies. The other fifteen percent minority stake is for The Program. The amount listed in the contracts needs to be paid by the end of the week.

"I want to thank everyone here for all your effort and sacrifice that you've made to make this happen. I appreciate everything that you have done for me, and I hope you share the same sentiment. I wish you guys all the best, and hopefully you could hit the ground running, and keep this success going. Now, you must work even harder to keep up the level of success individually, as we've done together," Jean-Jacque said.

Jean-Jacque's and his lawyer stepped away from the table, drank the rest of their champagne and walked out of the restaurant. He noticed a group of stocky well-built men walking towards the entrance of the restaurant.

"There must be a celebrity coming in here!" thought Jean-Jacque.

Jean-Jacque looked closer at one of the muscular men in the group and noticed one of them.

"Jamie?" said Jean-Jacque.

Jamie stopped, looked over in his direction, adjusted his posture, then raised his eyebrows.

"Oh shit, Claude! What's good brother! It's been a long time," Jamie replied.

"Oh my God, you look like you swallowed Arnold Schwarzenegger!" replied Jean-Jacque.

Both men embraced each other and laughed.

"Nah man, ever since Asia got into Med school; it was like I was in school too," Jamie said.

"Word, what type of doctor?" asked Jean-Jacque.

"She's studied cardiology, so, I've been helping her study for most of her exams and looking at those books on anatomy; I learned a lot. I learned about LDL, HDL cholesterol, what is the healthy amount of sugar intake. I started watching a lot of videos, and reading books on holistic medicine, and how to use natural foods to heal your body.

"Then, I started going to the gym and got myself a personal trainer. I started seeing results, so I went back to school to be a personal trainer myself. I competed in a few bodybuilding competitions and won first place in a few of them. Just this past year, my business partners and I started a natural food/holistic and fitness center to help other people in our community.

"In the center, we teach people how to eat natural unprocessed foods, and how to adjust their eating habits. Statistics have shown that in our neighborhoods, we are less likely to die by violence than obesity. Being unhealthy leads to hypertension, and diabetes, which are the top killers in our communities."

Jean-Jacque smiled at Jamie and shook his head.

"You look great man! I want to see Asia; I wonder how she's doing. But I don't know if you know, but I started a non-profit organization called The Helping Hand Initiative. What we do is help out people in our communities both here and internationally; learn ways on how to not be victimized by their circumstances. Health and fitness are other ways we could reach out to our people and help empower them.

"Jamie, I could introduce you to some of my business contacts that would help grow your business exponentially. You would definitely reach a lot more people in our communities here in the states and others like ours internationally. Trust me, it won't cost you anything, I don't want to invest in your company financially, I don't want anything from you; I just want to help your company grow. When we have time to talk, we will build more, kind of like those muscles you have."

Jean-Jacque embraced Jamie again and smiled.

"I can't believe it's you man! Have you seen Jena and the baby at all?"

"Nah, ever since my moms kicked her out the crib, she has been incommunicado."

"Man, I wonder how they're doing, it's like she dropped off the face of the earth."

Jamie shrugged his shoulders and shook his head from left to right.

"Well, look, here's my card, give me a call, we'll catch more, and I could explain to you more about my organization. It was nice seeing you brother," said Jean-Jacque.

Jean-Jacque walked away, and Jamie entered the restaurant.

He saw the guys at the table and walked over to them. Raphael saw Jamie and his friends walking towards the table and stood up on the chair.

"We haven't finished our meals yet, we are not shutting up, and we're not leaving. My boys and I come in here all the time and we spend hundreds, sometimes thousands of dollars in this establishment. We've been drinking, cause we're celebrating our success. We're all adults here!" said Raphael.

Raphael picked up the bottle of Dom Pérignon off the table, and a fork and tapped the side of it.

"Everyone here that didn't pay your bill yet, don't, we will pay for it; dinner is on me. Plus, I am buying out the bar, drinks are free for the remainder of the night. Whoever sent over security to kick us out; we ain't leaving."

Marques looked up at Jamie and his face lit up like a Christmas tree. He grabbed Raphael's arm and pulled him down off the table.

"Yo son, you're wilding out, chill! You don't recognize who this is?" said Marques.

Marques stood up and extended both of his arms like a condor soaring in the sky.

"Jamie! What's up brother? I haven't seen you in a while. You look like a black Lou Ferrigno. You look great man!"

Jamie and Marques shook hands, then he acknowledged everyone else at the table.

"Damn Jamie, you all swole and shit, have you been in any competitions?" asked Darrelle.

"Yeah, a few, I won a couple of trophies too! I see you all out here making a whole lot of money. Marques, your weed is pretty good; Asia is a heart surgeon, and the other doctors prescribe weed as an alternative to pharmaceutical drugs. A lot of patients have adverse side effects to other medications, and they feel extreme pain after surgery. They tend to lean more towards the homeopathic approach to healing, to aid with recovery, rather than the widely accepted allopathic way. So, they buy tons of weed from your dispensary.

"Asia has been telling me that a lot of people have been misdiagnosed and sometimes, going under the knife isn't necessary. A holistic approach works 7 times out of ten. Asia knows a lot more than I do, I know a lot of customers love your weed," Jamie replied.

"That's what's up man! I know Asia doing her thing as a doctor, and we definitely have a good business relationship!" said Marques.

"My pharmaceutical company is partnering up with Marques's dispensary to create an effective weed-based pain killer. As well as other marijuana-based drug alternatives to give people safer options.

"In our last meeting, we were discussing a possible marijuana infused tampon for cramping in women. There have been several studies going on, and the medical establishment has started to take notice and move forward with the times," Darrelle replied.

Kingston was quiet the entire time the guys were in the restaurant. He grabbed a bottle of Dom Pérignon, stood up and interrupted the conversation.

"Unnuh hear yuh selves! Fram long time di bwoy Claude ah rule yuh up an ah tel everybody wah fi du. Fram him kill Darren, mi nuh lakka dat bwoy! If a mi, eye an eye wud rinse mi gun inna him head. Marques, mek mi tek out dat bwoy fi yuh. Fram wah day him ah tell everybody nuh fi engage inna no illegal activities.

"Mi nuh waan go inna nuh office and work. Mi a thuggy, mi born an grow inna di garrison ah Tivoli Gardens, mi nuh tek talk, mi mek duppy; memba mi tell Unnuh. Yuh can gwan and mek him run all a yuh, him cyaan neva run me," replied Kingston.

Kingston lifted up his shirt and took out a nickel-plated desert eagle and put it on the table. Raheem stood up next to Kingston and put his arm around him.

"I agree with him, we've been soft since Claude started us doing this legal business. I hate being a mortician, let's give Claude what he wants, and we can then use our own connections and flood the streets with pure uncut shit and corner the market. Marques, don't you have a federal firearm license? Guns are worth a lot more on the streets than in the store.

"But first, we're going to have to kill Claude. I think that mother fucker had something to do with my Uncle Jasper's death. Fuck him, the acting mayor Marisol Velasquez and that bitch Jena. Nobody ain't seen her since some goons ran up in my uncle's spot, attacked him and left him for dead.

"Even with him not having any stake in our businesses, we're still going to deal with The Program," said Raheem.

"Tek yuh hand off ah mi bwoy! Yuh tink seh mi a matey? A dat mi ah chat bout, mek we move pan him now!" replied Kingston.

Marques took up Kingston's desert eagle and pushed it into his chest.

"Chill, Yo! Be easy, we're gonna do our thing just you watch!" said Marques.

"We back, we back, we back in business baby!" said the crew, simultaneously.

"We're going to have to mobilize, Raheem, don't Darnel come out of prison next year? We need him back on our team, cause he's a shot caller, a top dog in the Crip gang. He could help us distribute all of this weight out in these streets with one phone call. He won't need to be in them streets, either; we'll have workers for that," said Darrelle.

"I don't think so Darrelle, my cousin was locked up with that dude, and he told me that dude did a 180° turn around. Darnel ain't the same person that went in man. I heard that he's a holy roller now! He turned Muslim; he earned his master's degree in theology. Darnel is a certified Imam, he's really into that, "Save the world" through faith, angle.

"He's a motivational speaker and when he comes home; he's really going to try to change the community we live in. Darnel is gonna be on that original premise of what a Crip really was, (Community, Revolution, In Progress.) He's really into trying to do what Crip stood for when it started out in Chicago. Darnel is into building up the community, he not 'bout that life no more.

"Trust me, when he comes home, he won't be on our side. If anything, he will try to make sure that we don't make no illegal tender in these streets," Raheem said.

"Listen mi mon, Jamie yuh hab di gym ting ah gwan. Mi hab ah connect fram Mexico, mi can git di steroids injections yuh nuh!" said Kingston.

"Kingston, I'm not doing that, I'm promoting good clean health, the natural holistic approach to living. Straight vegan foods, 100% natural, nothing poisonous for the body. I'm not selling anything that's made in a laboratory in my place of business. The only thing I'm pushing, had to be cultivated from the Most High, herself. Quinoa, wheat grass, tropical fruits, and vegetables only," Jamie replied.

"Mi nuh care wah yuh ah seh, di people want fattening foods mon! Dem waan milkshake, hamburger, fried chicken, and pizza!"

"Shut up Kingston! You don't know what the fuck you're talking about!"

Kingston stood from the table, backed out his desert eagle, took it off safety, cocked it back and pointed it at Jamie.

"Wah yuh jus seh to mi? If yuh bad seh it again, pussy hole!" said Kingston.

"Yo chill!" replied Jamie and put his hands in the air.

"Either you wid di crew, or against di crew! Mek yuh choice, or mi mek it fi yuh!"

Kingston stood in front of Jamie with his fully loaded nickel-plated desert eagle, ready to fire rounds out of it at a moment's notice.

"Yo man, Kingston you need to calm the fuck down! You're making people nervous in the place, now is not the time to prove that you're a gangster. You're instigating fuckry, trying to excite these people to resort to violence. You are the catalyst for everybody here right now to get knocked, and all their legitimate companies to go belly up.

"Just because you want street money. All of you will go to jail if you follow this dick head. You all want to jeopardize your multi-million-dollar companies to push drugs, and guns out on the streets? Don't be stupid!

"Claude made everybody here legitimate businessmen, Chief executive officers of fortune five hundred companies. And you ungrateful bastards want to kill him? You all won't make 10% of what you all are making now, out on the streets," Jamie said.

"Yo wah dat Yankee bwoy ah seh?" said Kingston and looked away from Jamie.

Jamie knitted up his eyebrows, bit his bottom lip, reached inside his waistband and pulled out a .357 magnum pistol when Kingston looked away from him.

"Yankee? Memba mi tell yuh dat dis Yankee bwoy will blow yuh head off, clean, clean! Seh sumtin else! Yuh think mi nice? Yuh tek man fi toy? Seh sumetin nuh! Mek mi blow off yuh blood-clot head top, in front ah everybody. Yuh tink seh wen dem a mek gun, dem just mek fi yuh? Yuh deh yah a runoff yuh mouth! Yuh think mi fraid ah yuh bwoy? Eeeh!" exclaimed Jamie.

"Jamie! easy, easy, easy man! I didn't know you were 'bout it, 'bout it like that man! It ain't worth it! Don't do it, don't do it, don't do it!" replied Marques.

"Mark! Don't let this little bitch, get you all knocked, you're all business owners. CEOs of Fortune 500 companies; publicly traded companies! He's going to lead you all into ruin if you let him. Man, I am not messing with y'all, I am out!" said Jamie, and put his gun away as he walked out of the restaurant.

A couple days after that, the phone rang while he was working out. Annoyed, Jamie stopped, walked over to the phone, and he answered it.

"Hello!" said Jamie.

"Jamie, how are you doing man? This is Claude!" replied Jean-Jacque.

Jamie used a towel to wipe the sweat off his head and took a swig from his water bottle.

"Hey man, after you left the restaurant, the guys were saying some real off the wall stuff about you."

"Save it Jamie, I don't want to hear about those guys, they are all adults. Whatever plan they put together it's best I don't know what it is, spare me the details. All I know is that they signed the paperwork, and they paid me off. I don't have any relationship with none of those guys. I don't want to talk about them anymore, as far as I'm concerned, business wise, nor otherwise.

I called to see if you wanted to go hiking with me at Van Cortlandt Park and to do some meditation. Then we could build from there."

"Cool, I'll meet you there."

Jamie hung up the phone and finished his workout. Claude and Jamie met up at Van Cortlandt Park and walked along the trails up to the summit of the mountain. They were out of breath, so they sat down to meditate.

Five or ten minutes went by, Jean-Jacque opened his eyes and saw Jamie stretching out his shoulders.

"Hey Jamie, did you contact those people I told you about?" asked Jean-Jacque.

"Yeah, my business partners and I met with them last week. We discussed possibly getting a line of vegan supplements that we could sell at the center. Just waiting on FDA approval of these supplements before it hits the market. If that goes according to plan, then we are looking at distribution at the end of January," Jamie replied.

"That's cool man! See, one good turn deserves another. You know you are a good person."

"I appreciate that, Claude!"

"By the way, has Asia heard from Jena?"

"Nope, after she left, wherever she went; she hadn't

contacted anybody. I think it was from dealing with you. Her parents pretty much disowned her, and they forbade Asia from having anything to do with her. Ever since then, we never heard from her again.

"It broke her heart not having a relationship with her sister. Jena missed out on a lot of life events, she graduated Med school, we got married, we had kids. And all this is your fault."

"Thanks Jamie, for rubbing it in, I know what I did. I take full responsibility full responsibilities for my actions, but it takes two to tango though. I always said if I didn't come into her life, maybe shit would've turned out better. I don't regret our relationship, that's something that I am proud of; I just wished I could see her and my kid. But by not seeing her, I can't even atone for the trouble I caused, I broke up a happy home.

"But enough of that mushy stuff, I am proud of you and Asia being all responsible and contributing to society. I am glad that everything turned out great for Ms. Asiatic, excuse me, Dr. McCubbin!

"After I visited the cradle of civilization and saw Mount of good hope in South Africa. I had a premonition that I was going to be betrayed by someone. That's the reason why I wanted to cut ties with those guys. After visiting Blossom, I had a little affirmation that I must go out and visit all of the ancient sites of indigenous civilizations in the world. It's ironic that most of them are located in third world countries.

"There's a lot of history to be learned from these places. Like visiting a shaman, see pyramids everywhere there's one, and Stonehenge. I want to visit the caves in France, trek through Thailand, see the Dalai lama in the Himalayas, and visit Angkor Wat. I plan on going to Australia, Papua New Guinea, as close as I could get to the Andaman Island, and a lot more places in India to elevate my spirit.

"From now on, I will only associate with positive people. I don't want anything to stop this movement. I know that this non-profit is bigger than me; you know what I'm saying Jamie. I'm trying my best to push people down the right path, and make sure they have a secure mindset. It feels good to see people doing positive things and inspire other people to do positive things.

"I have been in the mayor's office working under Marisol, and I went to school and studied political science. I plan on running for governor one day. I've seen the politics; I made a lot of friends in high places; I got a decent amount of influence in the public eye to do it. Then from governor to senator, shit you never know, The White House."

"President Claude? Get the fuck out of here! You're Haitian Claude, you do know that the prerequisite of the candidate for the presidency, is that he or she must be an American born citizen; right?!" asked Jamie

"Okay Jamie, truth be told, I never told anybody this, but I wasn't born in Haiti. When my parents left Haiti, my mother was pregnant with me, and on the way to the states, my mother went into labor in the plane. The pilot made an emergency landing in Puerto Rico; and I was born in a hospital, in San Juan Puerto Rico. So technically, I am not Haitian, I am Puerto Rican," Jean-Jacque replied.

"Get the fuck outta here Claude! You're not Puerto Rican!"

Jean-Jacque reached in his pocket for his wallet and took out his birth certificate and presented it to Jamie.

"You see, place of birth: San Juan, Puerto Rico, which makes me a born American citizen. If memory serves me correctly, Puerto Rico became a Commonwealth after the Spanish American war. The U.S. gained all the Spanish territories, like Puerto Rico, Guam, and the Philippines. So, anybody born in those places, in my case Puerto Rico; becomes American citizens. Jamie, I am American, and I can run for president."

"Damn Claude! Okay, I see you!"

Jamie handed Jean-Jacque back his birth certificate, then they both got up and stretched before Yoga. Afterwards, they decided to jog down the trail. When they arrived in the parking lot where their cars were, they got inside their vehicles, and drove away.

While Jean-Jacque was in his car half-way into his journey back into the city, he wrestled with the idea of visiting Margot.

"Man, I haven't seen Blossom since I left South Africa. I wonder how she's doing; come to think of it, I haven't seen any of her conferences on C-SPAN or anything on television related to her company. I remember a segment on CNN about her becoming a UN ambassador. I have not seen any commercials, or any new ribbon cutting ceremonies of learning centers; she normally builds all throughout the world.

"I hope nothing has happened to her because, since news media outlets caught wind of her philanthropic work; other companies have been heavily scrutinized for their shady business practices in those same countries her companies operate in.

"Companies all throughout the world had been pressured to do the same thing Blossom had been doing for the local citizens. I hope they haven't sent anyone to put a stop to all the good she's done permanently; so, they won't have to continue to do the same," Jean-Jacque thought.

Jean-Jacque pulled out his flip phone and searched for Blossom's number. Then Jean-Jacque stopped and punched the roof of his truck.

"Shit! The last time I saw her we had sex, unprotected sex. She can't be…No, no, no! I hope I didn't get Blossom pregnant. It's been a little over a year, and she's supposed to actually be my guide throughout all the countries that I want my non-profit organization to expand to. Okay here we go, Blossom!" thought Jean-Jacque.

Jean-Jacque pressed the send button, and the phone rang until her answering machine picked up:

"Hi, I am unable to get to the phone right now, but if you leave your name, your number, and a brief message I will be sure to get back with you shortly; thanks for calling." (Beep!)

Hey Blossom, this is Claude! I haven't seen nor heard from you since I've been back from South Africa. We were supposed to travel the world together, and you promised to introduce me to your contacts. Enough about me, how are you doing? I hope you're not

321

embarrassed about what we've done together on your yacht. As far as I see it, what happened in international waters, stays in international waters. Blossom come on now, you gotta hit me up!"

Jean-Jacque hung up the phone, then it dawned on him that Blossom had a brownstone in SoHo not too far from his loft. He pulled up in front of Blossom's brownstone, and he noticed that lights were on inside. Jean-Jacque knocked on the door and rang the doorbell. He heard music blaring from inside, and the sound of a baby crying. He tried the doorknob, and the door was unlocked; so, he went inside. He walked through the foyer, and the stench of dirty diapers filled the air. Everything was in disarray, there were dishes piled up in the sink, loads of garbage in the kitchen, and duffel bags of dirty laundry overflowed inside the laundry room next to the kitchen.

"God damn Margaret! This place looks like a crack house. I hope this bitch isn't turning tricks inside the apartment," said Jean-Jacque.

Jean-Jacque heard crying from upstairs, so he decided to investigate. He took the steps two by two up the staircase to the second-floor landing. He noticed that the noise was coming from the double doors to his left. Jean-Jacque opened the doors, looked inside, and he saw Margot dancing to the music, wearing a robe and slippers on with her hair in rollers.

She had a cocktail in one hand, and a cigarette in the other hand. Jean-Jacque looked around, and the bedroom was in the same condition as downstairs. There were empty prescription pill bottles all over the place. Jean-Jacque heard a baby's cry, so he looked over at the bed, and saw a baby boy holding his feet in the air while looking up at his reflection in the mirror on the ceiling.

Jean-Jacque slammed the double doors behind him and walked into the room.

"Blossom! What the fuck is going on here?" asked Jean-Jacque.

She was intoxicated and almost dropped her cocktail. Blossom stumbled, turned around and faced Jean-Jacque.

"What the fuck are you doing in my house, Claude?" replied Margot.

She flung the glass at Jean-Jacque, and he dodged it like Neo from the matrix. The glass hit the door behind him and it shattered into pieces. The hard liquor streamed down the wall like rain on a windowpane. Jean-Jacque quickly closed the distance between him and Margot. She swung at him, he grabbed her by the arm, then tossed her down on the bed next to the baby. Margot was so inebriated that she rolled off the side of the bed and dropped on the floor faced down.

In pain from the impact Margot cried and held her elbow in her hand.

"I can't believe you just put your hands on me Claude; after all we've been through! Now, I know why Jena was afraid of you, and she never wanted you to know that she went to Vegas with your twins," Margot said.

Jean-Jacque walked over to the stereo system and turned off the music.

"Blossom, why do you have the place looking like this? And did I just hear you say that Jeneration went to Las Vegas, and that she had twins?" asked Jean-Jacque.

Margot dragged herself up from off the floor up onto the bed. Then she stood up and her legs were shaky like palm trees in a tropical storm.

"Yes, you ruined that girl's life, you bastard," Jean-Jacque replied.

He walked over towards Jean-Jacque and tried to hug her, and she attacked him. Margot slapped him and pushed him away from her.

"You ruined my life too Claude! Look at what you've done! I wasn't ready to be a mother, I don't know what the fuck I'm doing. I don't have anyone to turn to for help, I am all alone," Margot said.

Jean-Jacque grabbed her arms and held her close to him.

"Blossom! Why didn't you tell me you were pregnant? I

would have been there for you," Jean-Jacque replied.

"C'mon now, I didn't want to be chased out of town like they did to Jena. Your bad news Claude, I don't know why I got involved with you in the first place!"

"I don't know either! How do you know if this is even my kid, Blossom?"

"Trust me I know! You were the only man I have been with in the last two years."

"So, twins huh! I knew she was pregnant, but I didn't know she was pregnant with twins. Blossom, have you seen her and the babies?"

"Claude, I just told you that I had your baby, and your response was, 'Have you seen Jena and the twins?' So, South Africa meant nothing to you, huh?" asked Margot.

"Listen, this is some heavy information that you just dropped on me. Fuck all that South Africa shit for right now. You just drop the Goddamn bombshell, you just said Jena had my twins! Do me a favor and just start with the past, then we'll deal with the present later," Jean-Jacque replied.

"Okay, okay! She told me she went into labor after some goons tried to kidnap her inside her mother's building. She stayed at one of Raheem's Uncle's houses in the Bronx. Marisol paid her a visit, months after she'd had the twins. She told her if she valued her life and the lives of her kids; then she should leave New York and never return.

"She was terrified, so Jena packed up those kids, and she took the first flight out to Las Vegas. She has been out in Vegas ever since. She may return one day, but I doubt it, her parents disowned her for getting pregnant, and for messing with you. Jena's parents even forbade Asia from having anything to do with her either."

Jean-Jacque sighed, shrugged his shoulders, closed his eyes, put his hands over his face and sobbed.

"My goodness, I have four kids now! A son with Marisol, two daughters with Jena, and another baby with you!"

"Damn Claude, you get around! you have another son?" asked Margot.

"Yeah, I had a son with the acting mayor of New York. I was in The Program that I tried to recruit Jena in. I met Marisol at a young age, she was my first, and she got pregnant. She had a little boy, but nobody knew about that kid. She sent him off somewhere, I never met him.

"She's been raising him in secret on her own, nobody doesn't know that she has even had a kid; much less had a sexual relationship with a minor. From what she told me, he's a good kid. He's about to graduate junior high school. She's been having some health issues; the prognosis is that it's terminal; I don't think she's going to be around much longer.

"Marisol has been keeping it a secret for quite some time. She's been to several doctors and specialists; the treatment has not changed the diagnosis. But I commend her, she lived a good life, and she made a difference in people's lives. Marisol has come to terms with her fate, when it's her time; we'll be ready," Jean-Jacque replied.

Margot leaned over, put her arm around Jean-Jacque's shoulders and put head on his.

"That is some heavy shit Claude, but we are going to work through this. I'm sorry that I kept my pregnancy from you, but I promise you that I'll be honest with you from now on."

Margot grabbed Jean-Jacque's face and kissed him, on the lips.

"Thank you Blossom! But there's no way we are fucking, and your place looks like a pigsty! It stinks in here! Shit, you stink too!"

"Whatever Claude! I know, I know, I will clean up!"

Jean-Jacque turned around and picked up the baby off the bed and held him in his arms.

"Blossom, what's his name?"

Margot had already walked into the bathroom to take a

shower; she didn't hear Jean-Jacque's question. But Jean-Jacque noticed the letters over his crib spelled out Sebastian. Jean-Jacque walked over to the bathroom and knocked on the door.

"Margot, you named the baby Sebastian?" asked Jean-Jacque.

"Yes! I named him after my father, and his middle name is Jerome. I wanted to name him Adonis, but that wouldn't have gone over well with my parents; bad enough he's half black," Margot replied.

"I can't believe that you got a baby in this filth! You make all this money, and you don't have a nanny!"

"Claude, lay off me, okay! It's been a rough year and a half. I gave the nanny a few weeks off. I took some time off for myself, I've been under a lot of pressure; how could I have continued doing what I was doing pregnant and out of wedlock, huh? I think I've held up well considering the circumstances.

"I gained seventy-five pounds during the pregnancy, that baby weighed six pounds seven ounces, and he literally ripped me a new asshole. I had to sit on a doughnut for six weeks afterwards. I had a personal trainer, and I dropped off all of that horrible weight. My vagina has seen better days though, but I'll manage," Margot said.

"Listen, I'm gonna take little man with me for the weekend. I'm gonna bring him to my house Blossom, and when you are good in a couple of days, just stop by and pick him up. Besides, I haven't bonded with any of my children; I want to bond with my son," Jean-Jacque replied.

"Okay Claude, I guess I owe you that much. But you know why I couldn't you tell you that I was pregnant right? For God sakes you have two kids with my friend, and I doubt it would have gone well if I had called her and told her the truth: 'Hey gurl. You remember Claude? the love of your life, the person who took your virginity and got you pregnant. You know the father of your kids that they haven't seen yet, and he has never met them. He and I had sex, I am pregnant with his baby, and he's going to be there for me and my baby.' That wouldn't have sounded right at all Claude; we had an affair," Margot said.

"Blossom, we didn't have an affair! We were two consenting adults, who had sex. Jena was nowhere to be found; I didn't even know she was pregnant with twins. Everyone has been very deceitful; I'm the victim in all of this. But I won't play the victims role. Where are his clothes, diapers, car seat and diaper bag?" replied Jean-Jacque.

Margot finished bathing, she toweled off, then gathered Sebastian's things for Jean-Jacque.

"He loves his tickle me Elmo doll, so don't leave the house without it."

With the baby's things packed, Jean-Jacque grabbed the diaper bag, put it over his shoulder, picked up the car seat with the baby inside, then walked downstairs. Before he walked out of the brownstone, Margot bent down and kissed the baby on his forehead.

"You be a good boy, don't give your daddy a hard time Adonis."

"Adonis?! The baby's name is Adonis?"

"That is his nickname, his name is Sebastian. I told you that already, Claude."

Jean-Jacque opened the door and walked down the first step on the cobblestone stairs.

"Fatherhood looks good on you!"

Jean-Jacque grinded leaned in and kissed Margot on the lips. She opened her eyes, got up on her tippy-toes, and pushed her tongue in his mouth. Jean-Jacque pulled back and looked how Margot's robe barely covered her naked body.

"After you get this place in order we have to pick up where we left off back in South Africa," Jean-Jacque said.

Margot opened her robe, stepped back into the foyer unveiling everything she has to offer.

"I'm willing, ready, and able to commit to that request Baby

327

Daddy!" replied Margot.

Jean-Jacque smirked and walked towards his truck. He opened the back door on the passenger side and put the diaper bag and the car seat with the baby inside the car. He leaned in the car and strapped the car seat down with the seat belt and buckled it. Jean-Jacque closed the door, then walked to the driver's side door. He hopped in, started the car, and drove up the street towards the FDR drive south ramp.

There was a red light at the corner, so he waited until it turned green. As soon as it did, he accelerated into the intersection. Suddenly, a black van careened out of the shadows, and hit his truck on the driver side into a parked car. Jean-Jacque's head hit the steering wheel, then it ricocheted off the driver side window shattering it. His body slumped over to the side motionless, and his head flopped back like a tab on a soda can.

The van doors opened abruptly, two men got out the side of the van and dragged Jean-Jacque's limp body out the driver's side window. They dropped him down on the ground, put tape around his mouth, then zip tied his hands and feet together. As Jean-Jacque laid there unconscious, Sebastian sat in his car seat crying hysterically. The masked men wore black tactical garb and gloves; grabbed him by the shoulders and carried him inside the van with them. With a blink of an eye, the men closed the door, and drove off into the night.

The accident alerted a number of people in the area, but nobody was able to get to the scene fast enough to see what went on. The car alarm echoed throughout the neighborhood; loud enough that Margot heard it from her brownstone. She was startled by the sound of the loud sound the impact made.

"My baby!" said Margot.

A crowd of people gathered around the car and Margot ran down the street, barefoot only wearing a bra, panties and her robe. The bottom of her robe and the belt, flopped in the wind from side to side with each stride.

"My baby! My baby!" exclaimed Margot.

She pushed her way through the crowd and looked frantically inside the vehicle for her baby. She looked inside the back of the car, and she saw two people unhooking Sebastian's straps of his car seat. Margot opened the door, reached for her baby, panting and trembling.

"That's my baby! That's my baby! Thank God you're okay! It's okay Adonis, mommy's here! Come to me baby, Mama is here! I got you, don't you worry."

The two good Samaritan's handed Margot the baby and she held Sebastian close to her clammy bosom. Margot sobbed for a moment, then she looked into the driver's seat for Jean-Jacque.

"Damn it, Claude! What the hell have you gotten yourself into now?"

Moments later, the ambulance emerged on the scene, the doors opened and The Paramedic and the EMT came out of the ambulance. They both surveyed the scene and noticed that there was nobody in the car.

"Excuse me, is everyone here, okay? Who here was involved in the collision?" asked The Paramedic.

"I wasn't in a crash, but my baby and his father were," Margot replied, crying her eyes out.

"Mam, where is the man that was driving this vehicle?"

"I don't know where he is! I ran here from home and took my son out of the car. Oh my God please, please; could you check out my son?"

"Right away mam!"

The Paramedic quickly brought the baby with him to the rear of the ambulance and immediately started checking his vital signs etc. Margot closed the front of her robe and walked towards the ambulance.

"Mam, come on inside with us, we're going to take your baby to the hospital for further observation; just as a precautionary measure."

The paramedic closed the ambulance door behind Margot as the EMT turned on the siren and drove to the hospital.

Meanwhile, Jean-Jacque was still unconscious in the back of a van with a knapsack over his head and tape over his mouth. The four men that kidnapped him, had special mechanisms over their throat to disguise their voices.

"We have to make sure that we cut up his body after we kill him; then burn the remains. There can't be any trace evidence left behind, we gotta burn these clothes and the vehicle too. If there's no body, there's no murder, if there's no crime, there's no trial," one of the kidnappers said.

"Let's stick to the plan, alright, we got him, let's drive to the warehouse in Queens, and finish what we set out to do," another one replied.

"He ain't so tough, I bet I could take him down by myself," the driver said of the getaway van.

The men arrived at the warehouse twenty minutes later, took Jean-Jacque out the van, and carried him inside. There was a single light on, and under it was a chair with some restraints on it. The two men that carried Jean-Jacque inside, put him on the chair, bound him to it, then pulled the knapsack off his head. One man put down his gun on a table next to the chair that Jean-Jacque was being strapped to; pulled up his mask from his mouth and lit a cigarette.

After a few drags of the cigarette, he flicked it. He took up a small bucket filled with cold water, then abruptly doused Jean-Jacque with the contents. Jean-Jacque regained consciousness, then one of the men, ripped the tape off his mouth. Another man punched him in the face and stood towering over him.

"You thought that you were going to run New York, huh?" said one of the kidnappers.

"What? Who the fuck are you? How the fuck did I get here? Where's my son? When I get out of these restraints, I will kill everyone here, one, by one!" replied Jean-Jacque.

The man pulled back down his face covering and punched

Jean-Jacque in the stomach.

"Shut the fuck up! This is what's gonna happen, we're gonna cut off your fingers one by one, then we're gonna cut off your hands, and arms next. Then your toes, feet, and legs leaving nothing but your torso. Finally, we're gonna cut out your tongue because you talk a lot of shit. If you didn't have enough; we're gonna pull out each of your teeth one by one.

"We planned on cutting off your balls, but by the time we finished carving you up in pieces like a Thanksgiving turkey; you'd already bled to death," one of the kidnappers said.

"What do you want, huh? You want my money! Well, I ain't gonna give you shit!" replied Jean-Jacque.

"Here you go again talking shit! We got money already! We don't want your money; we just want to see you suffer," he said.

"I see four of you in here, covered in fatigues like a SWAT team! You got me all tied up; what are you scared of me for? Untie me, so I can go out like a warrior should; in a blaze of glory!" replied Jean-Jacque.

The men huddled around each other and whispered amongst themselves. One man approached Jean-Jacque, leaned close to his ear and pulled the mask up from his mouth.

"We are not afraid of anything Jean-Jacque, but in the next sixty seconds; you're gonna wish you were dead!" said the kidnapper.

Jean-Jacque didn't waste any time, he used his forehead and head-butted the guy in the temple sending him down to the ground. He pushed off the ground with his feet sending the chair backwards to the ground, shattering the chair he was in and unraveling his restraints in the process.

Jean-Jacque mustard up what little strength he had left and kicked at the knee of the man standing closest to him, breaking his knee cap. He grabbed one of the shards of broken wood from the chair and flung it at one of the men who pointed a shotgun at him. It went off in the air, and Jean-Jacque rushed him, tackling him over the table behind him.

Another man rushed at Jean-Jacque with a knife, but he ducked down and catapulted him over his shoulder down to the ground. Jean-Jacque used his legs and clamped down on the man's neck until his arms slumped to the side of his motionless body. Jean-Jacque released his grip from around his neck, took up the knife and cut off the straps off his ankles. Jean-Jacque stood there with the knife in his hand and the other guy with the shotgun, pointed it at him again. He threw the knife in his chest, and the shotgun went off into the chest of the first man on the ground he head-butted.

Both men laid there in excruciating pain gasping for air; then they stopped moving. The one man with his kneecap broken, got up and tried limping away: to no avail. He tripped over one of the dead bodies, turned over, pulled off his mask.

"If yuh gwan kill mi, just kill mi nuh! Mi nuh fraid fi dead," he said.

Jean-Jacque was surprised that it was Kingston, but he was glad it wasn't the mayor's tactical team, again.

"Yuh nuh hear wah mi seh bwoy! Yuh know seh, ah lang time mi supposed to kill yuh! Jah know star! Now mi cyaan avenge Darren's death," Kingston said.

Jean-Jacque picked up the shotgun, cocked it, and shot Kingston's head off. Jean-Jacque heard a loud bang, and a single shot was fired, hitting him in the right shoulder. The gunshot sent Jean-Jacque to the ground. He heard footsteps walking slowly over to him, Jean-Jacque looked over to his left shoulder and saw Kingston's desert eagle in his waistband. He took it and he waited until the last man standing came close enough to finish the job.

He laid there playing possum, then the man stood over him with the gun in his hand, then cocked it back.

The man pulled off the mask off his face, and it was Raheem! "Look at you, you ain't so tough now, is you! This is for my uncle, you son of a bitch." He pointed the gun down at Jean-Jacque and pulled the trigger. (Click, click, click.)

Jean-Jacque looked up, pointed the desert eagle at Raheem.

Surprised, and scared, Raheem dropped his gun.

"Look, it wasn't my idea! It was all Kingston's plan! Please let me go! You already killed him!" said Raheem.

Jean-Jacque didn't hesitate, he pulled the trigger and the gun shot lodged directly in between Raheem's eyes. The bullet exploded out the back of his head and his lifeless body dropped down to the ground.

Jean-Jacque slowly got up off the ground and spit out some blood on the ground. He reached inside his mouth, pulled out a tooth from it, and tossed it on the ground. He had a big gash over his left eye, and he was shot in the shoulder. He stumbled out of the warehouse, but he couldn't focus; his vision was blurred. Blood has spilled in his eye distorting his vision.

He saw the van door open, so he got inside. He looked inside, and the keys were in the ignition. Jean-Jacque started the van, put it in reverse, and backed out of the warehouse parking lot. He got to the main road, barely put the van in drive and drove away from the warehouse.

After about a half mile down the road. He felt woozy and fainted behind the steering wheel. The van accelerated faster and swerved into oncoming traffic. Jean-Jacque collided with a car head on, then the van hit a pole. The sound of the horn drowned out the high-pitched screams coming from the other vehicle. People ran out of their cars towards the accident and tried to save the victims stuck in the mangled vehicles.

Chapter 16:

Aftermath

The first responders arrived at the scene of the accident, where Jean-Jacque was unconscious behind the steering wheel of the very van that was just used to kidnap him. It was wrapped around a utility pole, and the other vehicle that was involved in the accident; was capsized on the sidewalk across the street from where Jean-Jacque was.

The firefighters jumped off the fire truck and rushed towards both vehicles. The first man that reached the van, failed to pull open the driver side door after a few attempts.

"Bring in the jaws of life!" said the fire fighter.

Two firefighters quickly brought over a gigantic saw, and placed it where the door and windshield intersected, and cut it open.

About five minutes of cutting through mailed metal to remove the door from the van; the firefighters were able to remove it. They deflated the airbag and The Paramedic reached inside the van and placed his fingers on Jean-Jacque's neck. He checked his pulse and placed a neck brace around Jean-Jacque's neck; then pulled him out of the van.

Jean-Jacque's entire face was swollen; He looked like someone who was in a state of anaphylaxis. The blood that oozed out of the wounds on his face had dried up and left a sheen on his skin like orange sauce on Peking duck. The FDNY paramedic, and the firefighters on the scene; placed Jean-Jacque on the gurney; then rolled him inside the ambulance and drove away without haste.

Meanwhile, across the street, the other first responders had a more daunting task to contend with. They smashed the windshield to get to the people trapped inside the car that was turned over on the side. The firefighters rushed over to help, as the windshield was being smashed in, and the airbags were being deflated. The men reached in and tried pulling the unconscious driver out of the vehicle, but he wouldn't budge.

"Damn, this guy is huge! He looks like a black Lou Ferrigno!" said one of the firemen.

They pulled the driver out of the vehicle, put him down on the pavement, and performed CPR on him.

The seatbelt of the person sitting in the passenger seat was stuck, so they had to cut it off her. After getting her out of the vehicle, they realized that she didn't have a pulse. The paramedic quickly brought out the (AED) defibrillator to revive her; but was unsuccessful; she was pronounced dead on the scene.

One firefighter who was inside the Jeep Wrangler checking the vehicle for more passengers, whimpered as he brought out the lifeless body of a young boy in his hand. "There's another kid still inside the car," he said.

Another fireman rushed in and pulled out the small body of a little girl, with the stature of a porcelain doll. He placed the little girl on the sidewalk next to the Paramedic, who was performing CPR on the young boy.

The fireman sprang into action without hesitation. He overlapped his hands and pumped on her tiny chest; (one, one thousand, two one thousand, three one thousand, breathe.) He tilted her little head back and blew his breath into her mouth; then repeated the process again. The EMT tapped him on the shoulder and shook his head from left to right. The fire fighter screamed out in agony that both kids were gone.

The Paramedic strapped the driver to the gurney, and put him inside an ambulance, and drove away. The firefighters took out sheets to cover the dead bodies of the passengers that died in the collision with Jean-Jacque.

A news media van pulled up on scene, a reporter, then a cameraman quickly exited it. The reporter walked towards a crowd of people that were standing behind yellow tape; police officers used it to square off a perimeter of the accident. The camera man turned on the camera, and the reporter pulled out her microphone. "Does anyone know what happened here?" asked Kim Lee.

A few bystanders filled the reporter in, on what transpired

there an hour before she arrived on scene. The reporter took a few more comments, then prepared with her camera man before going live.

"Three; two; one; this is Kimberly Lee, with channel 10 news New York, with an exclusive report, of a gruesome car accident, that left three people dead on the scene. I have someone here with me who claims to have seen the accident as it happened. Sir, could you tell us what you saw?" asked Kim Lee.

"Yeah, I saw the van driving erratically from out of that abandoned warehouse, about a mile up the street. The driver was swerving all over the road, until he collided with the vehicle, that they pulled those dead bodies out of. I heard that it was a woman, and her two children: a boy, and a girl. It was very sad you know; the guy driving was taken away in an ambulance. It always seems to be the person to cause an accident; that survives the accident," the witness said.

"Well, there you have it, Reporter Kim Lee signing off; if there's any new developments, I will let you know. Back to you Bill!" Kim Lee put her finger to her ear and listened to some new information from the news studio.

"This just in, the driver of the van that caused the crash, was none other than Henri Jean Jacque Cadet, the assistant to the acting Mayor of New York City, Marisol Velasquez. Sources have not disclosed the identity of the victims involved in the accident. Mr. Cadet was involved in an accident earlier today, but it was reported that he fled the scene of that accident.

"It was reported that as the paramedics were putting him into the ambulance, it seemed that Mr. Cadet sustained multiple injuries; that wasn't indicative of a car accident. And he had zip ties around his hands and feet; So, did he escape from a kidnapping? As soon as we find out, we will report it," she said.

The reporter put her microphone down by her waist, the camera man stopped recording, and they both got back into the van, and drove towards the warehouse, where apparently Jean Jacque was driving away from. Kim Lee arrived at the entrance of the warehouse and witnessed the police securing the perimeter. Kim Lee tried to walk past the beat cop standing at the entrance.

"Whoa, whoa, whoa! Hold it right there, mam there's no press allowed beyond this point," the police officer said.

"Oh, c'mon officer, my name is Kim Lee, I'm with channel 10; Is this a crime scene?" replied Kim Lee.

"Mam, I am not at liberty to divulge any information with the press."

"Officer, could you at least tell me if there were evidence of a kidnapping in there?"

"Ms. Lee, is it? All I could tell you is that this is an ongoing investigation, and the press will have the story when law enforcement officials learn what happened first. So, could you please leave, and allow us to gather all the details. The last thing we need is a media circus in this area, like vultures hovering over a dead caucus."

Detectives Richard Martins and Janis Cooper were walking outside of the warehouse towards the reporter, and the beat cop at the entrance. Kim spotted them, and she snapped her fingers for the cameraman to film their exchange.

"Detectives, detectives! Was there any evidence that Mr. Cadet was being held in this factory against his will?" asked Kim Lee.

"Mam, all I can say is that this is an ongoing investigation, and whatever development we learn; you will be the first to know. But for now, please leave, and don't report anything that you don't know!" replied Det. Martins.

"Officer, please don't allow anyone past this gate unless they are law enforcement," Det. Cooper said.

The detectives then walked past the reporter and the cameraman. Both of them got into their Crown Victoria, then drove off. They were following a tip that Jean-Jacque was at New York Presbyterian, in Queens. Upon their arrival, the detectives saw the acting mayor, Marisol Velasquez, entering the hospital. Det. Martins and Cooper, entered right after her, then stopped by the information desk.

"Good morning, I'm Det. Martins and this is my partner Det. Cooper, we're trying to locate Henri Jean Jacque Cadet; could you direct us to where his room is," he said.

"Good morning, detectives Martins and Cooper, his room number is 102, and it's directly down the hall to the left," the nurse replied.

"Thank you very much nurse Debbie!"

The detectives walked down the hall where the nurse directed them to go. After they arrived at room 102, they saw Mayor Velasquez, leaning over Jean-Jacque, and sobbing. They stepped back and gave the mayor her moment with Jean-Jacque. Twenty minutes later, Mayor Velasquez stepped out of the room, escorted by her security detail out of the hospital.

Det. Martins and Cooper didn't waste any time, they entered the room, and closed the door behind them. Jean-Jacque laid there in bed with his arm and leg elevated in a sling. His head was wrapped in bandages, and he had a neck brace around his neck.

"Knock, knock, knock! Son! Mr. Cadet, do you remember my partner and I?" said Det. Martins.

Jean-Jacque tilted his head towards the detectives and watched as the two detectives inched closer to him.

"Yeah, how could I forget! You both were at the scene of the incident that happened while I was a student at Alfred E. Smith high school. What could I do for you guys?" replied Jean-Jacque.

"Mr. Cadet, we won't take up too much of your time, but we just want to know what happened to you." Det. Martins took out

his pencil, and notepad awaiting a response from Jean-Jacque.

"Well, I was driving home with my son, when a vehicle came out of nowhere, and hit my car. Four men dragged me out of my car, zip tied me, and brought me to an abandoned factory in Queens. I don't even know what happened to my son. My God: I hope he's okay——

"After I came to, they told me that they intended to kill me. But they didn't anticipate that I could defend myself; even while I was tied up. I was able to escape, as I drove away in a van, I lost consciousness, and that's all I remember. I just came to, an hour ago, in agonizing pain, with my body in traction."

Det. Martins closed the notepad and sighed.

"Okay Mr. Cadet, we will be in touch; thanks for your time."

The detectives walked out of Jean-Jacque's hospital room and drove back to the abandoned warehouse.

In Jersey City, New Jersey, Jena was getting ready for her first day at work as a paralegal at Cadet Wilkins and Cadet. Jena got up off her bed and walked downstairs into the kitchen. She turned on the coffee maker and put a few eggo waffles into the toaster oven.

"Girls! Please come downstairs and eat your breakfast! I don't want to be late for my first day at work! Although both of you are the two smartest people I know, you both need to go to school; C'mon hurry up!" said Jena.

Jena picked up the remote control for the television in the living room and turned it on. The news was on, and the volume was turned up high. -

"Girls! How many times I have to tell you two not to watch the television so loud——"

"Breaking news: earlier this morning there was a car accident involving two motorists; both drivers are in critical condition at New York Presbyterian in Queens. And it was reported that there were three fatalities; one adult, Dr. Asiatic McClymont who was a cardiologist at Mt. Sinai hospital, and her two children. The driver..."

"Nooo! Asia, Nooo!" said Jena, then she dropped down on the ground.

The twins ran downstairs and saw their mother sitting down on the living room floor crying hysterically.

"Momma! We're ready, we're sorry for taking so long. We'll be ready in time tomorrow, we promise; just stop crying!" said Tiye.

Jena looked over at the twins, grabbed them both in her arms, and squeezed them tight.

"I'm not crying because of that, girls; I just saw on the news that my sister Asia, and her kids, died in a car accident today. I'm really sorry for scaring you," Jena replied.

"Momma, are you going to be alright?" asked the twins in unison.

"I hope so, but I need to call my parents, then I have to go down to the morgue to identify my sister. What a family reunion this is," Jena replied.

Jena got up, and walked over to the phone in the kitchen, and dialed up the number of her job. The phone rang, and the receptionist picked up.

"Good morning, law office of Cadet, Brandon and Cadet; how could I direct your call?" said the receptionist.

"Good morning, this is Jena McCubbin, and I am set to start today, but I just saw on the news that my sister Dr. McClymont, and her two children were involved in that fatal car crash. I won't be able to make it in today," Jena replied.

There was a brief moment of silence on the phone, then the sound of the receptionist sniffling broke the silence.

"I will let the lawyers know about what happened. I am sorry for your loss Ms. McCubbin."

She hung up the phone and looked in the rolodex on the counter to locate her parents' number. She found it and dialed up the number.

"¡Hola! ¡Buenos Dias!" said Mrs. McCubbin.

"Mom, this is Jeneration, Asia was involved in a car accident today; she didn't make it," Jena replied.

"¡A Dios mío, dime que estás bromeando!" (Oh my God, please tell me that you're joking!)

"No mamá, es cierto que Asia y los niños están muertos." (No Mom, it's true Asia and the kids are dead.)

"Wah gwaan Melba?" replied Mr. McCubbin.

"Come here, Jena is on the phone, and she said Asia, Jamie and the kids were involved in an accident. Asia and the kids didn't survive."

"Bumbaclot, ah wah cyar lik up eena har?" asked Mr. McCubbin.

"I don't know Easy, just come here."

"Jena, ¿estás de vuelta en la ciudad?" (Jena, are you back in town?) asked Mrs. McCubbin.

"Si, momma, I am in New Jersey, I am going to the morgue now; I will meet you there," Jena replied.

"Jeneration? Yuh aright?" asked Mr. McCubbin.

"Yes Dad, I am okay," Jena replied.

"¡Está bien Jena, nosotras te amamos!" (Okay Jena, we love you!) said Mrs. McCubbin.

"I love you too, mom and Dad!" replied Jena.

Jena hung up the phone and turned off the television. She grabbed her purse, car keys and walked towards the front door,

"Girls, put on your shoes; we have to go," Jena said.

Jena opened the car door and unlocked the doors so the twins could get inside.

"Put on your seatbelts! I don't want to lose you two also."

Jena started the car, grabbed her mobile phone, and dialed Margot's number. She put the phone on speaker, it rang as Jena backed out of the driveway.

"Hey, Blossom! Did you see what happened on the news today?" asked Jena.

"Jena, gurl, I heard the bad news! I'm sorry for your loss. Did you hear the entire news report of who was involved in the accident?" replied Margot.

"No, Blossom, as soon as I heard Asia's name, I tuned out everything else."

"Well, Jamie was driving the car, but he wasn't killed. Claude was the driver of the other vehicle that was involved in the accident."

"Are you fucking kidding me Blossom? I don't believe what you are telling me right now. You mean to tell me that Claude, the main person behind me getting disowned by my family, and being kicked out of New York; is responsible for killing my sister, and her two children?"

"I shit you not Jena, but you need to hear the whole story before you jump to conclusions. First off, he was driving from my house with my son in his car; when he was hit by surprise by a van at an intersection up the street and knocked unconscious. The people that hit him, dragged him out of the car, and kidnapped him.

"When he came to, he realized that his kidnappers were Marques, Darrelle, Raheem, and someone else named Kingston. He told me that they intended to kill him. The only thing that saved him was his martial arts skills. He was able to escape, and as he was driving away; he blacked out, and crashed into the car that Jamie, Asia, and the kids were in," Margot said.

"Blossom, you don't know what Claude is capable of; he could have orchestrated this whole thing. I'm on my way to the morgue now, I want to know what fucking hospital he is in; so, he can look me in my eyes, and tell me why he killed my sister!" said Jena and sighed.

"Jena, please calm down! Claude and Jamie are both at New York Presbyterian in Queens; I will see you there!"

Jena hung up the phone, and accelerated the car, maneuvering through traffic.

"Momma is Claude our Papi?" said Tiye.

Jena's facial expression immediately changed from being angry, and she looked at the twins through the rear-view mirror, and said, "Girls, you already know the whole truth; yes, Claude is your Papi! I have told you two nothing but the truth since you were able to understand me. When we get to the hospital, you will finally get the chance to meet your Papi."

"Okay momma! What about Abuela, and Abuelo?" asked Amanirenas.

"Well, your grandparents will be at the place we are going to see your Titi Asia. You will get to meet them as well as your Tio Jamie," Jena replied.

"Momma, why don't you ever talk about our Abuela and Abuelo?" asked Tiye.

"Girls, your Abuelo, disapproved of your father and I being together. When I became pregnant with you ladies; they disowned me. They didn't think I would amount to anything great because I had you wonderful ladies so young. I haven't seen or spoken to none of them since I was pregnant with you two," Jena replied.

"Okay momma, we love you very much, and if you need us to hold your hand while you view Titi Asia; we will be there for you," Tiye said.

Jena 's eyes welled up with tears, she used her sleeve to dry her eyes. Jena parked the car out in front of the chief medical examiner's office. Then she and the twins got out of the car and walked inside the building. Jena saw her parents in the hallway, and she walked towards them.

"Jay, Jay? Ah yuh dat? Lawd God ah heaven, mi only one daughter mi hab left. Yuh hear seh ah dat fucking bwoy, did kill Asia, and mi grand pickney dem. Mi did tell yuh fram long time nuh fi deal wit dat bwoy. And yuh si it deh, mi one good daughter, dead!" said Mr. McCubbin.

Jena's mother put her hands over his mouth to shut him up and stop any further insults. She turned to Jena and the twins and held her arms wide enough so all of them could get a hug from her. Jena walked to her mother and hugged her; the twins grabbed a hold of each leg; and all four of them stood there in each other's arms

343

crying and rocked from side to side.

"Girls, this is your Abuela Melba! And mom, this is Tiye and Amanirenas; your granddaughters."

Jena stepped away from the twins, and her mother as they shared a moment.

"Wow, you girls are so big! I'm so glad to have the pleasure of finally meeting you two," Mrs. McCubbin said.

Jena's mother hugged the twins tight in her arms and kissed them on their cheeks.

Jena turned to her father, raised her hand in the air and pointed at the twins.

"Hello Papi, these are your granddaughters, Tiye and Amanirenas. Now is not the time for I told you so, please, I just want to get through this. Can you tell me where Asiatic's body is?" said Jena.

"Jeneration, a dat alone yuh hab fi seh to mi? Eeh! Come yah gal, and gib mi ah hug nuh!"

Jena hugged her father for a brief moment and stepped back away from him.

"Asia right ova deh suh, inna dat room deh! Gwan go see yuh sister, an har pickney dem!"

Jena's father whimpered, as she walked into the room where Asia's lifeless body laid there on a metal slab. Jena's body trembled and tears streamed down her face as she approached Asia's body. She sobbed over Asia for a few minutes and lean in and laid her head on Asia's soulless body.

"I'm so sorry that I left you! I should have stayed here; I missed out on so much of your life, and all of your accomplishments. I mean you got married, became a doctor, and a mom. Three great things that I should have been present for. You were always there for me; I will never forget you, and I will always love you Asiatic."

Jena looked over at Asia's two kids, and put her hand over

her mouth, and dropped down to the ground. Her father came rushing into the room and grabbed her shoulders.

"Jeneration, cum off di floor mon, git up, dem gaan, wi cyaan do notten bout ih now. I an I jus hab to wull di faith."

Jena's father held her in his arms for the first time in a long time.

"Daddy, I am sorry for being disobedient when I was younger, my decisions in the past are the reason why we're here right now. If I had listened to you, we would not be here right now."

"Hush up yuh mout Jay Jay! Ah nuh fi I-yah fault, Eff di damn bwoy neva did lik her, ah chuck wud hab; sumetimes, ah suh Jah wuk yuh kno!"

Jena sighed and her body went limp in her father's arms.

"Papi, I'll bring the girls over later; there is something that I must do."

Jena walked out of the room, hugged her mom, and wiped the tears from her face.

"Mom, I will be back to see you!"

She grabbed the twins with the intention to make her way to New York Presbyterian.

It was a short trip, after she arrived at the hospital; Jena parked in the parking garage and walked inside the elevator with the twins by her sides. She pressed three because she remembered the floor that Blossom had told her that Jean-Jacque was on. The elevator stopped, and she exited it; as soon as she stepped into the corridor, Jena spotted Margot holding her baby.

Margot turned around and saw Jena and the twins and walked towards her. They met each other half the distance between them and embraced.

"Jena, how are you holding up? Did you see your parents?" asked Margot.

"Yeah Blossom, I saw them! But fuck all that small talk;

where's Claude?" replied Jena.

Margot pointed out the room that Jean-Jacque was in, and she walked towards it with the twins in tote. As soon as she entered the room, a range of emotions came over her, anger, rage, resentment, vengeance, and love. When she saw Jean-Jacque lying there in the bed; she sighed, stopped dead in her tracks and loosened the grip she had on the twins' hands.

"There he is the love of my life. I have never moved on, and I don't think that I can, or ever will," Jena thought.

But that's not what came out of her mouth: "Claude, you bastard! You killed my fucking sister, my niece and my nephew. What do you have to say for yourself?" asked Jena.

Jean-Jacque looked up and noticed the sight that was before his eyes and cleared his throat. "Jena, Jena baby? is that you? Are those——"

"Answer the fucking question, Claude! You don't get to weasel out of your responsibility this time," Jena replied.

"Jena, would you look at me! Do you think I did this shit on purpose? My arm is broken in two places, my leg is broken, my spleen is ruptured, my clavicle, and my ocular bone is fractured. I am sorry, but I had gotten kidnapped by my so-called friends; I was running for my life. And to think that I helped all of them become legitimate businessmen.

"If memory serves me correctly; I tried explaining to you the consequences and repercussions of our being involved with each other. So, I resent that you're blaming me for everything. I mean I've done some shady things in the past that I'm not proud of, but I thought that I had atoned for most of it.

"I guess not; look at the melee that ensued from me being involved with the company that I kept. I'm sorry for what happened, I truly am; I loved Asia too! I would not do anything to hurt her. Jena, don't pin this on me, you have to forgive me!"

A single tear streamed down Jena's face, and she wiped it away.

"Jena, are those the twins?"

"Ladies, I would like to introduce you to your father!"

Jena fought back all the rage that she felt toward Jean-Jacque and allowed the twins to go to him.

"Wow, girls, allow me to introduce myself, non mwen se, Jean Jacque," Jean-Jacque said.

The twins looked at each other in bewilderment. Jean-Jacque realized that maybe they didn't understand him, so he rephrased his statement.

"I'm sorry girls; mi nombre es, Jean Jacque! Did you two understand what I said to you?"

The twins smiled at Jean-Jacque and hugged him.

"Si Papi, you said, my name is Jean Jacque!"

"¿Cual es tu nombre?" said Jean-Jacque.

"¡Papi, mi nombre es, Tiye! ¡Y, mi nombre es Amanirenas, Papi," the twins replied.

Jena couldn't bring herself to interrupt them bonding, so she stepped out of the room. Margot was sitting in a chair outside in the hallway as she held her son in her hands. She sat down beside her and put her arm around her.

"I imagined the moment when I saw Jean-Jacque again, going very differently. Especially since learning that he's the person responsible for causing the accident; that took the lives of my niece, my nephew, and my sister. I tried being angry with him, but surprisingly; I'm not," Jena said.

"Jena, I know exactly what you mean!" replied Margot.

Margot turned and handed her son to Jena, and she smiled for a brief second.

"I know this is probably not the right time but, this is Claude son Sebastian; but I call him Adonis!"

Jena looked puzzled, until she realized what Margot implied.

347

"So, you and Claude huh?"

"Nah, Jena it's not like that at all! He visited me in South Africa for business, and we were drunk one night; and you're holding the result."

Jena gave Margot back her son and adjusted her clothes.

"Been there, done that! Blossom, we have been friends for years, we've spoken recently; why didn't you tell me this before?"

"Jena, I honestly felt that I had betrayed you! I didn't even tell Jean-Jacque until the day of the accident."

Jena looked at Margot and raised her eyebrows.

"I guess we're gonna be one big, blended family!"

Margot and Jena both smiled, as they embraced each other. Tiye and Amanirenas opened the door from Jean-Jacque's hospital room and ran to her.

"Momma, we are hungry, can we go see Tio Jamie now, then get some food on the way home?" asked Tiye.

"Oh, my goodness ladies, I almost forgot about your Tio Jamie!" said Jena.

Jena and Margot stood up and hugged one last time.

"Jena I'm glad you're back on the east coast again, now I get to visit you and the girls," Margot said.

"Me too, take care of little Adonis, hey Margot, before I forget; do you know what floor Jamie is on again?"

"Yes, he's on the fourth floor Jena, room 412!"

Jena and the girls walked by Margot and the baby, and both twins waved goodbye. Tiye pressed the elevator button, luckily, it was on their floor; so, after it opened, they walked right in. Amanirenas pressed the number four button and the elevator door closed. After the elevator stopped at the fourth floor, they stepped off, and walked towards the nurse's station.

"Excuse me, my name is Jena, and I am here to see Jamie; could you tell me where room 412 is please?" asked Jena.

"Sure, down the hall to the right, he should be awake now; the doctor just saw him," the nurse replied.

"Thank you!"

Jena and the twins walked down the hallway to Jamie's room, Tiye knocked on the door, and Jamie answered, "Who's there?"

"It's me, Big head!" replied Jena.

"Jena? No, it can't be she couldn't be here so soon," Jamie thought.

"Come in!" said Jamie.

Amanirenas pushed open the door, and they all walked inside.

"Well, well, well! Look at you all swole!" replied Jena.

"The doctors seem to think that me being this muscular saved my life. The impact would've crushed my chest plate otherwise. But forget about me, come here and give me a hug Jena, I haven't seen you in years. Are these the twins?" replied Jamie and smiled.

Jena walked over to Jamie's bed and hugged him.

"Tiye, Amanirenas; meet your Tio Jamie."

The twins ran to both sides of Jamie's bed and hugged him.

"¡Hola Tio Jamie! we're glad to finally meet you. Are you going to be, okay?" said the twins in unison.

"Yes ladies, the doctors told me that aside from a mild concussion, and some superficial bruises on my back, neck, and shoulders; I am okay! I can't say the same for your Titi Asia, and your cousins; they didn't survive the crash," Jamie replied.

"We know, momma went there earlier and saw Titi Asia and the kids. And we met Abuela and Abuelo!"

Jamie's eyes welled up with tears, he looked up at the ceiling and cleared his throat.

"Jena, it seemed like it was yesterday that I met Asia back in high school. I knew right away that she would be the love of my life."

Jamie sobbed like a newborn baby. Jena and the twins hugged him while he cried.

The television was on news channel 10, and the news anchor with a stern look on his face, waited to brief his viewers.

"In my ten years of covering the news I have never been so eager to report a story than right now. This is a story about a man who's a former gangbanger, who was convicted of involuntary manslaughter. He turned his life around in jail, and he was just released from prison. We are going live to his press conference:

"Good morning, ladies, and gentlemen, my name is Darnel, and I served seven out of ten years in prison. I was charged with murder, but it was self-defense. I earned my bachelor's degree in Theology, and a master's degree in Psychology. I began a gang reform program in prison called the Hand-to-hand Initiative.

"This program has helped reform hundreds of gang members from all over the tristate area in prison. Out of those men, 85% were able to get out of the penitentiary, after serving their debt to society and regain their place in the neighborhoods they came from.

"These men have given other known gang members an opportunity to get out of gangs. In conjunction with The Helping Hand Initiative, we have outreach programs in the Darren Chan Centers, all over the city.

"My main goal is to stop the influx of gang activity in the inner-city; one hood at a time. Of course, we won't eradicate crime in the 'hood altogether, but we definitely don't want to be responsible for any of it. It's up to us to protect our neighborhoods, and not destroy it.

"I am proud to say that I am a product of my environment; I want to give back to my community. Leading by example, is the way I could achieve this goal. I aim to teach people who are where I once was; that crime doesn't pay enough to throw your life away for a quick buck," Darnel said.

Jena and Jamie's eyes were glued to the television, and Jena applauded Darnel's press conference.

"That was one of the most important press conferences, I've had the pleasure of watching. Darnel's the most positive influencer to come out of where we're from. I'm so proud of him. What's this Helping Hand Initiative, Darnel was talking about?" said Jena.

"Jena, that is Claude's Non-profit organization," Jamie replied.

"Wow Jamie, are you serious! if he's responsible for Darnel turning his life around; I have a newfound respect for Claude now."

Chapter 17:

Laid to rest

Jamie sniffled and tears cascaded down the side of his temples, Jena and the girls held him tight and cried too. (Knock, knock, knock!)

"C...Come in," Jamie said.

"Oops, I am sorry! Jamie, I am Dr. Kaufman, and I was one of Dr. Asia... I mean one of your wife's colleagues. On behalf of Mt. Sinai hospital, I wanted to let you know that we're going to take care of all the funeral arrangements for your wife and kids. My condolences Jamie, Dr. McClymont was an amazing person, and it's a tragedy what happened to you, and your family," Dr. Kaufman said.

Dr. Kaufman walked towards Jamie's bed and extended his hand towards him. Jena grabbed him, hugged him, and kissed him on his cheek. "Thank you for being so considerate, we appreciate the gesture; Asia was my sister," Jena said.

"Oh, my goodness! So, you're Jena! Dr. McClymont spoke very highly of you. It's terrible that we are meeting under these unforeseen circumstances; please relay this message to your parents. Jamie, here's my business card, when you finalize everything; please give me a call," Dr. Kaufman replied.

Dr. Kaufman walked out of the room and closed the door.

Meanwhile, across town at the abandoned warehouse, detectives Martins and Cooper, were there mulling over the evidence collected from the crime scene. The crime scene investigators on the scene corroborated Jean-Jacque's story of what transpired there.

"I can't believe that Mr. Cadet was a victim in all of this; I believe that he orchestrated this whole thing," Det. Martins said.

Detective Cooper lifted up the masks off each of the bodies faces in the warehouse.

"Det. Martins, I recognize all of these men; they're CEOs of fortune five hundred companies. This is Darrelle Castillo of Castillo industries, this is Alejandro Martinez from Alejandro's growers and distributors, and this is Raheem Knight of Knight funeral home. I don't recognize this last guy, but something seems off about all of this," Det. Cooper said.

Detective Martins walked over to him and looked down at the body of the unidentified man. He reached inside his sport coat, took out his notepad, and shuffled through the pages. He stopped suddenly at a page, and read his notes:

"He was about 5'-10" tall, dark brown skin, low haircut, and a tattoo of the island of Jamaica on the back of his left hand; with the word "Kingston," written in script on it. This guy is Aloysius Covington III, aka, Kingston; the man who murdered Herman Brentwood; the first pick of the 1996 NBA draft.

"We've been looking for this guy for years. Now we get to contact Mr. and Mrs. Brentwood, and tell them that we found their son's killer," Det. Martins said.

Detective Martins looked up at the ceiling and noticed a surveillance camera.

"Officer, look around and locate where the security room is! I just hope that camera is operational. If my hunch about Jean-Jacque is correct; this is the break, we need to nail that son of a bitch!" said Det. Martins.

The police officer jogged out the room in search of the surveillance footage.

The crime scene investigators photographed the scene. While workers for the coroner's office, bagged and tagged each of the deceased men one by one afterwards.

"Detectives, you have to take a look at this; I found the security footage, and the security guards too!" said the police officer.

"Great police work officer!" said Det. Martins.

The detectives followed the officer to the security room, only to find two men shot, bound, and gagged.

Detective Cooper covered his mouth and nose with his tie and stepped over the legs of the dead bodies. He pressed the play button on the VCR and the footage showed; all the men that were found downstairs, breaking inside the warehouse. Soon after, they were confronted by one of the security guards.

They shot him moments after they entered the factory. The other guard followed suit after he heard the gunshots and met his demise as well. But not before the men forced him to take them to the security room. They carried the first security guard to the room; then they bound and gagged the two men.

Detective Martins fast forwarded the rest of the footage until the men brought in Jean-Jacque. The video footage corroborated Jean-Jacque's story exactly how it happened. Detective Martins stopped the tape and stepped back over the bodies. He paced back and forth, scratched his head and pointed at the monitors.

"This is ridiculous, why would these men throw away everything they had, just to kill Mr. Cadet? This is unsettling, their failed attempt to murder him backfired, and five innocent people are dead as a result. It still doesn't make any sense to me, even after watching the actual crime unfold.

"These men were multi-millionaires! Alejandro Martinez, and Darrelle Castillo's companies went public a while ago; they were on pace to become billionaires, sooner or later," Det. Martins said.

Detective Martins reached inside his pocket and dialed Jamie's phone number. The phone rang in Jamie's hospital room, and he adjusted himself in the bed and reached for the phone.

"Hello, who's this?" said Jamie.

"Hello, Jamie?" replied Det. Martins.

"Yes, this is he!"

"This is detective Martins; I am assigned to this case; we found surveillance footage of the driver of the other vehicle that crashed into you and your family; escaping from being held against his will. It's unfortunate that your family are victims of such a heinous crime. I am sorry for your loss!"

"Did you find the men that's responsible for all of this, detective?"

"Yes Jamie, their dead bodies were in the warehouse down the street from the accident! We will fill you in on everything when you get a chance to come down to the station."

Detective Martins hung up the phone, Jamie furrowed up his eyebrows and put the phone down on his chest.

"What's wrong Jamie? You look upset! Who was that on the phone?" asked Jena.

"Jena, that was Det. Martins, he said that they found footage of the man that crashed into my car. He told me that the person that crashed into me, was escaping from being kidnapped," Jamie replied.

Jena sighed and raised her eyebrows. "Jamie, do you know who was driving the other vehicle?"

"No, the detective didn't say who it was; he just said what happened."

"Well Jamie, it was Claude; he was kidnapped by Marques, Darrelle, Raheem and Kingston. Apparently, they were trying to kill him for whatever reason."

Jamie put the phone down on the nightstand and slouched down on the bed.

"Look Jamie, if you want to speak to him; Claude is on the third floor in this hospital. But I have to get back to the house and feed these girls. My parents want me to go to their house too. Here's my house number, and street address; give me a call when you get discharged."

Jena and the twins hugged Jamie and walked out of his room. He sat there pining over the information he just received. Jamie got up and walked towards the elevator, and as soon as it opened; his mother was standing there.

"Bwoy, you frightened me! Ah wah yuh ah duh out yah?

Cum, gwan back inside di room," Mrs. McClymont said.

Jamie sighed, then turned around, and walked back to his hospital room.

"Jamie, yuh aright? Mi kno seh, wen yuh fadda did dead; mi head did mash up bad. Mi cud ongly imagine how yuh muss feel tuh lose yuh fambily."

"Mom, I will be okay! I just have to focus on the funeral arrangements. I got to make sure that my wife and kids get a proper burial. One of the doctors that Asia worked with, came by earlier, and told me that Mt. Sinai would cover all the expenses; so that is a bit of a relief."

"Cum yah mi son, gib mi a hug. Mi love you! Mi glad seh yuh neva dead too! Watever yuh need fram mi, jus mek mi kno!"

Jamie just put his arms around his mother, and sniffled. "Thanks mom, for your love and support!" said Jamie.

"Yeh mon, wat mi muss do? Eeh! Yuh ah di washbelly! I cud not duh wid out yuh!" replied Mrs. McClymont.

Jena and the twins made it home, and the phone rang as she opened the front door. She rushed to answer it. "Hello!" said Jena.

"Jena! This is Felicia! I'm sorry for your loss! We saw the story about your sister's accident on the news; I've been trying to reach you all day! Are you and the twins, okay?" replied Felicia.

"Yes Felicia! We're okay, considering what happened! How's Nana?"

"Nana is okay, we're going to fly out there tomorrow to pay our respects to your sister, and her kids."

"Okay! Thanks for your support, I don't know how I am going to cope with this tragedy moving forward."

"We will always be there for you Jena, we're family. Our flight lands at 11 am, at Newark Airport; could you pick us up?"

"Sure, I will be there!"

Jena hung up the phone and sat down around the kitchen

table. The twins were too busy eating fast food to even ask who had called on the phone.

"You ladies must have been really hungry! Did you leave any food for your mother?" asked Jena.

Amanirenas used a napkin to wipe her hands and mouth, then she brought Jena an unopened bag with food to her.

"Awe, thank you darling," Jena said.

Jena ate her food, and she wiped her mouth with a napkin. "Ladies, when you are done with your food; go upstairs, wash your hands and brush your teeth. Remember that we have to visit your Abuela and Abuelo."

Jena finished with her food; then she cleared the kitchen table. By the time she went into the bathroom to freshen up; the twins were ready and waiting at the front door for her.

"Wow ladies, thank you for being so prompt," Jena said.

Jena hugged Tiye and Amanirenas, then they walked outside of the house towards the car. Jena locked the door to the house, then she unlocked the door to the car, and everyone got inside it.

Traffic was light, so it didn't take Jena very long to drive to her parents' apartment in the Bronx. Jena found parking not far from the front of the building. The trio, walked towards the entrance and Jena smiled and looked at the twins.

"Ladies, the last time I was here, I was pregnant with the both of you," Jena said.

They stepped inside the building and Jena stopped. Her heartbeat raced and cold sweat collected around her eyebrow. Jena exhaled, took out her keys, and faired the walk up the stairs like she was about to climb the Himalaya mountains. She tried to unlock the door to her parent's apartment. After struggling with the lock for a few minutes, her mother unlocked the door, opened it up.

"Sorry Jena, your keys wouldn't work; the super changed the lock the day after those men attacked you in the hallway.

"The good thing about it was, if it wasn't for him, you

would've gotten hurt; or worse.

"Come on in ladies! I just finished cooking dinner," Mrs. McCubbin said.

"Mom, we just ate before we came here!" replied Jena.

"Nonsense, you know you haven't eaten anything worth wild until you had my cooking!

"Girls, go and wash your hands in the bathroom, then come sit at the table," Mrs. McCubbin said.

Jena took the girls to the bathroom and went back to the kitchen table.

"Mom! Where's Dad?" asked Jena.

"Jena, your dad went out; he normally gets back home around 9pm.

"What's the matter? Am I not good enough to keep you company?"

"No mom, that's not it at all. I figured Dad would be home too!"

Mrs. McCubbin shared a plate of food and Jena bowed her head and prayed over it. while the twins, and her mother were engaged in deep conversation. Jena didn't pick up her head from her plate. She twirled the food around the plate with her folk. Jena shifted in her seat and tuned out her mother and the twins getting acquainted.

Jena put her fork down on the plate and got up from the kitchen table. She turned on the faucet in the kitchen sink and washed up her dish. "Girls, bring your cups and plates to me. Mom, we're going to leave now!" said Jena.

"What is it Jena, do you have a date?" said Mrs. McCubbin.

"No, I am very tired, I have been awake since 6 am this morning; I need some rest," Jena replied.

"Why don't you sleep in your bed? Your father and I always hoped that you would return home one day; so, we never changed it."

"Mom, I can't pretend that dad didn't beat up my boyfriend in this apartment; because I told him that I was pregnant. I cannot forget that you and dad disowned me and forbade Asia from having anything to do with me. This apartment brings back too many bad memories," Jena said, then turned off the kitchen faucet.

Jena walked over to the door and put on her shoes. There was a moment of silence, her mother wiped her mouth with a paper towel, took up her plate and put it in the sink. She turned on the faucet and walked over to Jena. "I am sorry for the way your father, and I dealt with the situation. We just wanted the best for you, and your sister. We didn't raise you two to be subservient to a man. We expected more from you; we didn't want you to settle on just being barefoot and pregnant," Mrs. McCubbin said.

"Girls let's go!" replied Jena.

"Mom, could I use your phone?"

Mrs. McCubbin sighed, then pointed out the location of where the phone was. Jena walked to the phone and dialed Margot's number. The phone rang twice, and Margot picked up.

"Hello!" said Margot.

"Blossom, I need to get out of this place! I'm at my parents' house; could I come over?" replied Jena.

"Yeah, come over, go to the address on that Christmas card I sent you last year. Do you still have it?"

Jena searched through her purse and found the envelope. "Blossom I will be right over."

Jena hung up the phone and swung her purse over her shoulder. "Mom, I am leaving now!" said Jena.

Mrs. McCubbin put her arms around each of the twins and looked at Jena. C'mon ladies, say goodbye to your Abuela," Jena said.

"Jena, if you have to go, I understand, but leave the girls here with your father, and I tonight; come back tomorrow morning and get them," Mrs. McCubbin replied.

Jena's shoulders slumped down, and she took in a deep breath. "Girls, behave yourselves, I will be back tomorrow to get you!"

Jena didn't even stop to hug the twin's goodbye; she just walked outside and slammed the door behind her.

As she walked downstairs, Jena saw her father walking upstairs. "Jay, Jay, ah wah yuh ah duh? Eeh!" said Mr. McCubbin.

"I love you daddy! I'll be back to pick up the girls later," Jena replied, hugged her father and kissed him on his cheek.

"Baby, tek care ah yuh self! Yuh ah mi ongle daughter mi hab left. Mi cud neva understand how yuh brain wok, but jus kno seh, mi luv yuh bad," Mr. McCubbin said, as Jena continued walking past him.

Jena continued walking downstairs, and out the building. She took in a deep breath of fresh air and exhaled. Jena got into her car, then she drove to the Bruckner Blvd expressway south, towards the FDR drive. When she got closer to the exit where she needed to get off; she looked at the address again and realized that Margot lived near to where Jean-Jacque did.

Jena got off the exit, then she turned down Margot's Street. She double parked outside her brownstone for ten minutes until someone moved from their parking spot. She quickly took the open spot and walked towards Margot's brownstone. Jena knocked on the door, and Margot opened the door right away.

"Jena, you got down here fast!" said Margot.

"Blossom, I just couldn't take it anymore, my mother is exactly how I remembered her. I felt like I was 17 again; still living under her roof," Jena replied.

"Awe! Please, come in! Jena, where are the twins?"

"My mother wouldn't let me leave with them. I will pick them up tomorrow morning."

"Jena, would you like some wine?"

"Yes, please! What I really want is some high-grade weed!"

"You came to the right place!" said Margot and laughed.

Margot took a small zip lock bag out of a draw in the kitchen and tossed it to Jena as she was opening a bottle of wine. Jena opened the zip lock bag and put her nose in it. "Damn Blossom! This weed, smells strong!" said Jena.

"Jena, this shit is the stickiest of the icky! It will surely mellow you out," replied Margot.

Margot poured out two glasses of wine while Jena rolled up a blunt in a backwoods leaf. "Blossom, this is a very nice place! Where are we going to smoke?" asked Jena.

"Thank you gurl, we're going out here, follow me into the back yard!"

Margot pointed towards the sliding glass door in the kitchen. "Besides, I could hear little Adonis from back there," replied Margot.

Margot led Jena outside, and they both sat down on the chairs of the patio furniture. Jena bent down and took off her high heels. "Oh, my goodness Blossom, my dawgs were barking. I had these shoes on all day."

"Hey Jena, light up the blunt, put your feet up; sit back and relax. You've been through a lot; take it easy gurl!"

Jena lit up the blunt with a lighter and sat back in the lounge chair. (Cough, cough, cough) "Damn Blossom, this shit is strong! Here take it!" (Cough, cough, cough.)

"It ain't that strong Jena, you're just a lightweight!"

Margot took the blunt from Jena, took a long pull off it, held it in for a few seconds, then exhaled. She inhaled again, then passed it back to Jena. "Hey Jena, do you remember when we first met back in high school?" asked Margot.

"I can't recall Blossom!" replied Jena.

"Well, I can remember it like it was yesterday, Jena; I was in the bathroom by myself, just minding my own business, and these

361

girls came in, and started teasing me. They were all calling me names like: 'Raggedy Anne, Trailer Park Trash, and Vanilla Nestle Crunch;' because I had bad acne.

"Then you came inside the bathroom, and said, 'Leave that white girl alone; she ain't did shit to you!'

"Then one of them walked up on you and said, "Shut the fuck up bitch; mind your own business!"

"Then she mushed you in your face. You didn't say a word to her; you just slapped the shit out of her. It was so hard that she fell back in the stall, hit her head on the edge of the toilet, cracking it open, and pissy toilet water spilled over on her face.

"The rest of those lame bitches tried to jump us, so we stood back-to-back in the middle of the bathroom like Charlie's Angels; then we regulated on all of them. We were punching bitches, kicking bitches, grabbing bitches by their ponytails, and smashing their heads together.

"You smashed this one bitch's face into the mirror; that left a huge gash on her face."

"Oh, my goodness, Blossom I have a vague memory of that day."

"Do you know that people still call her Medusa, due to that scar?"

"I can't believe that you still remember that Blossom!"

"Shit Jena, how could I forget! Anyone who's willing to bleed with me; will be my friend for life! That was almost ten years ago, and we're still close."

Jena reached over to Margot and hugged her with one arm. "Come here gurl, you're a great friend indeed. You could throw hands too!"

After they embraced, Jena sniffled on Margot's shoulder and tears welled up in her eyes. "I miss her, Blossom!" said Jena.

"I know gurl, I miss her too! But you know after you left, Jamie took real good care of Asia. As I recall he always did, he

362

looked out for all of us like he was our big brother; even though he was younger than you, and I. He must be going through it; he truly loved Asia, and those kids," Margot replied.

At that moment, Sebastian woke up, and the sound of him crying echoed through the baby monitor. "You better tend to your man!" said Jena.

"Ha, ha, ha! Very funny Jena! He's the closest thing to one though, but I don't need a man; I got a vibrator!"

"Blossom, I have to pee; where's your bathroom?"

"C'mon Jena, I'll bring you to the room you will be staying in; there's an on-suite bathroom in it."

Margot and Jena went inside and walked upstairs. Margot pointed to the room where Jena would stay, and she went inside the baby's room to tend to Sebastian. After Margot calmed the baby down and stopped him from crying; she walked back in the hallway toward Jena's room. "Hey gurl, do you have a change of clothes? If not, I can give you some of mine," Margot said.

Margot looked inside the room, and Jena was fast asleep. She entered the room, covered Jena with a blanket, turned off the light, and closed the door.

Jena woke up abruptly from the sound of a dog barking. "Oh, my goodness! How long was I out for?" Jena looked at her watch and saw that it was 7:30am. "Oh shit, I have to pick up Felicia, and Nana from the airport. I wonder if Blossom would loan me some clothes," Jena said.

Jena walked out of the room and followed the sound of Margot snoring. She entered her bedroom, and saw that Margot had the covers wrapped around her like a burrito. Sebastian was lying there beside her sleeping in the bed as well.

Jena closed the door and opened a door in the hallway next to Margot's bedroom. "Jackpot! I'll call her later on to let her know that I borrowed an outfit from her closet," Jena said.

She went back into her room and searched through her handbag. "Got it! Never leave home without extra pairs of underwear. You just never know what can happen," Jena said.

Jena went into the bathroom and took a quick shower. Before she left, Jena saw a notepad in the foyer, and wrote Margot a note:

"Dear Blossom, thanks again for your hospitality. I slept like a log; I really needed to unwind. It was fun reminiscing with you.

P.S. I borrowed an outfit from the closet in the hallway. I'll call you later!"

Jena walked outside and put on the slam lock on the front door before she closed it. She looked up the street where her car was parked, and saw a cream colored 1979 BMW 1 series, double parked there. As she approached the car, a man got out of it, and looked at Jena up and down. "Is this your car? I am on the phone with a tow truck company trying to get this thing towed. You can't just park anywhere you please, in this neighborhood. These are designated parking spots. Who did you come to visit anyway? They should have informed you that there is no public parking on this street," the man said.

"Hey! Calm down! First of all, good morning! Second of all, there's no signs posted anywhere, that any of these spots are designated. Third, it's none of your business who I visited. Now, move your fucking car out of my way; before I run that piece of shit over! Rude ass mother fucker!" replied Jena.

The driver of the BMW hung up the phone and reversed his car out of Jena's way. She started her vehicle and drove off.

"I hate privileged people, they're too pretentious and obnoxious for my taste. I hope I can pick up the girls and make it out to Newark Airport before 11 am."

Jena looked down at the time, and it was 8:30 am. By the grace of the traffic Gods, Jena made it back to the Bronx just minutes before 9:00 am. Jena double parked outside of her parents building, put her hazard lights on and ran upstairs to her parent's apartment. As she arrived on the second floor, she saw the superintendent. "¡Hola! Buenos dias, senior!" said Jena.

"¡Buenos Dias, senorita! ¿Como esta ustedes?" replied the

364

super.

"¿Bien, y tu?"

"I have seen better days Jena, but I am still performing my duties. I'm glad to see that you're okay, where's the baby?"

"Babies, Mr. Gonzalez! I was pregnant with twins. I never got the chance to thank you for saving me that day."

"Don't worry about its Jena! I'm happy you're safe. I'm sorry to hear about Asia, and her kids, such a tragedy. She was a kind, and beautiful person."

"Thanks Mr. Gonzalez!"

Jena hugged the super and knocked on the door. Tiye opened the door and smiled at Jena. "Buenos Dias, momma!" said Tiye.

"Buenos Dias, baby girl! C'mon, is Amanirenas ready? We have to go to the airport to get Felicia, and Nana," Jena. replied

"Oh wow! Nana, and Felicia is coming! Abuela made breakfast, can we finish eating before we go?"

"Yes, hurry up!"

Jena walked inside and closed the door behind her. She saw her parents, and Amanirenas sitting at the kitchen table, and she took off her shoes. "Buenos Dias, Madre, y Padres!"

"Ven, siéntate Jena y desayuna; ¡Hice mucha comida! Come algo de la comida de tu madre; Se que extrañaste tenerlo!" (Come sit down Jena and have some breakfast; I made plenty of food! Have some of your mother's cooking; I know you missed having it!) said Mrs. McCubbin.

Jena put down her purse and jacket on the standing hook in the hallway, then washed her hands in the kitchen sink. She dried her hands on the kitchen towel hung up on the oven handle, then walked over to the kitchen table. Jena hugged and kissed everyone sitting around the table. "Amanirenas, did you have a goodnight sleep?" said Jena.

"Yes momma, we slept in your room! Look, we have on

your old pajamas," Amanirenas replied.

"That's awesome baby, hurry up and finish eating; we have to pick up Nana and Felicia from the airport."

"Jay, Jay, how cum yuh always deh pan ah mission? Eeh! Jus sit down an relax nuh!" asked Mr. McCubbin.

"Dad, as much as I want to; I have to go! I live close by, there will be plenty of time for us to spend with one another."

Jena poured herself a cup of coffee, and made a bacon, and egg sandwich. "Mom, did you tell dad that Mt. Sinai, and Asia's co-workers were going to pay for the funeral?" said Jena.

"Yes, I did Jena! Eat up, you're withering away to nothing," Mrs. McCubbin said.

Jena took a few bites of her breakfast sandwich, tilted her head back and rolled her eyes. "Mmm, Mom, this is awesome, I forgot how great of a cook you were."

"Ya que ha vuelto, puede venir a comer para ganar algo de peso. Entonces puedes encontrar un marido; no puedes seguir criando a estas chicas tú solo." (Since you're back, you can come over and eat so you can put on some weight. Then you can find a husband; you can't continue to raise these girls by yourself.)

"Mamá, aprecio tu preocupación, pero nunca estuve sola; las personas que recojo del aeropuerto; siempre estuvieron ahí para mi." (Mom, I appreciate your concern, but I was never alone; the people that I'm picking up from the airport; were always there for me.)

"Mamá, abuela, ¿todavía se aman?" (Momma, Abuela, do you still love each other?) asked Tiye.

"Si, Por qué preguntas" (Yes, why do you ask?) replied Jena and Mrs. McCubbin simultaneously.

"Ambos siempre están peleando," (Both of you are always fighting,) Amanirenas replied.

There was an uncomfortable silence, you could cut the tension in the room with a knife. Jena finished her coffee and sandwich and wiped her mouth off with a napkin. "Ladies, please get ready; we have to leave." Jena looked down at her watch and saw that it was 9:30 am.

The twins got up and ran to the room to change their clothes. They quickly did and went into the bathroom to wash their hands and brush their teeth. "Ladies don't forget to make up the bed!" said Jena.

"We did already momma!" exclaimed the twins simultaneously.

Jena got up from the table and brought the dishes to the kitchen sink. She quickly washed them, put them in the dish drain, and dried her hands. Jena walked over to her parents and kissed them both on their cheeks. "Thanks for watching the twins!" said Jena.

"Bring them over whenever you want Jena," Mrs. McClymont replied.

The twins walked over and hugged and kissed their grandparents as well. "Bye Abuela, bye Abuelo; we'll see you soon!"

Jena, and the twins walked out of the apartment, and walked downstairs.

Jena, and the twins got down to the lobby as detectives Martins and Cooper entered the building. "Hey, are you looking for me detectives?" asked Jena.

"Excuse me?" exclaimed detective Martins, as he walked closer to Jena, and the twins.

"Your face looks familiar," Det. Cooper replied.

"Aah! You're Mr. Cadet's girlfriend, right! I remember now, you were waiting for him at the precinct, a good while back," Det. Martins said.

"I remember you two also; y'all wouldn't allow me to accompany Claude in the interrogation room when he came in for questioning. And he's not my boyfriend, we're not even friends anymore. He killed my sister, and her two kids," Jena replied.

"Oh wow! You're Asia's sister! We came here to see your parents, to give them the update on the case; are they home?" asked Det. Cooper.

"Yeah!" replied Jena.

"Okay, here's my card; give us a call!" said Det. Martins.

"My condolences mam; it must be a really rough time. Rest assured, we are working very hard to get you, and your family some closure," Det. Cooper said.

"Thanks, good to know!" replied Jena.

The detectives continued walking toward the staircase, and Jena put the card the detective gave to her inside her purse. She continued walking outside with the twins, then she opened the car doors with her transponder. She and the twins got inside the car, and she drove away.

"Oh, my goodness, we're going to be late!" Jena drove like a bat out of hell; it's a wonder that she didn't get pulled over for speeding by a state trooper. She arrived at the airport at 11:15am, Jena double parked outside of the airport, and walked towards the entrance.

As soon as she got to the front door, she heard a voice say, "Jena gurl! You're right on time!" said Felicia.

Jena looked over to the side, and there they were Felicia and Nana. She sighed in relief and smiled. "I'm so glad to see you two! How was your flight? Were you waiting long?" replied Jena.

"No gurl, Nana had to use the restroom; we just got our luggage, walked towards the exit, and poof there you were!"

"Good! Here, give me your bags Nana, and follow me; I'm just parked right out here!"

Jena, Felicia and Nana walked the short distance to her vehicle, and the twins were jumping up and down in their seats with excitement. Tiye and Amanirenas opened the door and ran towards Nana and Felicia. "Nana, Aunty Felicia! We're glad you made it here safe; we miss you!" said the twins.

"Oh girls, Felicia and I missed you too!" replied Nana.

They all hugged each other, then they packed the luggage in the trunk. Everyone piled up in the car, and Jena drove off.

"Wow Jena, this is a nice car! I love your outfit too!" said Felicia.

"Thanks, gurl, but this is a company car; perks of working at one of the top law firms in the nation. I want to thank you for turning me on to law; I am really intrigued by how this land is governed. This line of work is very fulfilling!" replied Jena.

"No worries gurl! But Nana and I are starving; is there some place we can stop to get a bite to eat before we get to your house?"

"Sure, I know exactly where we could go! It's a soul food restaurant up the street from the house; I will get us a to-go platter, with all the fixings."

Jena stopped by the restaurant, parked the car, and went inside to get the food. After ten minutes, she came back outside with a large platter, and two paper bags in her hands. Felicia got out of the car, and helped Jena get the food to the car.

"This is precious cargo gurl, I'm so hungry right now that if you dropped this food; I'm liable to eat it off the pavement!"

They both laughed, then got back inside the car, and Jena drove out of the parking lot. She drove a short distance and pulled into her driveway. "Here we go ladies, home sweet home!"

Everyone got out of the car, the twins helped Nana inside, while Felicia, and Jena brought the food and luggage inside the house.

Jena walked into the kitchen with the food and put it on the table. "Tiye, Amanirenas! Please get some forks, napkins, cups, and plates for Aunty Felicia, and Nana."

The twins gathered together each item and set the table.

"Wow ladies, I feel like I am at a restaurant; bravo!" said Nana.

Everyone sat down at the table and Nana clasped her hands

369

and closed her eyes. "Let us bow our heads for grace: Thank you, heavenly father for this plentiful bounty, and all of your blessings in our times of need. I pray that you bless us and continue to lead us down the path of righteousness; be that beacon of light during our darkest of time. And show us that it's always darkest before dawn! Amen!" said Nana.

Jena and Felicia shared out the food for Nana, and the twins. Felicia took a bite of the food and closed her eyes. "Mmm, Jena gurl, this food is very tasty; I don't know if it's the hunger talking, or this food is really good."

"Felicia, I asked the same question when I first had it, but I have to say that the food here is legit; every time I eat there, I taste a new flavor."

Everyone at the table laughed, and Jena poured out some sweet tea for everyone. "So, Felicia, tell me, do you still work at the hotel part time?" asked Jena.

"No, I gave that up! I met someone there who has a bounty hunter business, and he wanted someone to do the clerical work; it pays a lot more, and I get to do some private investigating too!" replied Felicia.

"That sounds great, before you stopped working at the hotel, did you see that, that little pipsqueak again trafficking girls?"

"Nope, Ted must-have went to a different hotel."

Everyone finished their meal, the twins cleared the table, and washed up the dishes. Jena escorted Felicia and Nana upstairs and opened the guest room door. "It's not much, but here it is, there's two twin beds in here, and there's a bathroom too, it's adjacent to the twins room. I think the realtor called it a Jack and Jill, or something to that effect. If you would rather use a different bathroom, there's one in the hallway. I'm going to take a shower and go to sleep; I will see you two in the morning!" said Jena.

"Okay Jena, thank you for everything, we'll see you in the morning!" replied Felicia.

Jena pulled up the door and went into her room. The twins

finished cleaning up the kitchen and went off to bed.

The next morning, Jena was awakened by the sound of the telephone ringing. "Hello, good morning!"

"Wake up Jena! This is your mother; your father and I decided that we would bury Asia and the kids at Kensico cemetery, upstate New York. We have an appointment with Ortiz funeral home at 9:00 am, so get dressed and meet us there," Mrs. McCubbin said.

"Okay mom, I will be there shortly!" replied Jena.

Jena hung up the phone and looked at the alarm clock on the nightstand; it was 6:45 am. "Damn, why this woman wakes up so early." Jena got out of bed, and went inside the bathroom to pee, wash her face and brush her teeth.

After she dried her face, and hands; Jena put on her robe and walked into the hallway. "Since I'm up, I should cook breakfast for everyone."

Jena sniffed and she could smell cooked bacon, and coffee in the air.

"Oh, my goodness! These girls are downstairs on my stove; I know I told them never touch the stove without my supervision."

Jena wrapped the front of her robe, tied it tight, and walked downstairs toward the kitchen. "Ladies, I thought I told you not to use the stove!"

Jena looked over at the kitchen, and saw Nana, and Felicia cooking breakfast.

"Good morning you guys, I was just coming down here to make breakfast! I guess you beat me to it. I thought it was the twins that were down here cooking."

"Good morning, Jena! The twins will be right down; c'mon, sit down, and have some breakfast," Felicia said.

Jena sat down, grabbed a piece of bacon, and poured herself a cup of coffee. "How would you like your eggs baby?" asked Nana.

"Sunnyside up Nana, and fried all the way through," Jena

replied.

Nana walked over with the pan and slid Jena's egg onto her plate. "Bon appétit!"

"Thanks Nana!"

"Jena, what do you have planned for today?" asked Felicia.

"Well Felicia, my mother just called me, and told me that she's going to finalize the funeral arrangements this morning at 9:00 am; so, I'm going to meet her at the funeral home," Jena replied.

Felicia put her hand on top of Jena's hand and winked at her. "Would you like some company gurl?"

"Yeah sure! I guess I have to ask Nana if she could watch the twins until we get back!"

"Nonsense baby girl! You don't have to ask; it would be my pleasure to stay with them. You two go ahead; it will be like old times," Nana said.

The twins walked downstairs and sat down around the kitchen table. "Good morning, Nana, momma, and Aunty Felicia! We overheard you talking about Abuela; where are you going momma?" asked Tiye.

"Your Abuela made arrangements for Asia, and your cousins' burial. Felicia and I are going to meet her at Ortiz funeral home in the Bronx. So, stay here with Nana until we get back," Jena replied.

"Okay momma!" said Tiye, as she poured out some fresh squeezed orange juice for her and Amanirenas.

Nana brought the pan over to the twins and shared each of them some scrambled eggs. "You remembered Nana, cheesy scrambled eggs; our favorite!" said the twins simultaneously.

"Enjoy babies, you two are going to have to show me your schoolwork after you're done eating your breakfast," Nana said.

"Yes mam!" said Tiye.

Jena and Felicia got up and went upstairs to get dressed as

372

the twins, and Nana ate their breakfast. Fifteen minutes passed, and both ladies returned downstairs, and Jena looked over at the twins. "Ladies, be on your best behavior; we'll be back soon!" said Jena.

Jena and Felicia walked out of the front door, they got inside the car, then Jena reversed out of the driveway, and drove off.

"I hope we make it in time, it's already a quarter to 8:00 am; even though it's the weekend, traffic can be a bitch getting into the city from the George Washington Bridge!" Jena exclaimed as she weaved in and out of the lanes.

Back at the hospital, Jamie lied there in bed motionless staring up at the ceiling. In the background, the television was tuned to a station that played an old rerun of Looney Tunes. The phone rang and Jamie took his sweet time to answer it. "Hello, good morning!" said Jamie in a low monotone voice.

"Buenos Dias Jaime! This is your mother-in-law, how are you feeling?" replied Mrs. McCubbin.

"Good morning, Mrs. Melba, I am doing much better; the doctors are going to discharge me tomorrow."

"That's great news! I just called to let you know that your father-in-law and I, decided to bury Asia at Kensico cemetery; isn't that where your father is buried?!"

"Yes, he's up there!"

"Are you okay with that Jaime?"

"Yes, that's fine with me, Mrs. Melba!"

"Okay great! We're on our way to Ortiz funeral home to finalize all of the arrangements. Rest up, I will see you tomorrow, Jaime, I love you son!"

Jamie hung up the phone, got out of bed, and saw that his mother was still there. He took a blanket and covered her up. He sauntered over to the bathroom and tried to pee, but it was still painful; the urine came out bloody. "Damn, this shit hurts! I don't know what that means, but I know it ain't good. I'll tell the doctor when he comes next time about this blood in my urine," Jamie said.

373

Jamie walked past the nurse's station and smiled at the nurse on duty. She looked up at him and stared as he walked past her toward the elevator.

"He's huge, he looks like a black Lou Ferrigno!" said the nurse.

Jamie pressed the up button for the elevator, it arrived, he got inside, and pressed the number 4. The elevator door closed and moved up one level; Jamie got off as soon as the door opened. He walked through the hallway looking inside each room for Jean-Jacque; until he finally saw him asleep in one of the rooms.

Jamie opened the door gently, closed the door behind him, and tip-toed toward Jean-Jacque's bed. He dragged a pillow from underneath Jean-Jacque's leg, placed it over his face, and pushed it down with all his strength. Jean-Jacque flailed his one good arm around, and a few seconds later, he stopped.

Jamie pulled the pillow away from Jean-Jacque's face, put his two fingers on his neck to check his pulse. "Wait a minute, you're still alive!" Jean-Jacque opened his eyes and jabbed Jamie in his throat sending him backwards to the food tray that was next to his bed.

"It should have been you that died in the accident, it should have been you, not my wife and kids. Everything that you touch turns to shit!" said Jamie.

Jamie stood there by Jean-Jacque's bed holding his throat and panting like a British bulldog trying to cool himself down in the summer.

"I'm sorry Jamie! It was an accident, if I could switch places with Asia and your kids, I would!" replied Jean-Jacque.

"Don't you dare speak their names! You're not worthy! You're a murderer Claude! You are a stone-cold killer!"

A nurse rushed inside the room with two security guards and stood by the doorway. "What's the commotion? Mr. Cadet is this man bothering you?" said the nurse.

"Bothering him?! Bothering him?! He murdered my wife

and kids; he should be in handcuffs. But nothing is going to come of it because he's a politician that works with the mayor's office. He's going to get away with murder!" said Jamie.

"Be that as it may sir, this is not the way to get justice. A vigilante has a short life span, it doesn't matter how much good you think that you're doing; you will never get the credit you deserve, and you will be vilified by law enforcement. Son, let the proper authorities deal with it; he should have his day in court, and be judged by a jury of his peers," the nurse said.

"I see how this is going, you're protecting him! This isn't over Claude; you're going to have to answer for your crimes against humanity one day. When that day comes; I will be there!" exclaimed Jamie.

Jamie backed out of Jean-Jacque's room as he wagged his finger at him. He strutted through the hallway like George Jefferson, from The Jeffersons; but he wasn't moving on up.

Jamie took the stairs down to the third floor back to his room. His mother and the doctor stood there talking amongst themselves. Jamie's mother saw him and raised her hands above her head. "Kiss mi nec back! Si him deh! Bwoy, wi deh yah a look fi yuh; ah weh yuh disappear tuh?" said Mrs. McClymont.

"I went for a walk mom! Replied Jamie.

"Yes, right!" replied Mrs. McClymont.

"Dr. Patel, I think that I have some internal bleeding; I peed earlier, and there was nothing but blood in the toilet," Jamie said.

"Come lay down on the bed, let me check you out Jamie," Dr. Patel replied.

Dr. Patel opened Jamie's hospital gown, then checked his abdomen for any abnormalities. "Hey Jamie, take a deep breath in, hold it, now exhale! Your right side is a bit bruised, and tender from the trauma that you suffered during the accident; it's a miracle that you didn't sustain any permanent injuries. You just need some rest; I have the nurse give you a diuretic to pass the clotting in your kidney, and some extra strength Tylenol for the pain.

"You'll be fine, kidneys are durable; they can heal themselves! Let me check your vision. Are you having headaches? Are you nauseated? Are you experiencing vertigo?" asked Dr. Patel.

"No to the first two questions, Dr. Patel, but what's vertigo?" replied Jamie.

"Vertigo is when you feel like you're falling, when you're not, and you can't keep your balance."

"No, Dr. Patel!"

Doctor Patel jotted down some notes and adjusted his glasses. "Tomorrow before you get discharged, y'all have to do a physical, okay Jamie!"

Jamie nodded his head in acknowledgement to Dr. Patel; so, he closed his clipboard, then left Jamie's room. "Jamie, yuh kno seh, di phone neva stop ring fram yuh lef. Yuh madda in law called a couple times well, an dat gal yuh carry ah mi house; she did call tuh!" said Mrs. McClymont.

"Mom, you know that Jena is Asia's older sister, right?!" asked Jamie.

"Watever! Eeh, tek dis, dem gib mi one numba fi gib yuh. Dem seh wen yuh cum back, call dat numba yah. Dem ah tell mi seh, dem ah go bury Asia at Kensico cemetery; where yuh fadda bury."

Jamie took the number from his mother and called it back. "Hello, my name is Jamie, and I missed a call from this number! My mother, father, and sister-in-law should be there making funeral arrangements for my deceased wife, and kids," Jamie said.

"Yes, good morning, Jamie! My name is Manuel, my condolences for your loss, we here at Ortiz funeral home, will ensure that your family will be well taken care of. Hold on, here's your sister-in-law," Manuel said.

"Hello Big head!" said Jena.

"Hey Jena! How's it going on your end?" replied Jamie.

"We're just about finished up here; I am going to pick up a

dress for Asia and Tatiana. My father is going to get a suit for Calvin."

"Man, I wish I could have been there for this. Thank you all for taking the time out to do this; I really appreciate it, Jena."

"Don't worry about it, Jamie! The funeral is scheduled for next week Saturday; that should be enough time for you to be out of the hospital."

"I will be out tomorrow, Jena! I'm going to take a taxicab home. I need to sleep in my own bed, these hospital beds are uncomfortable."

"Ok Jamie, I will see you soon!"

The next morning, Dr. Patel came into Jamie's room right on schedule. "Good morning, Jamie! Where's your mother?" asked Dr. Patel.

"She left last night, she claimed that I snored too loud; so, she had to go home to get some sleep," Jamie replied.

Dr. Patel laughed, then he and the nurse escorted Jamie to the therapy center, so he could go through the test. Although Jamie was in excruciating pain, he managed to pass the physical examination. "Mr. McClymont, I wish you all the best, and may God be with you, and your family; you're free to go."

"Thank you, Dr. Patel."

Jamie walked back to his room, to get dressed to leave. He had a difficult time getting the sweater over his head without grimacing in pain. His sides were extremely sore. He managed to dress himself, then he walked out of his room, and walked past the nurse's station. The nurse on duty was the same nurse that stepped in the room after he and Jean-Jacque had that little altercation. She looked up at Jamie and nodded. "Be careful young man; stay strong!" said the nurse.

Jamie smiled and continued walking to the elevator.

Jamie got off the elevator and walked outside the hospital. He hailed a cab from the taxi stand and the driver started the car.

"Good morning! I'm heading to the Bronx," Jamie said.

"Good morning, Sir! What's the address?" asked the driver.

"1022 Ward Avenue," Jamie replied.

Jamie got inside the taxicab and sat there quietly until he arrived home. He paid the driver $20, even though the fair was $10: "Keep the change," Jamie said as he got out the taxicab.

Jamie walked to the gate of his house, located his keys in his pocket, then he opened the door. Jamie closed the door behind him, then walked upstairs. He unlocked the door to his apartment and looked inside. It was just as he left it; Jamie stood there for five minutes and surveyed the place.

He took a deep breath, walked towards the living room, and sat down on the couch. There was a family picture on the bookshelf; Jamie took down the picture and stared at it for a few minutes. He cried and touched Asia, Tatiana, and Calvin's faces in the picture with his thumb. Tears and snot streamed down his face, he sniffled, inhaled, and exhaled like he was hyperventilating.

"Daddy loves you; I miss you so much. We're going to make sure that you get a proper burial, and I will always remember every single moment that I shared with all of you." Jamie hugged the picture in the picture frame, laid down on the couch, and cried himself to sleep.

A few days later, the doorbell rang, and Jamie jumped up out of his sleep. He turned over on his back, and just stared up at the ceiling. Ten minutes after, Jamie heard keys opening up the door downstairs, and footsteps walking up the steps. "Jamie!" yelled Mrs. McClymont, as she slowly crept upstairs.

She stood there at the door to his apartment shuffling through her set of keys, trying to locate the correct ones for his apartment. She finally found them, and opened the door; "Bwoy, yuh nuh hear mi ah call yuh?" Jamie's mother walked inside the apartment and looked around as she lurked closer to his bedroom. Jamie was lying there naked, with the sheet covering up his privates.

"Bwoy git up mon! Yuh deh yah ah sulk all week. Mi doubt it eff yuh nyam anyting since yuh cum fram di hospital. Git up!"

said Mrs. McClymont and grabbed a pillow and threw it at Jamie.

"Ok, okay! I'm getting up!" replied Jamie.

"Yuh friends dem cum tuh yuh! Clean up yuhself mon! Di funeral is tomorrow, yuh hab yuh suit ready?"

Jamie pointed at a chair that he had in his room with his black suit, white shirt, black tie, and shoes thrown down on it. "Aright gud! Mi ah go press dem fi yuh! Lively up yuhself, Asia wouldn't want to si seh yuh life come tuh dis. Mi luv yuh son! At least yuh kept di place clean. Mi did think seh di place would have been nasty; proud ah yuh!"

Jamie got up out of bed, and went into the bathroom to shit, shower, and shave. He quickly finished, got dressed and went downstairs. Jamie looked around, and didn't see anybody outside; so, he went inside his mother's apartment, and saw his business partners sitting down on her couch in the living room. "Hey, there he is!" Jamie took off his shoes before entering inside his mother's house, and then he walked over to each of his friends and shook their hands.

"What's up Kendall, what's up Blake! Thanks for coming guys," Jamie said.

"Yo Jamie, we were worried about you!" replied Kendall.

"I'm doing alright Kendall! I've just been going through the motions these past few days!" said Jamie.

"Understandable Jamie, I could only imagine brother!" said Blake.

"Blake this shit hurt more than when my father passed away! My son and my little daughter were filled with so much joy; they were innocent, and their future was bright. My wife was doing great work in the medical field, she was a very important part of a lot of people's lives; my life with them was cut short!" said Jamie.

There was a moment of silence, tears welled up in everyone's eyes.

Jamie got up and wiped his eyes with his handkerchief. "Enough about me and my situation, how's business going

379

Kendall?" asked Jamie.

"Same old, same old, Jamie! Those all-natural supplements are doing extremely well though," Kendall replied.

"That's great news! You guys coming to the service tomorrow?" asked Jamie.

"Yeah, that's why we came by, we tried to call you, but the phone kept going to voice mail. Your mother was kind enough to give us one of the programs. It has all of the information on it."

Kendall gave Jamie the program, he took it, and smiled. "This picture was from when we went down to Disney world; the kids had a blast. This was a great choice; they all look happy."

"Jamie, we're going to head out brother, but we'll see you tomorrow. Then we won't leave you alone again until you get back to normal."

Kendall and Blake walked towards the front door and put back on their shoes. Jamie shook their hands and they both walked outside. "Tell your mother we said goodbye, and thanks for the drinks," Blake said.

"Okay, I will fellas; thanks for stopping by." Jamie put on his shoes, stepped outside, and closed his mother's front door. He watched as his business partners drove away, then he walked up the street. Jamie was approaching the Brentwood house, and saw Meadow sitting down alone on the porch smoking a cigarette; so, he walked over to her. "Hey Meadow, how are you holding up?" asked Jamie.

"I'm doing alright Jamie, my condolences, I heard what happened to Asia and your kids; these tragic deaths keep happening to people around here. I need to move Jamie," Meadow replied.

"You could say that again! The service is tomorrow you know; are you gonna go?"

"Jamie, to be honest with you, I don't do funerals; that shit is too sad, Yo! I ain't even go to my brother's funeral!"

"Did they ever catch the mother fucker who did it?"

"Yeah, you obviously don't know, but he was with your peoples that kidnapped your friend Claude. Luckily, he escaped from them, but tragically he crashed into you, and your family during his getaway. The police found their bodies in an abandoned warehouse that was up the street from the accident. It was all over the news Jamie! The shitty part is you never know who's friend or foe nowadays."

Jamie now dumbfounded, sat down on the front steps next to Meadow; she nudged Jamie to give him a cigarette. Jamie looked at Meadow, held his hand up and shook his head from left to right. "Nah, I'm good; I'm not trying to start smoking cigarettes," Jamie said.

"One cigarette is not going to make you start Jamie. Here, it will help calm your nerves," Meadow replied.

Jamie took it, inhaled the nicotine latent cigarette, and exhaled the smoke up in the air. "Yo Meadow, you know who was involved in the kidnapping?" asked Jamie.

"If you go up to Boynton and Watson Avenue; you will see vigils for all of them; except Kingston. Did you know the detectives called my parents and told them that they found his body in that warehouse?" replied Meadow.

"I obviously don't, Meadow; this is all news to me!"

"Well, detectives Martins and Cooper, came by here a few days ago, and asked me if I wanted to gather up a few things from Kingston's apartment. I was shocked and appalled at first because Kingston wasn't my man; but I saw that they were serious. So, I said, fuck it, and I went with them. When I got there, the detectives escorted me directly into the bedroom, and there were two big duffel bags on his bed. I opened them both up, and there was two million dollars in cash, loose diamonds, and jewelry."

"Get the fuck out of here! How did you know that it was that much money?"

"I'm dead serious, the money was shrink wrapped in plastic, and the tags had the amount written on it. At first, I thought it was entrapment; 'cause they knew that shit didn't belong to me; I guess

381

they figured it was due to me, and my family for what he took from us. If I ever see Claude again, I will thank him for killing that mother fucker! No amount of money could ever bring back my brother though; but it's a start."

"That's cool! I guess that is a down payment for a new life."

Jamie put out the cigarette, hugged Meadow, and continued walking up the street. "Hey Jamie, good luck, and goodbye!" said Meadow.

"Take care of yourself Meadow!" replied Jamie.

Jamie walked up Ward Avenue and turn left on Watson Avenue towards the liquor store on Boynton. He saw Darnel surrounded by a small crowd of people; three graffiti artists were painting a mural of Asia, Tatiana, and Calvin. His wife was depicted as a nurturing shaman healing the community with natural medicine. Each of Jamie's kids were depicted as angels playing in various games with the neighborhood children.

After buying two small pints of Bacardi 151 from the liquor store; Jamie stood there and watched as the graffiti artists finished part of the mural. Darnel held a bullhorn in his hand, and he put it up to his mouth.

"The tragic events that took the lives of three of our own; Dr. Asiatic McClymont, Calvin McClymont, and Tatiana McClymont. Is all too familiar in this neighborhood, and hoods all across the city for that matter. I have been away for some time, but I used it wisely; with the ambition to come home to ensure that this situation doesn't happen again.

"I am working closely with Claude of The Helping Hand Initiative; to encourage our people to think before they act. It's not normal for our parents, and grandparents to bury their children. We have to work together to make that an anomaly again; our people need to be safe in these streets!" said Darnel.

Darnel put down the bullhorn briefly, acknowledged Jamie with a head nod; Jamie picked up on Darnel's nonverbal cues for him to come up and say a few words; but Jamie declined. Darnel tilted the bullhorn at Jamie and continued his speech. Jamie stood there and took a few swigs of the Bacardi 151, then he walked up Boynton Avenue, toward Westchester Avenue.

He saw three vigils out in front of the Bodega. There were at least two dozen candles for Marques, Darrelle, and Raheem. A graffiti artist spray painted each of their names and underneath it their birthdate and year of death.

Jamie looked at the vigil and opened the pint of Bacardi 151 and took a swig from the bottle. He decided to walk the exact path he used to with Asia, when they were kids coming from school. He stopped when he passed by the house where they were when he and Asia first kissed each other; Jamie took a few swigs. He walked by the fruit and vegetable store where Asia first scratched the middle of his hand as she held it; Jamie took a few more swigs. He walked by the bus stop where he used to meet Asia in the mornings before school and carried her Jan sport book bag as they waited for the bus to arrive; Jamie drank the last amount of liquor in the first pint, then he opened the other one.

After walking a few blocks, he stopped at Asia's parent's building, stood under her old bedroom window, and drank the entire pint of Bacardi 151. Jamie looked up at the window after he finished, dropped down to his knees, and wailed.

"Asia! Asia! Asia! I miss you baby! I'm sorry I didn't protect you, and the kids! I'm sorry!"

Mrs. McCubbin looked out the window and saw Jamie outside down on all fours on the sidewalk looking pitiful. She went downstairs, bent down next to Jamie, and hugged him to console him.

"C'mon Jamie, pull yourself together; get up baby; you have to go home. The funeral is tomorrow, you have to be strong. We're all hurting son; we just can't let this break us down," Mrs. McCubbin said.

Jamie wiped his eyes with his undershirt and got up to his feet. Mrs. McCubbin rubbed his back, and he walked up the street towards Ward Avenue. Somehow Jamie managed to make it home and mustered up the strength to climb up the stairs to the second floor. By the grace of a higher power, Jamie unlocked the door, walked to his bedroom, and laid face down on his bed.

The next morning, Jamie woke up from his drunken stupor with a splitting headache. He walked into the kitchen to make some coffee, and a plate covered with aluminum foil was on the table. He looked over at the coffee maker, and it was already percolating. "This is strange! The ones who would do this for me is my mother, and Asia," Jamie thought.

Jamie frantically looked in every room in the apartment; he didn't want to jinx it by saying her name; so, he didn't. But he didn't find anyone there; so, he just poured out a cup of coffee, and sat in front of the plate of food.

Jamie carefully unwrapped the aluminum foil covering off the plate, and voila! It was his favorite dish; yellow yam, green banana, ackee, salt fish, and callaloo. Jamie exhaled in relief.

After he enjoyed the hearty breakfast; Jamie went inside the bathroom for a quick shower. Five minutes later he heard the voices of Jena, the twins, and his mother-in-law.

Jamie finished bathing, got out the shower, and rushed into his bedroom. He knew that if his in-laws were already there; he had to be late. Jamie looked around for his suit, and it was hung up in the closet; steam pressed like it just came from the cleaners. "Damn mom! How can you get these sharp creases with just an iron? I will never get her technique down pat." Jamie put deodorant on and put lotion on his skin; before he put on his shirt, and pants. He tied his tie, put on his shoes, and put on a few spritz of cologne; before he put on his blazer, and sunglasses.

Jamie grabbed his wallet and keys, ran out his door, and jogged down the stairs. He opened the front door and saw a black limousine out in front of his mother's house. Tiye and Amanirenas saw Jamie and ran to him. "You look very handsome, Uncle Jamie!" said Tiye.

"Thank you, ladies, you both look very beautiful as usual!" Where's mommy, Abuela, and Abuelo?" asked Jamie.

"They're in your mother's house, eating breakfast!"

"Why aren't you inside eating breakfast too!"

"We did already, momma told us to get you; so, come on!"

The twins grabbed Jamie by his hands and pulled him inside his mother's apartment. Everyone was standing in the living room talking amongst themselves. "Good morning, everyone! Mr. McCubbin turned around and smiled at Jamie. "Mi think yuh cud not wake? We knock pan di door how many times; yuh madda opened the door, brought up yuh breakfast and yuh suit, and yuh still neva wake! How yuh can sleep suh mon?!" said Mr. McCubbin.

"I was very tired Mr. Easy, I'm still in a bit of pain you know, the doctor prescribed plenty of rest; so that is what I've been doing," Jamie replied.

Jena's father hugged Jamie, and her mother did the same afterwards. Jena was in the kitchen with Felicia, Nana, and his mother cleaning up. A few minutes later, they all walked toward the living room, and Jamie stretched out his arms. "Good morning mom! Good morning, Mrs. Melba! Good morning, Jena! Good morning, ladies!" said Jamie.

"Good morning, Jamie! You clean up nice, Big head! This is Felicia, and Nana; they're my friends/family from California!" replied Jena.

"Pleased to meet you! Thanks for coming all this way to pay your respects!"

No problem, Jamie, the pleasure is all mine, I'm Felicia, and this is my grandmother Mrs. Josephine. We both are sorry for your loss!" said Felicia, she and Nana, both hugged Jamie at the same time.

"Son, cum hugg yuh madda! Yuh enjoy di breakfast mi carry cum gib yuh?" said Mrs. McClymont.

"I Love you mom! Thank you for pressing my clothes for me." Jamie replied.

Everyone walked outside of the house, Jamie made sure that both doors were locked, and they got inside the limousine. Felicia and Nana got inside Jena's car and followed behind them. The drive to the funeral home was short and everyone else inside the limousine talked amongst themselves, while Jamie looked outside the window.

They finally arrived at the funeral home, and there were so many familiar, and unfamiliar faces outside. A few news media outlets were reporting the event. The driver pulled the limousine up close to the entrance and parked it at the reserved spot out in front of Ortiz funeral home. Jamie and everyone else in the limo got out and walked inside. The funeral director and his staff were inside ushering everyone into the right room where Asia, and the kids were. After everyone sat down, The Pastor started the service:

"Good morning, everyone! We're all gathered here today to pay our respects to three souls that are with our heavenly father. With a heavy heart I stand here presiding over this service for Asiatic McClymont and her two children, Calvin, and Tatiana. I remember baptizing Asia as a baby; that's how close I am to this family.

'Who will separate us from the love of Christ? Will hardship, or distress, or persecution, or famine, or nakedness, or peril, or sword? No, in all these things we are more than conquerors through him who loved us.

'For I am convinced that neither death, nor life, nor angels, nor rulers, nor things present, nor things to come, nor powers, nor height, nor depth, nor anything else in all creation, will be able to separate us from the love of God in Christ Jesus our Lord.

[Romans 8:35 37, 39]

'There is a time for everything, and a season for every activity under the heavens: a time to be born and a time to die, a time to plant and a time to uproot, a time to kill and a time to heal, a time to tear down and a time to build, a time to weep and a time to laugh, a time to mourn and a time to dance...'

[Ecclesiastes 3:1-4]

"I will open up the floor for people who wish to say a few words; Ms. McCubbin, you're up," the Pastor said.

"Good morning, everyone! Thank you all for coming to pay your respects. This is a very difficult time for me and my family, but we must stay strong. As it states in the bible:

'Oh, that my words were written! Oh, that they were inscribed in a book! That they were engraved on a rock with an iron pen and lead, forever! For I know that my Redeemer lives, And He shall stand at last on the earth; and after my skin is destroyed, this I know, that in my flesh I shall see God, whom I shall see for myself, and my eyes shall behold, and not another. How my heart yearns within me!'

[Job 19:23-27]

"I know my daughter and my grandchildren are safe in heaven with Jesus and all of our ancestors. Because it is written: 'Jesus said to her, "I am the resurrection and the life. The one who believes in me will live, even though they die.'

[John 3:25]

"I want to leave you with this quote:

'God is our hope and strength, a very present help in trouble.

'Therefore, will we not fear, though the earth be moved, and though the hills be carried into the midst of the sea.

'Though the waters thereof rage and swell, and though the mountains shake at the tempest of the same. 'There is a river, the streams whereof make glad the city of God, the holy place of the tabernacle of the Most-Highest.

'God is in the midst of her, therefore shall she not be removed; God shall help her, and that right early. 'Be still then and know that I am God; I will be exalted among the nations, and I will be exalted in the earth.

'The Lord of hosts is with us; the God of Jacob is our refuge.'

[Psalms 46]

Everyone in the room cried and hugged one another. Jena's mother walked away from the podium, Jamie and Jena stood up; and walked towards the microphone.

"Good morning, everyone! My name is Jeneration, and I'm

387

Asia's older sister. I haven't been here for the past few years, but the love I have for my sister never wavered. I just wished I could have been able to say goodbye to her, my niece and nephew. I am sorry!" said Jena.

Jena stepped away from the podium and put her hands over her face. Jamie stepped in front of the microphone and wiped tears from his eyes with his handkerchief. "I don't know if I can top what everyone else has said, but I guess I have to try! Good morning, everyone! My name is Jamie McClymont; Asia, Calvin, and Tatiana were my wife and kids. This is the hardest thing that I have ever done in my life.

"I hope no one in this room will ever have to bury their spouses, and young children prematurely. It's taking every fiber of my being not to have a nervous breakdown. But, like Mrs. Melba said, we have to be strong enough for each other.

"Asia was the strongest woman I knew, besides my mother, and Mrs. Melba.

"I remember when we first met as kids; my father had just passed away, and she was my rock! She was always a nurturing person; so, there was no surprise that she became a medical doctor. All respect due to Mr. Easy, her father; who's a healer/doctor as well.

"Asia used to come to the house so much that my mother raised an eyebrow. She pulled me to the side one day and told me: "Bwoy yuh beta marry dat girl wen yuh get older; she checks fi yuh!

"Asia was more than my lover, she was my confidant, my wife, the mother of my children...

"Asia was my friend...

"And I miss my friend! To my two angels, I know that you're in heaven telling God how to do his job. Just know that daddy loves and misses you too!" said Jamie.

Jamie stepped away from the podium, and The Pastor walked up to him and hugged him.

"Very well put son, we are all here for you, young brother!

Now, we're going to close, and if anyone is going to the cemetery; the address is on the program, or just follow the funeral procession. Anyone who isn't interested; there will be food and beverages served at Asia's mother's house across town in the Bronx after the burial. Thank you all for coming!" said The Pastor, and wiped tears from his eyes.

Everyone stood up and walked out of the room. Jamie, his mother, and Asia's immediate family stayed back to view Asia, and the kids one last time before they closed the casket. One by one everyone said their last goodbyes. Tiye and Amanirenas gave Tatiana and Calvin each one of their favorite toys to keep. "We're sorry that we never met before, but here cousins, take these with you to heaven; if you get lonely you will have something to play with," the twins said simultaneously.

The funeral director closed down each casket one by one, Jamie and the rest of the immediate family looked on with anguish and despair.

The limousine ride to Kensico Cemetery, in Valhalla, New York; was a somber tone. No one spoke a word the entire time. The twins were asleep on Jena's lap, and Mr. McCubbin held his wife in his arms the entire ride there. Mrs. McCubbin constantly wiped tears from her cheeks with a Kleenex. Jamie looked out the window of the limousine as Mrs. McClymont slept on his shoulder.

The thirty minutes' drive seemed like it took forever. Everyone in the limo got out one by one and stretched. "Look at all of those cars! Are all of them here for Titi Asia and our cousins?" asked Tiye.

Jamie looked around, saw at least fifty vehicles parked along the access road in the Cemetery.

Jamie held the twins' hands and walked them to the burial site. The pastor had already set up his podium and an array of beautiful floral arrangements. "Everyone please come closer, there is no need to be fearful. These graves are assigned for one! I wish to say a final prayer:

'Almighty God, in your great love!

389

Almighty God, in your great love

Almighty God, in your great love
you crafted us by your hand and breathed life into us by your Spirit.

'Although we became a rebellious people, you did not abandon us to our sin. In your tender mercy you sent your son to restore in us your image.

'In obedience to your will he gave up his life for us, bearing in his body our sins on the cross.

'By your mighty power you raised him from the grave and exalted him to the throne of glory.

'Rejoicing in his victory and trusting in your promise to make alive all who turn to Christ, we commend N to your mercy, and we join with all your faithful people and the whole company of heaven in the one unending song of praise: glory and wisdom and honor be to our God forever and ever.

Amen.

'Ashes to ashes, dust to dust; In the sweat of thy face shalt thou eat bread, till thou return unto the ground; for out of it wast thou taken for dust thou art, and unto dust shalt thou return.

[Genesis 3:19]

Everyone threw dirt that they picked up from the ground, and flowers on top of the caskets as they lowered them down into the ground. The gravediggers filled up the holes with dirt. It started pouring down rain, and everyone stood there peacefully until the graves were completely filled with dirt.

Chapter 18:

Reciprocity

The limo driver was beside himself with grief; the lives that Asia touched, was beyond measure. Jamie stood by the gravesite of his family alone, paying his last respects. One of the gravediggers walked over to Jamie and cleared his throat. "Excuse me sir! Are you going to take the rest of these floral arrangements; or do you want us to dispose of them?" asked the gravedigger.

"Do what you want to do with them! I will take the portraits of my family though!" replied Jamie.

Jamie took each of the enlarged photos of Asia, Calvin, and Tatiana, off the stands one by one. Then he walked over to the pastor, shook his hand and sighed. "I want to thank you for doing this; your sermon was beautiful," Jamie said.

"No need to thank me son; it was my pleasure, Jamie!" said The Pastor.

The pastor walked down to the limousine with Jamie. Jena and the twins were waiting outside of the limo for Jamie to come.

"Uncle Jamie! Come on; we saved a seat for you," Tiye said, as Jamie approached the limo.

Jamie saw the limo driver wiping tears from his eyes and raised his eyebrows. "You know conditions are critical when a stranger is affected by it," Jamie said.

"Nah Jamie, you don't understand; we grew up with Byron, he went to school with Asia. My dad is his Godfather; he's no stranger, he's family!" replied Jena.

"Oh wow! Okay Jena!"

"Pastor, are you coming to the house?" asked Jena, as she hugged The Pastor.

"Jena, honestly, I would love to as much as I love your mother's cooking. But I can't; I have a previous engagement," The Pastor replied.

Everyone got inside the limousine, The Pastor waved goodbye to them as Byron drove back to Melba's house in the Bronx for food. The ride back was a bit livelier than the ride up to the cemetery. Byron turned on the radio, and a Bob Marley, and the Wailers song was on:

"You're gonna lively up yourself, (lively up yourself), and don't be no drag!

You, lively up yourself, (lively up yourself), Oh, reggae is another bag!"

"Tun up dat tune deh driva!" said Mrs. McClymont, and Mr. McCubbin in unison.

Everybody began reciting the lyrics as the song blared in the limousine. Music has a way of making you feel Irie, at all the right moments. Song after song played, and all the hurt, and pain seemed to be a thing of the past. Jamie, and his family, got the closure that they needed to move on with their lives. Asia, Calvin, and Tatiana got a proper burial; and they can rest in peace.

The limousine pulled up to Jena's parents building, and people were already outside, eating plates of food, and drinking. Melba's sisters were at the house, and they prepared the food, so people could get food as they arrived from the funeral.

Jamie and the family got out of the limo and walked inside the building. On their way to the apartment, they passed by people in the lobby eating food. After they entered the apartment, Melba's sister Beatrice ushered everyone over to the kitchen table. They sat down and started chowing down on the food that she prepared for them before they came.

"Damn BB! You put your foot in it!" said Mrs. McCubbin.

"Thanks Melba, I learned from the best!" replied Beatrice.

Everyone at the dinner table continued to enjoy their food, as everybody else inside the apartment; talked amongst themselves. People came into the apartment sporadically to offer their condolences, and to get a second plate to take with them as they left. As the night went on, less and less people were left at the apartment. Jena, and Felicia, started clearing off the kitchen table, and washing up the plates, glasses, pots, pans, and utensils.

Jamie, and Mr. McCubbin, were sitting in the living room smoking weed. Jamie inhaled the smoke from the blunt, covered his mouth and coughed.

"Mi memba wen Asia first bring yuh cum yah, an mi tell mi wife; how comes dat bwoy deh so fat. But yuh come inside, an yuh did hab manners; very respectful. Yuh did win we ova! Jamie, mi glad seh yuh did deh inna Asia's life. Mi glad seh yuh ah mi son in law. An dat can neva change," Mr. McCubbin said.

"Mr. Easy, that means a lot to me, thank you for your support all these years. I love you and Mrs. Melba very much, Big up yuhself!" replied Jamie.

Jamie sat there mellowed out from the effects of the marijuana, and Mrs. McClymont walked into the living room, put her hands on her hips with her mouth wide open. "Bwoy yuh ask if yuh can bun weed in front ah mi? Eeh! Yuh nuh too old fi mi tek mi belt off an beat yuh!" exclaimed Mrs. McClymont.

Jamie, and everyone laughed, and Mrs McClymont walked over to him, and hugged him, then kissed him on his cheek. "Ah joke mi ah mek! Mi glad tuh si seh yuh ah full-joy yuhself!"

"Mi kno mummy, mi luv yuh tuh!"

Jena, Felicia, Nana, the twins, Jamie, and his mother; all said their goodbyes, and left the apartment after a long day. It all seemed so surreal, starting with the terrible news of Asia, and the kid's deaths, to their burials. Felicia offered to drive, so Jena could rest. But Jena stayed awake, so she could give Felicia directions back to the house. Nana, and the twins got some much needed shut eye, due to the early start of the day.

They made it back to New Jersey sooner than they anticipated. Felicia, pulled in the driveway, and Jena turned around and nudged the twins. "Ladies! We're home now; c'mon get up, go inside, and prepare for bed," she said.

Nana, and the twins woke up, as Jena unlocked the front door. They both walked inside, took off their shoes, and trotted upstairs to their rooms like they were prized thoroughbreds at the Meadowlands.

"Ladies, please no running!" said Jena.

Felicia helped Nana get out of the car and helped her inside the house. "Whew! Felicia gurl, what could I do without you! I'm so tired, I'm gonna go upstairs, climb into bed, and sleep until next weekend," Jena said

"We're always gonna be here for you, and the twins Jena; we love you!" replied Nana, and they all laughed, and Nana slapped her knee with her hand.

"We love you too!" said Jena.

She kissed Nana on the forehead and hugged her tight. Jena sauntered upstairs, went inside her bedroom, and closed the door.

The next day, Jena woke up earlier than usual; so, she could make a special thank you breakfast for Nana, and Felicia. While she was inside the kitchen preparing food; the phone rang. Jena turned down the burner on the stove, picked up the receiver and held it to her ear with her shoulder. "Hello, good morning," Jena said.

"Hey, good morning, Jena. This is Mr. Walker; how are you doing today?" replied Mr. Walker.

"Good morning, Mr. Walker. I'm doing well, how is everything going down there at the office?"

"Not very good Jena, that's why I am calling you. Our client is the prime suspect in the murder of his family. He is facing three life sentences, for a triple murder he didn't commit. The dilemma is the evidence that we have thus far, proving his innocence; is circumstantial. Could you please come in Monday morning and help us figure out this case; our clients' life depends on it."

"Since you put it that way Mr. Walker; I guess I have no choice. I'll be there bright and early Monday morning."

Jena hung up the phone and continued preparing breakfast. Tiye, and Amanirenas, walked downstairs moments later, and saw Jena setting the table with place mats, utensils, and glassware.

"Good morning momma, it smells good in here," the twins said, as they sat on their usual chairs around the kitchen table.

"Good morning, ladies did you two have a goodnight sleep?" replied Jena.

"Ah huh! We did," the twins said in unison.

"I dreamt about being at a carnival with Papi, and he won me a huge teddy bear!" said Tiye.

"Wow! Was your sister there with you Tiye?" asked Jena.

"Ah huh! Papi bought her a ginormous pink cotton candy on a stick. Around her mouth, and her nose was pink; she looked like a clown. Amanirenas, got it all over her hands; her fingers were stuck together, like a duck with webbed feet."

Nana, and Felicia, came downstairs as Tiye was telling Jena about her dream. "Good morning, everyone, I could smell those grits and eggs from upstairs," Nana said.

Nana sat around the table and Felicia, kissed the twins on the top of their heads, and began helping Jena, serve the plates of food to everyone else sitting at the table.

"Good morning, Jena, you were out like a light last night. By the time Nana, and I got upstairs; we could hear you snoring through the door," Felicia said.

Felicia grabbed the pitcher and poured out some orange juice for everyone; before she sat down at the table. Jena, walked over to her, and poured Felicia, out a steamy cup of coffee; then sat down at the opposite side of the kitchen table.

"Let us bow our heads and say grace:

"Bless us, and this food oh Lord, we thank you for these gifts that we're about to receive from thy bounty through Christ our Lord and savior. Amen," Nana said.

After everyone unclasped their hands, they all passed around the breakfast items to one another at the table. The sounds of the silver ware clanging and scratching the plates drowned out them chewing their food. "Hey Felicia, my boss called me this morning, and asked me if I could come in tomorrow morning to help with a case. Could you, and Nana, watch the twins until I get back?" asked Jena, then she took a sip of coffee and used a napkin to wipe her mouth.

"Sure, Nana, and I will be delighted!" replied Felicia.

After breakfast, the twins cleared the table, put the dishes in the sink and turned on the faucet. "I am so proud of those girls; they're so mature, and well behaved. Most kids their ages are so bratty, I hope what happened to your sister, niece, and nephew doesn't have a negative effect on them; it would be a shame," Nana said.

"Nana, I hope and pray that won't happen to either of them," Jena replied, as she wiped off the kitchen table and chairs.

The rest of the Sunday morning, and afternoon were uneventful. Jena, and the rest of the ladies in the house; just lounged around in the living room, watching various reruns of 70s sitcoms on television. Around 6 pm, after noshing on fruit, cheese and crackers.

"Hey Felicia, have you ever had New York style pizza?" asked Jena.

"Jena, not only have I not had New York style pizza; I've never had pizza in my life!" replied Felicia.

"Really! I'm going to order a pizza pie from Giovanni's pizzeria."

"Okay, it sounds like a plan."

"Nana, would you like to have some pizza?" asked Jena.

"Baby girl, I'd rather eat spaghetti and meatballs," Nana replied.

Jena, got up from the recliner, and walked over to the phone in the kitchen from the living room. She took Giovanni's pizzeria's take-out menu from the refrigerator and dialed the number off it. The phone rang twice, and someone answered: "Hello, Giovanni's pizzeria; what would you like to order?"

"Hey Giuseppe, this is Jena, I want to order an extra-large, half meat lovers, half Hawaiian pizza, and a small spaghetti, and meatball dinner," Jena replied.

"Hey Jena, my father, and I are sorry for your loss, how are you, and your family holding up? We saw it on the news last week."

"Thanks Giuseppe, my family and I are doing better, considering the situation; thanks for your concern."

"Okay Jena, I will send over your order in about thirty minutes; take care."

Jena hung up the phone and went upstairs to use the bathroom; to make room for dinner. Those grits, eggs, and sausage she made for breakfast was coming down the bend like a racehorse passing by the fifth furlong. Before she knew it, the doorbell rang. "Oh, my goodness, that was quick. It must be a slow day," Jena said.

Jena, finished up, flushed the toilet, washed her hands, sprayed some air freshener, and walked downstairs. Felicia, and Tiye, were standing at the door holding the food. She got to the door and took out her purse. "Hi Bobby, how much do I owe you for the food?" asked Jena.

He put his palms up out in front of him and shook his head. "Mr. Giovanni told me to let you know that the food is on the house," Bobby said.

"Thank you, Bobby, tell Mr. Giovanni that I really appreciate it," Jena replied.

Jena closed the front door, then Felicia, and Tiye, brought the food to the kitchen table. Jena took out a paper plate that came with the food and put a slice of pizza on it for Felicia. "Here gurl, you get the first slice; tell us what you think," Jena said.

Felicia took the plate from Jena, and bit into the slice like an alligator chomp into its prey.

"Mmm, this tastes awesome Jena, I didn't think cured meat, tomato sauce, and mozzarella cheese; would taste so good together," Felicia replied.

Jena smiled and shared a plate of food for Nana; as the twins, helped themselves to pizza. Everyone enjoyed their meal and continued watching television.

Jena looked over at the clock in the kitchen and saw that it was fifteen minutes of nine. "Oh, my goodness, look at the time. I have to get to bed; I have an early meeting tomorrow morning." Jena, got up, walked upstairs to her bedroom, and closed the door. She got underneath the covers and nestled into the mattress.

The alarm echoed throughout Jena's room like the sounds of a rooster on a farm at the crack of dawn. When Jena turned off the alarm, it was 6:02 am; she got up and walked directly into the shower to bathe. Afterwards, she got out of the shower, walked back into her room, and took out her pants suit she planned to wear for work.

Standing there in her birthday suit, Jena, admired the sight of the sun rising over the horizon through her bedroom window. She relished the moments the sun rays took to creep along the carpet in her room towards her, then she basked in all its glory as the sunshine glistened over her wet skin. Feeling fully energized, Jena, quickly got ready for the day, and made her way to the kitchen to put on a pot of coffee. Much to her amazement, the coffee maker was already percolating. Feeling delighted and appreciative, Jena, poured out a cup of coffee, and drank all of it before leaving for work.

Jena arrived at the lawyer's office ten minutes early. She got out of the car, locked the doors with her transponder, and walked inside the building. Jena whispered good morning to Gertrude, the receptionist, at the front desk because she was on a call. Gertrude, kindly replied to Jena, with a greeting of her own; then she pointed Jena, to conference room three, as she walked by. There were a team of lawyers inside the room, mulling over the case files.

Jena knocked on the glass door, Mr. Walker, looked up, and welcomed her inside with a come-hither motion of his left hand. Jena opened the door, and he pointed at an open seat for Jena to take. "Gerald, what do we know so far about our client?" asked Mr. Walker.

Mr. Walker got up, tucked his tie inside his silk grey pinstripe vest and paced around the table as his team read from the case files.

"He was happily married to his wife of fifteen years. He was a father of two. There was no trace evidence on his person, linking him to the scene of the crime. There were no defensive wounds on his arms or face. There was no sign of false entry; so, the killer had access to the house. And the police have yet to find the murder weapon.

"Mr. Walker, we also know that the family was bludgeoned to death with a heavy object. All of the bodies were found in different areas of the house. So, the killer took them out, one by one. The only alibi that our client has is that he was at a baseball game at the time of the gruesome murders of his family," Gerald said.

"Thanks Gerald, our client, is facing three counts of murder in the first degree. The Prosecutors are seeking three consecutive life sentences. If we can't substantiate his whereabouts, our client will be up shits creek, without a paddle. So, brainstorm guys; what aren't we seeing?" said Mr. Walker.

Jena sat down on a chair and opened the case file. Mr. Walker leaned over the table with his palms pressed so firm on it that you could see the whites of his knuckles. Jena skimmed through the documents, saw the baseball tickets, and her face light up like a light bulb. "Did he use a credit card to purchase these tickets?" asked Jena.

"No, they were bought with cash," Mr. Walker replied.

"Did anyone watch the recording of the game? These were great seats; they were seated right behind the dugout. The recording of the game would show him, and his guest in the stands. If he did indeed attend this baseball game; it would exonerate him of any wrongdoing," Jena said.

Mr. Walker pressed the conference call button on the phone. "Gertrude, bring over the monitor, and the video of the game into the conference room III," he said. As the game played out, sure enough, at the bottom of the 3rd inning, there he was, catching a pop fly ball with his baseball glove.

Mr. Walker, and the other lawyers looked at the footage with glee. Everybody in the room cheered in excitement like it was the winning shot made by Michael Jordan, in game 6 of the 1997 NBA finals.

"This is exactly the smoking gun we were looking for. Jena, you're a heaven sent! We've been here racking our brains over this evidence, and here comes Ms. McCubbin, the new kid on the block, in the 25th hour with a new set of eyes, straight out of left field like Ricky "Wild thing" Vaughn, from that movie, "Major league." Jena, you blew this case wide open. This meeting is adjourned; Gertrude, get me the prosecutor's office," Mr. Walker said.

The rest of the lawyers closed their folders and high five each other. They banged on the conference table with their clenched fists and open palms. Then they all chanted the lyrics to the song, "Wild thing," by The Troggs: "Wild thing, (doo, doo, dum, dum, doo, doo.) You make my heart sing. (doo, doo, dum, dum, doo, doo.) You make everything groovy. (Doo, doo, dum, dum, doo, doo.) Wild thing…"

Everyone patted Jena on the back, for a job well done as they left the conference room. Jena closed her folder and walked towards the entrance.

Mr. Walker held the receiver to his ear and whispered, "Good job Jena" and he extended his hand for Jena to shake.

She shook his hand and smiled as she exited the conference room. Jena got into her car and drove off feeling like she accomplished something worthwhile. Jena pulled into her driveway behind a brand-new Toyota Rav4, parked close to the garage. "Who the hell is this parked in front of my house?" said Jena.

She slammed her car door and opened the front door. Jena walked inside the house with the intentions of taking on whoever had the Cajones, to park in her driveway without her knowledge.

"Hello, I'm home; Tiye, Amanirenas, Felicia, Nana! Anyone know whose car is that outside?" asked Jena.

She looked over into the living room and saw Jamie sitting on the couch. "Oh, hi big head, is that your new car?" said Jena.

"Hi Jena, nah, it's a loaner from the dealer, until my Camry is ready," Jamie replied.

I thought it was some stranger in here," Jena said as she took off her shoes by the front door. She walked over to Jamie in the living room and kissed him on the cheek. "How long have you been here for Jamie?" asked Jena.

"About twenty minutes ago, the twins told me that you went into the office early this morning. Are you back to work already?" replied Jamie.

"Yes, my boss called me yesterday, and asked me to come in today. What brings you to Jersey?"

"I received a call from Claude, a couple of days ago; I almost hung up on him. But I'm glad I didn't, he advised me to sue the companies of Marques, Darrelle, and Raheem, since they're responsible for my family's deaths. So, he told me about a lawyer friend of his named Gerald Johnston, who he claimed is a shark in the courtroom. I am supposed to be meeting him out here at a restaurant called Giovanni's. Do you know him?"

"Yes, he's a big-time lawyer over at the firm that I work for. You're in good hands Jamie, he knows his stuff; anyone out of that firm is fit to be a lead on any case. What time is your meeting with him?"

"I'm supposed to meet him in a half hour; he told me that he just got out of an important meeting at the office."

"Yeah Jamie, that's where I'm coming from; what a coincidence. The place is right down the street, so you have about fifteen minutes before you have to go."

"How's the slices there Jena?"

"Great! I just ordered from there last night. Tell Giuseppe, that you're my brother-in-law; he will take care of you."

Jena got up, and went inside the kitchen where Nana, and Felicia, was preparing dinner. Hey Nana, hey Felicia," said Jena, as she hugged and kissed them before she washed her hands in the sink. "What are you ladies cooking in here?"

"Hey gurl, we just made some baked chicken, green beans,

401

mac and cheese, and cornbread," Felicia replied.

"That sounds great Felicia, I smell something else coming from the oven. Nana is that your famous apple cobbler I smell?" asked Jena.

"Yes Jena, you're like a bloodhound. you can't get anything passed you, and that nose of yours," Nana replied.

Jena grabbed a banana from off the table and walked back into the living room. "Jamie, after you finished your meeting with Mr. Johnston, come back for dinner," Jena said.

"Okay Jena, I will." Jamie got up, walked towards the door, and put on his shoes. "Hey Jena, you blocked me in," Jamie replied.

"Take my car, just don't scratch it Big head."

Jamie took Jena's car keys off a hook by the door and left. He got inside the car, backed out of the driveway, and drove two miles down the block to Giovanni's pizzeria. Jamie walked inside and looked around the restaurant. Jamie saw a waitress and walked over to her. "Hey, excuse me, do you know of a Gerald Johnston, waiting for Jamie McClymont, by any chance?" asked Jamie.

"Yeah sure, he's over there in the booth," the waitress replied.

"Thank you!" Jamie, walked over to the table, and leaned over the table. "Gerald Johnston?" asked Jamie.

"Yes, Jamie McClymont, I presume. Pleased to meet you; Jean Jacque, told me so much about you. I am sorry for your loss, and I will do everything in my power to get the restitution that you deserve," Gerald replied.

"Thank you, I appreciate it."

"Please sit down, what are you having?"

"I'll have a glass of wine. I've been off the painkillers for a couple of days now; I think it's time to celebrate. I'm getting closer to a semblance of normalcy each day that passes by."

"Okay great, hey, excuse me waiter, could we please get a bottle of Sassicaia San Guido, and two glasses. Thank you," Gerald

said.

"Right away sir!" replied the waiter.

"So, Mr. McClymont, before we get into the nitty-gritty; how are you holding up?" asked Gerald.

"Please, call me Jamie, Mr. McClymont, was my father. I am doing better as each day passes by," Jamie replied.

"Great, so, what we have here, is a civil suit; so, we won't be in a courtroom per say; we will conduct what we call a deposition. Since Jean-Jacque, will retain ownership of these companies; the lawyers that will be present at the deposition, would only be representing the company as a formality. So, we're seeking 300 million in compensation for pain, and suffering; 150 for Asia, and 75 for each child."

"Yes, that sounds about right, but you know, there's no amount of money that could silence my pain or bring my family back to me. Only time could heal all these holes left in my heart."

"That's very true Jamie, but it's a start. Of course, I will be waiving my retainer, I will be doing this pro-bono."

Jamie, leaned back in his seat, and sipped the glass of wine that was brought over by the waiter. "When will this deposition be?" asked Jamie.

"I set up the meeting for 9:00 Monday morning. And since there would be no dispute from the companies; you would receive the check for 300 million dollars then. How's that sound?" replied Gerald.

"It sounds too good to be true."

"Trust me on this one, there's no gimmicks Jamie, you have my word. Ask anyone about me, my reputation precedes me."

At that moment, a large cheese pizza was brought to the table by the waiter. "Please Jamie, you have to try a slice of Giovanni's, famous pizza; it's the best pizza in the state."

Jamie, and Gerald, ate their slices like it was their last meal before surrendering themselves into police custody, to serve time after sentencing.

"Gerald, I am pleasantly surprised, this pizza is pretty good," Jamie said, with his mouth half full of semi chewed pizza.

While they were enjoying their food, a man wearing a white apron walked over to their table and threw a towel over his left shoulder. "Excuse me sir, my name is Giuseppe, my father, and I own this restaurant, and I am sorry to interrupt you while you enjoy your meal. But aren't you the man that met in the horrific accident a few weeks ago? The accident in Queens that killed a doctor, and her two children?" asked Giuseppe.

"Yes, that would be me," Jamie replied.

"So, you're Jena's brother-in-law then?"

"Yeah, she just informed me how great the food was here; I concur." Jamie raised the last slice in the air like he was about to propose a toast at a wedding; then, he bit into it.

"Okay, great, well, I am glad you enjoyed it. I will get you guys each a pie to go on the house. Any family of Jena's is a family of ours. My condolences to you and your family."

After Giuseppe brought over the pies, and Gerald paid the bill, he and Jamie walked out of the restaurant.

"So, Jamie, 9:00 am sharp Monday morning?!" asked Gerald. He extended his right hand for Jamie to shake it as he held his briefcase in the other.

Jamie stuck out his right hand, shook Gerald's hand. "I will see you then Gerald, I appreciate you doing this for me," Jamie replied.

"That's not necessary; any friend of Jean-Jacque is a friend of mine." Jamie put the pizza on the front seat and drove out of the parking lot. A few minutes later, Jamie arrived at Jena's house less than it took to go down to the restaurant. Jamie got out of the car, grabbed the pizza box, and put it in his car.

Before he could ring the doorbell, Tiye opened the front door, raised both her hands above her head and jumped over the threshold. "Boo, did I scare you Uncle Jamie?"

"Yes Tiye, I was terrified."

Jamie, hugged Tiye, and walked inside, took off his shoes, and put Jena's keys back on the hook. "Honey, I'm home! I always wanted to do that."

Jena, Nana, and Felicia were standing in the living room in front of the television watching the news. "Breaking news: this just in, prominent New York City judge Aaron Black, has been arrested for his role in a statewide sex trafficking ring. He will be charged as a co-conspirator alongside Rodolfo Meléndez (former mayor of New York City,) Arthur Rosenbaum, (venture capitalist,) several prominent politicians, and businessmen in the tristate area. More on this story as it develops."

"This shit is deeper than we thought it was Jamie. Claude, tried to warn me, I wonder if he was privy to this nugget before news broke, Jena said.

Jena, walked over to the phone, and dialed the number to Jean-Jacque's room at the hospital. The phone rang a few times, then Jean-Jacque, picked up. "Hello!"

"Claude, have you seen the news about Aaron Black, the judge?" asked Jena.

"No, but mayor Velasquez, called earlier to brief me of what was going to happen. The FBI might try to link her to this as a co-conspirator too," Jean-Jacque replied.

"What about you Claude, you've been working with them for over a decade."

"I can't discuss this over the phone Jena, but I will be getting discharged from the hospital on Monday; I will contact you when I get out."

Jean-Jacque hung up the phone on Jena, and she stood there holding the receiver in her hand, frozen in a state of shock.

Chapter 19:

From whence they came

Amid everything that has transpired so far, Jean Jacque surviving several attempts on his life; is nothing short of miraculous. A team of specialists entered Jean-Jacque's room, led by Dr. Patel. (Knock, knock) "Good morning, Mr. Cadet, it's Dr. Patel, how are you feeling today?" asked Dr. Patel

"Come in Dr. Patel, I'm feeling great this morning," Jean-Jacque replied.

"Well, all the tests that my colleagues and I have conducted, have come back negative. It's amazing how quick you have recovered."

"Dr. Patel, it's mind over matter. I owe it all to martial arts training."

"Either that or mechanical engineering, the van took the brunt of the collision. Anyway, Mr. Cadet, you are free to go. Here are your discharge papers and the prescriptions for the pain. Enjoy the rest of your day. I hope I don't see you in this capacity again."

"I couldn't have done it without you and your staff's help Dr. Patel."

Dr. Patel closed the door, and the phone rang. Jean-Jacque picked up the receiver and put it at his ear.

"Good morning," he said.

"Claude, what up! It's Jamie," he replied.

"Hey Jamie, how was the deposition?"

"It went exactly the way you said it would. Gerald Johnston was able to get me 300 million dollars from Marques, Darrelle, and Raheem's companies. When Mr. Johnston first told me how much he could get me, it sounded too good to be true. I am looking at a check for that amount, as we speak."

"I am glad Jamie, you deserve it, I considered that you received double that amount, but I figure that it would be better for us to earn triple together."

"Claude, having a family is priceless. A month ago, I felt like I was worth ten times that amount. Truth be told, I hate you for taking them from me, Claude. Whether you were complicit in any wrongdoing or not, you were driving the van. Only time will tell if these wounds would heal enough for me to forgive you. Even if the day comes when I do, I will never forget."

Jamie hung up the phone on Jean-Jacque and he slumped down in bed. A single tear streamed down his face, until he saw acting Mayor Marisol Velasquez on the news. He turned up the volume with the remote and stood in front of the television.

"Kim Lee here at Gracie mansion and the FBI took acting mayor Marisol Velasquez, in for questioning. Since this investigation is ongoing, there's not much we can report. We will fill you in as the news develops, back to you Bill."

"Damn, not you too Marisol! It's only a matter of time before they come knocking on my door. I have to see my parents before everything boils over. I haven't seen my parents since I started The Helping Hand Initiative. I have not had my mother's cooking for far too long. I hope it's not too late for me to travel back home to Haiti. Let me call Jena, and Blossom, to see if they would allow the kids to travel with me."

Jean-Jacque dialed Jena's number, but the phone rang until her answering machine picked up. He hung up the phone, dialed Margot's number, and it rang a few times.

"Hello," Margot said.

"Hey Blossom, I am planning a trip to Haiti, would you let Sebastian join me?" said Jean-Jacque.

"Claude, have you been watching the news? How in God's name, are you considering traveling at a time like this? You're still a patient in the hospital, for God's sake."

"Blossom, trust me, I won't be implicated in all of this, the federal government doesn't want, nor do they need anything from me. There have been attempts on my life, and all those people who were responsible, are either dead, or in custody. Please, I want my parents to meet Sebastian. I want Jena and the twins to travel with us as well."

"I would have to travel with you and our son this time. The last time I allowed you to take Sebastian; your so-called friends kidnapped you, and he was left for dead."

"Great Blossom, I will make the arrangements, as soon as I get home, I'll call you with the itinerary."

Jean-Jacque hung up the phone, and he heard familiar voices in the hallway. The door opened abruptly, and he saw dozens of balloons, a floral arrangement, and a familiar face poked through the guise of the balloons. "Jean, cousin, how are you feeling? I am sorry that Latrice and I couldn't visit sooner. We have been swamped with work these past few weeks," Patrice said.

"It's okay, Patrice, better late than never. The doctor just discharged me from the hospital, so you wonderful ladies came just in time," Jean-Jacque replied

Latrice, Patrice, and Jean Jacque walked out of his hospital room to the nurse's station. The nurse Lauren was waiting there with a wheelchair for him. "Now, you know we're going to miss you, Mr. Cadet. Please take care of yourself, come back to visit us after you recover," nurse Lauren said.

"Thank you, nurse Lauren; I am going to take things slow; I know the road to recovery is a long one," Jean-Jacque replied.

Jean Jacque sat down in the wheelchair, and Patrice pushed him to the elevator. The elevator doors opened after Latrice pressed the down button, and they entered inside. Latrice pressed the P button, and the movement of the elevator startled Jean-Jacque. The elevator stopped, the doors opened, and Patrice pushed Jean Jacque in the wheelchair out of it to their car.

"Latrice, with all of the major players in the program now in custody, do you think the FBI will come after me?" asked Jean-Jacque.

"There's no way for us to know Jean, the only way to know for sure is if the FBI flip Marisol, and she gives you up. Former mayor Rodolfo Meléndez, has been in custody for some time now, and I highly doubt that Arthur Rosenbaum will say anything to them about you either. They both have everything to lose, and nothing to gain. The only one of those four you need to worry about, is Judge Aaron Black," Latrice said.

Patrice drove to their loft and pulled into the garage. Latrice attempted to help Jean Jacque out of the car, but he declined the offer. "I have to do this by myself Latrice, that's the only way to really start rehabilitation," Jean-Jacque said.

Latrice stepped back and watched as Jean Jacque struggled to exit the car. After he finally got out of the car, Jean-Jacque looked up at the staircase, and sighed. Patrice opened the elevator doors, and smirked, "Over here 'Billy goat,' you're not ready to climb that mountain just yet," Patrice said.

Jean-Jacque, Patrice and Latrice, rode the elevator to their floor, and Latrice pulled open the doors that led them into their apartment. Patrice helped Jean Jacque out of the elevator, Latrice turned on the light, and the television. The news was on and covering the trial of former mayor Rodolfo Meléndez and the opening statement for his defense.

"All rise, Judge Lolita Smith presiding," The bailiff said. Everyone sat down after the Judge sat down on the bench.

The defense attorney stood up and walked up to the stand. "What we have here is a classic case of, 'who done it.' Mayor Rodolfo Meléndez, was accused of leading a crime syndicate, that preyed on the innocence of boys and girls, as young as thirteen years old. Mayor Meléndez was arrested and held without bond for crimes he didn't commit. I understand the severity of the crime he's accused of, but mayor Rodolfo Meléndez is innocent. I hope that by the end of this trial, you twelve in the jury would find my client innocent," he said.

"Kim Lee here with channel 10 news, outside the courtroom of the trial of former mayor Rodolfo Meléndez. His defense just finished their opening statement, and FBI agents are walking inside the courtroom behind me with acting mayor, Marisol Velasquez. I wonder if the prosecutors subpoenaed her so they could put her on the stand. Who knows for sure if the information she might have pertaining to this case; would help or hurt the former Mayor? We will find out soon enough; back to you Bill," she said.

Jean-Jacque shook his head in disbelief, as he sat on the couch looking at the news, as Marisol was being escorted inside the courtroom by the FBI. "Patrice, what do I make of this cousin? It's only a matter of time before they come looking for me," Jean-Jacque said.

"Jean, trust me, Marisol Velasquez won't incriminate herself or say a word about you. Her freedom and credibility depend on it. Relax, and focus on your rehab," Patrice replied.

Jean-Jacque reached over the side of the couch, picked up the phone, and redialed Jena's number. "Come on, Jena, please pick up the phone," Jean-Jacque said.

"Hello Claude, Is everything okay with you? I just came home from work, and I checked my messages and saw that you called earlier today," Jena replied.

"Everything's fine, Jena. Would you allow the twins to travel with me to Haiti to visit my parents? Ever since the accident, I had an epiphany that tomorrow isn't promised today. I don't know anything about the twins. I've missed so much of their lives thus far. I promise I won't make anything come in between us ever again."

Jena paused for a moment, then she sighed. "Claude, that sounds like a great idea, but it's bad timing. I just went back to work. This is a new job, and I already had a week off. I don't think my boss is going to be okay with asking for another week off, just so the twins can travel with you to Haiti."

"Jena, I asked Blossom if she would let Sebastian go with me, and she said she would only let him go if she went too. So, she could watch over the twins if you don't trust them to travel with me by themselves."

"Let me think about it Claude; I'll call you back tomorrow."

Jean-Jacque smiled like a Cheshire cat and hung up the phone. Latrice and Patrice looked at him with their eyebrows knitted up and their hands akimbo. "Who was that on the phone? We have

410

not seen you this happy since your high school graduation," the twins said in unison.

"It was Jena, and I think she's going to allow the twins to travel with me to Haiti. ——

"Hey, why don't you two come with me too? I doubt you've been back home since; you first came to America," Jean-Jacque replied.

Latrice looked at Patrice, and they both laughed at the notion. "Jean, we haven't been on vacation since we made partner at the law firm," Latrice said.

"Hold on, Latrice, I think a little 'rest and relaxation' would be good for us. Besides, Jena just helped a client beat a murder rap in one of our cases. The lawyers at the firm can handle things while we're gone," Patrice replied.

"So, it's settled then. Mom and pop will be excited to see all of us. And I bet Uncle Clyde will be happy to see the both of you too," Jean-Jacque said.

News coverage of the trial came back on the television, and the prosecutor called Marisol Velasquez to the stand. She stood there and raised her right hand and placed her left hand on a bible. "Do you plan to tell the truth, the whole truth, and nothing but the truth; so, help you God?" asked The Bailiff.

"Yes!" replied Marisol.

"You may be seated."

The prosecutor stood up, walked up closer to Marisol, and put his hands behind his back. "Good morning, Mayor Velasquez, I have a few questions, and I need some help clarifying some information about 'The program.' Misses' Mayor, did you attend Fordham University on a full academic scholarship?" asked the prosecutor.

"Yes, I did, I graduated summa cum laude," Marisol replied.

"Your parents must-have been extremely proud of you and your achievements."

"I believe that they were, academics weren't top priority for them; they just wanted me to find a good paying job. My parents were immigrants from Guatemala, they sent home 20% of the money they earned to keep family members out of poverty. They always planned on going back to Guatemala after their retirement. They didn't plan on planting roots here in America."

"So, they took your ambitions to achieve higher learning as an insult?"

"I wouldn't go so far as to say that, but they worried about the incurred costs of college."

"How did you become so ambitious? I mean, your father was a day laborer, and your mother a domestic worker," the prosecutor asked.

"My parents may not have had an ivy league education, but they encouraged me to become more educated than they were. They never wanted me to struggle," Marisol replied.

"So, is that why you joined the program!"

"Objection your honor, prosecution is leading the witness," the defense attorney said.

"Your honor, I just want to show how these young unsuspecting students get lured into the program," the prosecutor said.

"Overruled, Ms. Velasquez, please answer the question," the Judge said.

"Yes, getting a good education was the main reason why I joined The Program," Marisol replied.

"Was sex the other reason Ms. Velasquez?" asked the prosecutor.

"Objection your honor, he's badgering the witness, and that's hearsay," the defense attorney said.

"Sustained, please rephrase the question," the Judge said.

"Okay, your honor, Ms. Velasquez, was there any sexual contact between you and the individual that recruited you into The

412

Program? Or did the sexual contact occur between you, and your recruits."

Marisol looked down at her hands and it had droplets of blood on them. She noticed that there was blood dripping down from her nose, so she tilted her head back and the Judge reached over to hand her a Kleenex, and Marisol fainted. Everyone in attendance gasped and the bailiff ran to the stand to her aid. "We need a medic!"

"Court will be in recess until 8 am tomorrow morning," The Judge said and pounded the gavel.

A Paramedic and an EMT ran inside the courtroom with a gurney in tote, directly towards the stand where the bailiff had stabilized Marisol. People in attendance were walking outside of the courtroom as Marisol was being strapped to the gurney.

Jean-Jacque, Latrice, and Patrice had their eyes glued to the television. They were shocked by what just happened to Marisol. "That didn't look good, she has an inoperable brain tumor, I hope and pray it is not as serious as it looked," Jean-Jacque said.

Latrice and Patrice hugged Jean-Jacque, as he sat there with tears cascading down his cheeks. An hour later, the phone rang, and Jean Jacque picked up the phone. "Hello, this is Jean," he said.

"Mr. Cadet, this is Olivia, Marisol Velasquez is in Mt. Sinai hospital, it doesn't look good. I think you should make it down there before it's too late," Olivia said.

Jean-Jacque hung up the phone, got up off the couch, and grabbed his crutches. "Latrice, that was Olivia, my secretary, Marisol is at Mt. Sinai, I have to see her before..."

"Jean, you don't have to say another word, we understand, we will take you to the hospital to see Marisol," Latrice said.

Jean-Jacque and the twins made it downstairs to the parking lot, all three of them got inside the car, and Patrice drove to the hospital where Marisol was admitted an hour earlier. Jean Jacque could not wait until Patrice parked, he hopped out the car, and moved as fast as he could inside the hospital. He approached the information desk and tapped on the counter. "Excuse me, I'm Henri Jean-Jacque…"

"Mr. Cadet, I know who you are, Mayor Velasquez is in room 106."

Jean-Jacque limped down the hallway toward Marisol's room. Olivia and two security guards were standing outside her room when he arrived at room 106.

"How is she doing?" asked Jean-Jacque.

"Mr. Cadet, she's heavily sedated, the doctors say that the tumor is causing swelling on the brain, and there's nothing more they can do," Olivia said as tears welled up in her eyes.

Jean-Jacque put his hand on his head, looked down at his feet, and leaned back on the wall. It didn't matter how hard he tried; he couldn't stop himself from crying. After a moment he looked up and mustered up the strength to go inside Marisol's room. Before he entered the room Jean-Jacque noticed a little boy by Marisol's bedside. "Who's that in there with Marisol?" asked Jean-Jacque.

"Mr. Cadet, that is Marisol's son Dominique," Olivia replied.

Jean-Jacque stared at Olivia, raised his eyebrows, straightened up his posture, and limped inside the room. He cleared his throat and the young boy turned around and faced Jean-Jacque. He was taken aback how much Dominique resembled him. Jean-Jacque regained his composure and cleared his throat. "Hey, how are you feeling?" asked Jean-Jacque.

"Who are you?" replied Dominique.

The young man looked at Jean-Jacque with a blank stare, while tears dripped from his eyes like a leaky faucet. Dominique wiped the tears off his chin and squeezed his mothers' hand.

'What is the correct answer at a time like this? Do I blurt out 'Dominique, I'm your father,' or is a subtle approach more fitting,' Jean-Jacque thought.

"Well, I am the deputy mayor of New York City," Jean-

Jacque replied.

"Oh, okay, my name is Dominique, my mother spoke very highly of you Mr. Cadet. I am pleased to meet you." Dominique put out his hand, and Jean-Jacque shook it.

"You have a very firm handshake young man, please, call me Jean, Mr. Cadet is my father. Did your mother tell you anything more about me?"

"She talked-about you a lot, but more in the context of how disciplined you are, and how being the that way made you a well-rounded person. My mother is a great woman, and I am grateful for all she has done for me."

Dominique looked away from Jean-Jacque, hugged Marisol, and cried like a baby without a pacifier. Jean-Jacque walked over to him and rubbed his back. The severity of the situation was too overwhelming for him to contain himself, tears poured out his eyes like water from a broken fire hydrant.

Olivia walked inside the room, and didn't say a word, she just about faced, and left Marisol, Jean-Jacque, and Dominique alone.

The next morning, a loud noise from Marisol's EKG machine, woke up Jean-Jacque. He got up and walked over to her bedside from the couch in the room. Dominique woke up, as a team of specialists rushed into the room to attend to Marisol. A nurse ushered Jean-Jacque, and Dominique out of the room, closed the door, as the doctor used a defibrillator to revive her from flat lining. The doctor made several attempts but was unable to revive Marisol. He looked up at the clock on the wall and called out: "Time of death 8:03 am."

The nurse covered Marisol's body, and the doctor opened the door, walked over to Dominique and Jean-Jacque. "I… I'm sorry, she didn't make it," he said.

Dominique leaned back on the wall and dropped down to the floor on his butt. He lowered his head down on top of his arms that he folded on his knees and sobbed. Jean-Jacque put one hand on his hip, and the other on top of his head, as he walked away from the

415

doctor after he delivered the news. The doctor put his hand on Dominique's shoulder and it his head down. "I'm sorry son."

Jean-Jacque paced in the hallway, until he returned to where Dominique was slumped on the floor. He looked up at Jean-Jacque with the veins in eyes visibly red, and his eyelids plump as tulips. Dominique wiped snot from his nose with his forearm, and sniffled. "What am I supposed to do now? My mother meant everything to me, she was the only parent I knew!" asked Dominique.

"That's not entirely true, you know me, it's my responsibility to take care of you now, I am your father," Jean-Jacque replied after he took a deep breath and exhaled.

Dominique looked away from Jean-Jacque, nodded his head up and down, then sniffled. "I... I figured as much. She kept bringing you up in conversations with me as if she was hinting at that conclusion. It's comforting to know that you're willing to take me on as your responsibility."

At that moment, Jean-Jacque heard a familiar voice from the doorway. "Mr. Cadet, it's detectives Martins and Cooper, could you please come with us?" asked Det. Cooper.

Jean-Jacque looked up at the detectives, and one of his crutches dropped on the floor. "Have you no compassion? Can't you see that I am grieving over the death of the mayor? Have some respect, you sons of bitches!" replied Jean-Jacque.

"We're sorry for your loss, but we need to tie up these loose ends. The only way to get that done is to get you down to the courtroom to hear the testimony of former Judge Aaron Black. I bet that he'll incriminate you while he's on the stand. When he does so, and there are other witnesses to corroborate his side of the story, Jean-Jacque, y'all get put in handcuffs on felony charges for sex trafficking."

"You two must like the taste of crow. After today, I will appreciate a little more respect."

"Respect, respect, Mr. Cadet, you're lucky we don't just hall your ass down to the precinct right now. You won't pass go or collect $200."

"I'll go with you, but he gets to come with me."

"It makes no difference to us. Get your things, and let's go."

"Have you ever been to court before?" asked Jean-Jacque.

Dominique shook his head from left to right.

"Good, there's a first time for everything."

Detectives Martins and Cooper escorted Jean-Jacque and Dominique to their car, and they got in. Sirens blared as they raced through the city to the courthouse. The detectives escorted Jean-Jacque and Dominique inside the courtroom, where several news media outlets were in the middle of their trial coverage.

"Kim Lee here, and this is breaking news, acting mayor Marisol Velasquez, has died earlier today. Cause of death is unknown; we will report it as soon as we gain further information."

Det. Martins opened the door, they walked inside one at a time, and stood in the rear of the courtroom, as the prosecutor called Arthur Rosenbaum to the stand. He approached the bench and was sworn in by the bailiff. the prosecutor walked up to the witness stand and buttoned his double-breasted suit. "Mr. Rosenbaum, you're "The," go-to venture capitalist, to all the wealthy and powerful people in this great state of New York, aren't you?!" asked the prosecutor.

"I plead the fifth; I exercise my right to not incriminate myself under the advice of counsel," Mr. Rosenbaum replied.

"Okay Mr. Rosenbaum, but are you or are you not a major player in The Program, along with Rodolfo Meléndez, Marisol Velasquez, and Aaron Black?"

"I exercise my right to not incriminate myself under the advice of counsel, I assert my Fifth Amendment privileges."

"Mr. Rosenbaum, isn't it true that you have 'groomed' several under aged girls as a member of The Program."

"I Plead the fifth, I exercise my right to not incriminate myself under the advice of counsel."

"No further questions, your honor."

"Defense, your witness."

"I have no further questions your honor," the defense attorney said.

"Okay Mr. Rosenbaum, you may step down," the Judge said.

Arthur Rosenbaum got up and walked away from the stand.

Jean-Jacque, Dominique, and the detectives stood in the back of the courtroom like flies on the wall, watching as the attorneys displayed their case. Jean-Jacque looked at a group of men seated in the courtroom and noticed that they were members of the Rubber Band Gang. Jean-Jacque leaned over to Det. Martins and grit his teeth. "You're so adamant that I'm guilty, that you allow members of the Rubber Band Gang to roam the city with total autonomy."

Detective Martins leaned over to Jean-Jacque and displayed his detective shield. "There's a time, and a place for everything; your time, and your place is now."

The defense attorney stood up to address the court. "The defense calls to the stand, Judge Aaron Black."

The Judge got up from the audience seating area, buttoned his double-breasted designer blazer, and walked towards the stand. The bailiff put a bible in front of the Judge, he placed his left hand on the Bible. "Please raise your right hand, do you plan to tell the truth, the whole truth, and nothing but the truth, so help you God?" said the bailiff.

"Yes," Judge Aaron Black replied.

"You may be seated."

"Counselor, your witness," the Judge said as the defense attorney walked closer to the stand.

"Mr. Black, or should I address you as Judge Aaron Black?" asked the defense attorney.

"Mr. Black is fine," Judge Aaron Black replied.

"Mr. Black, how many years did you serve as a Judge in the

state of New York?"

"I served as a Judge for twenty-five years."

"Out of those two and a half decades, how many incidents did you face for misconduct unbecoming of a federal Judge?"

"In all my years on the bench, I have never faced such egregious accusations as the ones I currently face."

"Are you now, or ever have been the leader of 'The Program,' that many unsuspecting youths have fallen victims to over two decades?"

"No."

"Thank you, Mr. Black. No further questions, your honor."

The defense attorney for Rodolfo Meléndez, walked back to his seat and sat down. The prosecutor jotted down some notes, then he walked over to the stand, "Mr. Black, you claimed that you are not the person who called the shots in The Program, if you're not the leader; then who is?" asked the prosecutor.

"I followed orders from, former Mayor, Rodolfo..."

Everyone in the courtroom gasped, and indiscriminate chatter amongst the attendees drowned out Judge Aaron Black's answer to the question. "Order in the court," Judge Lolita Smith said and pounded the gavel twice.

The prosecutor nodded to the bailiff, and he walked out of the courtroom. He rolled a TV stand with a television and VCR on it, back inside with him. The prosecutor reached for the remote control, pressed the on button to the tv, and the play button on the VCR.

"This is exhibit A; you can see ladies and gentlemen of the court; this is video footage of former Judge Aaron Black leading an underage girl to a back room in the jazz club Divvy Divvy's. The man that you see being coerced, is former Mayor Rodolfo Meléndez. Ladies and gentlemen please be advised that the footage you're about to see is graphic.

"There is former Mayor Rodolfo Meléndez entering the

419

room, sat on the bed, and an underage girl preformed fellatio on him. She stopped moments later, and you see that innocent underage girl exiting the room with her head down. There she was stopped in the hallway and berated by former Judge Aaron Black. The underage girl burst into tears and ran away.

"I ask you members of the jury; if this footage of former Judge Aaron Black's display of his power as leader is not concrete proof that he is in fact the boss, I don't know what will. And there's hours of footage like this one, showing him exert his dominance over everyone, and everything that he surveys."

Judge Aaron Black stood up from the stand and applauded the prosecutor's video evidence of his involvement in The Program.

"So, your whole entire case relies upon exposing me as the bad guy. Let me let you in on a secret. The Program, that you have denigrated to the court as a child sex trafficking ring, has done more for this city than you will ever fathom. Since you asked the question, I'm obliged to answer. This organization prides itself on excellence, and its members associate themselves with nothing less than overachievers. High ranking members duties are to recruit new blood into the fold, individuals who are groomed to replace their counterparts when it's appropriate.

"The way we fill our ranks with the cream of the proverbial crop, is to seek out virgins. There's an unbreakable bond that's shared between you and someone who gives their innocence to you. Their loyalty and devotion are beyond measure. For their sacrifice, new bloods are given an opportunity to get an ivy league education. In some situations, they're so grateful that they recruit newer bloods, for The Program. Then those members move up in ranks, and the cycle continues.

"There are rear cases when new bloods' fall short of the expectation from The Program. For instance, the new blood, is not intelligent enough for an ivy league education or they lose their innocence to someone who didn't groom them. Then they are indebted to the program indefinitely," Judge Aaron Black said.

"Could you elaborate further, Mr. Black?" asked the prosecutor.

"Sure, the person or persons are relegated to facilitate menial duties of The Program. Those duties include, but are not limited to, security, drug dealing, and enforcement of rules of anyone who steps out of line."

"Mr. Black, you're telling the court that The Program is responsible for the high crime rate in New York City?"

"No, I'm telling you that the public service that The Program has provided many citizens in this city should be commended and not vilified."

"So, all these dangerous gangs have been failed recruits that have to pay back The Program for being stupid?"

"I wouldn't be so blunt; once we ascertain that they won't make it through The Program, they're relegated to, for lack of a better term, mere sexual objects. There only to fulfill our sexual desire. At the end of the grooming process, and the relationship is consummated, the recruit is adorned with a colorful rubber band around their wrist."

One of the members of the Rubber Band Gang stood up and flung a chair at Judge Aaron Black. "Mother fucker, you ruined our lives," The Band leader said.

The chair shattered on the wall after it hit former Judge Aaron Black in the head and knocked him out cold. Judge Lolita Smith pounded the gavel several times, after the melee ensued. "Order in the court, order in the court; another outburst like this and I'll have you all in contempt. Bailiffs, please clean up this mess, detain that man, and remove him from my courtroom," the Judge said.

The Rubber Band Gang member went with the bailiffs and didn't resist arrest. Jean-Jacque turned to Det. Martins and smiled. "In the immortal words of reporter Kim Lee, 'Now, there you have it," Jean-Jacque said.

Jean-Jacque smirked, put a business card in the front sport jacket of the detective, and walked out of the courtroom. Det. Martins took out the card, and it read: "Get out of jail free card." The detective smiled and plucked the card with his finger. "Touché,

Jean-Jacque, touché," Det. Martins replied.

The reporters standing outside the courtroom, approached Jean-Jacque, stuck their voice recorders in his face, and unloaded a barrage of questions:

"Jean-Jacque, Jean-Jacque, how do you feel about being appointed Mayor now since the acting Mayor Marisol Velasquez died earlier today?"

"With Judge Aaron Black's confession, will today be the deciding blow that ends The Program's reign in New York City once and for all?"

"Although willful ignorance is not a crime, will you be charged for participating in The Program?"

"Will all of the current members of The Program be arrested?"

Jean-Jacque didn't speak a word to any news media outlet, as he and Dominique covered their faces with their arms, blocking the flashing lights. The clicking of the shutters from the cameras, sounded louder than the migration of Cicadas. Photographers were clamoring over each other, fighting for position to get the best shot.

They managed to shuffle their way through the sea of reporters and made it outside the courthouse by the skin of their teeth. Jean-Jacque hailed a taxicab parked on the curb. The driver started the car, they both claimed in the back and shut the door.

"Where to?" asked the taxi driver.

"SoHo, I will let you know exactly where, just drive," Jean-Jacque replied.

Jean-Jacque and Dominique sat in silence the entire taxi ride to his loft. Jean-Jacque paid the driver with a twenty-dollar bill and told him to keep the change. They stepped out of the taxi and walked inside the building. Jean-Jacque turned to Dominique and put his arm over his shoulder. "Did you know that this building belonged to your mother?" asked Jean-Jacque.

"No," Dominique replied.

"I've been living here since the age of fifteen with my cousins Latrice and Patrice. And now, it belongs to you, son."

Jean-Jacque squeezed his arm around Dominique's neck, hugged him, and led him to the elevator. The united duo stepped inside the elevator and Jean-Jacque pulled the doors closed.

"How soon will my mother be buried?" asked Dominique.

"Well son, under normal circumstances a week after a person has died, but if their parents, and next of kin isn't able to make the ceremony; it could take a while longer," Jean-Jacque replied.

"My mother spoke to me about her wanting to be buried back in Guatemala. Since she was the acting mayor of New York City, would that even be possible?"

"I think that if Marisol had a will stating that she wanted to be buried in Guatemala, then that is where she will be buried."

The elevator stopped on Jean-Jacque's floor, and he pulled open the doors to the loft. Jean-Jacque and Dominique walked inside, saw Latrice and Patrice in the kitchen. They were drinking coffee, and Jean-Jacque took a deep breath and nudged Dominique in front of him. "Medam, mwen ta renmen prezante ou pitit gason m ', Dominique," (Ladies, I would like to introduce you to my son, Dominique,) Jean-Jacque said.

Latrice knitted her brows, Patrice stood next to her with her hands and arms akimbo. "Kisa ou te jis di, Jean?!" (What did you just say, Jean?!) asked Patrice.

Jean Jacque gripped Dominique's shoulder, exhaled, and raised his eyebrows. "Marisol Velasquez and I had a son that she hid from me for a long time, since she is no longer with us; I thought it was about time we had a relationship together," Jean-Jacque replied.

"Jean, Ou te gen yon lòt pitit salo? (You had another bastard child?) How long have you known about him?" asked Latrice.

"Latrice, he's not a bastard; Marisol told me about him after that ordeal I had with former mayor Rodolfo Meléndez, over Jena. She told me that it wouldn't be safe for me to have a relationship with him back then; things didn't exactly get better," Jean-Jacque

423

replied.

"Let me get this straight, you had a love child with the former acting Mayor of New York City, and you're just telling us this now," Patrice said.

"Patrice, I know it looks bad, but it was all for his safety, her safety, and mine," Jean-Jacque replied.

They all stood there in silence, Latrice and Patrice looked at Dominique, then they both walked over to him and stretched out their arms. "Welcome to the family Dominique, we're pleased to meet you," the twins said in unison.

Dominique smiled, put out his hand, and Latrice and Patrice pulled him closer to their bodies and they both hugged him instead.

"Now we're one big happy family. I hope Mama will be as accepting of this as you two are," Jean-Jacque said and wrapped his arms around everyone.

The phone rang and interrupted the family moment. Jean-Jacque walked over to the phone and picked up the receiver: "Hello, this is Jean, how can I help you?" replied Jean-Jacque.

"Hello Claude, this is Jena, why so formal? Are law enforcement there at your place?" asked Jena.

"No, no, nothing like that, how are you and the twins doing Jena?"

"We're doing well, I saw on the news that Marisol Velasquez died; how are you holding up?"

"I'll be alright, but I'm not so sure about our son."

"Excuse me, did you say our son? We don't have a son together."

"Yes, I know Jena, Marisol and I had a son together, and his name is Dominique."

"Claude… forget it, I won't even ask…Anyway, my boss cleared the time off for me and the twins to go to Haiti with you."

"That is great news, my parents are going to be surprised to meet everyone."

"You mean… Go figure, I wouldn't expect nothing less from you. When are we flying out to Haiti?"

"In a few days, first, I am going to fly out to Guatemala with Dominique to bury Marisol."

"Claude, you be careful, I will see you when you get back."

Jena hung up the phone on Jean-Jacque, and he stood there holding the receiver in his hand listening to the dial tone until a prerecorded voice came on. "If you'd like to make a call, please hang up and dial again."

The next morning, Jean-Jacque woke up out of his sleep by the loud sound of the phone ringing next to his ear. He grabbed the receiver and cleared his throat before he answered. "Good morning, this is Jean, how can I help you?" said Jean-Jacque with a raspy voice.

"Mr. Cadet, this is Olivia, your secretary; I just got off a call from the medical examiner, he said that the autopsy is complete, and we're all set to retrieve Ms. Velasquez's body," Olivia replied.

"Okay, great, she wanted to be buried in Guatemala. Will you be traveling with Dominique and I there?"

"Yes, I am well aware of Marisol's request to be laid to rest in Guatemala; I've contacted her parents, all of the arrangements are taken care of there."

"Okay, great, we will see you tomorrow."

Jean-Jacque got up off the couch and walked upstairs to his bedroom. With Dominique still asleep, he tiptoed past the bed into the bathroom and closed the door. He rushed to the toilet and pissed like a racehorse. Averting being embarrassed by pee stains on his trousers. Those drugs Dr. Patel prescribed had him urinating more frequently than usual. He looked at his watch, it was 8:30 am.

"I have to stop using these drugs, if Olivia didn't call me, I'd still be asleep. This pain is unbearable though, but it's mind over matter Jean, mind over matter," Jean-Jacque said.

Jean-Jacque flushed the toilet; then, struggled to pull his shirt over his head. He grimaced in pain, but still managed to get his clothes off. Jean-Jacque turned on the faucet, put his hand underneath the water until it warmed up, and then got into the tub for a quick shower. He dried himself off with a towel, opened the door, and shut off the bathroom light. With the towel wrapped around his waist, Jean-Jacque noticed Dominique sitting on the edge of the bed.

"Good morning, son, did I wake you up?" asked Jean-Jacque.

Dominique stretched, yawned and rubbed his eyes. "Good morning, Jean, no, you didn't wake me up. I have to use the bathroom," Dominique replied.

Dominique got up off the bed, stepped past Jean-Jacque, and closed the bathroom door behind him.

Jean-Jacque went into his closet, picked out some clothes, and put them on the bed. "I hope you had a goodnight sleep son; we have a busy day ahead of us. We have to go out and sort out some things before your mother's funeral. Do you have a suit?"

Dominique flushed the toilet, opened the door, and turned off the bathroom light. "No Jean, I don't have a suit for this occasion."

"That's okay, I'll buy you a suit before we leave tomorrow morning for Guatemala. Get dressed, we'll get a bite to eat off a food truck on the road."

Time was of the essence, Jean-Jacque got ready and waited for Dominique to do the same. Five minutes went by, and Dominique was all set to go. "Come on son, I made an appointment with my tailor, he's going to take some measurements of you for a suit. Ever been fitted for a suit before?" asked Jean-Jacque.

Dominique shook his head from left to right and started at his father with a blank look on his face. "I prefer clothes off the rack Jean," Dominique replied.

Jean-Jacque laughed, and they got into the elevator. There was a black Lincoln Town Car waiting outside of the building. The driver opened the rear passenger door for Dominique and Jean-

Jacque as they exited the building.

The driver drove a few blocks and stopped in front of a brownstone, and Jean-Jacque opened the door and pointed at a glass door. "Son, this is Mr. Verona's tailor shop, this little old Italian man is the best tailor in the city."

Jean-Jacque led Dominique down a set of stairs, through a glass door, and into the store. Me. Verona saw Jean-Jacque and his face lit up. "Sonny boy, glad to see you again! I have been following the news about the goings-on in the mayor's office. I knew from the get-go that you were innocent. I'm sorry about Marisol; she was a nice woman. So, what can I do for you today?" said Mr. Verona.

"Mr. V, I need a suit for him, his name is Dominique, and his mother was Marisol," Jean-Jacque replied.

Mr. Verona gasped and put his hand out. "Pleased to meet you. Sonny boy, give us some room. I will take care of him right away."

Jean-Jacque backed away from Mr. Verona, and Dominique stepped up on a platform in front of a floor-length mirror. Mr. Verona took his measuring tape from off his neck and placed it on Dominique's back.

"Stretch-out your arms, young man."

Dominique stood there with his arms outstretched like the Christ the Redeemer statue. Mr. Verona strapped the tape around Dominique's neck, arms, chest, and waist. The old man walked back over to a notepad and jotted down his measurements. He walked over to Dominique and wrapped the tape around his legs, then took his inseam measurements. Mr. Verona looked at the numbers and frowned. "Huh, that's strange, his measurements are exactly like yours when Marisol first brought you here to me."

Mr. Verona looked Jean-Jacque in his eyes and shrugged his shoulders. "You're in luck Sonny boy, I still have a suit that I made for you all those years ago."

He opened a closet and pulled out the suit and handed it to Dominique. "Here, young man, go into that dressing room, and try this on."

Dominique took the suit from Mr. Verona and walked into the dressing room. Jean-Jacque looked at the old man. "M... Mr. Verona..."

The tailor put his hand up in the air, turned his face. "Don't you say another word, Sonny boy, the less I know, the better."

Dominique stepped out of the dressing room with the suit on, and Mr. Verona clapped his hands together. "Vestibilità perfetta. What about shoes? He's going to need shoes," Mr. Verona said.

"Yeah, sure, what do you have?" asked Jean-Jacque.

"I have these Salvatore Ferragamo, wingtip tassel loafers, size 11 in the closet. Here young man, try these on."

Dominique put on the loafers like Cinderella, slipped on the glass slipper.

"Bellissimo!"

Jean-Jacque reached in his pocket, took out a wad of money and Mr. Verona wagged his hands at him. "Don't you dare, this is on the house Sonny boy, your money's no good here. Besides, you're going to need a lot more suits; whenever you're ready, you come back and see me; I'll be here."

Dominique changed clothes and Mr. Verona put the suit and shoes into a garment bag. "Here you go my boy," Mr. Verona said.

"Thank you for the suit, Mr. Verona," Dominique replied.

"It was my pleasure, call me Mr. V, all of my friends do."

"Arrivederci, Sig Verona."

"Parla Italiano, eh!"

"Si"

" Sonny boy, I like this kid, he's smart like you were at his age," Mr. Verona said.

"I hope he'll become a hell of a lot smarter than I ever was," Jean-Jacque replied.

"C'mon let's go, son." Dominique and Jean stepped outside the shop, and Jean-Jacque clapped his hands together. "So, there's a food stand up the street; do you want a shish kebab, son?" asked Jean-Jacque.

"Sure, I've never had one before, but 'There's always a first time for everything,'" Dominique replied.

"Okay, cool, Mahmud has the best kebabs in the city."

Jean-Jacque led Dominique a short distance up the street to Mahmud's food truck. "Son, my secretary called me before we left the loft and told me that she made all of the arrangements for your mother, so it's just you and I today, kid. Is there anything you want to do in the city?"

"No, I'm not fussy like that; spending time with you is fine."

"Hey Jean! I haven't seen you in a while. Sorry about everything that happened to you and Mrs. Velasquez; she was a nice woman," Mahmud lamented.

"Hey Mahmud, thanks, I appreciate your concern. Let me get the usual," Jean-Jacque replied.

"Good choice, I just made a fresh batch of Adana and Urfa, what about the kid?"

"I'll have whatever Jean is having. Is the meat Halal, sir?" asked Dominique.

"Always young man, anything less is uncivilized," Mahmud replied.

Mahmud prepared the dishes for Jean-Jacque and Dominique, then handed them the containers. "Hey, anything to drink?"

"Yeah, a "Fruitopia. You want one son?"

"Sure, I'll have one," Dominique replied with a mouth full of food.

"Hey Jean, this kebab is pretty good," Dominique said.

"I'm glad you like it," Jean-Jacque replied.

Hey Mahmud, how much?" asked Jean-Jacque.

"For you, $10," Mahmud replied.

Jean-Jacque smiled and handed Mahmoud a ten-dollar bill. "Thanks for the hook up, Mahmud."

Walking back to the car, Jean-Jacque took Dominique's garment bag. "Slow down son, you're gonna eat the stick if you're not careful."

"I'll try my best, but I cannot promise anything."

They both got into the car, and the driver took them back to the loft. "Thank you, Raymundo, I'll see you tomorrow morning," Jean-Jacque said.

The driver nodded his head as he held the door open for Dominique and Jean-Jacque. "Thank you for the suit, the shoes and the kebab, I appreciate it, Jean," Dominique said.

The father and son duo walked inside the building, and Latrice and Patrice were walking outside at the same time. "Hey Jean, Dominique, where did you go?" asked Latrice.

"Hey Latrice, I took him down to Mr. Verona's Tailor shop to get fitted for a suit," Jean-Jacque replied.

"It looks like you two bonded over Mahmud's too," Patrice said.

"It appears so, Patrice," Jean-Jacque replied.

"We'd love to stay and chat, but we're going shopping. Could we use your car service, Jean?" asked Latrice.

"Sure, ladies, make sure you tip my driver," Jean-Jacque said.

"We will see you two when you get back; have a safe flight," Latrice and Patrice said simultaneously.

"Son, we have to get some shut eye for our trip tomorrow. You're going to meet your grandparents in Guatemala too. Did you ever see or speak with them before?" asked Jean-Jacque.

"Yeah, plenty when I was little, but not since they moved

back to Guatemala," Dominique said.

"With your mom gone, I will make sure that you see them more often."

The next morning, Dominique snuggled up against Jean-Jacque's chest on their way to the airport. "I guess little man trusts me now," Jean-Jacque thought and exhaled a temporary sigh of relief. This moment was the quiet before the storm, there's a lot more work to be done until he could relax, relate, and release. All the burden he incurred over the past ten years culminates at this point.

The plane ride to Guatemala was peaceful. Olivia brought all of Dominique's travel documents and clothes along; she had everything taken care of as promised. It was a rocky landing, but everyone on board was safe, thanks to the pilot.

Jean-Jacque, Olivia, and Dominique de-boarded the plane, and dozens of locals were standing there with lit candles in their hands. The pilot and a few men took Marisol's casket out of the cargo bay of the plane. Per Guatemalan traditions, artisans constructed her coffin of pine back in New York. The men placed the casket on a truck bed adorned with an assortment of flowers. Marisol's family didn't waste any time, and the funeral was in session as soon as the plane landed.

Marisol's parents approached Dominique and Jean-Jacque as they walked to the burial grounds. "Welcome to Guatemala! Although the reasons for visiting our great country are sad circumstances, we must rejoice, for death is an integral part of life. Pardon my bad manners; I am Marisol's father, Pedro, and this is her mother, my wife, Guadeloupe. We are pleased to meet you, Jean. Is this Dominique?" asked Pedro.

"Yes sir, he is, Dominique, say hello to your grandparents," Jean-Jacque replied.

"Hola Abuelo, y Abuela!" said Dominique.

"Hablo español mijo?" asked Pedro.

"Si"

"Marisol told us that she adopted you because your parents were too young to take care of you. And that her secretary's sister was left the task of his caregiver, while she performed her duties as deputy Mayor. Although we consider you to be our grandson; we were under the impression that it was not biological."

"Well Pedro, I hate to break it to you like this, but I am one of those young parents, and your daughter was his biological mother, understand."

"I'm confused, so you mean that you and my daughter were... Oh! I'm glad for the clarification. At least Marisol had a child that we now know is one of us."

The funeral procession sang "Cruz de Madera" by Michael Salgado, as they walked down the road from the airplane. Everyone stopped a mile down the road, men lifted the coffin off the truck bed, and put it next to an opened grave. Locals sang "Un Dia A Las Vez" by Los Tigres del Norte.

"Did any of you bring Marisol's belongings for us to bury her with?" asked Pedro.

"Yes," Olivia and Dominique said in unison.

"Please, take them out, so we can add them as we lower Marisol down into the ground."

Several men lowered the casket in a pre-dug hole in the earth, and locals placed pennies, Marisol's belongings, and hands full of dirt that they kissed on top of the casket. Once the coffin reached the bottom, grave diggers used shovels to fill the hole with soil. Many locals poured water on the soil with each toss on top of Marisol's casket.

The priest stood there over the mound of dirt next to a large vigil and raised his hand in the air. "We are gathered here today to celebrate the life of Marisol Velasquez, and commit her body into the soil," The Priest said.

'In the sweat of thy face shalt thou eat bread, till thou return unto the ground; for out of it wast thou taken; for dust thou art, and unto dust shalt thou return.' (Genesis 3:19)

432

"Her soul has already risen to be with our heavenly father. Jesus Christ said:

'Whoever eats my flesh and drinks my blood shall live forever.' (John 6:54)

'The LORD is nigh unto them that are of a broken heart; and saveth such as be of a contrite spirit.' (Psalms 34:18)

[3] 'Blessed be God, even the Father of our Lord Jesus Christ, the Father of mercies, and the God of all comfort.

[4] 'He who comforteth us in all our tribulation, that we may be able to comfort them which are in any trouble, by the comfort wherewith we ourselves are comforted by God.' (2 Corinthians 1:3-4)

"Is there anyone here who wants to say a few words about the departed?" asked the Priest.

The grief-stricken crowd wailed as the mariachi band played their instruments in the background.

"Marisol was a brave selfless soul. Her mission in life was to help people fulfill their full potential. Baby girl, you will be missed," Pedro said and held Guadalupe in his arms as she wept.

The crowd of mourners dispersed and only Pedro, his wife Guadalupe, Jean-Jacque, Dominique and Olivia were left standing there. "Jean, are you and Dominique, staying in Guatemala for a few days?" asked Pedro.

"Sure, Pedro, what about my secretary Olivia and our pilot?"

"We have plenty of space for them."

"Okay then, we'll stay through tomorrow and leave late the next day. I scheduled a trip to Haiti to visit my parents with Dominique," Jean-Jacque replied.

"Great, follow me to the house; you guys must be hungry."

"How far is the house from here, Pedro?"

"Oh, it's only fifty yards up this hill. This burial ground is a family cemetery. We've buried our dearly departed here for

433

generations. Come on, Dominique, follow me. I will bring you to your mothers' room."

Jean was amazed at how grand The Velasquez house was. It sat on a fifty-acre compound, equipped with a rose garden and a vineyard. "What a beautiful house Pedro, why did you ever leave this to live in the United States?" asked Jean-Jacque.

"Thank you, Jean, but this is all Marisol's doing. The original house that my wife and I lived in before Guadeloupe had Marisol, is over there past the rose garden. But to answer your question, I wanted Marisol to get a better education than she would have received here in Guatemala," Pedro replied.

Pedro led the group to the courtyard, where friends and family members were eating food. "Please, sit down. I'll have some food brought to the table."

Two young men brought two trays of food over to the table and Jean-Jacque took in a deep breath of the pleasant aroma. "Mmm, smells good, what is it?" asked Jean-Jacque.

"Well, this dish is called 'Pepian,' and these are 'tamales.' Jean, have you ever tried Guatemalan cuisine before?"

"Yes, I ate Guatemalan food before, Pedro."

"Fantastic, enjoy."

Dominique, Jean-Jacque, the pilot, and Olivia ate the food, and Guadeloupe poured licuados in their glasses for them to drink.

"Mmm, Abuela, this food tastes fantastic," Dominique said.

"I'm glad you like it mijo," Guadalupe replied.

After dinner, Pedro noticed that his foreign guest looked exhausted. "You all must be very tired, come on let me show you to your rooms."

They all got up and went into the house; Jean-Jacque, the pilot, and Olivia's rooms were close to the front entrance of the house. Then Dominique followed Pedro upstairs to a large room with double doors.

"Wow, Abuelo, this room is like a presidential suite at a

fancy hotel. Look, there is my mom's porcelain doll collection, vaulted ceilings, and a Jacuzzi tub. Was this my mother's room when she was little?" said Dominique as he stood there in amazement.

"Ha, ha, no Dominique, she built this house for you when you were two years old. Your mother wanted to bring you here every summer, so you could experience Guatemala firsthand. Marisol loved when we brought her here for the summer as a young girl. She promised that she would build a castle for us to live in. Marisol kept her promise…," Pedro replied.

Pedro turned his face away from Dominique, and he sobbed like a baby. Dominique put his arms around him and hugged him. "It's okay to cry Abuelo, I miss her too."

Dominique yawned, and Pedro wiped away the tears from his face. "Come on mijo, I know that you are tired, get some sleep."

The next morning, Jean-Jacque was awakened by the sound of laughter coming from outside his bedroom. He got up out of bed, looked out of the glass sliding doors to his bedroom, and saw Dominique stomping on something inside of a huge wooden barrel. He smiled and went into the bathroom to freshen up and walked outside to see what the commotion was.

"Good morning, son, what are you doing?" said Jean-Jacque as he stood there squinting from the sun shining on his face.

"I am stomping on grapes, Abuelo said that these grapes from the vineyard are used to make wine and cognac," Dominique replied.

Jean-Jacque sat down next to Pedro in the courtyard, and the table was filled with fresh fruit, bagels, muffins and an espresso machine.

"Good morning, Jean, would you like to have some espresso?" asked Pedro.

Jean-Jacque nodded yes to Pedro, and he took an apple off the table, rubbed it on his shirt, and bit into it. "It is more beautiful here now than it was yesterday when we arrived."

435

"Yes, Marisol had big plans for this property, she wanted to raise cattle, horses, and geese here."

"Hey Pedro, what are those green thorny plants over there?" asked Jean-Jacque.

"Oh, that is agave plants. Marisol wanted to make tequila, wine and cognac here too. She was a very ambitious person. Two miles down the road, is a school where she built for the local children here. Marisol was big on educating the next Jeneration. She wanted the next great mind that led the free world, to come from Guatemala," Pedro replied.

"I know Pedro, she inspired me to do the same thing. Was Marisol born here in Guatemala?"

"No, Jean, my wife and I made sure she was born in the United States of America. We wanted her to take full advantage of being a citizen."

Jean-Jacque spent the rest of the day sipping espresso, cognac, wine, eating Guatemalan food, and relaxing. The next morning, Jean-Jacque, Olivia and Dominique woke up early to fly back to the U.S.

"Pedro, Guadeloupe, thank you for your hospitality."

"Jean, thank you for bringing Marisol back to Guatemala, and our grandson too."

"No problem, I will make sure Dominique visits you every summer."

Dominique hugged his grandparents and they both squeezed him tight in their arms. "Te amo Abuela y Abuelo, Los voy a extrañar a los dos," Dominique said.

"We love you too mijo, and we're going to miss you even more! Have a safe flight back home!" replied his grandparents in unison.

Jean-Jacque, the pilot, Olivia, and Dominique, boarded the plane, it jetted down the runway, and took off into the air back to the United States.

Jean-Jacque picked up the phone in the airplane and called Jena. She picked up the phone after it rang several times:

"Hello, this is Jena!"

"Hey Jena, this is Jean. I'm on my way back to the U.S, could you and the twins meet us at the private hangar at JFK airport?" asked Jean-Jacque.

"Sure, how would I know what gate to go to once we get to the airport?" replied Jena.

"You are going to the Fixed Base Operation hangar; I'm sending a car service to pick you and the girls up. I instructed my driver where to take you once he arrives at the airport."

"Okay, Claude, what time should we be ready for?"

"Seven o'clock in the morning, the flight leaves for Haiti at 8:37 am sharp."

"Does Blossom know about these flight plans?"

"No, I will call her after I hang up the phone with you. And remember to bring everybody's travel documents with you."

Jena hung up the phone, and Jean-Jacque dialed Margot's number. The phone rang a few times and Margot picked up the phone:

"Hello, Claude, how are you doing?" asked Margot.

"Hey Blossom, how did you know it was me?" replied Jean-Jacque.

"I have caller I.D. Claude; your name came up on the phone before I picked it up."

"Oh, okay, the reason for the call is that I'm on my way back to the U.S, so I need you to meet us at JFK airport."

"Ok, Claude, will I be going to the private hangar?"

"Yes, I'm sending a car service to pick you and Sebastian up in the morning, be ready for 7 am."

"Ok, Claude, how was Guatemala? Jena told me that you

took Dominique there to bury Marisol."

"It was all too surreal; I knew Marisol since I was twelve. She was an exceptional person, and I am going to miss her dearly. Marisol was the driving force in my life that aided me to become the man that I am today."

"I know it's hard Claude, how is Dominique holding up?"

"He is a resourceful young man; he just needs guidance. I am the only parent he has left, so I have to be there for him."

"I know that you will live up to that assertion. Sebastian and I will be there at the airport tomorrow morning."

"Okay Blossom, I will see you then."

Margot hung up the phone, and Jean-Jacque called home. The phone rang once, and Latrice picked up the phone.

"Hello, this is Latrice, how can I help you?"

"Latrice, I am on my way back to the U.S with Dominique, and I want you and Patrice to be ready for 7 am tomorrow. I am sending Raimondo to pick you all up."

"Ok Jean, we will be ready!"

Jean-Jacque hung up the phone, shut the shade down at his window, and went to sleep.

The plane landed 5 am the next morning at JFK international airport. The pilot announced their arrival: "Welcome back to New York, it was my pleasure piloting this plane to Guatemala and back; whenever you need my services, I'll be more than happy in serving you."

Dominique woke up and saw Jean-Jacque, and Olivia zipping up their carry-on bags, and putting their shoes back on. He did the same and they all walked off the plane. "Mr. Cadet, the maintenance crew here will service the plane, and it will be all set and ready to go at 8:45. There is a lounge over there, and they serve breakfast. I suggest you take advantage of the complimentary meal," the pilot said.

Jean-Jacque and Dominique we're heading towards the

lounge, and Olivia hugged Dominique. "Mr. Cadet, have a safe flight. I will see you when you return from Haiti. Take care Dominique, enjoy your trip," Olivia said.

There was a breakfast buffet in the lounge, Jean-Jacque, and Dominique went to the bathroom to freshen up before they helped themselves to the buffet. The news was on the television in the lounge, and Jean-Jacque heard:

"Reporter Kim Lee here with channel 10 with breaking news. Judge Aaron Black, Rodolfo Meléndez, and Arthur Rosenbaum were found guilty of all charges. Sentencing will be in one week. This verdict is the deciding blow to The Program that will stop its grip on the city of New York, once and for all. Back to you Bill."

Jean-Jacque and Dominique shared themselves breakfast and sat down around a table at a window by the entrance. Jean-Jacque made tea for himself, poured out some orange juice for Dominique, then they sat there and ate breakfast.

The bartender changed the channel from the news to a station that aired an old rerun of Looney Tunes, and Dominique puckered up in his chair to watch the television set. Jean-Jacque picked up the newspaper and skimmed through most of it, only to stop at the crossword puzzle. He was perplexed because most of the questions pertained to day-time soap operas, which he held no prior knowledge.

Three black Lincoln Town cars with dark presidential tint on the windows pulled into the hangar next to the private airplane. Raymundo opens the rear passenger door, and Latrice and Patrice stepped out of the car. He opened the trunk, took out their luggage, and the baggage handlers stored them onto the plane.

Jena and the twins got out of the car, and the baggage handlers put their luggage on a cart and rolled it to the plane. Margot stepped out of the car, Jean-Jacque helped her out, hugged her, kissed her on the cheek, then he took Sebastian from her arms. He fussed a little until he saw Jean-Jacque, then he gave him a toothless smile with the pacifier in his mouth.

"Hey Adonis, how are you doing buddy? I'd like to introduce you to your brother Dominique," Jean-Jacque said.

Dominique waved at Sebastian, then put his finger in the baby's palm, and he squeezed it. Tiye and Amanirenas walked over to Jean-Jacque and hugged him. "Good morning, ladies, you both look beautiful today. I love your 'Shirley temple' curls Tiye. Amanirenas, who did your hair? I love it, you look like a treasure troll," Jean-Jacque said.

"Thanks, Papi, Mommy did it for us," the twins said simultaneously.

Jean-Jacque kissed Jena on the cheek and hugged her with one arm. "Good morning, Jena, you look nice," Jean-Jacque said.

"Thank you, Claude, you look spiffy as usual," Jena replied.

"Okay, enough of this mushy stuff. I want to hold this adorable baby of yours Jean, what is his name?" said Latrice as she reached for the baby.

"His name is Sebastian," Margot replied.

"Ladies, I want you to meet your older brother Dominique and your younger brother Sebastian. Dominique, I want you to meet your twin sisters Tiye, and Amanirenas," Jean-Jacque said.

The twins and Dominique hugged one another, and they all touched Sebastian.

Patrice shrieked with excitement and took out her camera. "Everyone, squeeze in close to each other. I want to take a picture," Patrice said.

"Give me the camera, I'll take it!" said the pilot.

Everyone got into place, and the pilot held the camera up to his face. "Now, say cheese."

The pilot snapped the picture, then Latrice shrieked. "Okay, everyone, get out of the frame, and let's take a few with Jean, and the kids, then him with each mother and their child," Latrice said.

All of the children stood juxtaposed to Jean-Jacque, then they interchanged positions like a game of musical chairs. The pilot photographed Jean-Jacque, and the kids posed like he was Andy Warhol.

Dominique and the twins stepped away from Jean-Jacque, Margot stood by him, and the pilot took their picture while he held the baby in his arms. Margot took Sebastian and moved out of the frame. Jena coaxed the twins into position, and the pilot snapped the shot.

Jean-Jacque noticed Dominique with his head down, so he called to him, and he looked up at his father all teary-eyed and sniffled. "My mother can't be here; how could I take a picture without her?" asked Dominique.

Latrice and Patrice sighed then put their hands on their chest. "We'll take one with you and your dad, Dominique. Will that make it better?" asked Latrice.

Dominique sauntered over to where his dad was, and the pilot snapped the last picture of them. Jena and Margot walked over to Dominique and put their arms around him.

"We know not having your mom here is tough on you, but we will always be here for you, Dominique," Jena said.

"Consider us as your second and third mom's. We will love you like our kid," Margot said.

The pilot looked at his watch, and it was 8:15 am. He raised his eyebrows, then handed Patrice back her camera. "This photoshoot is officially over; it's getting late. We have to board the plane now," the pilot said.

Jena walked next to Jean-Jacque as the group boarded the plane. "Cute kid Claude, you better watch him; he's going to be a lady killer like his dad," Jena said.

"Ha, ha, ha, that's very funny. I hope and pray that Dominique amounts to much more than that," Jean-Jacque replied.

All jokes aside, Claude, I won't lose any sleep over what happened to Marisol. But is Dominique having a hard time coping with his mother's death?"

"It appears so; I have to be there for him, Jena. I'm the only

441

living parent he has left."

"He's welcome at my house, and I know Blossom feels the same way too."

"Thanks, that means a lot."

"Oh Claude, let me tell you what Jamie said to me before I forget. He told me that a Jamaican girl he dated in high school, named Precious, contacted him and told him that he got her pregnant way back then, and they have an eleven-year-old son together," Jena said.

"Wow, I remember Precious Stone, she was Mikey Dread's niece. He had a Jamaican Bakery across the street from Alfred E. Smith H.S.," ean-Jacque replied.

"He also said that he was flying down to Jamaica to meet her and his alleged son."

"Well, I hope it works out for him, considering…"

"Yeah, me too!"

"Good morning, folks; this is the captain speaking. I'm happy to be your pilot during this flight to Port-au-Prince, Haiti. It's clear skies and excellent weather today. We will be flying at an altitude of 35,000 feet at approx. 430 knots. So, sit back, relax, and I will have you down there in no time," the pilot said.

"Hey Claude, my girlfriend, Felicia, said she and her mom would've come along, but they didn't have their passports with them. By the size of this group, the plane couldn't have accommodated two more people and their luggage anyway," Jena said.

"This is a 'Gulfstream V Ultra-long-rang jet,' this plane could accommodate 19 people. Trust me; we would've had space, Jena," Jean-Jacque replied.

The plane took off the tarmac on time, and the flight took five hours to reach Haiti. Upon the pilot making the final descent, the twins woke up. Tiye rubbed the sleep from their eyes, then she pulled up the shade on the window. "Look, look, it's 'Beast's Castle' from 'Beauty and the Beast.' Did we fly to France, Papi?" asked

Tiye.

Jean-Jacque laughed and shook his head. "No ladies, we are not in France, and that is not Beast's Castle from Beauty and the Beast. We are in Haiti, and that is my house that we're going to be staying in," Jean-Jacque replied.

"Wow, Papi, are you a prince or something?" said Amanirenas.

"No, I'm not a prince, I'm a king, and you ladies are my princesses, and your brothers are my princes," Jean-Jacque replied.

"Is mama and Aunty Margot, your queens, Papi?"

Margot crossed her arms, and legs, then waited for Jean-Jacque to answer. Jena blushed, and Jean-Jacque stammered a bit before he answered.

"Niña, tu mamá y tu tía Margot siempre fueron reinas. No estoy seguro si quieren ser míos nunca más," (Baby girl, your mama and aunty Margot always were queens. I'm not sure if they want to be mine anymore,) Jean-Jacque replied.

Margot and Jena raised their eyebrows and tilted their heads off to the side, as the plane slowed down to a screeching halt. The pilot left the cockpit, opened the side hatch, and let down the stairs. Latrice and Patrice exited the plane first, and they both raised their hands in the air. "Sak pase Hayiti, mwen lakay mwe!" (What's happening, Haiti? I am at home!) said the twins in unison.

"Cousin, you are home indeed," Jean-Jacque said as he stepped off the plane and walked down the stairs.

Latrice and Patrice dropped their bags and ran to two figures in the distance approaching the plane.

Margot, Jena, and the twins surveyed their surroundings in awe, walked down the stairs, and with Sebastian on her hip, Margot put on her sunglasses and the Caribbean breeze wind blew her hair off to the side. "Claude did your private jet just land in your backyard?" asked Margot.

"Yes, and No, this is the headquarters for the Helping Hand

Initiative, Blossom——

"Look who's coming!" said Jean-Jacque as he diverted his attention. 'Mama, Papa, mwen pa wè ou de depi lontan.'"

"JJ, we haven't seen you in a long time either. What are you doing here so soon? We weren't expecting you until next summer. Who are all these people? Whose kids are those?" said Flora.

"Mama, I'd like to introduce you to Jena, Margot, and these are my kids: Dominique, Tiye, Amanirenas, and Sebastian."

"Eh, eh, kisa wap di mwen? Henri, èske ou te konnen pitit gason ou lan gen pitit?"

"Yes, my wife, I knew JJ had kids; he told me so," Henri said.

"My son, I'm happy to see you. My condolences on Marisol's death. Is this your son Dominique?" said Henri.

"Yes, Papa," Jean-Jacque said as he hugged his father.

"Son, come, say hello to your grandparents."

"Alo grann, ak papa," Dominique said.

"Eh, eh, ou pale Kreyol?" asked Henri.

"Yes, grandpa, I speak Haitian Creole."

"I'm glad pitit pitit."

Margot walked over to Jean-Jacque's mother, kissed her on the cheek, and handed Sebastian to her. "Hello, I'm Margot, here is your grandson."

Flora looked at the twins and gritted her teeth. "Latrice, Patrice, ki jan ou ta ka kite JJ fè timoun epi yo pa di manman l'? Li te devwa ou a pran swen l'," Flora said.

"Aunty, Jean doesn't listen to us. We just found out that he had all these kids. I'm sorry, but we are just as surprised as you are," Patrice said.

Tiye and Amanirenas ran over to their grandparents, and each of them hugged their legs separately.

444

"I achieved the American dream. I accomplished all of my goals, and I have everything and everyone that I love here with me right now; what more can I ask for," Jean-Jacque said and stood there with a big smile from ear to ear.

Made in the USA
Middletown, DE
25 August 2023